# Billionaire Mogul–Beckett

## Scarlett Avery

# Dedication

*For my readers who are unapologetic about their addiction to smut, but also need all the feels.*

# Get the BILLIONAIRE MOGUL—BECKETT Secret Chapter

Join my mailing list and grab the Exclusive Secret Chapter or Storyboard for this romance.

Great extra goodies. Hot deals. Zero spam.

**www.MyRomanceAddiction.com**

# Chapter 1

## *Beckett*

E ven though I'm sleep deprived and my balls are still aching from last night's wild sex marathon, I have to report for duty.

Adulting isn't an option when you're the CEO.

After greeting the security team at the gate, I step into the building, take the elevator, and head to the executive floor. Since it's early, the place is blessedly quiet.

As I stride to my office, I can't help but smile. There's always a sense of immense pride that washes over me when I trail the hallways of the five-story Culver City building my business partner and I own when it's empty like this. Photos in black frames of our milestones and achievements line the walls.

Our vision.

Our creativity.

Our boldness.

Our empire.

Our freaking dream come true.

We built this.

I enter my office, not bothering to close the door. I remove my suit jacket and place it on the back of one of the guest chairs.

My phone rings.

*Already?*

I fish it from the pocket of my jacket and check the name on the screen.

"Good morning, Valerie," I say, accepting the call.

"I'm not sure it's going to be a good morning, boss," she says.

"Are you okay?"

"I am."

"Did something happen to the kids?"

"No. Everyone on my end is safe and sound."

"Okay, so why the gloom and doom?"

My executive assistant Valerie Hurst is usually a cheery person. I don't recognize the person on the other end.

"Are you heading home from LAX?" she asks.

I was on my private jet at five this morning after three nefarious days in Sin City. Technically, I was there to work, but at night, all bets were off.

"I just walked into the office." I round the desk and take a seat. "There's too much for me to catch up on to waste time in traffic. Not to mention, I have to head out to a meeting with the agency in a couple of hours."

"I gather you haven't checked social media?" Valerie asks.

"No."

"What about the entertainment news?"

"No."

"The newspapers?"

"No! What's going on, Valerie?"

"You might need to hire a new publicist. Fast!"

The former publicist who had been with me forever, hung

up her PR boxing gloves to become a full-time mom upon the arrival of her fifth child. After a month of working with her replacement, I couldn't handle the woman's overdramatic nature and bitchy attitude. I fired her ass.

"Why?" I ask.

"I was about to turn off the TV as I was rallying my three rambunctious boys to get them into the SUV so I could drop them off at school, when the news broke."

"What news?"

"It has to do with..."

"Spit it out, Valerie."

"It has to do with a woman you were with while you were in Vegas. The radio host was going on about it. Apparently, it's spreading all over social media like wildfire."

I frown into the phone. "The media has a shit fit because I was with a woman? It must've been a slow news night for them to focus on something as mundane as two people hooking up."

"It's more than that, Beckett. You're going to need an expert who's able to reframe this delicate situation before it turns into a blood bath."

"Delicate situation? Blood bath?"

"It seems you pissed off someone with a lot of weight and leverage."

I flash back to my time in Vegas, my thoughts scrambling to make sense of what Valerie just divulged. I'm stumped.

"None of this makes any sense, Valerie!"

"Turn on your computer and do a search."

I do just that.

I secure the phone between my shoulder and my ear. With quick fingers, I type my name in the search bar.

"What the hell?"

Screaming headlines flash on my screen.

It's never a good thing when you see *BREAKING NEWS!* in front of your name on countless results.

*'BECKETT CHRISTENSEN STOLE MY DAUGHTER'S VIRGINITY!'*

*'BECKETT CHRISTENSEN CORRUPTS PASTOR'S DAUGHTER!'*

*'SEX SCANDAL MIGHT CAUSE BECKETT CHRISTENSEN TO LOSE IT ALL.'*

*'EIGHTH RICHEST PASTOR IN AMERICA GOES AFTER CEO ROCK STAR.'*

I blink.

I blink again.

"What the fuck?"

"I'm on my way." Valerie's voice breaks through my hazy thoughts. "In the meantime, I'll call security to make sure they beef up their presence. I'm sure paparazzi and reporters will surround the building in no time. Fucking piranhas."

"Good idea," I say. "Thanks for having my back."

"Always, Beckett."

"I'll see you when you get here."

"See you soon."

I drop my phone on the desk and stare at the screen in disbelief.

Las Vegas is always a blast... even when it's for business.

I was in Sin City for the Monday night finale of a show I'm a co-judge on. The after party was over the top. It was all very PG because the room was swarming with reporters and celebrity bloggers. Last night, I was the MC at Bella Lusso's extravaganza televised fashion show. I ended the night on a bus packed with gorgeous supermodels clad in skimpy, expensive Bella Lusso lingerie, driving up and down the Las Vegas Strip.

It was all in the name of publicity.

A smoking-hot Brazilian bombshell model with dark eyes and long, dark hair caught my attention. After the ride, I went up to her room. If this modeling career doesn't work out for her, she has a future as a Cirque du Soleil artist. Man, that woman was flexible. It'll be a few days before my body recovers.

Where does the pastor's daughter fit in?

I exhale and pinch the bridge of my nose.

*Coffee. I need strong coffee.*

I'd already had two cups on the jet, after that conversation, I need to shoot more caffeine into my veins. Drinking hard liquor at this early time of the day is ill advised.

I push away from my desk, ready to stand up when a violent tornado bursts into my office.

"What the fuck, man?" My good friend and business partner Rhys shouts at me, waving an iPad over his head. "Seriously?"

"Did I make the front page of the entertainment section, Hartford?"

"In every newspaper, on every entertainment website, and on every fucking celebrity blog, Beckett!"

"There's no such thing as bad publicity, Rhys."

He shuts the door with the heel of his foot and stalks towards me, his eyes burning with a mix of anger and annoyance. He drops the iPad on my desk and does a slow clap.

"Once again, your penis is the star."

"Sorry yours doesn't gather as much interest." I'm pissed off he'd accuse me without knowing the facts.

"When *I* fuck a woman, it doesn't make the front pages of the entertainment section," Rhys says between gritted teeth.

"For some reason, when it comes to you, your dick always ends up an international sensation."

"Well, it's a pretty formidable dick. Perhaps yours doesn't measure up," I say.

"Don't make me pull out a ruler, Christensen. Your forbidden Vegas escapade trumps everything out there. And you're trending under #ZelBeckEpicFuck. No one is talking about *our* company, Beckett. It's all about *you*, the bad boy with the insatiable sexual appetite. A virgin *and* a pastor's daughter? There were no other damn choices?"

"Listen, Rhys, I take full responsibility for my actions, but one thing is certain, Zelda was no virgin." I point an angry finger at him. "I'm willing to back it up with my entire fortune."

"That's not what her father claims."

"This is a publicity grab on the pastor's part," I say. "Zelda is as much of a virgin as I'm about to be canonized as a saint."

"Why would her father risk his reputation if it wasn't true?" Rhys asks.

I'm about to retort when a memory surges.

"It all makes sense now." I slap my forehead with my palm.

"What are you talking about?"

"Zelda was adamant. Fucking her pussy was a dealbreaker. Her father claims she's a virgin, but it's semantics—"

"What the hell does that mean?"

"That woman's ass is well used, looser than many pussies I've fucked. She gets fucked in the ass to pretend she's still untouched."

Rhys lifts his hand. "Too much information."

"I'm not going to sit here and be accused."

"What about last month's presidential fuck with the President's daughter? What was your excuse again?"

"I have none," I say. "Trust me, her father's *former position* was the last thing on her mind as she was begging for my cock."

Always aim higher, is my motto.

I graduated from *almost* fucking the former Vice President's daughter and her two best friends in a club in London to fucking the former President's daughter. Honestly, that almost foursome in London could've cost me everything. If it wasn't for the fact my three playmates invited a few friends—who only party with drugs—to join us without my knowledge or consent, my dick might've put me in some hot water. Going on pure instinct, I bailed out just as a reporter was making his way to the room where the fun was happening. It was a close call... way too close for comfort.

"In my defense, she kept insisting *once you go to Texas, you never go back,*" I say.

That woman knows how to show Southern hospitality.

Rhys shakes his head and lets out a sarcastic laugh.

"What?" I demand.

"I get this isn't your first real taste of success, but it is for me. And right now, your dick is fucking it all up—for me, for you, and for all the hard-working and dedicated employees who believe in our vision. You owe them more than that!" He jabs the air with a finger.

We stare at each other long and hard like two silverback gorillas about to engage in a brawl, his blue eyes burning into my own.

Alpha versus Alpha.

"Beckett, you're the CEO of a multibillion-dollar company." He rakes a hand through his hair. "I'm the lucky bastard who gets to ride this along with you. You need to start thinking with your other head."

"I can multitask." I sneer.

I hold his defiant gaze.

The fury dissipates from his eyes, replaced by an air of defeat.

This company is his *raison d'être*. Sometimes he forgets it's also mine.

I get up, plow my hand through my hair and take a seat on the edge of my desk, my gaze never leaving his.

"I wash my hands of Zelda. She's lying. That said, I'll curb my appetite for the next week," I say. "By the time I get back from New York, this fake scandal will be water under the bridge."

He lets out a forced breath.

He holds my gaze. "That won't do."

I knit my eyebrows together. "What are you talking about?"

"I want more than words, Beckett."

"You want me to sign my pledge in blood?"

"A little too medieval for my taste. If you don't have any skin in the game, you'll have forgotten about this conversation by end of the day. God knows what kind of debauchery you'll indulge in while you're in the Big Apple."

"I won't—"

"Please don't insult my intelligence. You love women. I get it—"

"And you don't?" I shoot him an incredulous stare.

"My fucks never end up becoming liabilities," he says. "Yours often do."

"What do you expect from me, Rhys?"

He narrows his eyes. "A challenge."

"A challenge?"

"You keep your cock under lockdown for the next thirty days."

My eyebrows hit my forehead. "Come again?"

"No sex for a month."

"I know it's way too early for you to be drunk, but for the record, what's coming out of your mouth is preposterous."

"If you value this company as much as I do, you'll take me up on my challenge."

"You're crazy."

"Since you fired your personal publicist, allow me to step into the role. You need an image rehab, Beckett."

"Fuck off!"

"Just because you'll be on the east coast, doesn't mean the media won't be after you," he says. "This story won't die down anytime soon. You abstain from temptation for the next month and the spotlight moves to another scandal."

"Please. This is LA. Another celebrity will fuck up before lunch." I scoff.

"Yeah, but Zelda's father is just getting started. It's clear he'll keep fanning the fire. He'll be on CNN tonight."

*Fuck.*

"I'll counter on WNN." Wire News Network's Enews, aka WNN's entertainment program, has always been good to me.

"Your focus needs to be on the company. Not on a misguided pastor dead set on protecting his slutty daughter's long-gone honor."

*Wait. What?*

"You're taking my side now?"

"#ZeldaNotSoVirgin is trending faster than #ZelBeckEpic-Fuck. So is #BackdoorZelda."

I shake my head.

"You're not off the hook that easily."

"You can't be serious about this challenge, Rhys."

"I am." He taps me on the shoulder. "You lie low for a while... and you get a nice prize for your effort."

I'm skeptical, but I bite.

"What kind of prize?"

"My most valued bike."

My eyes grow wide.

"You're willing to part with your Legendary British Vintage Black?"

"The one and only."

Rhys has a stellar collection of expensive bikes, but in the world of motorcycles, he struck gold. He may not have much left from his first career, but he was able to hold on to a coveted ride released in 1948. It has an estimated value of four hundred thousand dollars. That baby is pure mechanical genius.

"It shows you how much this company means to me." He sticks his hands in his pockets. "I hope it's the same for you."

I consider him for a long beat.

"Abstinence for a rare gem?" I ponder. The first word leaves a bitter taste in my mouth.

"Yes." Rhys's cocksure grin irks me.

"You think I can't do it?"

"Prove me wrong, Christensen," he says.

"You're so certain of yourself."

"I am," he says with supreme confidence.

I shoot him a side gaze. "Your bike as bait?"

"Pretty much."

"Thirty days?" I keep repeating myself, but I'm weighing the pros and cons here.

"Four *very long* weeks," he says.

I nod, pensive.

"You can only engage with women in a professional or friendly manner."

"I can do that." Something tells me my eagerness will come back to bite me in the ass.

"Let me make sure we're on the same page here," Rhys says. He lifts a hand and fans his fingers out. "One"—using his other hand, he points to one of his fingers—"your cock can't be inside of a woman's pussy. Two, same for her ass. Three, it also applies to her mouth. Four, titty fucking is cheating. Five, handjobs aren't a way around the rules. I doubt you'd waste your time putting your mouth on a pussy if you aren't getting anything in return. So, that's a non-issue. And I don't have to mention kissing since you never do." By the time he's done with his long list of stipulations, my jaw is hanging open.

"Any questions, Christensen?"

"I can't even get a blowjob?"

"Not unless you're flexible enough to suck your own cock."

I roll my eyes.

He flashes me a row of white teeth. "You can jack off as much as you want."

I glare at him.

It's not like I have an issue with jerking off. I love stroking my cock. The problem is, I've never gone that long without sex.

My mind is spinning.

"You're not man enough, Christensen?" he asks.

It's going to take me a few weeks to find a new publicist, so keeping it zipped up is a good idea. Not to mention, he damn well knows I've never been one to back down from a challenge.

His triumphant grin grows wider.

*Fucker. No way am I letting you have the upper hand.*

"I can live without pussy for a month!" *I think.* "You're on!"

"Good! Let's shake on it."

And we do.

"Just so you know, I'm not worried," he says, his hand still in mine. "That bike will remain in my secure storage facility where it belongs."

I laugh. "I wouldn't count my chickens—"

There's a knock at the door.

My gaze moves away from Rhys's face. "Come in!"

Valerie pokes her head in.

Her features are tense. Somber, even.

"What's wrong?" I ask.

"Yeah, what's going on?" Rhys asks.

"Sorry to interrupt, but something else came up," Valerie says. "There's a life-and-death situation you need to be aware of."

*Good Lord.*

*What a morning.*

# Chapter 2

## *Arianne*

'GLACH TECH BOASTS ANOTHER EYE-POPPING RECORD QUARTER.'

The photo of the man smiling above the caption, 'CEO EXTRAORDINAIRE', makes me want to poke my eyes out with a fork.

*More like CEO douchebag.*

As I keep scrolling through the article, I can't help but shake my head.

There are thousands of other business articles I could be reading right now as I wait for my turn at the coffee shop, but no, I decide to mark my return to California by pouring salt on the wound that apparently hasn't quite healed.

*Don't do it.*

*You're stronger than that.*

*Don't do it.*

I will myself not to scroll down the article, but the masochistic part of me wins. The evil grin of a woman wearing inch-thick makeup, hanging off Glach Tech's CEO's arm in another photo makes me want to smash my newly acquired iPhone to pieces.

*I hate you, bitch. You're nothing more than a stupid tart.*

I scroll down further.

More photos of the *happy* couple—my scumbag cheater ex and my backstabbing cousin.

I want to vomit.

The urge to run away sparks.

I'm this close from turning on my heel, return to the sublet I'm renting, pack my suitcases and hop on a plane far away from LA—never mind if I arrived two days ago.

It's futile because the internet knows no borders.

*Breathe.*

*Don't let them get to you.*

I swallow the sour taste of my bitterness.

*And this is why I stay away from men.*

God knows I'd love to rewind the movie of my life, but I can't. My heart doesn't cry anymore, but the humiliation... time doesn't seem to dampen the crushing feeling.

*Focus on the now, Arianne.*

With a sigh, I type the name of the company I'm about to meet into the browser to see if anything new surfaced since I last checked.

*Nothing.*

*Good.*

Sinking my teeth into a new challenging project will erase Glach Tech—its CEO and his girlfriend—from my memory bank.

"Next!" A barista's loud voice yanks me back to the present.

The guy in front of me steps up to the counter.

I tuck my phone back into my handbag and do a mental check to make sure I haven't forgotten anything.

Nope.

*I got this.*

I smooth down my hair pulled back in a tight chignon. I do the same to the fabric of my three-piece light summer wool suit, congratulating myself on my selection. It screams *business.* My expensive high heels are the only touch of rebel on an other-wise conservative outfit. I'm going for the supremely buttoned-up version of Grace Kelly, since Mom always says I could easily pass for one of Princess Grace's heirs.

Dressing the part is half the battle.

"Next!"

I step up to the counter.

"What can I get ya?" the barista asks.

I order an extra tall, extra hot, one percent milk latte with two shots of espresso and three packets of sugar. The barista asks for my name and then punches in my order. I pay and wait, already starting the mental countdown.

As she prepares my coffee, a child starts yelling.

"Let go, Mommy!"

I turn around.

A mother wrestles with a little girl.

"We don't want to disturb the nice people," the mother says.

Ignoring her mother, the child starts running around in circles, grabbing random items from shelves before throwing them to the floor.

Her mother tries harder to calm her down.

"I hate you, Mommy!"

The child's tantrum escalates.

I move my attention away from the drama.

"Here you go," the barista says, placing my coffee on the counter.

"Thanks."

I'm just about to grab the cup when a mass hits my legs full force before little arms wrap around them, rooting me in place.

*Shit.*

I jerk forward, tipping the cup over and dark liquid splashes all over the place.

*No, no, no.*

I let out an exasperated sigh as I lower my eyes to a pair of big brown ones. There's nothing innocent about the face looking up at me. The child flashes me an almost evil grin.

"Buy me coffee, lady," she says.

My gaze lifts to her mother's.

"Is this your child?" I ask, irritation coating every word.

"Don't talk about my sweet angel like that."

*Sweet angel?*

"Your words are negatively tainting her aura, possibly scarring her for life."

*This woman is off her tree.*

I give her my best resting bitch face in response.

"Come on, angel. The mean lady doesn't like children."

*No, I don't like your child.*

Her daughter doesn't let go immediately, but with some forceful coaxing, she does.

*Thank God.*

"It'll be a few minutes for me to make you another coffee," the barista says, snapping my attention back to her.

*Great.*

～

My luck sucks this morning.

I'm starting to regret my decision to stick around until I got a fresh cup. The other three baristas were hogging everything in sight because each of their customers were on a multi-coffee

run of complicated concoctions that could rival the most decadent desserts, which resulted in backlogging my straightfor-
ward order.

*Lovely.*

So now, I'm hustling.

Conscious of the time, I make my way to my meeting—with
a fresh extra-large latte in hand—as fast as I can in my high
heels, careful not to break my ankles in my haste. The Cedrics,
aka Cedric de Seignard shoes, were a good idea this morning,
but now, I curse them. On the plus side, I didn't get a spot of
coffee on my suit or on my designer shoes. *Thank God for small
favors.* Although, I'm certain the sweltering heat will cause
sweat stains to form under my armpits. I weave through the
mob of people heading to work, dropping *I'm sorry* along the
way. The construction crew, heavy machinery, big trucks, and
Jersey barriers redirecting traffic are a nuisance. Yeah, the
morning commute is a bitch.

*Dammit.*

I don't let that deter me. I pick up the pace a little.

When I arrive at my destination, I let out a long breath. I'm
cutting it close, but at least I'm not late.

*Now isn't the time to rest on your laurels, Arianne!*

Ignoring my achy feet—pounding heart, sweat drizzling
down the middle of my back, and the puddle forming inside my
bra—I hurry forward and thank my lucky stars when the elec-
tronic doors open. Both hands are full. I'm gripping the cup in
one and I'm firmly gripping my bag and laptop case in the
other. When I arrive at the lobby, I panic. There must be a
thousand people waiting to use the elevators.

*I can't be late for this meeting.*

There are bodies to my left and bodies to my right, forcing
me to move at the same snail's pace as the crowd.

*Shit.*

I do a quick mental calculation.

*Crap.*

The coffee is going to be a liability if I hope to squeeze inside a packed elevator. Staining my suit or my crisp white shirt would be the kiss of death.

"Excuse me," I say. No one seems to hear me. "Excuse me," I say louder. "If I could just get through." A few kind souls get out of the way. I rush towards the sign that says 'garbage'.

What I'm about to do is sacrilege, but what other choice do I have?

*Bye-bye, dark goodness. You'll be missed.*

Resigned, I dump the cup and rush back to the elevators.

After what seems like an eternity, the group of people in front of me moves forward.

*Yes!*

A few more elevator cars descend to the lobby, and I'm finally able to inch close enough to step into one of them. I let out a relieved breath when I do.

The car is packed, and I'm the last one in.

*Of course.*

I hold my breath to make it easier to squeeze right in front of the dashboard. As testament to an already frantic morning, I hit the jackpot.

A dozen lights shine back at me.

*This cannot be happening.*

I'm tempted to jump out of the car and into another one, but I brush away the idea. I'm cutting it close as it is. Tardiness isn't my trademark.

The ride up to the nineteenth floor is a slow punishment. People don't seem to be in a rush to get off, which only delays the door closing again. After the third floor, I can't take it anymore. I start pressing the buttons on the dashboard with urgency as a wave of people step off the elevator.

*Come on. Close!*

A few people grumble behind me, but I ignore them.

I check my watch.

*Fuck.*

I'm ten minutes late.

*Not good!*

When we hit the eighteenth floor, I'm almost giddy with joy.

My turn next.

Two people exit together, taking their sweet old time, chatting like they're sitting at a coffee shop, catching up.

*Really?*

Impatient, I press the button like a maniac to force the doors to close.

"It doesn't make much of a difference if you keep doing that," a deep voice says from behind me.

"I'm severely late," I say, jabbing the button some more.

"The elevator is on a timer." The man's retort is swift. "It's pre-programmed."

"This *makes* a difference."

"It really doesn't."

"Well, thank you for your expert opinion, Mr. Elevator Mechanic, but you're not the boss of me."

"If I were, you'd be in trouble."

*Why does that sound like a tempting promise?*

I don't grant him a glance, but I dart my eyes to the right to confirm it's just the two of us.

*Tough luck, buddy.*

I jab the button with a vengeance.

Finally, the doors close.

*Hallelujah!*

*Take that, Mr. Know It All.*

I'm already in the end zone, close to scoring a touchdown. I even do a stadium wave in my head, with the obligatory sports-caster's voice echoing loud, '*Gooooooo Buchanan!*'

My triumph is short-lived.

The elevator jerks hard.

I lose my balance and stumble back.

*Shit.*

I reach out to hold on to something. Anything.

"I got you." The man's voice is amused.

A large hand settles in the middle of my back, preventing me from landing on my ass. The warmth of Mr. Know It All's touch travels through my body.

*Whoa.*

Just when I'm about to turn around to thank the guy, the elevator jerks again.

I shriek.

Everything comes to an abrupt stop and darkness settles around us.

*Oh no.*

# Chapter 3

## *Beckett*

My phone nearly slipped out of my hands when the elevator lurched. It felt like we dropped twenty feet. It was pretty freaky.

Now, it's pitch black and other than our heavy breathing, you can't hear a sound.

*My shitty morning just got shittier.*

"Oh my God, the power is out," the woman says.

*You think?*

"Thanks to you, we're now trapped."

"Thanks to me?" She has the gall to sound shocked.

"Yes! You were the one pressing the buttons like you were on a mission."

"I *told* you I was late," she says.

"And I *told* you hitting the 'close door' button wouldn't make a damn difference."

"What do you know about elevators?" she asks.

I may not be able to see her, but the warmth of her body radiates near mine. And her floral scent... she smells divine.

"Not much, but Google does. While you were losing your shit on that poor button, I did a quick search. I was right."

"Good for you." Her tone suggests she's rolling her eyes right now.

"No, not good for me, because now I'm stuck in damnation with you." I cross my arms over my chest. "Had you been a little more patient, I'd be walking into my meeting on the twentieth floor."

I have an appointment with our advertising agency. Now I'm going nowhere.

A series of bells ring and voices shout from around us.

"People are calling out for help," I say.

"Thank God."

"If there's a building-blackout, it won't do us much good," I say. "We might be stuck here for a while."

"Maybe we should call 911?" she says.

"I'm certain someone already has."

She lets out a huff of resignation.

"Since we don't know how long we're going to be here, it's best to conserve the battery life on our phones."

She lets out a frustrated groan this time. "Why the hell do they have a button on the dashboard if it doesn't even work? I'm pretty sure it's not for decoration."

"In many ways, it is."

"That's stupid!"

"It's about perceived control."

She snorts. "That's ridiculous."

"From where I was standing"—*and thank you for the exquisite view, by the way*—"I could see it all play out."

"What are you talking about?" she asks.

"By believing you were in control of your fate—or at least how quickly you got to the nineteenth floor—your stress level diminished. It was all an illusion. How's your stress level now?" I couldn't help myself.

"You're a comedian, aren't you?"

"Something like that." I chuckle. "Since we might be trapped in here for God knows how long, we might as well relax and enjoy the downtime."

"Relax? Relax?"

I sense she disagrees.

This woman is wound up so tight.

I'd taken great pleasure in checking out her fine ass in her snug pencil skirt that hits her below the knee. I could develop a fetish because of that skirt. And those shapely calves, thanks to those killer high heels...

*Damn.*

I wish I'd caught a glimpse of her face. At least I was able to appreciate her beautiful profile.

Maybe if her hair wasn't pulled that tight, she wouldn't be this stuck up.

I'm sure I can help in that department.

I'd love nothing more than to fuck up her hair to find out how long it was before wrapping it around my wrist and pulling—

"I can't relax!" She exhales a long breath. "I'm supposed to be at a meeting as we speak."

*You and me both, babe.*

"God, I hate being trapped in a small space." Her hand slaps against what sounds like her thigh.

She's frustrated.

So am I.

"Are you claustrophobic?" I ask.

The last thing I need is for her to be jittery on top of being bitchy.

"No. I just don't like not being in control."

Her need for control is what got us into this mess in the first place. No point in reminding her.

"I doubt we'll be the only two people to arrive late to a meeting," I say.

"I don't make it a habit of being late, sir."

*Sir?*

I like how it sounds on her lips.

"Tardiness isn't in my DNA. I'm always on time. Always."

I let out a laugh.

"What's so funny?" she asks.

"You're new to LA."

"What makes you say that?" I'm not imagining the guardedness in her voice.

The darkness intensified my senses, making me that much more aware of the melodic timbre of her voice, despite the edge.

*I wish I could see her.*

"Down, girl—"

"I'm not a girl!" she says. "That's such a prehistoric way of referring to women. Newsflash, this isn't the Stone Age, Tarzan. Cavemen no longer roam among us."

"Ouch." That was below the belt.

"You asked for it," she says.

It's a good thing I made a vow of chastity for the next month. I thought Rhys had lost his marbles this morning, but now, I'll have to thank him when I get back to the office. This woman's walls are erected so high, not even an invasion of grand proportions would bring them down. Flirting with her would be a big fat waste of time, which means I should erase all images of the unmistakable curve of her ass from my memory.

I ignore her snide remark. "To answer your question, the nightmarish traffic in this city isn't an overused cliché," I say. "You never know when you'll get to your destination."

"Well, I was on time, but some unexpected drama at the

coffee shop caused me to be late." She sighs. "It's one of those mornings."

"I can sympathize. I'm having a hell of a morning myself."

"What happened? Your *girl* burnt your toast this morning? Or maybe your *girl* didn't make your coffee at the right temperature?"

*She's a tough cookie.*

"Are you always this friendly?"

"I don't have to be friendly. We'll be out of here in no time and I'll never see you again," she says.

"Never say never."

"Oh, now you're quoting James Bond?"

"There's no winning with you."

"Men. It's always about the win."

"That remark wasn't directed at me, so I'm going to ignore it. You should redirect all that pent-up anger to the asshole who did you wrong."

"You know nothing about me!" she says.

"You're right." There must be a way of cracking this tough nut. "Maybe we should get to know each other a little better since we're roommates. My name is Beckett. And you?"

"I'm not giving my name to a complete stranger," she says.

"I give up."

Did she sweeten her coffee with battery acid? Nah, I bet she laced it with hydrogen peroxide.

A few short minutes tick away and although I know I should shut the hell up and leave her be, I don't. Instead, I try a different approach.

"Are you going to chew my balls off if I ask where you come from?"

Silence.

"My name is Ari and I'm from Philadelphia."

I'm sure it's a nickname, but at least it's something.

"Pleased to meet you, Ari," I say. "First time in LA?"

"No."

"Do you live here now?"

She sighs. "Are we playing twenty questions?"

"What's wrong with a pleasant conversation with a stranger?"

She doesn't answer.

"Don't you want to know anything about me?" I ask.

"Not really."

I should be licking my wounds right now, but you know what they say about a dog with a bone. Backing away from a challenge isn't something I'm capable of and right now winning this woman over would be like climbing Mount Everest barefoot.

*Challenge. Accepted.*

"Why not? I'm a loveable guy." I deliver the line with my trademark charm and panache, adding an extra lightness in my voice since she can't see me.

"They all say that, don't they? Then, the truth slaps you across the face and knocks you off your feet... and not in a good way."

*I guess that fell on an unimpressed audience.*

I allow her words to hang heavy around us.

"If you give me his name and address, I can get someone to take care of him," I say. "Not even the elite police force will be able to find the body."

I expect another smart retort but she surprises me.

"Don't tempt me," she says. "I suspect you aren't part of the mafia, so chances are, we'll get caught. Since orange isn't my color, I won't entertain the thought."

*Yikes.*

"Maybe I gave you a fake name. How do you know I'm not

the most wanted mob king on the FBI's list? Remember, you said you didn't want to know anything about me."

She doesn't answer, but I feel her moving away from me.

"I'm pulling your leg. I'm an honest citizen. There are no bodies hidden under my pool."

"Good to know."

"For what it's worth, I'm sure he'll get what's coming to him."

"I doubt it. Some people are like Teflon," she says.

*He really did a number on her.*

Isn't it ironic?

She's unwilling to share her full name, yet, she just shared something far more personal.

A long stretch of silence passes between us.

"I wonder how much time we have left before the oxygen runs out," I say.

"What?!"

"I'm pulling your leg again."

"You're just mean." There's lightness in that statement.

"Not at all. I just wanted to get a reaction out of you since it seems it's all I can get."

She lets out a low laugh.

"Are we friends now?" I ask.

"Not even in your wildest dreams, loverboy."

"Look at that, you stumbled onto something."

"What are you talking about?" I'm sure she's sporting a frown.

"I'm a lover, not a fighter."

"Moving right along," she says.

I chuckle.

Feeling like we've made progress, I take a chance.

"You smell lovely, by the way."

The closed space traps the exquisite floral scent of her perfume.

"Thanks," she says. "I'm lucky you didn't eat garlic, yogurt, or sardines for breakfast. Halitosis is so unattractive."

I chuckle again. "Is that your way of saying you like how I smell?"

"You're putting words into my mouth, loverboy."

"I'm going to savor this moment because you just went from hating my guts to calling me loverboy. Twice."

"Don't get the wrong idea, I still hate your guts, but that was smooth."

"It's my trademark, along with my dazzling white smile and baby blue eyes."

"Oh, someone is so full of themselves."

"Not at all," I say. "I'm simply describing my best assets while keeping it PG. Feel free to do the same."

That gets me a laugh. It's contained, nonetheless, it's a laugh.

"I'm sure your charm must go over well with the women you try to seduce—"

"Try? I'm insulted. The word isn't even part of my vocabulary."

"I guess women drop their panties for you every single time."

"Wouldn't you want to know, cupcake?"

I don't know how far apart we are, but I take a small step closer to her.

Her clothes shuffle and then there's a thumping sound. "Shit!" she says.

"I guess you can't run very far."

"Don't you dare touch me," she says. "I've taken self-defense classes."

"I wouldn't dream of touching you unless you begged for it."

She gasps.

I grin wide.

"Only a woman who has no sense of her worth would beg a man to touch her," she says.

"I can assure you, they beg for much more than that."

She clears her throat.

A million questions bounce around in my head.

*Is she a screamer in bed?*

*Would she dig her fingernails into my ass as I drive into her?*

*Does she prefer doggie style, or woman on top, or maybe reverse cowgirl.*

What am I thinking about?

She's not that wild.

I bet I could change that in an instant.

"Wow, Romeo. You have a hell of an ego."

"Perhaps you've never had it good enough to beg for it," I say.

"Women fake it all the time and men are none the wiser."

*Feisty.*

"There are certain telltale signs women can't fake. A good lover knows that."

"You're so full of—"

The elevator jerks just as she's about to rip me a new one.

The lights flicker back on and static screeches from the ceiling speakers before a voice blares. "This is the Los Angeles Fire Department. Hold on tight. Everything should be restored soon."

I shield my eyes from the brightness.

Eager to know what she looks like, I lower my hand and turn my head.

To say I'm shocked would be an understatement.

*Holy shit, she's fucking hot.*

I don't mean made-up hot. I mean, born-hot, the kind that's practically an oddity in my circle where hair, lashes, nails, tits, and asses are more often than not, grossly fake. True, I can't attest to every part of her being the real deal, but I'll tell you, God was smiling down on her the day she was born.

She's tiny.

The top of her head barely reaches my shoulder—even in her sexy skyscraper heels.

*What a turn-on.*

Her face is striking.

Her fair skin suggests she isn't from southern California.

Images of me gliding my hands across her body as I discover her soft, pale skin assail me.

*Oh yeah.*

Even her earlobes are sexy.

If there's such a thing as a perfect nose, hers is it.

And those lips... hmm. They're painted in a soft shade of pink with a slight shiver that accentuates her pout. No duck lips for her. Thank God. I bet those perfect lips would look fucking sexy wrapped around my cock.

I had pictured her differently.

I guess you can't judge a book by its cover any more than you can judge a voice in the dark by its clipped tone.

My eyes sweep up and down the length of her body in one glance.

So many women put it all out there. They leave nothing to the imagination because there's no subtlety in the way they dress.

Not her.

She's like a chocolate bar covered in foil I'm dying to unwrap.

*I like the mystery.*

Expressive wide brown eyes stare up at me.

With a slow, deliberate gaze she takes me in from head to toe.

A smile is firmly planted on my lips when our eyes meet again.

She looks me up and down again as if I'm a figment of her imagination.

*I'm all real, baby.*

Her eyes widen, and she sucks in a gasp, her cheeks ignite in flames as redness colors them.

"Hey roomie!" I wave, pinning my warmest smile on my face.

She shakes her head as if breaking free from a trance.

"Seems to me, you like what you see."

Her mouth falls open.

"It's okay. You can admit it. I like what I see." *A lot.*

She glares hard, as if she wishes she could make me vanish in a cloud of smoke. Poof! Be gone.

She rolls her eyes. "As if!"

I push the envelope. "What's wrong with us admitting how we feel about each other?"

"Don't look so pleased with yourself, *roomie*," she says. "This is the last call for us."

Then it hits me.

*Not a trace of recognition.*

*Her accent sounds American, but maybe I'm wrong.*

She doesn't give me that, *Oh my God, it's you! It's you!* look most women do when they meet me.

I've been high profile for the better part of my life. Having someone oblivious to who I am is a refreshing change. And another turn-on.

"You're right," I say. "This," I say, waving my finger between us, with a cocky grin stretching my lips, "is like when the lights come back on in a club or a bar... just before we decide if we'll leave together and spend the night enjoying each other's company."

Her cheeks flame up and her eyes grow as wide as saucers. I can't help the sly smile when my eyes fall to her neck. Her pulse thrums in her throat, the rapid rise and fall of her chest is so, so seductive.

A touch of unexpected vulnerability.

I like it. A lot.

She clears her throat.

"I'm never out late. Ever." My jaw drops. "I wouldn't know what it's like to pick up stray dogs... who might or might not have unsavory diseases I'd rather stay far away from. STDs... so nasty!" Her lips pull up in a triumphant grin.

I ignore her snide dig and zoom in on what's important.

"No random hookups?" I ask.

"Nope."

I'm dumbfounded.

"Ever?"

"Nope."

"And you've never closed a bar or a dance floor?" I ask, because who the hell is that goody two-shoes?

"Never," she says.

"How come?"

"I value my sleep."

"How old are you? Ninety-five?"

She shoots me an unimpressed gaze.

*We're back to being cat and dog.*

She lifts her chin up. "A rested mind is a productive mind."

My eyebrows draw down in confusion.

*What kind of answer is that?*

"Sleep over fun?"

She nods. "Always."

"Even on weekends?" I should drop it, but I can't.

She narrows her eyes. "I gather it's the complete opposite for you?"

"It is." Even though my former reckless career is behind me and I sit at the helm of a formidable company, I still like to party hard.

"Why am I not surprised?" Sarcasm laces her words.

My eyes travel down the length of her body, searching for clues.

They're glaring at me.

She's young, but she hasn't lived.

*Maybe she's a virgin.*

Her hair is pulled back tight. Too tight. The color is a perfect blend of blonde and brown meshes. There isn't a strand out of place. The conservative form-fitted three-piece gray suit she's wearing isn't something you see often in LA. Her white blouse is buttoned up all the way. No flash of skin or cleavage— not even a hint. At first glance, it all screams, *Stay the hell away.* A second glance tells a different story.

She's in desperate need of someone to ruffle and mess up her ordered life. A big injection of chaos into her overly controlled universe, a cocky sabotage to loosen her up.

I take little pleasure in popping a cherry. That said, I'd make an exception for her. I'd sacrifice myself to fuck the prim and proper out of her.

Another time, another place, I'd say I was that guy, but not today.

*Thanks for nothing, Rhys, for cock blocking me.*

She'd be fun to unravel. Alas, I'm forced to rein in my cock and suppress my needs for the next thirty days.

My eyes are on the prize.

That bike is mine.

Not to mention, she comes across as the kind of woman who would want to break my balls instead of licking them.

*Yeah, I'll stick to my fist.*

"You need to let your hair down once in a while," I say. "You might enjoy it."

She squints. "I'm afraid you're mistaking me for one of your *girls—*"

The elevator jerks into motion.

"Thank God this is over," she says before tearing her gaze away from mine, staring in front of her. "Not a minute too soon."

"We finally agree on something," I say.

# Chapter 4

## *Arianne*

*'IS YOUR VAGINA INCENSED? BITTER, MAYBE? MEN CAN SMELL IT.'*

I snort, reading the headline.

"Yeah, well, my vagina is also infuriated, indignant, angry, and spitting fire," I say, before taking another sip of my coffee. "Cobwebs? My vagina is well past that. It's a minefield at this point and I bet it lets off a strong signal and smell, telling men, *Stay the hell away.*" I let out a sarcastic laugh.

I wonder if my *roomie* from this morning could smell my angry vagina?

As I scroll down the article, my lightheartedness dissipates and a familiar discomfort sets in. I sigh. "My vagina is also very, very lonely."

Now I'm depressed.

*Thanks for nothing, Cosmo.*

I flip the iPad over, uninterested in letting a nonscientific-based article in a woman's magazine, written to make you feel sorry for yourself, affect my mood.

"There's a reason I stick to Cosmo quizzes and stay away from the flimsy articles."

My phone rings.

I answer the call, a grin already stretching my lips.

"Are you finally in LA?" my best friend Phoebe asks.

"Yes, I'm officially an Angeleno!" I say.

"YAY!"

"My ears!"

"Well, excuse me for being excited."

"I'm just teasing. I love your reaction."

Phoebe Pedersen and I have been best friends since we became roommates in college.

"Welcome to the City of Angels, *chica!*"

"What kind of lame welcoming committee is this?" I ask. "No *Glad you're back* banner. No champagne. No wine. No charcuterie board. No chocolate fountain. Not even cake. You're on the other side of the planet. We can't even go for coffee or drinks to celebrate."

"Someone is demanding," she says. "I may not physically be present in LA, but I haven't forgotten. The only reason I didn't call sooner was because I was in the air and landed in Hong Kong three hours ago."

"You're the best, Phoebe."

"Of course I am." I can see her beaming smile from here. "Jetlagged?"

"It's ridiculous."

"I'll be in the same boat when I come back next week," she says.

"Hong Kong isn't as far. It took me nearly fourteen hours and a stopover at Heathrow Airport before I landed at LAX from Stockholm," I say. "I must've slept twelve hours straight when I arrived two days ago."

"What a pain, but am I ever happy you're back in California!"

"After gray and dreary cold weather for months on end in Europe, I'm looking forward to the hot Cali sun. I'm sure the warmth will perk me up. There's a pool—"

"It's not the ocean, but at least it's water," Phoebe says. "The building is pretty anal about keeping the pool clean. Same goes for the entire property."

"Good to know, but I don't own a bikini. I've been way too jetlagged to leave the apartment since I got into town."

"I see a shopping spree in your future," she says.

"Definitely. I'm pasty white and desperate for some color. Over the weekend, I'll make sure to give my visa card a good workout."

"Amen to that!" she says. "How's the apartment?" Phoebe asks, changing the subject. "Is the cleanliness up to your standards?"

"The place works. It seems like the original tenant is even more compulsive than I am. Thanks so much for being my eyes."

"You're sure it's okay?"

"I am, Phoebe."

"Sorry I couldn't get you an affordable apartment with an ocean view."

"You did a great job."

"Good. I was so nervous you'd hate it."

She knows me well.

She was instrumental in helping with my move to LA. I live in a color-coded and well-organized world. She doesn't, but that doesn't stop me for loving her to pieces. Through her boyfriend, Phoebe caught wind of a sublet in El Segundo. It's fully furnished, well decorated, comes with floor to ceiling windows, located in a great neighborhood and available for a year. Bonus,

I pay half of what I normally would for a place like this. Since I only have three suitcases to my name, this is perfect. For the past two years, my suitcases have been my only possessions in the world after leaving everything behind.

*Starting over is a bitch.*

"It's exactly what I need until I find my bearings."

"I wish you'd stay with us," she says.

"Phoebe, you just moved in with a wonderful man—a boyfriend I haven't even met yet. I refuse to be the third wheel."

"You wouldn't be," she says. We've been arguing about this since I decided I had healed enough to return to California.

"I'd be in the way."

"You're my best friend. Oscar knows that. I'd never allow him to come between us—not that he's that kind of guy."

Her loyalty and her friendship mean everything to me.

"God, I've missed you so much," I say, swallowing down my emotions.

"I've missed you, too, Ari," she says, choking up. No amount of text messaging, FaceTime or Skype can replace being close to people you care about the most. "I really wanted us to spend time together."

"Newsflash. We both live in the same city now. We *are* going to spend more time together. I'm just unwilling to be in the way of you and copious amounts of sex."

She laughs.

"Oscar and I have been seeing each other for eight months. We *can* keep our hands off each other."

"It's different when you live together, you can have sex in every room, at any time of the day, whenever one of you feels horny."

She laughs harder.

"Truth be told, I love the idea of a live-in cock," she says.

"And I'm grateful my latest obsession is attached to a normal man and not a freak or an asshole. I swear, I savored a bottle of champagne the day after Oscar asked me to move in with him as I was gleefully deleting my profile from all those dating websites. God, how dreadful. No more bad dates—Shit. I'm sorry, Ari. That was insensitive of me."

"Not at all," I say. "I don't intend on having a profile on any dating or casual hookup sites. I can live without the headache. Statistically, you have less than a one percent chance of meeting someone who isn't carrying a plane full of luggage."

Okay, that's a fly by the pants rationale since I haven't Googled the data, but she doesn't need to know that.

"I won't argue with you. Online dating makes you seriously consider joining a nunnery. I was this close." We both laugh. Phoebe has a trunk full of freaky stories. "It's much better to meet a guy the old-fashioned way." There's a smile in her voice. Not surprising.

After months of striking out with unsuitable—and often, horrible—matches, Phoebe met her Peruvian boyfriend, Oscar Alcóver, at the bar he owns.

"Oh no, that door is closed shut," I say. "I'm so not going down that road any time soon."

Case in point, my roomie. Sure, the man is unbelievably hot, but he's a man. And that right there is a big strike against him.

"I thought coming back to California was about new beginnings—a renewal."

"It is. Career wise," I say.

"It can't only be about work, Ari."

"According to Cosmo—"

"You're so left brained and factual, why do you keep doing those illogical fashion magazine quizzes?"

"They're my guilty pleasure," I remind her. "Not to mention, I needed a pick-me-up after this morning's trauma."

"What happened?"

"I was trapped in an elevator for over an hour on my way up to a meeting with prospective clients."

"That's terrible."

"It was a freaky experience."

"Were you alone?"

"I wasn't."

Nope. I'm not telling her about my sexy roomie clad in a perfectly cut suit with ocean-blue eyes you could lose yourself in. It would only give her false hope. Since it's unlikely I'll ever see him again, why go there? Not that I'm interested or anything.

"Thank God."

"I know."

As much as I hate to admit it, the man's presence was comforting. Without him, I would've freaked out.

"How was the meeting in the end?"

"It never happened."

"Were they pissed off you were late?"

"Once the elevators were working again, I raced to the meeting, mortified by my tardiness. The prospects weren't at the office."

"How come?"

"Their executive assistant said it was confusion on their part, which I don't understand since I triple checked with her to make sure the meeting was still on. Still, I didn't argue."

"That sucks."

"It really did... especially after the elevator incident."

"Is the meeting rescheduled?" Phoebe asks.

"It is. I'm meeting them again in twelve days."

"Knowing you, it'll only give you more time to perfect an already pristine presentation."

"I guess." I'm still really annoyed by their forgetfulness.

"So, Cosmo was your cure for this morning's mayhem?" Phoebe veers the conversation to the original topic.

"It was! Before you called, I was reading an article that explained my predicament."

"Care to share?" There's resignation in her voice.

"You seem so excited."

"I already know you're going to find a million reasons to stay stuck."

I ignore her comment.

"Men can smell my angry pussy a mile away," I say. "All the festered disillusionment I foster is more pungent than the most expensive perfume. So, you see, I'm a lost cause."

"Don't say that!"

I know where this conversation is going.

"Just because you met *the one*, doesn't mean we're all destined to be as lucky."

"Give it a chance—"

"Pun intended?"

"Crap. Chance is your ex's first name."

"Ironic, right?" I sneer.

"Wrong choice of words, sorry. But Oscar has a lot of really handsome and available friends. And they're all normal."

I doubt any of them look nearly as drop dead gorgeous as the guy I was trapped with this morning. No one should have such mesmerizing eyes. No one. That shade of blue could make a girl do a lot of crazy things. Good thing I have my wits about me.

"It sounds like you've psychoanalyzed them," I say.

She's quiet for a long beat.

"These are good men. Solid men, Ari."

"Unless I can secure one of them as a client, I'm not interested."

"What about a friends with benefits arrangement?" she asks. "It can't be about work twenty-four-seven."

Okay, so my life is sixty percent work, thirty percent thinking about work and ten percent sleeping, but at least I devote zero percent of my time thinking about men.

"It still involves being with a man. I'll pass."

"Ari—"

"You're wasting your time, Phoebe."

She lets out a long sigh.

"Work doesn't stampede all over your heart and it sure as hell doesn't backstab you." Anger bubbles up inside me.

"Arianne, please—"

"I'm sure you have a lot to do since you landed not long ago. I'm going to go head out and work on my tan." And clear my head.

"Arianne, don't shut the door in my face," Phoebe says. "By letting Chance and his trashy girlfriend win, you're punishing yourself."

So she keeps reminding me.

"It's called self-preservation," I say. "We'll talk to each other tomorrow."

I hang up before she can argue.

# Chapter 5

## *Beckett*

I follow the maître d'hôtel through a bustling bar for a late-night drink with a friend. The spacious room mirrors the décor reminiscent of old-fashioned British gentlemen's clubs, a close resemblance to the well-appointed style of one of my favorite hangouts in LA—The Study, the private gentlemen's club annexed to the Quintus Hotel.

A tall, elegant man stands up as I approach, a broad smile already stretching his lips.

We greet each other with a bro hug.

"Beckett Christensen," he says, stepping away from me.

"Prince Easton," I say.

"Just Easton," he says with a laugh. "Brielle isn't my wife yet."

"Speaking of the stunning beauty, how is she?" I ask.

"Perfect in every sense of the word."

"I can't believe you're off the market." And I still can't believe your fiancée is a bona fide princess with royal blood running through her veins.

"I'm in love." I swear his eyes twinkle. He's pussy whipped.

It seems to be a contagious disease running rampant in my circle these days. Lucky for me, I'm immune. "I was never a bad boy like you, Christensen. I'm just a finance geek who got really lucky."

Geek? He means, genius.

"I can't believe you're going to be a bona fide prince," I say. "Once it's official, do we have to bow in your presence, Your Grace?"

"I'll expect nothing less," he says.

"Don't hold your breath, Winchester."

We both laugh.

"Sit down," he says.

A waitress approaches.

Easton suggests the cheese and charcuterie platter, an assortment of croquettes, and the meatball flatbread as appetizers. I don't argue. We both opt for top shelf vodka on ice as a drink.

The waitress scurries off.

I scour the room before meeting his gaze. "This is a cool hangout."

"Bygone is where I meet friends. I keep the more overrated Manhattan establishments for clients and prospects."

"Glad to see I'm still on your good list," I say.

We first met at a conference in San Francisco. He knew who I was before I introduced myself. Turns out, he's a huge fan. Many moons ago, I was a rock god and lead singer of one of the bigger rock bands of our time. As an angel investor, Easton is a billionaire many times over. He has a flair for buying and selling companies at the right time. He took an interest in our company early on. Over the years, I've relied on his expertise.

"Always," he says. "So, how was your stay in New York?"

After last week's craziness, I couldn't wait to get out of LA fast enough. My time in the Big Apple helped me regain my equilibrium. My sexy little stuck-up roomie is no longer on my mind. Bonus, Zelda is in my rearview mirror. I'm not sure how the conversation with his daughter started, but the pastor ate his words and shut the hell up about suing me after #Backdoor-Zelda exploded on social media, causing an embarrassing number of men to share their stories.

"Ten whirlwind days, but they were really productive," I say.

"Good," he says. "How's life as a CEO treating you?"

"Hectic. Demanding. Stressful. Relentless at times. But it's also humbling and incredibly rewarding. It's more than I signed up for, but I wouldn't give it up for the world."

"From singer to kickass executive, who would've thought?" Easton says, not for the first time.

I'm about to shoot off a smart repartee, but the waitress is back with our drinks and food.

With a nod, we thank her.

"The American dream... anything is possible," I say once she's gone.

"I'll drink to that," Easton says, lifting his tumbler.

I mimic him and we clink our glasses.

For the next few minutes, we enjoy exceptional food and sip on smooth as velvet vodka.

"Wow," I say, pointing at my plate after taking another bite.

"I know. This place is a gem."

"Although this is your hangout, I hope you don't mind if we talk business?" I ask.

"I'm willing to make an exception for you, Christensen."

"I'm special?"

"You are," he says with a laugh. "Seriously, you had a lot of questions and since you were going to be in town, meeting in person made more sense."

"Thanks. I appreciate it."

"You're a CFO short?" he asks.

"Two, actually."

He knits his eyebrows. "What am I missing?"

"Our CFO has been on maternity leave for two weeks now. We went through an executive agency to hire an interim, but the day before she was due to start, the agency called to let us know her son was rushed to ICU after a bad car accident. Eleven days later, he's still in a coma."

"I'm sorry to hear that," Easton says.

"It's a tragedy. Understandably, she stepped down before she even started."

"So now, you're looking for a replacement?"

"Yes and no."

Easton frowns. "How can it be both?"

"The executive agency went into action to find us another CFO, but Rhys, who was at a conference in Dallas while I was in Vegas, made suggestions that prompted us to put everything on hold."

"Conferences spark new ideas that can set a company on a lucrative path. What kind of suggestions?"

"We're flying high, so the idea of selling the company is off the table. That said, Rhys suggested we hire a merger and acquisition expert for a thorough fitness assessment," I say with air quotes. "What if we're leaving millions of dollars on the table, but we're unaware of it? We want to know so we can fix the issues and boost profits."

"Forward thinking. Great idea."

"I'm glad we're on the same page," I say. "Correct me if I'm wrong, but a CFO has a different mission than a consultant whose main objective is to shape a company for a potential buyout or an IPO."

"You're right," Easton says.

"Our closest competitor sold their company to a computer giant for over three billion dollars—

"Since then, sales have doubled with no signs of slowing down."

"No one else in the marketplace has a buzz-worthy brand like theirs... other than us." I steeple my fingers together. "We want to dominate the market!"

Easton nods.

With his eyes still trained on mine, he grabs his tumbler and takes a long swig of his drink.

I do the same.

"We don't measure up?" I ask when he remains silent.

"Your company is worth well over three billion dollars," Easton says.

I like the way this conversation is going.

"The superior bass on your headphones trumps the competition. No one comes close. I wouldn't dream of listening to music on anything else since I discovered your headphones."

"That's a huge compliment coming from a guy like you."

"It's the truth, Beckett," he says. "You have a solid brand, a former rock star status—hence, instant name recognition—and a product customers gobble up—even though it's a luxury item far from being within everyone's reach. I'd say your company is worth five billion dollars. With the right consultant, that number could skyrocket to six or seven billion."

I nearly choke.

The news hits me like a slug to the chest, forcing my back against my seat.

Rhys and I figured we could get a little over two billion, making us instant billionaires, but this blows my mind.

"Seven billion dollars?" I ask to make sure I heard him right.

"Absolutely," Easton says.

"Wow."

"I know exactly who you need," he says.

I rub my hands with excitement. "I'm all ears."

"Have you ever heard of Glach Tech?"

"No."

Easton pulls out his phone and does a quick search before handing me his device. I scroll through Glach Tech's product catalog.

"Still doesn't ring a bell." I hand him back his phone.

"Amassing funding through a crowdfunding campaign is an art. Many try, few succeed. Of those who get traction, not all reach their campaign goal because it takes extraordinary vision and a solid plan. It also takes a kickass and aggressive social media campaign. You need all the pieces to work together. One weak link could spell failure."

"I assume Glach Tech is the exception."

"Glach Tech pulled a hattrick." He places his elbow on the table and flashes me three fingers. "Three massively successful crowdfunding campaigns, each amassing several millions of dollars. They went from an insignificant company with fledging sales to a market leader in five years."

"I gather you know who orchestrated those campaigns?" I ask.

"After their first noteworthy campaign, I did some digging. I also had my intelligence team poke around. Turns out, it wasn't a consultant who masterminded Glach Tech's rise to success. It was an employee. She was a young woman at the time, barely out of college—"

"You want me to poach one of their employees?"

"She no longer works for them," Easton says.

"Is she working for another company?"

He shakes his head.

He's piqued my interest. "I'm surprised she isn't one of your consultants."

"When she was still working for Glach Tech, she made it clear her allegiance was with them—which I respected. We stayed in touch. I was fascinated by her brilliance. Then two years ago, out of the blue, she contacted me. She needed to get as far away from Silicon Valley as possible."

"Sounds like there's a story there."

"It's not mine to tell," Easton says.

"Fair enough."

"When she came to me, I was considering investing in a number of tech companies across Europe. I bought her a first-class ticket to Stockholm. From there, she hopped around Europe, working for me and other angel investors."

"You're saying she knows her stuff."

"She was instrumental in helping me avoid money pits," Easton says.

"Is she still in Europe?"

"After a couple years away, Arianne decided it was time to come back stateside."

This sounds promising.

"I know she's talking to a few companies for possible consulting work, but I'm not sure if she settled on anything yet."

"Arianne," I nod. "Pretty name."

"Don't let the softness of her name fool you. She's tough as nails, sharp as a whip, and she doesn't take bullshit from clients. She tells it like it is, so you don't waste time or money."

"All good things," I say. "I'm excited."

"You should be. She started her undergrad degree at seventeen—"

"Holy shit!"

"Yeah, she's extremely smart. She has an analytical mind

like I've never seen before. If you look up 'sexy brain' on Google, her photo appears."

I laugh.

"After completing an honors bachelor of business finance degree, she graduated at the top of her class at the tender age of twenty-three with an MBA/CFA degree. The CFA is one of the hardest degrees to earn. The prep work is punishing. The failure rate is extremely high, yet Arianne nailed it on the first try while finishing her MBA."

"I barely finished high school," I say.

"I've never met anyone with the ability to reshape a company like her."

"Wow."

"Earlier this year, Glach Tech was bought out for a ridiculous sum, making the CEO an extraordinarily rich man. Without the crowdfunding hattrick and Arianne's foresight, they would never have sold for that kind of money. She single-handedly brought back the company from the dead—"

"Sold!"

"Without even meeting her and without talking to your business partner?" Easton asks.

"It takes a lot to impress you, Easton," I say. "You only have accolades for this woman. Her only fault might be she can't walk on water."

He laughs.

"She's a free agent?"

He nods.

"I want her!"

"I can make the introductions."

"Is she in New York?"

"It's your lucky day, Christensen. She just moved to Los Angeles."

# Chapter 6

## *Arianne*

"Stupid idiots." I rage under my breath as the packed car zooms down from the nineteenth floor.

*Twice! Twice, they are a no show!*

*How can people be this disrespectful?*

I let out a sigh.

Fool me once, shame on me. Fool me twice and don't expect me to take your calls ever again.

When the elevator doors open, I stomp out, still angry as hell, muttering a string of four-letter words.

All this preparation and sitting in traffic for no good reason. I was up at five-thirty this morning to slap makeup on my face and get ready.

*Thanks for nothing.*

I exit the building in search of a cab when my phone rings.

I fish for it inside my handbag.

"Hey, Easton!"

After Phoebe and my parents, Easton Winchester was the fourth person to get my new phone number.

"Hey, Arianne!"

"I got your message. I was going to call you back after my appointment."

"Is this a bad time?" he asks.

"No, it's not."

I move out of the way to avoid getting run over by a mass of people rushing towards the entrance of the building.

"Did your prospects hire you on the spot after a stellar presentation?" he asks.

"They'll never get to hear the presentation I slaved over for days," I tell him.

"I detect frustration," he says.

"You detect correctly, dear friend."

"What happened?" he asks.

"Twelve days ago, I had an appointment with the same company. On my way up, I got trapped in the elevator—"

"Oh, no."

"I know, right?"

"How long were you trapped in there for?"

"About an hour. The heavy construction right outside the building was responsible for a temporary power outage."

"Were you trapped alone?"

"No, there was another guy in there with me." A very cocky, tall hunk with mesmerizing ocean-blue eyes and a dazzling smile I barely noticed. As much as I hate to admit it, I haven't been able to stop thinking about him. My roomie was the kind of man who makes a lasting impression.

"Thank God for small favors," Easton says.

"Yeah."

"If this is your second meeting, why didn't your prospects hear your presentation?"

"I booked a seven-thirty meeting instead of a nine-thirty meeting to bypass the heavy morning rush," I tell him. "Just like last time, I triple checked the appointment.

Just like last time, they confirmed. Their executive assistant also confirmed. Just like last time, there was confusion on *their* part, aka, another early morning golf game."

"That's highly unprofessional," Easton says. "Do you have any other prospects on the list?"

"Not really. There are a lot of tire kickers. The landscape in LA is different from Europe, New York or Silicon Valley. Maybe I made the wrong decision by coming here." I let out a defeated sigh.

"Maybe not," Easton says.

My ears perk. "You have a project for me?"

"A friend of mine does."

"Tell me more." I'm practically salivating at the idea of working again.

"This isn't high-tech—"

"I'm okay with that!"

"Down, girl," Easton says.

"Sorry. I'm just not good at being idle."

"Then the timing couldn't be more perfect. This project was made for you, Arianne. It's the kind of opportunity you can really sink your teeth into and make your mark."

*Interesting.*

"Here in LA?"

"Yes. My friend isn't a tire kicker."

"I like the sound of that."

"He already has a hugely successful company worth multi-billions of dollars."

I frown my confusion into the phone. "Why would he need me?"

"He's seeking an expert willing to take a look under the hood of his well-oiled top-of-the-line ride and turn it into a speeding bullet. In other words, he needs you to take his company to the next level. This is more about ballooning his profits than a potential buyout."

*Right up my alley.*

"I'd love to meet with your friend."

"Good. I was hoping you'd say that. He flew overnight from New York to LA. He just called me to find out if I got in touch with you. He's eager to meet with you. Are you available today?"

I hesitate. "Err... I like to have a complete picture of a prospect's company before meeting with them." I sigh. "I don't want to give off the wrong first impression by being unprepared."

"Arianne, your mind works faster than a processor."

I laugh. "You've always been such a great supporter."

Easton was my ticket out of Silicon Valley when I needed to run away.

"From my understanding, you already have the job."

*What?* "How can that be?"

I'm dumbfounded.

"I relayed my experience. You've never disappointed me."

*Incredible.* "Wow."

"This is a relaxed face-to-face. You'll have plenty of time to crunch numbers and prepare complicated, colorful Excel spreadsheets."

"Are you making fun of me, Easton Winchester?"

He laughs. "I wouldn't dream of it."

"I should hire you as my publicist," I tell him. "Here I thought I could do it on my own, but I keep stumbling on losers. One call from you and you hand me a winning lottery ticket."

"I didn't do a thing." That's a lie, but I won't argue.

"Thanks for vouching for me, but I still feel uncomfortable walking into a meeting with nothing more to offer than a smile."

Nervous trepidation grips at my core.

"Arianne, stop overthinking. You could nail this contract with your eyes closed."

I think of how much time I've sunk into proposals that no one really cares about since I landed in LA.

*New city. New attitude.*

*Throw caution to the wind, Ari.*

"Let's do it!"

My butt barely hit the backseat of the cab when we're already in Culver City. Normally, I'd leaf through the pages of my presentation during the ride to a meeting. I considered Googling as much as I could, but decided against it. I'm not a half-full kind of girl. I dive deep or not at all. Bits and pieces of information would only end up giving me a panic attack. Easton assured me I had this one in the bag. Why stress when I don't have to?

After a thorough screening when the cab rolled in front of a security booth, we inch to the front of a modern building where a row of security guards awaits. Another round of checks later and I enter the building.

*They don't skimp on security here.*

As my Cedrics heels click against the polished concrete floor, I take in the impeccable décor. This place is dripping with luxury. It's understated, but impossible to ignore. I gasp in admiration when my eyes catch an edgy ceiling lamp, consisting of eight large black globes, that looks more like a work of art than a utilitarian item. It's a great complement to the modern water wall.

*Wow.*

Whoever is behind this has flawless taste.

From the opulence, it's apparent I'm not dealing with wannabe bubble gum CEOs who are nothing more than time-wasting teenage boys dressed in suits.

*Amen to that.*

The thought of a certain man in a suit brings me back to my extremely attractive elevator roommate. Considering the solemn promise I made to myself, that guy has no business occupying my thoughts like he has.

*Focus.*

"Hello and good morning! Welcome to SCORE MAX Audio Bass! I'm Paula. How can I help you today?" a thin jovial redhead with a slick bob, wearing a white blazer, says in one breath as I approach her desk.

"Good morning. My name is Arianne Buchanan. Valerie is expecting me."

"She told me to be on the lookout for you." Paula gives me a onceover, her smile widening. "I love your suit. I've never seen a woman wear a vest under a jacket before," she says when her green eyes meet mine.

"It's a little conservative, I know."

"It's good, honey," she says. "So many young women these days walk around with dresses that are as short as t-shirts. It's slutty."

"It's not my style," I tell her.

"Your beauty should speak for itself," she says. "And God was good to you, honey."

"Thank you," I say, blushing. "Valerie mentioned the meeting was on the fifth floor. I should go upstairs. I don't want to be late."

"You're right. You better go before I talk your ear off," Paula says. "I'm from Minnesota. We've been accused of being too friendly." She laughs.

"Friendly is good."

"Aww... I like you already," she says, placing her hand against her heart. "If you head right up to those elevators," she points to her right, "I'll tell Valerie you're on your way up."

"Thank you."

"Knock 'em dead, honey! You're surely dressed for the part!"

# Chapter 7

## *Beckett*

"**A**rianne is here," Valerie announces when I pick up my landline. "She's in the 1916 Traub conference room. I'll let Rhys know."

Given our mutual penchant for bikes, all of our conference rooms are named after rare motorcycles.

"Perfect!" I say. "Did you order breakfast?"

"I got a breakfast board from Blond Pistachio. Your favorite."

"You're the best. Coffee?"

"It goes without saying. Lattes from Thoroughly Hot should be arriving any minute now, the fridge is already stocked full with Perrier water, catered lunch will be delivered at one, I have a dessert board and more lattes scheduled for four, and finally, dinner reservations are set at Le Specialità for seven o'clock."

"You're the picture of efficiency," I tell her.

"Of course I am."

I chuckle.

When Easton told me he'd gotten hold of Arianne, I

cleared my schedule. Rhys did the same. We're eager to get the ball rolling.

"If we're going to hold Arianne hostage for the day, we might as well make it as pleasant as possible," I say.

"Although, I'm happily married and you're my boss *and* we have a non-fraternization clause in our contract, may I take some liberties?" She continues before I can answer. "I doubt any woman in her right mind would be opposed to having you and Rhys as her captors."

I laugh.

"Do I have to call Emmett and tell him about your secret fantasy?" I ask.

"He already knows."

"Moving right along."

She laughs.

"Let me gather my things and I'll head to the conference room."

"Excellent!"

I get up, but my phone rings.

I debate whether to let it go to voicemail.

*Let me get this.*

"Mom!" I say when I pick up.

"How's my baby boy?"

My success has no bearing on the way she sees me.

"I'm fine, Mom."

"Just fine?" Concern colors her voice.

"I'm unstoppable!"

"Now you're talking!" We both laugh. "New York was good?"

"It was a worthwhile trip."

"Did you get back yesterday?"

"No. I just got back a few hours ago. I extended my stay by a day to meet with Russian distributors who happened to be in the Big Apple. I flew overnight so I could be back at the office first thing."

"Beckett, I don't care if your fancy jet is equipped with those lounging beds, that's not proper sleep," she says. That's the topnotch doctor in her talking. "At this rate, you're going to burn out—"

"Mom, is there anything urgent?"

"I was at a medical conference in Baltimore before you left for New York, so we haven't talked in a while and you know how I feel about text messages, Beckett," she says. "I miss my baby boy."

I chuckle. "I miss you too, Mom, but I have to go. I have someone waiting for me for a meeting."

"When will Dad and I see you?"

"Mom!"

"All right. All right. I get it," she says. "Go do your CEO thing." There's laughter in her words.

"I'll talk to you later," I say.

"I can only hope," she says with a sigh.

"A little dramatic, much?"

She laughs.

"Big kiss, baby."

"Right back at ya, Mom."

I hang up and rush to the conference room. As I approach, the sound of laughter erupts.

I'm glad Rhys is entertaining our new consultant.

"Oh God, that's so funny, Rhys," I hear Arianne say. "I can't believe that actually happened."

*There's a melodic timbre to her voice—*

I'm hit with my tragic reality.

I have to keep it to my fist for another eighteen days.

I won't hear the soft, helpless whispers of a woman's voice in my ear as I take ownership of her pussy, pounding into her forcefully. For another excruciating two-and-a-half weeks, I'll have to live without hearing a woman scream out my name at the top of her lungs as I push her over the edge.

*Fuck.*

I haven't been able to forget the smart mouth I was trapped inside the elevator with. These past twelve days have been torturous. The memory of her only heightened my misery.

And of course, Rhys is enjoying every minute of my suffering. He took cruel pleasure in texting me daily reminders of my vow of chastity, each time carefully including photos of the coveted bike from different angles.

*Asshole.*

I ignored his taunting subterfuge, preferring to lose myself in work in the hopes of ignoring my hungry cock. I can't count the number of times I've jerked off since agreeing to this ridiculous challenge. It's so obscene, I should be arrested. By the time he hands me the keys to his Legendary British Vintage Black, I'll be a wild beast.

I sigh.

I'm just about to enter, but freeze.

*Shit.*

I forgot my iPad.

I race back to my office.

"Is everything okay?" Valerie asks when she sees me zooming by her.

"I'm not as organized as I'd like this morning," I say over my shoulder.

With my device in hand, I make my way to the conference room.

Arianne is still laughing her head off.

*Sounds like Rhys and her are hitting it off. Good.*

I enter without knocking.

Rhys stands up, a huge grin stretched across his face, malice twinkling bright in his eyes.

*What is he up to?*

Then, it all seems to happen in slow motion.

Arianne pivots on her chair, ready to get up, but freezes.

The warm smile on her gorgeous face dissipates, replaced by sheer confusion.

I'm dumbfounded.

I squint, certain I'm seeing things.

She mirrors my bewildered expression.

*Ari is Arianne?*

*Whoa!*

*I didn't put two and two together.*

"Well, well, well," I say, when I recover.

She stands up.

She's wearing another suit of armor. This three-piece suit is navy-blue with white pinstripes. I catch a glimpse of her pencil skirt that hits her below the knee.

I swear I'm going to develop a fetish.

Just like last time, the look is strait-laced.

*What are you hiding underneath that armor?*

She's staring at me.

I lift an expectant eyebrow.

She tilts her head back as if to take a better look at me.

"You?!" she says.

"Yes, me."

"Nooooo..."

My grin widens in amusement. "Yeeees..." I mimic her.

She shakes her head. "How can this be?"

Talk about coincidence.

"Small world," I say.

"Small world."

"You two know each other?" Rhys asks.

"She's my roomie from the elevator incident," I tell him.

He stares at us with astonishment. "Her?!"

I nod before turning my attention to the stunned woman in the room.

"Wasn't it you who said we were never going to see each other again?"

"You can't be the man Easton referred me to," she says.

"I am. Beckett Christensen, please to meet you." I extend a hand.

Wide eyes bounce from my hand to my gaze.

"You're my new client?!" *Basically, your boss.*

My lonely hand is still stuck in the air.

She hesitates, but she shakes my hand.

Her touch is as soft as silk.

"I am. And you're Arianne Buchanan."

"I—I am."

"You're sure about that?" I ask.

She flashes me an unimpressed stare and pulls her hand from mine.

I take a step closer and lean in, forcing her to look up.

Pleading brown eyes flutter at me.

She comes across as a woman unaware of her beauty.

I take my sweet time milking the moment before speaking.

"Looks like we'll be working *really* closely together. Like I said, never say never."

She swallows hard.

# Chapter 8

## *Arianne*

I *do not appreciate your sense of humor this morning, God.*

I exchange a few words with the big guy up above as I stare bewildered at my new boss-slash-client—the incredibly handsome man I haven't been able to forget. Of all the companies in a massive city like LA, I had to land here.

What are the odds?

And this is why I never walk into a meeting unprepared.

Easton said I have nothing to worry about. Judging from the outrageous baby blue eyes looking down at me, I'd venture to say he's dead wrong. Forget about being caught off guard. I was caught with my panties around my knees. Not good.

*You're a professional.*

No way am I allowing long, dark lashes framing dreamy blue eyes to set me off course. I have a reputation to maintain, regardless if my boss-slash-client tips the hotness meter on the Richter scale.

*You're immune.*

"It appears I stand corrected," I say. I take the high road.

"I forgive you," Beckett says.

"Excuse me?"

"You were wrong. I forgive you," he says.

"I wasn't asking for forgiveness," I tell him.

"I forgive you for causing us to get stuck in an elevator for an hour and I can forgive you for misspeaking just now."

"You know as well as I do, I had nothing to do with the power outage."

"I'm playing with you," he says in a low voice.

My cheeks flame.

I take a step back, but my ass hits the conference table.

"Are you two going to be at it all day or can we get started with the meeting?" Rhys reminds us of his presence.

I straighten my jacket and my vest. "That's a great idea."

"What she said," Beckett says.

*Cocky bastard.*

I ready myself to sit down, but Beckett pulls my chair out. I didn't expect the gallantry.

"Thank you."

When I look up, Rhys is observing us with the same curiosity he would two rare pink dolphins.

I gather Beckett picks up on that because he rushes to a seat next to his business partner. Both men stare at me with different shades of piercing blue eyes for a long beat. I blush under the observation.

*Is it warm in here?*

Worried I might suffocate, I undo the first button of my blouse and fan myself as discreetly as possible.

*Breathe.*

Beckett's head tilted to the side is making me feel very self-conscious. I fumble with the buttons, but he stops me with a few words.

"It looks better undone."

I must've undergone a lobotomy when I crossed the

threshold of the building because I drop my hands to the table like a docile child.

He flashes me a blinding smile.

My cheeks burst into flames all over again.

Rhys clears his throat.

"Maybe we should start with our background since it's linked to the creation of this company," he tells me.

Beckett points a finger at his partner. "Yes, let's start from the beginning."

"That's a great idea," I say, slipping back into the shoes of the intelligent woman I am. I open my notebook and click on my trusted pen, ready to take copious notes.

"Are you going to write everything down?" Beckett asks, surprised.

I look at him confused.

*Of course I am.*

"This is an unusual situation for me," I tell him. "I'm normally well versed on a company before I step into a meeting. Easton mentioned you wanted to get the ball rolling, and I agreed, but I'm not about to let you down. I have standards."

"You're hard on yourself," Beckett says.

"Time is money, Mr. Christensen," I reply.

He arches an eyebrow and his lips form a lopsided grin.

*What did I say?*

"Touché, Miss Buchanan..." My name has never sounded so sexy. "Given what Easton had to say about you, you shouldn't worry about letting us down," Beckett says.

"I have to agree with Beckett," Rhys says. "You're exactly what we need. This meeting is just us talking."

"Exactly," Beckett says. "You'll have plenty of time to dazzle us."

"Thanks for the vote of confidence," I say, holding his gaze.

"If you two need a moment, let me know..." Rhys chuckles.

"Idiot," Beckett says.

"Do you want me to start?" Rhys asks.

"Run with it," Beckett says.

"Beckett and I met in rehab," Rhys launches into story mode.

"Oh, wow," I say.

"It's a cliché given our first careers," Rhys says.

"What do you mean?" I ask.

"Have you ever heard of Random Misconception?"

"No. Never."

"What about Hijinks?"

"I'm afraid not," I say. "God, this is so embarrassing. I should know these things—"

Beckett reaches across the table and places his large hand over mine.

A jolting electric shock had run through my body when we shook hands, but now... holy volcano.

"Relax."

The simple word passes Beckett's beautiful lips like a soft caress.

"It's not like you're going to fail a test, Arianne," he says.

The mention of my name slaps me back to reality.

*What the hell is wrong with me? He's a client! And the boss! Snap out of it!*

"You're already hired." He offers a warm and reassuring smile. "Rhys and I are putting things into context."

"Thank you for saying that," I tell him.

He nods, that seductive smile still stretching his lips.

"Beckett was, slash is, Random Misconception's lead singer," Rhys says.

I furrow my eyebrows.

"Random Misconception had a comeback six months ago as the backup band for Stasia van Gameren."

"I see," I say.

"Back in the day, the four guys behind the band dominated the charts. The exposure from the band's recent comeback exploded our business. We couldn't keep up. Beckett acquired a whole new generation of fans overnight. His guest appearance as a co-judge on Jam Session—a popular entertainment talent show—also helped boost sales—"

"So, you're juggling all three—the business, the TV show, and your rock star career?" I ask Beckett.

*When does this guy sleep?*

"The TV show isn't a full-time gig," Beckett says. "The comeback was a favor to my cousin Jagger. His girlfriend needed a band, so the four of us reunited. Random Misconception no longer goes on the road, but we'll do the occasional late-night show appearance."

"Who are the other members?" I ask.

"Rod Wolfe is on drums, my older brother Holt—who heads a successful record label in his spare time—is on bass, and my cousin Jace is on guitar," Beckett says. "I'm also on guitar and I'm the lead singer, as Rhys pointed out."

"I'm not into rock music, which explains why I've never heard of you," I say. "I've never met a professional musician before. That's impressive."

"Beckett isn't a professional musician. He's a rock god—same for the other three members of the group," Rhys says.

"We used to be." Beckett chuckles. "Past tense. We traded our instruments for business suits. We're all busy execs now, hence why I'm running this small business with you!" Beckett points to his business partner.

"Small?" Rhys laughs.

"It's all relative," Beckett says with a smile.

"A lot of companies would like to be as *small* as you," I say. They both laugh.

"What about you, Rhys? Are you a musician?"

"I used to be a rapper. My stage name was Hijinks."

"What does that mean?"

"Hijinks–all one word, is the less common spelling of high jinks. It was a popular eighteenth-century drinking game in Scotland. Basically, it's another way of saying mischievous."

"Cool name!" I say.

"Cool name for a very short-lived career."

"Oh."

"I'm what you call a one-hit wonder. I skyrocketed to the top of the charts overnight and then, I crashed and burned."

"I'm sorry to hear that," I tell him.

"There's a handful of well-known white rappers who have name recognition. I had the rhymes, but I wasn't street enough."

"Street?" I ask.

"I didn't grow up in poverty—we were middle class. I was never part of a gang, I never sold drugs, I never shot anyone, I wasn't part of any drive-by shootings, my face wasn't—and still isn't—covered with tattoos, and my teeth aren't stapled with diamonds or plated in gold."

"Oh God, that sounds painful."

"It's all part of having a shtick—something that makes you memorable, unique, and edgy. I thought my strong emceeing skills were my ticket to fame... for a while, they were. With hours of practice, I could out-rhyme anyone who challenged me. My flow was smooth. The delivery, impeccable—"

"You should hear him spit," Beckett says.

"Spit?" I ask, confused.

"It's when rappers drop clever verses or rap ridiculously fast," Beckett says.

"I see." I nod.

I know nothing about rap music.

"That's how I caught the attention of a producer," Rhys says. "That kind of verbal speed is an art form. Still, the music industry chewed me up and spat me out."

"That's horrible," I say.

"That's show business."

I let his words sink in.

"You didn't know each other before rehab?" I ask.

"I knew who Beckett Christensen was—everyone knew who he was—but it wasn't reciprocal," Rhys says.

"I'll make sure to Google both of you after the meeting," I tell them.

"I guess it's game over for you, Christensen, once Arianne discovers your skeletons," Rhys says.

"My former life is an open book," Beckett says. "There isn't much I can do about it."

The glee in his eyes is dangerous.

"Former life?" Rhys asks, incredulous. "You made headlines two weeks ago."

"Whatever!" Beckett rolls his eyes.

Rhys's jab piques my curiosity.

I guess Beckett's expensive tailored suit hides more than meets the eye.

Not that it matters, but it's a good thing I've always steered far away from reckless bad boys. They're too unpredictable. I value order and frown upon chaos. Walking into a meeting unprepared is my idea of living on the edge.

"Rehab connected you." I veer the conversation back on track.

"That's where we became fast friends," Beckett says.

"That's also where the company started—"

"They encourage business startups in rehab?" I ask, interrupting Rhys.

Beckett and Rhys laugh.

I blush. "I guess my inexperience shows."

"Don't apologize for not knowing how rehab works," Rhys says. "Not everyone develops an addiction to drugs like we did."

"I wouldn't know. I've never done drugs," I say.

"Never?"

"Never."

"Wow," Beckett says. His expression is unreadable.

"Not even marijuana?" Rhys asks.

"Oh, God, no," I say, horrified.

They both cock a surprised eyebrow.

"I'm sorry, I interrupted you, Rhys." I'm eager to move the spotlight away from me.

"This guy here"—he points to Beckett—"was complaining about the nonexistent bass on the four-hundred-dollar head-phones he bought." Rhys grabs a pair of well-worn headphones from the tray of samples in the middle of the table and lifts them up. "Beckett fell for the glitzy marketing."

"The multimillion-dollar marketing campaign for those was omnipresent!" I say, recognizing the brand made famous by a rapper turned billionaire. "Every big shot celebrity, singer and athlete was photographed wearing them."

"Exactly," Beckett says. "I'm surprised they weren't able to get the Pope to deliver the Easter sermon with them wrapped around his neck."

We all laugh.

"Their reach was phenomenal," I say.

"Aesthetically, the headphones are perfect," Rhys says. "Regrettably, if you're a music lover, they don't offer the best audio experience. I should know. I bought a pair of each model to test. In fact, we have a sample room with our competitors' products."

"You do?" I ask.

"The bass makes or breaks a song," Beckett says.

I'm impressed.

I draw my eyebrows together. "Forgive my naïveté, but how does a former rapper and a rock star who met in rehab create a company that rivals that one." I point to the headphones Rhys is still holding. "I assume a certain level of sound engineering knowledge is required, and then there's the whole production and manufacturing side. Those things can't be easy to figure out."

"You're right on the money," Rhys says.

"She's sharp." Beckett smiles wide.

"I'm a good listener," I say.

"Easton said you have a sexy brain... I see why," Beckett says.

My cheeks burst into flames.

*A sexy brain?*

"To answer your question." Rhys gets my attention. "I was in and out of rehab as my career slid into an abyss. I was surprised Beckett Christensen talked to me, let alone hung out with me. He wouldn't stop complaining about the headphones. He had his brother buy him new ones with each visit, but none of them measured up. Jokingly, I told him my dad created the perfect headphones. In fact, a few of his prototypes were kicking around at the house, collecting dust. That got his attention."

"So, your dad is the creative genius?" I ask.

"Was," Rhys says. "He died of a sudden heart attack. I couldn't cope without drugs. Heck, I couldn't cope *with* the drugs. Mom implored me to go back to rehab. That's when I met Beckett."

*Great. I just put my foot in it.*

"I'm so sorry," I say.

"Don't be," Rhys says. "You didn't know."

"To your comment"—Beckett forces my attention to him—"Rhys's dad was a talented sound engineer with a knack for tinkering with any piece of equipment until he could bring out the bottom end, aka the perfect deep, low-pitch range in a song. Before he died, he came up with the technology that's become the foundation of our business. He secured the patent and the trademark, but the investment required to bring the product to market was equivalent to the GDP of a less developed country."

"My dad was risk averse," Rhys says. "But he was willing to dish out money for a few prototypes—with an element of pride. I got my mom to bring me a pair of his headphones when she came to visit me in rehab. I still remember Beckett's shocked expression when he listened to one of his songs."

"I told him it was wrong for this kind of technology to sit dormant in a closet," Beckett says. "It wasn't my first time in rehab either. Random Misconception had decided as a group to step out of the limelight while we were still on top. I didn't handle retirement very well. In the first few weeks of the program, I wondered what the hell I was going to do with myself once I was done. It's never a good thing when my mind is idle—"

"Same here," I say.

"I can't believe we have something in common, Miss Buchanan," Beckett says.

"I suspect we don't find joy in the same things, Mr. Christensen."

He squints his ocean-blue eyes, staring at me through a sliver of determination as his nostrils flare. "I'm sure, in time, we'll find more things we share in common... perhaps things that bring us mutual joy."

*Oh, shit, the temperature in the room rises again.*

"I can step out of the room if you two need a moment." Rhys repeats his offer.

"You were saying, Beckett?" I'm grateful Rhys's question breaks the spell I'm under.

"When I listened to music with Rhys's headphones, I knew without a shadow of a doubt what the next phase of my life was going to look like. I just had to convince this guy to join forces with me." He pats his business partner's shoulder.

"I was clueless about my own future," Rhys says. "I was happy to jump on board."

"That's an amazing story," I tell them. "And you were able to figure out the ins and outs of the business side on your own?"

They both laugh.

"Hell, no," Rhys says. "We're musicians. We're not like you. We stopped learning after high school. One plus one equals two, I think—"

"No!" Beckett shakes his head. I'm confused. This is pretty basic math. "It's three. You have to account for inflation."

I laugh.

"See what I mean?" Rhys says. "We can't handle big numbers."

They chuckle.

I look around the room, extending my arms open. "You're exaggerating, gentlemen."

"Careful, Hartford, we can't pull the wool over her eyes," Beckett says.

"You understand that means she won't fall for your bullshit, Christensen?"

Beckett rolls his eyes.

Their constant banter is making me blush.

"My dad has had a string of companies in his lifetime—some big successes, some huge busts," Beckett says. "The same applies to many of my uncles. Rhys and I relied on their expertise. They became investors early on and they were rewarded with handsome buyouts. For the marketing, I figured why fix it if it ain't broke. We copied what worked. I approached musicians I knew and asked them to give us some feedback. They were blown away. In no time, their hordes of fans were rushing to buy SCORE audio bass headphones, propelling us to the number two spot. Five years later... here we are."

# Chapter 9

## *Beckett*

"What a kickass day," I say before taking another swig of my vodka on the rocks.

"I'll drink to that," Rhys says before gulping down his vintage bourbon.

"We'll have to get Valerie and my executive assistant to work together to find an expensive gift to thank Easton."

"What do you get a billionaire and future prince?"

"I don't know. A new castle?"

We laugh.

"Whatever it takes, we'll go the distance," Rhys says. "Arianne is worth it. She's exactly what we need."

*In more ways than one.*

It was a long day for our prim new consultant. After dinner at Le Specialità, Arianne declared she was exhausted. As much as I would've loved to hang out with her more and get to know the woman behind the genius, I had to let her go. After putting her in a chauffeured car, Rhys and I made our way by foot to one of our favorite hangouts—the Quintus Hotel. We kept it low key tonight. We ditched the gentlemen's lounge in favor of the bar for late-night drinks.

"She blew me away by how fast she picked up on everything," I say.

"Same here. I was even more shocked when she agreed with Easton about the potential valuation of our company," Rhys says. "I thought he was pulling your leg. Six to seven billion?"

"I still can't believe it myself," I tell him.

"After today, I can see how we can reach—if not surpass—that, thanks to Arianne's expertise," Rhys says.

"I agree."

"We threw a lot at her, but she didn't seem fazed at all."

"She's something else," I say.

We bombarded her with a tsunami of information. In our defense, she was insatiable. The more we threw at her, the more her eyes lit up with excitement. That's the kind of enthusiasm we were hoping for.

"There's one thing, though," Rhys says.

"What's that?"

"Shame on Easton for misleading us."

My eyebrows hit my forehead. "In what way?"

"Didn't you say Arianne describes herself as a nerd and finance geek?"

"That's what Easton told me," I tell him.

"Hmph." I expect Rhys to elaborate, but he moves his attention to his bourbon.

"What am I missing?" I ask.

"Nerds didn't look like Arianne when I was in high school. If they did, I would've joined the chess club, reading club, and campus Mensa group."

I laugh, shaking my head.

"You had me going there."

"My jaw dropped when I walked into the conference room and saw her."

This is the first time we've had a chance to talk since this morning.

"Mine too," I say, "I'm sure I did a piss poor job at hiding my shock."

"Your expression was priceless." Rhys chuckles.

"This may sound gauche, but I've never met such a striking combination of brains and beauty before," I say. "Some might argue it's a reflection of the type of women I tend to go for... I guess it is."

"You're not going after her, right?" Rhys asks.

*Well, I was planning on it.*

"Did you hear me say that?" I ask him.

"I just want to confirm. You couldn't shut up about the woman in the elevator after your first encounter. Had it not been for the fact you were on the east coast, I bet you would've gone back to that building every single day at the same time in the hopes of bumping into her again—"

"Like I have nothing else to do," I say.

I'm unwilling to admit how many times it's crossed my mind.

"Knowing you, I bet your cock couldn't wait to say *Welcome aboard* when you stepped into the conference room and recognized your sweet-smelling, short-lived roomie."

"What do you take me for?"

"The manwhore you are, Christensen," he says. "Your threshold for resisting beautiful women is fairly low—like nonexistent."

"It isn't a crime to appreciate beauty."

"Regardless of how gorgeous Arianne is, she isn't your type."

"Why do you say that?"

"She doesn't come across like the kind of woman who would fall all over herself just because you're a pretty boy, and she isn't impressed by your rock-star status. That's very rare." He's right on both counts. It's usually easy-peasy to get a woman to drop her panties in a heartbeat. "She's never watched the entertainment show you co-judge." Yeah, the show opened the door to a whole new generation of hot, young women. "Not only are you two complete opposites—"

"Like you're two peas in a pod."

He ignores me. "Arianne seems to be one of the rare gems who's immune to mighty Bad Boy Christensen."

*Fucker.*

"I'll take it one step further, I'm not even sure she likes you."

I came to the same conclusion within ten minutes of officially meeting her.

"I have no problems charming a woman," I say.

"You don't get it, do you? Your fucks are easy lays, too eager to spread them wide—"

"Hey, I take offense to that."

He flashes me a *Are you fucking kidding me* look before continuing. "Beckett, it's going to take *a lot* more than a little cocksureness, pearly white teeth, and baby blue eyes to get a woman like Arianne on her knees."

*Fuck! He had to go there.*

Every time she stepped out of the conference room to go to the bathroom, my eyes couldn't help but caress the roundness of her ass. My cock stiffened each and every time. I had to suppress a moan to avoid Rhys's already suspicious gaze. I won't lie, I prayed she'd keep drinking liquids. The struggle between wanting to bite said fine ass and bend her over my knee to leave my imprint for daring to taunt me like that was real. It was a brutal mental battle, but in the end, I had to suppress the urge... and ignore my hard-on.

*Damn her.*

When Rhys wasn't watching, I tested the conference room table for sturdiness. In my defense, twelve days without pussy is a bitch. Once we'd parted ways after the power outage, I resigned myself she'd remain a mystery I was destined to elevate to a full-blown fantasy. Now, she's a temptation within reach... one I can't have.

"You don't know what the hell you're talking about, Hartford."

"Do you think I'm blind? You were hanging on her every word."

"What she had to say was insightful."

"You were laying it on thick, as if your life depended on it."

"I'm always charming."

"You were lathering her with charm."

"Like you weren't trying hard."

"I was concerned your intense focus would scare the poor woman away."

"Oh, give it a break." I roll my eyes.

"I'll concede, she's incredibly attractive, she has a banging body—despite the conservative suit—and her brain is damn sexy, but at least *I* can control myself, unlike you."

"I can control myself!"

He gives a small smile.

He's unconvinced.

"Just make sure to remember she's untouchable," he says.

"I don't need a lecture, Dad."

"Glad to hear we're on the same wavelength, son."

I should let it go, but I can't.

"For the record, my interest in Arianne is strictly professional." I can't believe I managed to say that with a straight face.

"Never mind she's on contract and doesn't fall under the non-fraternization clause—"

*Shit.*

I curse my mouth.

"I knew it!" Rhys's smile is dangerous. "You've been obsessing about her all day long."

"I haven't!" I say, a little too quickly.

He shoots me an incredulous side gaze.

A few short minutes pass as we focus on our drinks.

"Thanks for reminding me of the terms of our office romance policy," Rhys says, breaking the silence.

My head whips in his direction.

"I'd love to take her out for drinks when you're not around. Three's a crowd."

"Don't you think that would be unprofessional?"

"I'm a gentleman, Christensen. I was talking about taking the time to get to know her. That's how connections are made."

"Connections?"

"Yeah, a word you can't spell."

"I planned on taking the time to get to know her as well." *Not that I'd know where to start.*

He laughs.

He fucking laughs.

"You know what they say, once a playboy, always a playboy." He mocks.

I'm a once and done kind of guy, and I make no qualms about it.

You have one chance to impress me.

If you blow my mind, I'll grant you a second ride. Don't expect a third.

I don't do birthdays or Sundays at your parents'.

Connections are for people who are looking for commitment—another word I can't spell.

"Here's a word you can spell, *hiatus*." Rhys grins. "You don't pose a threat since for the next eighteen days, you agreed to be a good boy and keep your cock zipped up."

"Fuck off."

"I'm simply reminding you of our bet," he says.

I narrow my gaze.

"You set me up, Hartford."

"You're the one who just said your interest in Arianne is strictly professional. Mine isn't. She's fucking delicious. The somewhat conservative three-piece suit is alluring... a refreshing tease. It makes you want to peel it off to discover what's hidden underneath..."

*And I have. Many times today in my mind.*

"Can you imagine loosening that tight bun and running your fingers through her silky hair?"

*Yes.*

"In my experience, the toughest nuts to crack... are the wildest."

*My past conquests have been easy. Too easy.*

Rhys's vivid description is like audio-porn. I'm as revved up as I was earlier in Arianne's presence.

*Damn him.*

"You can't go after her," I tell him.

My argument is weak. I know it. He knows it.

"I can and I will." He stands up and pats me on the shoulder. "It's a win-win, Christensen. You get the hot bike, and I get the hot girl."

If I don't see red.

# Chapter 10

## *Arianne*

After peeling out of my clothes, untangling my shoulder-length hair from the tight chignon and taking a long, soothing bath, I make my way to my laptop, a second glass of sauvignon blanc in one hand, the bottle in the other. Nothing screams unprofessional bubblehead like drinking too much in front of clients. I prefer to be in control of my senses at all times. In the refuge of my sublet, it's a different story. It has been a long day and my brain is a little mush. Wine is a must!

Wrapped in an expensive silk robe I bought on a whim in London, I sit down and hit Google with a vengeance to learn everything I can about SCORE's two executives.

I start with Rhys, and then, focus on Beckett.

I click on photo after photo as I sip more wine.

I even check their music videos.

*Now, I know what spitting means.*

Not that I understand a word, but Rhys kicks ass. The crowd in the background at a live performance is freaking out. He exudes such confidence.

Beckett is equally talented. His guitar skills are impressive, he has an incredible voice and his stage presence shines. The way he almost makes love to the microphone when he sings, his eyes closed as if connecting with every word of the song, is mesmerizing.

They're both tall with thick, brown hair and stunning blue eyes, but they couldn't be further apart.

*Holy. Smoking. Hotness.*

Something inappropriate, unseasonable, and very foreign—since it's been a long while—stirs inside me.

I'm too consumed to fight it or deny it.

I lose track of time, pretending it's all in the name of research and preparedness.

I may have my walls erected high, but I'm not blind.

Beckett and Rhys have the world at their feet, and by God, they wear their success well. I've always had a soft spot for men at the helm of an empire.

As I bask in an ocean of gorgeousness, my phone chimes. With a smile stretching my lips, I accept the video call.

"Hey!" I say when my best friend's beautiful face comes into view. Her big brown eyes are twinkling with excitement. Her coffee-colored hair is pulled back, but the slick bangs remain.

"Hey, you!"

"It's ten past eleven here. What time is it in Australia?" I ask.

"It's ten past two in the afternoon in Perth." After Hong Kong, she's in Down Under. "These conferences overseas are brutal. I just about reached my quota. I decided to hide in my hotel room so I could call you to find out how your meeting went this morning."

Phoebe is the director of manufacturing for the leader of a natural kettle-cooked potato chips company.

"You're the best. We could've texted each other."

"Not the same," she says. "So, did they hire you?"

"Yes and no. The first meeting was shit. The second... I still can't get over it."

"You had meetings with two different prospects today? You didn't mention that when we talked yesterday."

"The second meeting came out of the blue."

For no apparent reason, I start giggling uncontrollably.

"Are you drunk?" Phoebe asks.

"Nope. Just a tad tipsy."

"You're a lightweight, Ari. A tad tipsy means, you're drunk."

"I'm not," I say. "I had a good buffer. I had a huge Italian meal, followed by a decadent dessert with my new bosses-slash-clients."

"Your hazy eyes betray you, but I'll let it slide. Congratulations on the new clients!"

"Thanks!"

"I can't wait to get back to LA so we can celebrate and I can hug the hell out of you!"

"Ditto!" I say.

With Phoebe in LA and in a new relationship, and me living in Europe, we haven't seen each other in person in a long time.

"On a side note, I love it when you remove your armor." She laughs.

I roll my eyes. "If I could wear my hair pulled back tight and my three-piece suits to bed, I would. It's just not very comfortable sleeping attire."

Phoebe shakes her head.

"You might get your wish," I tell her.

"Which one? You opening yourself up to a man again?"

"Ha. Ha. Funny. LMAO. But, no. The three-piece suits

worked in Silicon Valley, New York and in Europe, but in LA they're a liability. It's as hot as Hades in this city."

She laughs. "Well, I can't say I'll be complaining to see you wearing something a lot less... guarded. I'll be back Thursday, middle of the night. Let's go shopping!"

"You're on!"

"I can't believe you gave me that win so easily."

"It's not a win, Phoebe. It's either I get a new wardrobe or I melt in a pool of sweat."

She laughs again.

"The tide finally turns in my favor just when I was losing faith," she says.

"Whatever."

"Tell me more about this new contract."

"Without Easton I'd be drinking for a whole other reason right now."

She frowns.

I tell her about my no-show prospects and the phone call from Easton that turned my day from shitty to fantastic.

"The man is your savior, Ari," Phoebe says when I'm done.

"He truly is."

"Who will you be working for?"

"SCORE headphones."

"That's a departure from your usual roster of clients."

"One I'm enjoying by the minute."

Another fit of giggles.

*Great. Working with two attractive bosses-slash-clients means I revert to being a teenager again.*

"What do you mean?"

"Are you in front of your laptop?"

"I can be."

"I'll wait."

She squints. "This better be good, Ari."

"Trust me, it is."

She gets up from where she was sitting. I watch as the images go blurry and she moves from a couch to a table.

"Okay, what's the deal?"

"Open two tabs in a browser. In one of them type, Beckett Christensen. In the other, type Rhys Hartford." I spell both their names.

"Please hold," she says in her best phone operator voice.

"Holding!" I giggle.

I should stop drinking, but instead, I take advantage of the moment to sip more wine.

Her facial expression precedes her exclamation.

"Mother of God!" Her wide eyes move back to her phone.

"I know, right?"

"You're working with those two guys?"

"Yup!"

"Seriously?"

"I signed all the papers late this afternoon. It's official!"

"Better you than me."

"Why do you say that?"

"I love Oscar with all my heart, but come on. Your clients are smoking hot. I couldn't work with them. I'd be drooling all over myself and lose focus."

"I'm a consummate professional."

"Fuck being a professional. Did you see what they look like?"

"I sat across from them all day long and well into the evening, so yeah, I know exactly what they look like."

"And you didn't drool all over yourself?"

I offer a one-shoulder shrug.

"Puh-lease." Phoebe doesn't fall for my bullshit. "The only reason you wouldn't have a physical reaction to those two men is if you were made of tin foil. Even then."

"Okay, I ogled.".

"So, you do have a pulse."

I flatten my lips into a thin line. "Don't quit your day job."

"Seriously, Ari. This is a huge step for you."

I tend to stick my head in the sand and pretend I don't see men.

"It takes a lot to ruffle my feathers—"

"Or flutter your vagina."

"Phoebe!"

"Just sayin'."

"I'm immune to men—"

"Seems to me like those days are behind you." Her wide eyes are fixed on her laptop.

No doubt, she's scrolling through a wall of deliciousness.

"Oh, videos!" she says.

The edgy sound of Random Misconception blares in the background.

"Holy Jesus! Beckett can sing."

"I can't say rock music is my thing, but the man has an insane voice—"

The wine has mellowed me out, removing my barrier to overshare.

"God! Beckett has a sexy ass in those jeans!"

"Are you sure you're in love with Oscar?"

"Don't you dare question my love for my man," she says. "I'm just being a good friend by evaluating these two for you."

"They're *clients*."

"Whatever helps you sleep at night," she says before moving her attention away from me. "Let me check out your other hunky client." Her fingers are already flying on the keyboard.

"Oooohhhh!" she says. "Rhys could get me to listen to rap music."

"You kill me."

"This display of manliness bears the question again. How in the world can you work with—Dear God—"

"What?"

"These two redefine suit porn!"

"I know." I take another sip of wine.

"Holy shit! Did you see the photo of them in a tuxedo?"

"Trust me, I did."

"They're tall?"

"I'd say six-one to six-three."

"Nice!" She nods. "And those blue eyes... how can you stare at them without losing yourself?"

"I managed." *Barely.*

"Those dazzling smiles should be on billboards across the country."

"God didn't skimp the day they were born," I say. *That's for sure.*

"Imagine what they're hiding *under* the suit or tux."

My cheeks burst into flames.

"Oh, someone has been having some naughty thoughts at work," she says.

"You're blowing this way out of proportion. They weren't naughty thoughts. They were curious ones."

"Which one makes your pussy flutter the most?"

"Phoebe! That's a horrible word."

"Okay. Quiver, pulsate, palpitate, convulse, tremor, shatter. Pick the word you prefer and pick a guy," she says.

"All of those words are over-the-top."

"You want to play it like that?" She continues before I can answer. "Which one of those two will you fantasize about tonight while you play with yourself?"

"Phoebe!" I'm sure my cheeks are ten shades redder.

"You may have given up on cock—because it's attached to a

man—but orgasms? Come on, Ari. A girl needs two to three of those per day." *Unbelievable.*

"Two to three?"

"I hit the jackpot with Oscar."

"Evidently."

"Until you meet *your* Oscar, I suggest you take matters into your own hands. How long has it been?"

"Why do I tell you so much?" I shake my head.

"Because I'm your best friend."

"Well, listen here, best friend, there will be no fluttering or quivering pussy," I tell her. "The same goes for fantasizing about the men who will be signing my paychecks."

"You say that now, but I'm sure in time, you'll change your mind." She seems so certain of herself.

I hesitate, weighing if I should give her more ammunition or not.

She squints at me. "Are you holding back on me? Did you already have a hot make-out session with one of them?"

"I just started today! What do you take me for?"

"Given the chance, there isn't a woman in the world—who's single, of course—who wouldn't want to get down and dirty with one of those guys... or maybe both. They say ménage romance is the new black."

"I can't imagine being in a relationship with one man, let alone two."

"Don't knock it till you try it!" She's on a roll.

"You've lost your mind."

"No. I'm just excited for you, Ari," she says. "A week and a half ago, you were going on and on about the infuriating guy you were trapped inside an elevator with. Even though you wouldn't admit to it, I bet he was hot." I should've kept my mouth shut. "The old Arianne wouldn't even have mentioned it because in her world men don't exist. LA-

Arianne takes notice of hot men. Bravo! You're making progress."

"Speaking of the hot guy from the elevator—" *Damn*.

I blame Beckett's mesmerizing eyes and blindingly obnoxious good looks for my slip up.

"Ah-ha! I knew it!" she says. "What about your hot roomie?"

I chew the inside of my lip.

"Don't tell me he works at SCORE," Phoebe says.

"No."

"Phew. That would've been a freaky coincidence."

"He co-owns the company."

"WHAT?" Phoebe's brown eyes are as big as saucers.

"Yes."

"Which one is it?" she asks.

"My short-lived elevator roommate is Beckett Christensen."

"So, your dirty wet dream is a reality now and he has a name... one that screams self-assuredness. I like it!"

She's right about Beckett's almighty confidence. Rhys has it too, but it's a bit more toned down.

"He was never a dirty wet dream." *Lie*. "He was simply a distraction."

"One that reminded you you're a woman with needs, Ari. It's okay for your lady parts to flutter again."

"Stop it with that ridiculous word!"

She grins wide.

"Anyway, you're getting way too excited—"

"There you go—"

"There are certain professional conducts I adhere to—"

"There should be some leeway when God delivers such irresistible temptations."

I open my mouth to respond, but I freeze when my eyes

catch a headline in the column of the *USA Today* Entertainment page that's open on my laptop.

"What the fuck," I say.

"What is it?" Phoebe asks.

I blink in disbelief.

"What is it, Ari?"

I read the headline out loud.

## *'GLACH TECH CEO ANNOUNCES ENGAGEMENT TO GIRLFRIEND. HOLY MASSIVE ROCK!'*

"Oh, shit," Phoebe says. "I can't believe this farce of a relationship has lasted this long."

"Neither can I."

"I'm so sorry, Ari."

"It's not your fault."

"I know, but you didn't need to find out this way."

I let out a disgusted sound. "I didn't need to find out at all, but it is what it is."

A tidal wave of harsh reality shatters the lighthearted moment I was sharing with my best friend.

There it is in black and white.

It's indisputable.

I'm assaulted with memories I'd rather forget. The effect is the same as torrential rain dosing a raging California bush fire, leaving behind shards of debris where life once existed.

"If this ridiculousness goes through, I'm sure the wedding will be as gaudy as *she* is," Phoebe says. "The bitch has zero taste or class."

Phoebe is being a good friend, but that doesn't change the facts. The bitch got exactly what she wanted.

"Talk to me, Ari," Phoebe says when I remain frozen in silence.

"This is why I stay the hell away from men."

No more relationships.

No more tears.

No more drama.

And no more trusting someone who will stomp all over your heart.

Love sucks.

The pain may have subsided, but the humiliation... it's still vivid enough to keep me steadfastly bound to the promise I made to myself when I got the hell out of Silicon Valley.

# Chapter 11

## *Beckett*

*S*eventeen more days...
    *You can do it.*
*Damn right you can!*
*You can do anything you set your mind to.*
I pump myself up, with each step I take.
But I don't even believe my own bullshit.
*No. I. Can't.*
*I won't survive this.*
Rhys's bike is a lot less appealing with each passing day.

I'm strung up tighter than the tightrope acrobats walk on. As crazy as it sounds, I've jerked off more in the past week and a half than I have in all of my teenage years combined.

My balls are aching.

My cock is desperate.

Self-gratification when it's all you're getting is almost pointless and cruel.

And dare I say porn quickly becomes lackluster.

Thirteen excruciating long days without pussy.

*Fuck, this born-again virgin shit is torture.*

Last night, I dreamt of begging a woman to sit on my face so I could devour her pussy for an hour straight. And I'm not talking about just any woman. The pussy I wanted to ravish was Arianne's.

There. I said it.

What I wouldn't give to get my mouth on her and feel the swell of her clit against my tongue and taste the sweetness of her slickness.

*Dammit!*

I'm hard again.

Aware of eyes on me, it's impossible to adjust myself.

It's like walking with a third leg.

*Fuck!*

As I stroll across the executive floor, I nod left and right, dropping *good mornings* and flashing a warm smile, as I make my way to Arianne's newly appointed office. Rhys is going to learn the hard way; you don't challenge me unless you expect to lose.

If he thinks I can't charm a woman, he's going to get whiplash. I'll make sure to send him a nice catalog of selfies of Arianne and I, sitting on his prized bike.

"Knock, knock, knock," I say, my knuckles rapping against the door of Arianne's new office.

"Come in!"

"Good morning, Arianne, I thought you'd—"

I freeze.

She isn't alone.

She's sitting next to Rhys.

He flashes me a shit-eating grin. "Good morning, buddy," he says.

"Good morning," I say, unwilling to return his smile. I tear my attention away from him. "Good morning, Arianne."

"Good morning, Beckett," she says.

One glance tells me she's been in the office for a while. There are stacks of paper piled on her desk. Competitors' headphone samples litter the small, round conference table in the corner of her office. The two pens sticking out from the back of her head like chopsticks are another indication she's hard at work.

I guess I should say, *they're* hard at work.

"Is that for me?" Rhys asks, pointing. "You shouldn't have."

I don't grant him an answer. Instead, I focus on the woman who consumed my dreams last night.

"I brought you coffee and breakfast," I say, lifting the tall cup and bag I'm holding.

"Wow," she says. "Does everyone get this kind of royal treatment when they work for you?"

I knit my eyebrows in confusion.

Rhys crosses his arms across his wide chest and leans back against his seat. "We're already on our *second* Thoroughly Hot latte of the day and I've already taken care of breakfast and morning snacks."

"Second cup of the day? Breakfast and morning snacks?" I ask.

"Yes, we've been at it since six a.m.," Rhys says.

"How come?"

"Arianne called me last night just as I was getting into bed," he says.

I try my darndest not to show my surprise.

"We had a really great conversation. You know... getting to know each other better."

*Fucker.*

"I found out so many insightful things about her."

*I bet.*

"Did you know she's a Philly girl, an only child, and her Scottish parents own a couple restaurants?"

*Oh, he's so proud of himself.*

"I also found out that although Ari was in Europe for two years, she chose to explore Italy from top to bottom and never discovered Paris."

*Thank you, Mr. Travelocity.*

"How did she get your number?" I bypass his bullshit.

A facetious smile lifts the corner of his lips. "We exchanged numbers while we were waiting for you yesterday. I figured she might need it. I'm glad she had it on hand."

*What. The. Fuck?*

"Really?"

The desire to revert to a backward-thinking, Neanderthal-chest-beating caveman, is strong.

"Why did you need to call him?" I ask Arianne, fully aware of my accusatory tone.

She blushes. "I hope I didn't do anything wrong." *It all depends.*

"I'm just curious." I attempt to soften my abrasiveness.

"I called Rhys to find out if I could get to the office early," Arianne says. "I wanted to hit the ground running first thing this morning."

Sure, Rhys and I get in that early when we need to plow through work, but she just started. "Isn't six a little early?"

"You hired me for a reason," she says, lifting a defiant chin. "I could live with not being prepared yesterday when I first met you, but that's not my MO. Since my goal is to have preliminary reports to you before the end of the week, there isn't a minute to waste."

I don't know how to respond to that.

On one hand, I'm grateful for her dedication, on the other, I hate that she went to Rhys instead of me.

"I see," I say with a slow nod.

I should keep my gaze trained on her, but my eyes drift to Rhys. I guess he takes that as an invitation.

"I picked up Arianne at her place and we drove in together," he says.

*He knows where she lives?*

"She's already picked up on a few things we can improve."

"That sounds promising," I say.

"Very. Promising." Rhys is playing me.

"If it's okay with you, Beckett, I plan on spending the next three days working closely with Rhys," Arianne tells me. "I want to have a good grasp of the ins and outs of your manufacturing to see where I can trim costs."

"Three days? That's—"

"That's the core of the business," Rhys says. "Any savings could be allotted to more marketing and advertising dollars."

*Like I couldn't figure that out on my own, Einstein.*

"It makes sense," I say with a tight smile.

Arianne's eyes drop to my hand, reminding me I'm still holding on to the breakfast I brought her.

I close the door with my foot and stalk to her desk, my eyes glued to my business partner.

I drop the coffee and the bag in front of her. "Just in case you want another coffee and you need a shot of sugar before lunch."

"Thank you," she says.

"It's my pleasure. I'm not a fan of reheating coffee in the microwave, but Thoroughly Hot is worth the exception. Tall latte with two shots of espressos and three sugars, just the way you like it, accompanied by an assortment of my favorite French pastries. Since you've never been to Paris, I guess this is so *apropos*."

Rhys rolls his eyes hard.

*You think you're the only one who has game, buddy? Think again.*

"I don't know what to say." Arianne blushes.

*Damn, I love the color of her cheeks.*

"You two are so attentive."

I shoot Rhys another threatening glare.

He returns the favor.

I fish for my phone in my suit jacket.

"Why don't we exchange numbers? You never know when you might need mine."

"She already has mine," Rhys says.

"Just in case you're not available," I tell him.

"I'll *always* be available for Arianne." He pauses. "Day... or night."

He's rattling my cage.

I keep my cool.

"Shit happens, Hartford," I say.

"I'm reliable, Christensen."

"So. Am. I."

Arianne's eyes ping-pong from mine to Rhys's, confusion painted on her beautiful face.

"I feel like I did something wrong," she says. "If you want me to wait until nine when the office opens, it's okay. I can knock off a couple hours of work at my place."

"Nonsense," I tell her. "If you have my phone number, you have another point of contact."

More eye-rolling from Rhys.

"That's a great idea," she says, grabbing my phone.

With quick fingers, she punches in her number.

*Much better.*

Rhys narrows his gaze at me.

The slow triumphant smile that curls up my lips doubles as a big *fuck you.*

There's a knock at the door.

"Come in," Arianne shouts.

"Rhys, I'm sorry to interrupt," Cecilia, his executive assistant says, poking her head around the door.

"That's okay," he tells her. "What's up?"

"It's Leland," Cecilia says.

Rhys checks his phone. "Why is he calling the office line?"

"He's here," Cecilia says. "He says it's urgent."

Rhys's worried eyes shoot up, mirroring my own concern.

"Did Leland want to see both of us?" Rhys asks.

"He said this is production related and it's best if he talks to you first."

We exchange another worried glance.

"Okay, I'll be right out," Rhys tells her.

"Should I show him to a conference room or your office?" Cecilia asks.

"My office is good," Rhys says.

"Got it," she says.

With that, Cecilia closes the door.

Rhys turns his focus to me. "I wonder what's wrong."

"I'm sure it's nothing. You know how anal Leland can be."

"He wouldn't show up here if it was nothing, Beckett."

"You're not in this alone. Let me know what's going on and we'll nip it in the bud asap."

"Divide and conquer," Rhys says with a slow nod.

"Divide and conquer," I say.

The tension between us has dissipated. We're back to being two buddies with a dream instead of two idiots showing each other up to earn the attention of a gorgeous woman.

"I have to go," he tells Arianne. "I don't know how long I'll be tied up for, but if you need anything at all, ask Cecilia and she'll get it for you."

"Sounds good," she says. "Have a great meeting."

"Are we still on for lunch?" Rhys asks Arianne.

"Absolutely!" she says.

*Breakfast and lunch?*

*Someone works fast.*

"You don't want to keep Leland waiting," I say.

"In a hurry to get rid of me?" Rhys asks.

"Your executive assistant said it was urgent."

He nods.

And... he's off.

"Leland is your point person, right?" Arianne asks.

"That's right. We partnered with Tekknika Audio, a manufacturer based in Brisbane, California, to develop and manufacture SCORE headphones right here in the good ol' USA. Leland Kastner is the team leader for all our products."

"Thanks for helping me keep it all straight."

I smile as I take her in.

Today, she's wearing black armor with a crisp white blouse. Alas, it's all buttoned up. I hope she's wearing another one of her sexy as all fuck pencil skirts.

Not a strand of hair is out of place.

Her makeup is soft and feminine.

Everything is almost identical to yesterday, except for the sparkle missing from her big brown eyes. I may be reading into this, but she looks tired. And sad?!

"Is everything okay?" I ask.

"Yes."

"You're sure?"

"As okay as it'll ever be, I suppose," she says. Her tone is a little too flippant.

I try a different approach.

"If you were here at six, that means it was a short night for you."

"I didn't expect to sleep much." She doesn't say more, but her clipped tone suggests there's a hell of a lot more.

"Wanna talk about it? I'm a great listener. If you need an impartial ear, I'm your guy."

"No thanks..." She shakes her head. "It's nothing worth wasting time over."

That's all she says.

No further explanations.

She's hard to read and nearly impossible to figure out.

*Why does that intrigue me so much?*

I can't remember finding the last dozen women I fucked nearly as fascinating. It's more than finding out how sweet her pussy tastes, it's about understanding what makes her tick.

My eyes are still glued to her soft pink shapely lips.

*Damn.*

I have the pressing urge to suck them between my teeth, to fucking own them.

"You're staring, Beckett."

"Am I?"

"You know you are."

My brain is telling me to drop it, but since most of the blood in my body is flowing to my crotch, I'm oblivious to the warning. My starved cock does all the thinking. And talking.

"I'd love to take you out for dinner," I say. "Eight o'clock? We can leave together. There's this incredible restaurant—"

"Unless it's *strictly* business, I'll pass."

Talk about slamming the door shut.

Undeterred, I soldier on. "What if I wanted to thank you for your hard work?"

"I haven't even rolled up my sleeves yet, Beckett. It's a bit premature, don't you think?"

*Okay. Strike two.*

"We both have to eat, might as well do it together? It would be great to get to know each other outside the office."

"That's not a good idea." She shakes her head, her lips pressed together, as an angry blush creeps up her cheeks. Another time, another place, and I'd say pissed off looks sexy on her, but not in this case. There seems to be a shit load of baggage behind her refusal. "I prefer to keep the lines unblurred." The fury in her eyes is unmistakable. "Anything else and people get royally screwed."

Her gaze moves to her computer, dismissing me in the process.

*Well, hell.*

# Chapter 12

## *Beckett*

$S$*he turned me down.*

> *She fucking turned me down.*

My hard-on wilted in a blink.

She's the only woman to turn me down flat like that.

*Have I lost my touch?*

A wink and a smile is enough to get women to drop their panties.

With this whole abstinence bullshit, I'm starting to question my manhood.

I lost my virginity at sixteen to my next-door neighbor. She was seventeen. That summer I learned everything I needed to know about pleasing a woman. I hit rock star status a few months before I turned eighteen. Since then, it's been a never-ending supply of willing pussy.

And now, I've hit a wall.

Since I met Arianne in the elevator, it's been a constant push and pull.

I've never had someone challenge me like this. Never.

*She's okay warming up to Rhys, but not me?*

What the hell?

After getting shot down like a schmuck who doesn't have game, I made my way to Rhys's office with my tail between my legs. As I was entering, he was stepping out. With a serious expression on his face, he informed me we had some problematic quality control issues with all the shipments we received so far this week from a major outsourcer in Vietnam. He was rushing off to Tekknika Audio with Leland in tow to assess the damage with his own two eyes. He assured me I'd get a briefing later.

*Divide and conquer.*

I stroll to my office, still confused by the irrational need to seduce a woman who prefers a rapper to a rocker. Instead of sitting down and knocking off things on my to-do list, I pace my office back and forth like a trapped panther, plotting wicked ways to seduce Arianne and outwit Rhys.

My pacing comes to an abrupt stop.

*What the fuck am I doing?*

*I have a company to run, for God's sake.*

I remove my jacket and fling it on the couch. I undo my cufflinks and roll up the sleeves of my shirt. Determined to stop obsessing over Arianne, I round my desk and sit my ass down.

Two hours later and I've proven why I deserve the title of CEO.

*Thank fuck my head is screwed back on straight.*

I'm just about to call Valerie to ask her to step into my office when my phone rings. I reach for it when a text message comes flying in.

*Rhys.*

*I'll get back to him.*

I answer the call.

"Easton!" I say.

"Beckett! Am I catching you at a bad time?"

"I always have time for you," I tell him.

A chime lets me know I've received another text.

I ignore it.

"I'm honored," Easton says.

"Are you kidding me? You hand-delivered a secret weapon."

"Arianne?"

I spare him the details of my teenage duel with Rhys and get down to the nitty-gritty.

"She's already brainstorming ideas to take us to the next level," I say. "The ink has barely dried on the contract. Talk about dedication."

"I told you."

My phone vibrates with another notification.

"You sure did. Thanks for the recommendation."

It's important to keep things in perspective and remember why we brought Arianne onboard. It was never to be my plaything.

"Anytime," he says. "I'm glad to hear Arianne is already knee deep because I have something that's about to blow your mind."

I sit up straight in my chair. "I'm all ears."

There's a knock at my door.

"One second, Easton."

"All right."

"Come in," I shout.

Valerie pokes her head in.

"I'm sorry to interrupt, Beckett. Rhys is on the office line. He can't get through to you. He says he needs to talk to you right now. It can't wait."

*Shit.* "Transfer the call."

"Okay."

She leaves, closing the door behind her.

"Easton, I'm really sorry—"

"I overheard. Is everything okay?"

"We have a situation with the company that takes care of our production. I'm not sure what's going on. This is Rhys's department."

"All right. Go play CEO and call me back later."

"I will."

I barely have time to hang up with Easton when the phone on my desk rings.

"Hey, Rhys—"

"You need to get down here right the fuck now!"

# Chapter 13

## *Arianne*

Valerie just called to let me know Beckett was back in the office. With a nervous tremor lodged deep in the pit of my stomach, I trail down the hallway to his office.

"Knock, knock, knock," I say, rapping on the door.

"Come in!"

I open the door, but don't step inside. Instead, I stick my head and shoulders in his office. It's best, just in case I need to make a run for it. After all, I was a little short with him earlier.

"Is it safe to come in?" I ask.

He sits back against his seat, his arresting blue eyes staring straight at me.

"It all depends on you," he says.

I put my big girl panties on and step inside his office.

I close the door behind me and lean against it, still hesitant.

I had the whole spiel rehearsed in my head, but when my eyes drop to his forearms, I lose my ability to speak.

*Wow.*

My gaze travels up Beckett's defined wide chest. Even to the blind eye, it's evident from the way his crisp white shirt hugs his torso, every muscle of his body is well sculpted. I can just picture the perfect body hiding underneath the shirt.

In my momentary bewilderment, I continue my careful inspection.

My eyes slide down to his exposed forearms.

*Holy hell.*

"Your tattoos... the photos online don't do them justice—" *Shit.* My mouth runs away from me. "Oh, my God, I'm sorry. I was so out of line. And unprofessional." I close my eyes in dread.

I brace for the hatchet to fall on my neck, but it never comes.

I open one eye, then the other.

"You're stalking me?" A wide grin stretches his lips. "Bad girl." The mischievous sparkle in his eyes is dangerous.

"Err..." My mind speeds up in my attempt to save face. "It was for research. It's important to know the man—in this case, the men—behind the company." I'm almost convinced by my own bullshit.

Beckett lets out a boisterous laugh. "That's a valiant attempt, Miss Buchanan, but it's too late. The cat is out of the bag. I won't tell a soul you have your eye on me, if you don't." His cocky playfulness is doing things to me. "This can be..." He waves a finger between us. "Our little secret."

It's my turn to laugh. "You're impossible, Beckett Christensen."

"You already knew that, but I suspect that's not why you're here."

My dread returns full force.

"You're right." I let out a heavy sigh. I take several steps forward until I'm standing in front of his desk. "I'm really sorry—"

"For chewing me up and spitting me out?"

"For redirecting my anger towards you, yes. I was rude. You didn't deserve it. It's not your fault I'm in a pissy mood."

"Whose fault is it?"

I hesitate, dancing from one foot to the other.

"My ex."

"Ah!" He nods. "What did the asshole do?"

"He announced his engagement—in a public spectacle—to the backstabber responsible for the demise of my relationship two years ago. Granted, it takes two to tango, but the woman he cheated on me with weaved her way into our lives"—and *our* bed—"and he didn't say no. There are other things, like my ex reneging on his word and finding out he never was interested in me—" Something catches in my throat. "He was only interested in what I could do for him." I shake my head, dispersing the bad memories. "Regardless, none of it justifies how I spoke to you. I'm sorry."

I bite down a wave of humiliation.

He nods. "I accept the apology."

I expect him to say more, but instead, he stares at me, considering me.

"Maybe you dodged a bullet. Your ex sounds like a royal douchebag."

"That's what my best friend Phoebe keeps reminding me."

"I don't know the guy and I don't know this backstabber, but from what I know about you, I speak with confidence when I say, your ex got shortchanged." Beckett pauses. "He picked the wrong woman." He flashes me a boyish smile.

My cheeks burst into flames.

My whole body combusts.

"You don't have to say that to make me feel better."

"I'm not. Contrary to your ex, I don't talk shit."

"Thank you." I lower my eyes. "I should've kept my emotions in check. I only found out last night about the engagement. It was a fluke, but the side effect was real. The headline was like a drive-by shooting to my brain. I'm not in love anymore... it's just..."

"Hurtful and upsetting?" Beckett completes my sentence. I nod. "No one wants to be betrayed."

"Exactly."

"Don't you wish you were a Red Priestess with blood-magic powers, capable of giving birth to a full-blown shadow baby to take care of your ex and the backstabber?" he asks.

I didn't see that coming.

I explode in laughter.

"You know what I'm talking about?" He chuckles.

"Yes," I say when I regain my composure. "I'm a huge fan of the epic series."

"So am I. And here I thought we were complete opposites. Turns out we have another thing in common."

"Turns out we do." I return his smile.

He has a great sense of humor.

"I'm sure I screwed things up, but if the dinner invitation still stands..." I let my sentence trail.

"Really?" His gorgeous eyes light up.

"Really," I say. "As you pointed out, we both have to eat and, to be honest, I don't know if I can handle being alone tonight. My best friend Phoebe is in Australia. She won't be back until tomorrow and I don't know anyone else in LA."

I can't believe I'm willing to be this vulnerable and transparent with a man I barely know.

Beckett gets up and rounds his desk until he's standing next to me.

I almost lose myself in his beautiful blue eyes.

This close, they're like two fiery aquamarine stones staring back at me. His gaze lingers on me long enough to make me blush. I lower my gaze, chewing my lower lip in the hopes of regaining my bearings as a rush of hot shivers runs through me.

A man has never elicited this type of pull before.

"I'm sorry, Arianne, but dinner is a no go."

"Oh."

*Good job, Arianne.*

"Earlier, you said dinner between us had to be strictly business. After what you shared, I can't agree to that. You have to decide if you're okay deviating from that stipulation or if you'll stick to your guns."

Confusion causes my eyebrows to knit together.

"I was going to take you to a notable restaurant, but not anymore," he says. "We need to have a kickass dining experience followed by a wild night out on the town. It's the best remedy to say a big fuck you to your ex and flip the middle finger to that backstabber."

His words are wishful thinking.

"It's not like they're going to know," I say.

"True, but you'll know, and you'll feel a hell of a lot better. If I do a good job—and push you out of your comfort zone—you'll forget their very existence."

*From his lips to God's ears.*

"I'm almost afraid to ask what you have in mind."

"Remember when we were roommates in that elevator?"

"You'll never let me live that down, will you?"

"No. Never. I'll milk it for all it's worth," he says. "Going back to that day... When the lights turned back on, you told me you had never closed a bar or a dance floor."

"It's true."

"We need to change that. Let's go out and paint the town red!"

"But it's only Wednesday."

"This is LA, baby! The city that never sleeps."

"Isn't that New York?" I ask.

"Please. They wish."

I laugh.

"Are we on?" Beckett asks.

I shake my head and nod at the same time. My thoughts, a jumble.

"Are you turning me down again?"

"I'm not! I came in here to apologize. This turnabout is beyond my expectations."

"So, it's a yes, then?"

"Beckett, I can't keep up with you."

He takes a step closer. It's so intimate, I feel the warmth of his body radiating through mine. *Dear God.*

"You're underestimating yourself," he says. His eyes are almost hooded beneath his thick, dark eyelashes.

*Am I imagining things?*

A jarring thought hits me.

"I don't have anything to wear. My wardrobe consists of pantsuits, skirt-suits, and an infinite number of vests. Nothing appropriate to hang out with a former rock star."

*God, that sounded so geeky.*

*Really, Arianne?*

*A hot guy suggests a carefree night and that's your lame excuse?*

"Weren't you here at six this morning?" Beckett asks.

I knew sleep would evade me the second I read that headline last night. Coming in early was a way of distracting my mind.

"Yes," I say.

He looks down at his impressive watch. Just like the rest of him, it screams power and money. "It's a little past one right now, which means you've already clocked seven hours of work. I suggest you pack up your things and hit a couple stores."

"Seriously?"

"Absolutely. Does dinner at eight work?"

"It does."

"I'll pick you up."

"That sounds great!"

"Now we have that settled, let's talk about Rhys."

# Chapter 14

## *Arianne*

"Pick up. Please, please, please," I say, my eyes glued to the screen.

After nearly sprinting back to my office, I called my best friend.

When Phoebe accepts the video call, I let out a sigh of relief.

"What's up?" she asks. "You just bombarded me with ten text messages."

"You weren't responding, so I took the liberty of calling you. I know you're a night owl."

"I just got out of the shower," she says. "Why do you look so freaked out?"

"Help! I have nothing to wear!"

She squints at me. "You're fully clothed," she says. "Are you drinking on the job?"

"No, silly. Beckett asked me out and I have nothing to wear."

She tilts her head to the side. "I gather this isn't business related?"

I tell her the whole story.

"That's exactly what you need!" Phoebe says. "You won't be able to spell Chance's name by the end of the evening. Same for Slut Mariah."

"I shouldn't admit this, but I'm dying to do something crazy," I tell her. "I'm tired of being so *regimented*. Slut Mariah used to take pleasure in mocking my disciplined life. That's what gave her the upper leg. Remember? Chance kept singing her praises for being so fun, bubbly, and lighthearted. I want to be the fun one for once... even if it's only for one night."

"Puh-lease!" My best friend rolls her eyes. "Don't you dare compare yourself to trashy-extension-wearing Mariah. That would be lowering yourself, and I won't hear of it. She's not fun. She's vapid. And easy. Chance wasn't talking about her personality. He was talking about her vagina—her very well used vagina." The way Phoebe stretches out the words is hilarious. "Am I right or am I right?"

I explode in laughter at the expression of disgust contorting Phoebe's face.

"You won't get an argument from me," I say. "I really need this night out."

"I totally agree."

"I can't thank Beckett enough. He's the perfect man for operation 'forget Chance and his slut'."

"Speaking of perfect, what about Rhys?" Phoebe asks.

"What about him?"

"Weren't you considering a ménage with both attractive men?"

"That's how fake news starts!" I say.

She laughs.

"They're my clients. Beckett is being a gentleman by not allowing me to wallow in self-pity. That's it."

"In other words, Beckett is the chosen one."

"Are you not listening?"

"Both blue-eyed gods are scorching hot, but I'm willing to bet every dollar to my name Beckett is edgier, more imperious, and more domineering. Turbulent, even."

Leave it to Phoebe to come up with shit like this.

"Turbulent? This isn't a flight on his private jet."

"Perhaps, but I bet he can get you off. HELLO!"

"Why are we friends again?"

"Hear me out. I'm onto something here." She's undeterred. She scares me when she's like this. "You don't have to sleep with sexy Beckett—although I would fully support you if you did let him dip his cock into your pussy because God knows you need a really good fuck—"

"Seriously, Phoebe?"

"Make sure to landscape before your date—"

"It's not a date! It's dinner—"

"Whatever you say. My point being, throw caution to the wind. Live a little! Get crazy with the bad boy!" She stands up. "You know, *Livin' la Vida Loca*." She actually gyrates her hips.

"What is wrong with you? Is it something they put in the water in Australia? Because I swear to God, you have a screw loose."

She laughs as she sits back down. "Sue me for being excited that my bestie is finally getting some."

"Which part of *he's my client*, don't you understand?" I ask.

"You're exempt from the office fraternization clause, and if you're both consenting adults... why should the night end with dinner and a little bar hopping? I'm just sayin'."

"Moving right along. To answer your question, Rhys is getting ready to board a private jet to Vietnam to deal with a production crisis. There's a strike with no end in sight. Then, he's heading to South Korea to source out other reputable manufacturers. He'll be gone for a while."

"God made the decision for you. Sexy Beckett it is."

"Phoebe!"

"Okay, okay. No more clowning around. Going back to the reason you called. You're right. Your whole wardrobe screams unapproachable. Same goes for your hairstyle."

"The look says professional."

She shakes her head. "I disagree. The look says *Stay the fuck away, asshole!* I've told you that a million times."

Okay, she has. I just chose to ignore her.

"I understand you have nooooooo interest in Beckett, but if you want to be the fun one—the playful one—you have to dress the part."

# Chapter 15

## *Beckett*

I park my red Alfa Romeo 4C Spider in front of Arianne's El Segundo complex building. Lucky for me, she lives in a neighboring city, therefore traffic wasn't too much of a bitch. After Arianne buzzes me in, I take the elevator and get off on the fourth floor and head down the hallway to her sublet.

I knock.

She opens.

When she does, I take a step back, stunned.

*Whoa.*

If it weren't for that gorgeous face and those sparkling brown eyes staring back at me, I'd think I had knocked on the wrong door.

Talk about dramatic transformation.

The woman standing in front of me isn't as guarded as the one who left my office hours ago.

*No more armor?*

I take in every single delicious inch of Arianne's body.

Her outfit doesn't show much skin, but wow, wow, and wow.

Since the elevator incident, she's been a fascination. Before her, I was never this obsessed with longer skirts. In fact, I don't even know women who wear them. The skirt she's wearing now still hits below the knee, but it's a lot flirtier than the one she wore earlier. It's demure and sexy as all fuck at the same time. The latter, because I'm dying to know what she's hiding underneath.

Thong? G-string? Boy shorts? Lace or satin panties? Whatever she's wearing, I'd love nothing more than to rip them off with my teeth.

My blood scalds, turning to lava in my veins, which rushes hot and thick to my cock. The fucker is dying to say hello.

Arianne tilts her head. "You're staring, Beckett."

*No. I'm gawking openly and stupidly.*

"Your hair. Wow! You're stunning!" I say.

So far, I've only seen her with her hair pulled back tight in a severe bun. It's still up, but this sexy messy look enhances her features and showcases her eyes beautifully. Her makeup is a little more dramatic tonight. Those dark-red pouty lips are inviting to no end.

"The way I usually style it screams, unapproachable... so my best friend tells me. I don't want to come across that way."

"Tell your best friend she's wrong. The pinned-up hairstyle screams, challenge."

"What do you mean?"

I cock an eyebrow. "It makes a guy wonder what it would take to be lucky enough to run his fingers through your hair."

Her eyes are so fucking huge right now, I bite off a smile.

She blushes.

"Same for the skirt." I lower my gaze. "I love the longer length on you." My eyes brush up and down her body. "It's also a challenge... I'm not even going to tell you what's been running through my mind since I saw you in that elevator."

"Is this appropriate talk, Mr. Christensen?" she asks.

"We're no longer at the office, Miss Buchanan. We're just two friends about to go out and have a great time."

"Friends?"

"Friends."

"Do playboys have female friends?"

"Don't believe everything Google tells you."

"A picture speaks a thousand words. And there are a lot of photos of you on the internet."

"Fair enough," I say. "In that case, you'll be my first female friend."

"That's a tall order."

"Something tells me you can manage... you're certainly dressed for the part." I wink.

She beams. "Really?"

Arianne's tempting body is adorned in a black shimmery pleated skirt. She's wearing a gunmetal gray fitted t-shirt with a slogan printed across her chest that reads '*Holy Chic*' traced in black sequined letters. Her feet are strapped in a pair of laced-up, black high heels.

*Holy chic, indeed.*

I lean into her until my lips flirt with her earlobe. "Own it, Arianne. You. Look. Fucking. Hot."

This close, I smell every note of her light-scented perfume.

She clears her throat.

"It's just clothes."

"You look fucking hot in *just clothes*."

*Fuck, I'm dying to know what you look like out of them.*

"Thank you," she says with a touch of shyness.

"My best friend Phoebe's boyfriend has a cousin who is a personal shopper at Beverly Hills' Neiman Marcus. A few text messages later, and Andrea had all my measurements. By the time I got there, she had a rack full of options. Thank God she didn't try to make me look slutty."

"Slutty is for women who have nothing more to offer."

She seems surprised by my comment.

"Google tells me you've dated your fair share of *slutty* women," she says in air quotes.

"Which makes me an expert," I tell her. "About those Google searches. If there's anything you want to know about me, ask."

She considers me for a beat.

"I will. No more late-night searches." Her eyes grow wide at her slip of the tongue. "I don't mean late night, late night. I mean... it's for research." She shakes her head. "Forget it."

*Late night?*

My cock twitches at the visual of her slipping her fingers between her wet pussy, thinking of me. I push the thought aside, if I don't, my cock will become an impediment to my ability to walk.

"I'll allow the late-night searches as long as it's the last thing you do before going to bed. It's even better if you conduct those searches while you're in bed..."

Her jaw drops.

My inner voice was dying to be heard.

"You did not just say that."

"I did." No point denying it.

Interest shines bright in those big brown eyes.

This evening is very promising.

"As for the compliment, I'm flattered," she says changing the subject. "I guess I'm rocking the chic/fashionably nerdy look Andrea was going for?"

"Nah." I shake my head. "Drop the nerdy. You're chic *and* fashionable."

She smiles.

"You don't have to butter me up, Beckett. I'm sure you must be used to stepping out on the town with actresses and supermodels."

"And you fit the part beautifully."

That shy smile just turned into a beaming one.

"If we're exchanging compliments, you look good—"

"Good?"

She giggles.

"You look great—" She gives me a onceover, taking in my head-to-toe black attire. "Okay, you look incredible even when you aren't wearing a suit."

"You've been checking me out?"

"Nowhere in my contract does it stipulate I'm obligated to bare my soul to my client."

*There's a hell of a lot more I'd love for you to bear.*

"We can keep bantering all night or we can have some fun," I say.

If we don't get out of here, I'll be balls deep inside her pussy within the next five minutes. There's only so much a sex-starved man can take.

Thirteen days of celibacy and I'm at my breaking point.

"Let's do it!" she says.

# Chapter 16

## *Arianne*

If I allow myself to forget all about Chance, the betrayal, the lies, and the deceit, I'd be willing to admit I'm sitting across from the perfect man.

Beckett Christensen is what every woman dreams of—a gentleman, an influencer, a force, and an Adonis oozing with charm. His devastatingly good looks and those insane blue eyes make him all the more irresistible.

I gave myself a good talking to before he arrived and I was determined to stand strong in my belief I was immune to my client's charms. That's until I opened the door. He'd ditched the bespoke suit, but he still looked delicious. The head-to-toe black look is a classic among men. Rare are those who exude the level of raw masculinity Beckett does.

I don't know what his cologne is, but it smells like Eau de Pheromone.

It didn't go unnoticed how women salivated all over themselves as we followed the waiter to our table. I swear, some had whiplash from craning their necks to catch a glimpse of the tall, sexy man trailing behind me. Beckett is being a kind soul by preventing me from spending the evening deep diving in a pint of Wunderlust ice cream, but I must say, knowing I'm the envy of all these women is pretty thrilling.

I'm not completely delusional, I know at the stroke of midnight, it all ends. But for now, I'm willing to step into the fairytale.

We're at C'est Si Bon inside the Quintus Hotel.

It's upscale dining experience at its best.

A lot of clients wined and dined me at five-star restaurants before, but they all take a backseat to this. Everything about the Quintus Hotel spells upscale.

Beckett tells me the restaurant is packed with Hollywood's Who's Who. I believe him. People here look like they're made of money.

"This is exquisite," I say, finishing the last drop of my drink. "The red wine and the restaurant."

"Since you've never been to Paris—and Rhys made a point of highlighting it this morning—I thought this would be perfect," he says.

"The way you say that makes it sounds like you two have a rivalry going on."

"There's no rivalry here," Beckett says. "He's sweating his balls off somewhere in Vietnam while I'm sitting across from the hottest woman in the restaurant. I win hands down."

I laugh. And blush.

The man has my head spinning.

"Stop it," I say. *Or keep going.*

"Flying to Paris overnight is a bit of a stretch—even when you own your own private jet."—*Of course.*—"C'est Si Bon is the second-best thing. The food is spectacular, the wine list is refined, and the attentive service is irreproachable... in other words, it's very *holy chic.*"

"You find clever ways of twisting things around."

"I get that a lot."

*Why did that sound borderline perverted?*

After tasting some of the most refined champagne in my life at Flûte Champagne Bar, we made our way to the second French restaurant in the hotel.

"You enjoyed your meal?" he asks.

"I believe I've been quite vocal about it since the first bite."

"Yes, you have, but it would be ungentlemanly of me not to double check."

"I enjoyed the meal immensely. So far, this evening rocks."

"And to think it's only getting started."

Something I can't make out veils his eyes.

*Stop reading too much into things.*

"Should we order another bottle of red with dessert or would you prefer white?" he asks.

Since Beckett is driving, I've been doing most of the drinking. I should hold back a bit, but this wine is so freaking amazing. Not to mention, the rich French meal serves as a buffer, right?

"Waltzing into work on my third day on a new contract with a massive hangover might send the wrong message. I wouldn't want my client to think I'm irresponsible."

"What kind of tyrant do you work for?" He winks. "What about another glass?"

I hesitate.

"You're going to dance it off," he says.

"Who says we're going dancing?" I ask, surprised.

"As if a night of fun would exclude dancing," he says in a matter-of-fact way.

"Rock stars can dance?" I ask.

"Rock stars are invincible. We can do anything."

"Your ego is huge, Beckett Christensen."

His eyes, which match the iridescent blue of the Ionian Sea, turn dark.

"What did I say?" I ask.

His half smile should be a precursor.

"That's not the only thing huge about me."

My cheeks flame up.

My lips part in shock.

My brain can't even come up with a response.

"Did I say that out loud?" The amusement in his eyes is evident.

"Yes, you did," I say. A vision of his naked glory and his hugeness flashes in front of my eyes. I shake the thought away before I start drooling all over myself. If I could fan myself in an inconspicuous way, I would, but he's still staring straight at me. "A client shouldn't reveal that much about himself."

"We're friends, remember?"

"In that case, I know way too much about my new friend."

"You don't know nearly enough."

"You're right, a bottle might be too much. We're definitely keeping it to another glass."

He laughs.

My client is a dangerous man.

A part of my brain is cautioning me to keep my wits about me, but another part of me doesn't care. I can't remember the last time I enjoyed an evening out with a guy.

Beckett's sexual track record must be as long as the Mississippi River, but right now, he makes me feel like I'm the only woman in the world.

# Chapter 17

## *Beckett*

I'm taking great pleasure in pushing her buttons. Sure, my straightforwardness is like drinking from a firefighter's hose, but she hasn't asked me to tone it down. Still, I don't want to smother her with my dirty talk... not yet, anyway.

I grab the menu. "Let's order dessert."

"What do you recommend?" Arianne asks.

"Crème brûlée, and the profiteroles are—"

My ringing phone interrupts. I normally set my phone on silent mode when I'm having dinner, but I wanted to be available just in case Rhys needed to reach me. I check my screen. It's not him.

"I apologize," I tell her. "I'll be a minute."

"That's okay," she says.

"Hey, Cesar, what's up?" I say when I answer.

"Christensen, *hermano*, you're still coming, right?" my friend asks.

I search my memory bank. *Shit.* "It's tonight?"

"Don't tell me you forgot."

"I apologize, but it slipped my mind. I was in New York for

ten days. I got here yesterday. Since then, it's been nonstop," I tell him.

"I see," he says. "Was Rhys in New York with you? I tried calling him, but he isn't answering."

"No. He's in Vietnam. It's very last-minute. We're having some issues with production."

"Shit. I'm sorry to hear that," Cesar says. "I guess you can't make it?"

"It's an important night for you. I'll be there. I'm afraid I didn't get Diana a gift."

"She'll be thrilled to see you. Gift or no gift. The Cuban band I flew in for the occasion hasn't started playing yet, so get your pretty ass over here, *con rapidez*."

"I'll make up for the gift later."

Cesar chuckles.

"I'll be coming with someone. I hope that's okay."

"One of your boys?"

"No." My gaze shifts to Arianne. *A sexy little thing.* "A woman."

It's dead silence on the other end.

"Cesar?"

"I'm still here. I thought we had a bad connection because I swear I heard you say you were coming with a woman."

I know where he's coming from. I don't present women I fuck to my friends. Then again, Arianne doesn't fall into that category.

"Idiot."

"Is she a model you hired as arm candy for an event?" Cesar asks.

"She's as gorgeous as a model, but no, I didn't hire her." Arianne's face turns a bright shade of red. "We're friends." She averts her gaze. Okay, she works for me, but tonight, all bets are off.

"*¿Amigos con derecho?*" Cesar asks. *Not yet, hermano.* Until he fell head over heels for Diana, Cesar only had *friends with benefits.*

"Just friends."

"You don't have female friends, Christensen."

"I do now."

He lets out a boisterous laugh.

"If it wasn't for Diana, I'd hang up on you."

He laughs even harder.

"This, I have to see with my own two eyes," he says when he regains his composure.

I shake my head.

"We're just about to order dessert," I say. "I'll see you soon."

"See you and your *lady friend* when you get here."

"Fucker."

I hang up.

I meet Arianne's expectant gaze.

"Is everything okay?" she asks.

"I know this is last-minute, but my buddy Cesar is throwing a big party for his girlfriend. Diana turns twenty-seven today. She doesn't know it, but it's a double whammy tonight. He's going to pop the question."

"That's so exciting!" Arianne claps.

"Yeah, it's a huge leap for him. He's a consummate bachelor—"

"Says the playboy sitting across from me."

I laugh. "I told you not to believe everything you read on Google."

"Sure."

I shake my head.

"Cesar is a good friend. In rehab, it was Cesar, Rhys, and me—the three misfits," I tell her. "If there was trouble to be found, we usually did. He runs a hot sauce empire these days, but he's still the featured artist on many chart-topping Latin hits. Back in the day, he dominated reggaeton—"

"Oh my God!" She lifts a hand up like a traffic cop, as she draws her eyebrows together. "Are you talking about Gran Herminio, aka Great Soldier, aka Puerto Rican reggaeton king Cesar Navarro and his gorgeous pop star girlfriend from the Dominican Republic, Mayté, aka Diana Estevez?"

I'm surprised by her answer.

"Yes. You know them?"

She bobs her head up and down. "When I was in college in New York, I got a crash course in Latin culture."

"This, I have to hear."

"My best friend Phoebe fell hard for this hot guy from the Dominican Republic. He didn't know she existed, but she was hopelessly in love. She decided to learn everything related to DR and the Hispanic-slash-Latin culture, so when he *did* finally notice her, she would be ready. She enlisted me as her sidekick. She never caught his eye, but we had a hell of a semester that year. That's the only reason I can dance salsa, eat hot sauce without my mouth burning, and the reason why I have as many Latin songs as I do on my playlist, even though I don't understand the lyrics."

"You dance salsa?"

"Don't look so shocked."

This woman has so many layers.

"I was worried this was going to put a kink in our evening, but I guess I was wrong."

"Although Phoebe and I started out with two left feet, months of perseverance paid off. I can salsa like the best of them," she says with a tinge of pride.

"The party is taking place at one of Cesar's salsa clubs. You're okay with us dropping by?"

"Absolutely!"

~

After enjoying our desserts, we zoomed to Cesar's main club. He's usually closed on Wednesday nights, so the place is packed with friends and family. Still, given his, his girlfriend's, and the status of a few big names, security is tight. The guy spared no expense. The interior of his club is reminiscent of a flamboyant Vegas show. We arrived right before he dropped to one knee. Cesar didn't want to wait any longer than he had to. Diana was elated and she couldn't stop crying.

After he slipped a big ass ring on his girl's finger, the four of us hung out for a while in one of the private lounges. A few glasses of champagne, too many desserts and a shit ton of selfies later, I weave my way through the crowd, holding onto Arianne's hand. Cesar is about to welcome the band.

"I still can't believe I'm here on such a big night." Arianne shouts her comment over the music when we come to stand in front of the elevated stage. "Thank you so much for bringing me. Phoebe is going to be so jealous."

The vivacious woman standing in front of me is a far cry from the stern, pinned-up consultant who cut me at the knee earlier today.

"One, we're friends."

She grins wide.

I wink. "Two, I promised a night of fun. Three, I hinted at us closing a dance floor. It doesn't get better than Club Impacto."

"No, it doesn't," she says. "Do you know how to dance salsa?" she asks. Skepticism colors her eyes before I even answer.

"While we were in rehab, Cesar challenged me. I had two left feet. With rock music, there's more jumping around than dancing. The thing is, I don't shy away from a challenge and I play to win!" I drive my point home with a cocksure dance move.

"I'm suitably impressed," she says.

"Suitably?" I arch an eyebrow. "What would it take to make it just straight up, impressed?"

"Once the band starts, your ranking *might* improve."

"Tough jury." I chuckle.

She laughs.

"This night is so unlike me," she says, looking around before settling her gaze onto mine.

"Is that a good thing?"

She pulls her lower lip between her teeth and nods. "You're rubbing off on me."

I cock an eyebrow. "You dirty girl."

"I said, you're rubbing *off on me. Not* you're rubbing me off —" Her eyes grow wide and she covers her mouth. Her shock is evident.

*What a slip of the tongue.*

"That can be arranged," I say.

I expect her to avert her eyes, but she doesn't.

She holds my daring gaze and her tempting lips part.

It's like she's about to say something, but her brain can't come up with anything.

I'm in big trouble.

Rhys's challenge is a cock blocker I could do without.

*Fuck.*

"Can I get your attention, please," Cesar says into a microphone, walking up onstage.

"The show is starting," Arianne says before tearing her gaze away from mine.

The moment is gone.

Cesar invites *Cienfuegos* to the stage. A short black guy sporting a dyed platinum blond afro introduces the group. In heavy, accented English, he lets us know the first song is a salsa rendition of an old chart-topper. Something about a special request. After roaring applause, *Cienfuegos* kicks things off with a bang. The second the song blares through the speakers, everyone, including Arianne, recognizes it and cheers. I'm clueless, but I can handle the animated beat.

I grab my dancing partner by the waist and we start moving to the music.

I make out the words of the bridge.

*Amigos con derecho.*

The irony is uncanny.

I search the crowd for Cesar. He's dancing with his fiancée. That ridiculous grin stretching his lips says it all.

"Fucker," I mouth.

"Friends with benefits," he mouths back with a wink.

I shake my head.

Thank God, Arianne is oblivious to our sparring.

She's already lost to the music.

*Wow. She can dance.*

She can really dance.

There's no hesitation in her bold movements.

I could watch her body sway so bewitchingly to this seductive beat for the rest of my natural life.

*Damn.*

It's like she's in a trance. My cock is this close from busting a vein just from watching her.

I can't even adjust myself inconspicuously.

After an hour of feverish dancing, my cock is aching, an annoying reminder of my vow of chastity.

*I shall not succumb to temptation.*

I keep repeating the mantra over and over in my head, although I know I'm only kidding myself. The woman dancing in front of me is on fire. Her messy updo is a lot messier.

Strands of hair caress her cheeks. Without thinking, I unlace our fingers and brush a few of them behind her ears.

Arianne's eyes move up to mine.

I read something I haven't seen so far.

*Lust.*

With a soft touch, I allow my fingers to glide down to her mouth. I trace her lower lip with my thumb, smearing her perfectly applied lipstick. She shivers but doesn't ask me to stop. What she does next surprises me. She grabs hold of my wrist, closes her eyes, and allows her lips to part.

*An invitation?*

*Goddammit.*

The need to slip my thumb between those plump lips is overwhelming, but I resist. We're surrounded by too many people—and too many phones—and the last thing I need is to give Cesar more ammunition.

*It's just a dance.*

To my regret, the song ends.

Arianne opens her eyes.

The black guy with the platinum blond hair makes an announcement in Spanish. Judging from the reaction of the crowd, it must be another favorite. A petite brunette with waist-length hair wearing thigh-high sparkly silver boots and a white micro mini dress steps up to a mic. With one nod, the band starts playing. The frantic tempo of the previous song slows down to a more melodic salsa.

*Fuck, it's about to get worse for me.*

"*Probablemente,*" Arianne says. "I love this song. Especially, Daniela Darcourt's version."

The beat is dangerously sexy, only enhanced by the smokey-timbre of the female vocalist.

Arianne lets go of my hands and to my utter shock she goes for it.

I stand back and admire her in awe.

I can't peel my eyes off her.

*Fuck, she's beautiful.*

Beautiful in an unassuming way.

Beautiful because she's clueless to her natural beauty.

Beautiful because she's oblivious to the sensuality buried deep inside her.

I'm so wrapped up with her, everyone around us ceases to exist. Not that it matters because every single person here seems caught up in the bewitching notes of the song.

The woman who seemed so distant—so in control—loses herself in a series of outrageous and dizzying dance moves, matching *Probablemente's* enraptured tempo. Every movement is an assault, fraying my weakening resolve. Glistening pearls of sweat trail across her forehead, testament to her feverish dancing.

A standoffish Arianne is a challenge that gets my engine roaring, but this carefree version is intoxicating, and I'm not quite sure what to make of her yet.

As the tempo increases, she lifts her skirt up just enough to bring more attention to her slender curves. My head jerks back, astounded when she slaps each ass cheek as her hips suggestively sway left to right.

*God, those hips.*

My cock throbs to the beat of her dancing.

My pulse is racing faster than a well-built automobile breaking three hundred miles per hour on the track.

I'm turned on beyond belief.

And fuck if I don't want to drop to my knees and find out how sweet she tastes. I want to lick my way down her stomach and look up to see that same cock-hardening expression on her face while I devour her pussy.

I want to hear my name on her lips when she comes.

*Damn challenge.*

When the bridge hits again, I reach out and pull her to me.

She doesn't resist.

I slide a hand around the dip of her waist, resting it against the small of her back. I mentally warn myself not to slide even lower because right now the only thing I want to do is grope that fine ass and force her body to grind against my impossibly hard cock.

*Too many witnesses.*

We're pressed so close together, I'm sure I can feel her heart beating.

And she can feel every inch of me.

There's no mistaking what's happening here.

Our eyes lock onto each other's.

A second ticks by.

Another.

And another.

The air is filled with an intense tension. No, raw passion.

She doesn't stop dancing.

She keeps fucking tempting me.

With my hands resting against her hips, I feel the sexy sway of every undulation.

The way she rolls her tempting hips suggests there's a bad girl trapped inside her delectable body, dying to be unleashed. She just needs a willing soul to coax her out to play.

Lucky for her, I'm in a very giving mood.

I lean into her until my mouth is so close to hers, I can nearly taste the champagne on her breath. "We can keep dancing, or we can go back to your place and become more acquainted as *friends.*" I'm using the same low rasp I use to tell a woman to spread her legs wide for me so I can have access to her pussy. I haven't used that voice in a while.

I pull away from her.

Even under the dim lights, the heat radiating from her eyes is unmistakable.

"I vote for the latter," I say when she remains silent.

This can go either way.

She can shut me down again or she can give me what I want.

I've never had my ass handed to me before. Not even once. I can't imagine it happening four times on the same day.

A slow smile curves her lips as she tilts her head back.

Her half-lidded eyes are scorching, her desire as palpable as mine.

"*Friends* who work together could be a dicey, slippery slope," she says.

It's a valid point.

"This is uncharted territory for me, Arianne. You're exempt from the fraternization clause, so we aren't breaking any rules. As for us working together, we're adults. I'm sure we can handle it."

"You didn't want to be *friends* with any of the other consultants in the past?"

"The men are automatically eliminated."

She laughs.

"As for the other women, no. None of them looked as fucking hot as you," I say. "I hope you'll be my first *friend*."

"Something tells me you haven't said that to too many women."

"You're right. See how special you are?"

She considers me.

I pull her to me, fusing us together. Not that I know how that's possible considering we're already breathing the same air.

She gasps.

I've been good so far. I'm done being good.

I grind my impossibly hard cock against her. It's provocative. There's no mistaking the message.

"Jesus."

"Is that a yes?" I cut to the chase.

"Yes."

One word.

Endless possibilities.

# Chapter 18

## Arianne

E very cell in my body is on high alert. My skin is prickling with an all-encompassing electric current. Although my feet have barely touched the ground from this enchanting evening, there's a voice yelling at me.

*Mayday! Mayday!*

*Pending invasion!*

*Abort mission.*

*I repeat. Abort mission. Now!*

*Do you copy, Buchanan?*

*Extricate yourself from this perilous situation before it's too late!*

*Do not try to be a superhero. You will get burned!*

*You are no match for the irresistible scorching-hot boss-slash-client.*

*Save yourself, girl.*

*SAVE YOURSELF!*

The sophisticated security system I've carefully spent two years building to protect me from the enemy—aka, men—falters. All the circuits are cross-wired, which explains why I'm so helpless now. When I perfected the code, I didn't take Beckett Christensen into account.

I know firsthand an office romance can be disastrous.

I shouldn't be in this predicament again.

I promised myself I never would.

But here's the thing, it may be past midnight, but I'm still wearing my glass slippers, and the ocean-blue eyes staring down at me are making me dizzy with need.

I don't lust over men. Until the incident in the elevator, I couldn't spell the word.

I'm too levelheaded for that, but here I am.

Lustful and desirous.

I can laugh at Phoebe as much as I want, but right now, my pussy is fluttering-palpitating-pulsating-quivering-throbbing so much, I'm this close to coming.

The ride in Beckett's pricey sports car to my sublet is excruciating. We don't say much, but the complicit side gazes we exchange speak volumes. Same goes for that sexy smile stretching his lips.

"You haven't changed your mind?" he asks, cutting the engine of his sports car.

I can play it two ways tonight. I can retreat to my usual MO and spend the night alone, or I can let one of LA's most notorious bachelor playboys have his wicked way with me.

I shake my head. "No. I still want this." *I want you.*

Fire lights his eyes.

"I would've been thoroughly disappointed if you didn't."

"I'm sure my sublet isn't what you're used to—"

"I'm not coming up to your place for the décor. I'm coming up for *you!*" He taps the tip of my nose.

We ride the elevator from the guest parking lot up to my apartment in silence.

I'm so nervous, I wouldn't know what to say, anyway. Not

to mention, the wetness pooling between my legs renders me speechless.

No man has ever had this kind of hold on me before.

I barely have time to lock the door and turn on a few lights when Beckett has me spinning around. My back lands against the door. His hands come to rest on either side of my head, making me his hostage. His willing hostage.

"I'm going to enjoy getting to know my new friend," he says.

The flames burning from his blue eyes, his roughened breathing and the overwhelming nearness of his tall, hard body is too much to handle. My back arches against the door, drawing his gaze down to my breasts and back up to my eyes.

My chest heaves as I struggle to breathe.

*I can't believe he's looking at me this way.*

I swallow as he edges closer, my throat suddenly dry.

"I don't want this to come across the wrong way... but I need to know. Are you a virgin?"

"No, I'm not..."

"I'm listening," he says.

"I'm really flattered, Beckett, but I..." I hesitate again. "I'm sure I don't have the same level of experience as the women you've been with."

"Experience means you know more tricks. It doesn't make me want you more, and it does zilch in terms of attraction. I don't think I'm wrong in assuming our attraction for each other is pretty explosive."

I avert my gaze.

Beckett places two fingers underneath my chin, forcing my attention back to him. His eyes bore into mine, making me feel naked. "I expect an answer, Arianne."

"You're right."

He leans down, his mouth stopping a mere inch away from mine. "We're on the same page?"

"Definitely."

He brushes his lips along the underside of my jaw. The blistering contact on my skin sends a thrill of shivers coursing through my body. My nipples harden, aching with need, just begging for his touch and his mouth.

*Oh my God, I'm going to melt.*

"I like the sound of that," he says. "Do you know what I've been dying to do all night?" His gaze never leaves mine as he lowers his mouth, touching his lips to mine. "I bet you taste real good."

His stunning blue eyes are consuming me.

If he doesn't kiss me, I'm going to go insane.

His mouth comes crashing down on mine, hard, hungry and unwavering. A soft moan escapes my throat and my lips part. He slips his tongue into my mouth, searching for mine. The dance that ensues is mind-blogging. My hands cup his face before they travel to the back of his head until my fingers tug at his hair. He responds by threading his fingers through my hair and fucking up my messy updo.

"You should let it down more often," he says, pulling away from me, his fingers still interlaced in my strands. His lidded eyes are dangerous. "I can just imagine what it would be like to fuck you from behind while fisting your gorgeous, silky hair." His words cause my clit to tingle, but when he tugs on one lock, pulling hard at the nape of my neck, I close my eyes and let out a low desperate moan.

Just when I think things can't get any better, Beckett ratchets the passion factor by kissing the hell out of me.

*God, yes.*

I didn't know it was possible to make love with your mouth because that's exactly what Beckett is doing. It's been so long, I would've been happy with a peck. This all-encompassing, combustive kiss is more than I could ever wish for.

I lose myself with no hope of ever finding my way back.

And right now, I really don't want to.

The kiss is so potent, we both pause for a shuddering breath. We exchange a lop-sided grin before Beckett assaults my lips again. He devours my mouth in a primitive display of possessiveness I'm unaccustomed to. It makes me feel sexy as hell.

After what seems like a blissful eternity, I break free of his embrace, gasping at the sheer size of him pressing against me. Desperate to get closer, I fling my evening bag across the room. It goes crashing somewhere, but neither of us care. I pull up my skirt and lift a leg before circling his waist. I let out a small yelp when he pushes against me with his hips, holding my ass in place with strong hands.

*Mother of God.*

I've never had sex standing up before. I'm not sure this qualifies as sex, but I'm sure it qualifies as a holy-Jesus-yes-yes-yes. Beckett's heavy breath warms my ear, punctuated by each hard thrust that pins me to the shaking door. It's like he's fucking me with our clothes on.

I'm almost embarrassed by my naïveté and inexperience.

*Wow. I didn't even know this was a thing.*

When his mouth finds mine once more, I surprise us both when I bite his lower lip.

"You're a wild one," he says.

"You make me do wild things."

"This is only the warm-up, baby. You'll be a beast when I'm done with you."

I giggle.

He doesn't crack a smile.

"I want your other leg around my waist." I frown, unable to comprehend how that's going to work. "Do as you're told."

When I follow his command, Beckett uses the door as an anchor. He runs skilled hands down my thighs and hooks his arms underneath my legs, pulling them apart until they nearly reach my shoulders.

*Holy shit, he's strong.*

My skirt slides around my waist, giving him full access.

I'm wide open for him.

I pant, my heart beating at an infernal rate.

On a loud groan, Beckett resumes the kiss, ravishing my mouth, sucking my tongue until I'm writhing against his insanely hard cock. He presses hard against me in response, hitting me where I need it most. My fingers are no match for the precise way he grinds against my clit.

*God, I'm close.*

Then, everything stops.

# Chapter 19

## *Beckett*

"No! Beckett, please," Arianne says when I pull away from her.

"It would be a waste of a good load—and fairly embarrassing—if I came in my pants."

I drop her legs and let her slide down my body.

"Oh my God, I do that to you?"

"How many times do I have to tell you that you're fucking hot?"

Her eyelashes flutter like crazy.

"I... I thought..." She shakes her head. "This is too much."

"You want me to stop?"

"No. It's just my brain can't quite catch up."

"But your body surely can."

We grin at each other.

Call me a greedy bastard, but I want both—the girl and the bike.

Rhys made sure to text me the terms of our agreement every single day since he got on that jet.

I have them memorized.

Since kissing is an anomaly in my world, he left it off the list.

It's been so long since I've tasted a woman's mouth, I was worried I'd forgotten how. I couldn't get enough of Arianne's soft lips. And the way she responds to me... damn. If you had told me I could get off by ravishing a woman's mouth and dry humping, I would've said you're fucking crazy. But here I am, a few breaths away from spilling my load.

As for Rhys's other cock-blocking rules... as much as I'd like nothing more than to drag Arianne to the floor and fuck her sweet pussy into submission, pounding an orgasm—or four—out of her, I can't. That would be cheating. I always win fair and square. But there's no way I'm leaving Arianne's place without tasting her.

"We're about to blur the lines," I tell her.

"I thought we were well past that," she says.

I weigh my next words. "You're okay if we make it a little depraved?"

"I've never done depraved."

"Do you want me to take you there?"

She ponders my question.

"I'd love to know what it's like," she says in a soft voice.

*Game on.*

I drop her to her feet.

"Come on, we're going to your bathroom." I grab her hand.

"There's a bedroom and a couch."

Poor little lamb, she's used to predictable. I'm anything but.

"I'm glad to hear it, but we're going to the bathroom."

She frowns.

"Depraved, remember?"

"Right." She worries her lower lip.

Given I haven't seen a woman's naked body in thirteen days, she should be worried.

As expected, the bathroom isn't big, but it'll do.

"Strip!" I tell her.

"Ah, a shower before sex. Of course," she says.

*What?*

"That's not what I had in mind."

"Oh, I just thought..." She shakes her head. "Never mind."

"Finish that thought."

She averts her gaze.

"Arianne," I say.

She lets out a shaky breath. "My ex is an engineering scientist and a bit of a germaphobe. Well, that's what he proclaimed at the time we were dating. He believed—" She pauses. "This is so embarrassing."

"You can tell me. I'm not going to judge," I tell her.

"He believed a woman's *vulva*—because pussy is vulgar and vagina is anatomically inaccurate—contains more bacteria than a toilet in a high-traffic airport that hasn't been cleaned in twenty-four hours."

I'm so dumbfounded, I don't know how to respond.

"So, a shower before and after sex was the norm," she says. "Same with washing sheets and towels afterwards. Oral sex was inconceivable. I was always responsible for my... you know... orgasms."

My jaw drops.

"What about fingers?"

"And spread bacteria-filled bodily fluids all over the place? Never."

"Blowjobs?"

"Well..."

I motion a hand, coaxing her to continue.

"Ejaculating in a woman's mouth is repulsive. All those germs. Sucking him off for a few strokes was okay, as long as I brushed my teeth and used mouthwash before we continued because kissing me after his cock was in my mouth was a big no-no."

*No fucking way.*

I'm stunned into silence.

I want to ask her why the hell she dated someone incapable of bringing her pleasure, but I refrain.

"He's the only man I've ever been with." She answers my unspoken question. "Once he hooked up with his current girl-friend-slash-fiancée, all of a sudden, receiving head and eating pussy became his favorite things. Said girlfriend-slash-fiancée made sure to let me know by sharing explicit photos and videos of them in action." She lets out a suffering sigh. "Maybe it was me."

*No, sweetheart, it was your loser ex.*

"Maybe my *vulva* wasn't to his liking."

*I'm willing to bet your pussy is perfect.*

"For the past two years..." she lets her words trail.

"You haven't been with anyone?"

She shakes her head. "You're free to bail out now. I wouldn't be offended."

I hook a hand behind the nape of her neck and pull her close to me. "Not a chance."

She places a hand against my chest before dropping her forehead. "I don't want you to be disappointed, Beckett."

"Look at me."

She does.

"You're a dichotomy, Arianne. A very sexy dichotomy. I saw the way you danced. Fuck"—I shake my head, flashing back to those hips rolling—"you're incredibly sensual. It isn't forced. You're not trying to wrestle a reaction out of me. What makes it so disarming is how much you're oblivious to your sensuality. There's a force hiding inside you. You simply haven't found the right guy to coax it out of you—"

"Which is why you should run while you still can—"

"I want to be that guy."

She looks up at me like I have two heads. "Really?"

"Tell me you don't want that, and I'll go—"

"I want that."

I brush my lips over hers. "Good answer, baby."

She grins, threading her fingers through my hair. "I'm not used to being your *friend* yet and you've already elevated me to *baby* status? It's a bit much for a girl to handle."

"The next level for you is hot little lover."

Her eyes grow as wide as saucers.

"No pressure," she says.

"I believe in you." She sucks in a breath. "Strip. Keep the shoes and the underwear." She reaches between us and pulls her t-shirt over her head and tosses it onto the floor.

I take a step back to allow more maneuvering room. When her skirt pools at her feet, she kicks it to the side.

"Turn around." I come to stand behind her. My half-lidded eyes meet hers in the mirror before traveling down her delectable body. Her smooth creamy skin is a departure from the tanned—and overly tanned—women I usually fuck. "I like this a lot." I take in her black sheer lace combo with red flower appliqué. It's sexy, in a good girl kind of way. "Who did you wear this for?"

She averts her gaze.

I tilt my hips forward.

She gasps.

Let's try that again. "Who did you wear this for?"

"If I answer, I might come across as presumptuous."

"So, you were hoping for more tonight?"

"Nerdy girls like me never end up with bad boys like you, Beckett—"

"'Nerdy girl' sounds like a putdown when you say it." I

cock an eyebrow. "You can be both—highly intelligent *and* incredibly beautiful. It will be my pleasure to remind you that you're a fucking gorgeous woman over, and over, and over again until you believe it."

She responds with a shy nod.

"About the lingerie..." she says, "in a moment of sheer delusion, I listened to my best friend's advice, believing her when she said this night should be more than just dinner and bar hopping."

"I like Phoebe. A lot."

She laughs.

"I'm glad I listened to her. I suspect white cotton granny panties and matching bra wouldn't have the same effect."

My eyes glaze over her as they land on her taut stomach before bouncing back to hers. "Something tells me you could make it work."

Her cheeks flush. "You have a way with words."

"I tell it like I see it, Arianne. Your scientist-engineer-douchebag-ex didn't know what to do with you. I do." I reach for her bra, releasing the clasp and freeing her tits.

"Damn, those are beautiful," I say.

Her tits are a perfect size—without being too big—with small pink nipples. Unable to resist, I cup them in my hands, palming them before circling her perky nipples with my thumbs. She relaxes into me, eyes closing. I take my time until the pressure of her ass against my cock is excruciating and sinful at the same time.

I give those rock-hard nipples a little tug and her moan reverberates to my balls.

I'm skirting the rules by exploiting the loopholes.

Rhys never anticipated my undeniable obsession with Arianne or my newfound selfless mission to bring her pleasure and make up for her ex's shortcomings.

"When do I get to see you naked?" she asks, meeting my gaze in the mirror.

"You feel like you're missing out?"

"Definitely."

"Fair enough." It pains me to let go of her tits, but there's so much I want to do to her.

She watches in the mirror as I unbutton my shirt, remove it and throw it on the floor. I undo my belt buckle, unzip my fly and push my pants down. I step out of them and kick them out of the way. In a dramatic sweep, I push my boxer briefs down my legs before removing them. I stand behind her wearing nothing other than a cocky grin. My erection is pointing straight up at my stomach, a little past my bellybutton, ready to play.

A gasp slips from Arianne's luscious lips.

She turns to face me.

"Oh..." A glimpse of what I'm packing makes her shiver with lust. She blinks, her gaze bouncing from my cock to my eyes. "You weren't exaggerating when you said you were huge."

"No, I wasn't."

"The massive size is intimidating."

"Remember, I believe in you."

"I'm going to need more than your faith in me. I'm going to need an act from God."

She reaches out for my cock.

I swat her hand away.

"Did I say you could touch?"

Confused eyes search mine.

"Until I give you permission, hands-off."

I can tell she doesn't know what to do with that order. It takes a beat, but eventually she nods like a good girl.

If she were to touch me, I'd come in her hand with only a

few strokes. Since a hand job is on Rhys's no-no list, it's best not to go there.

"You can look, but you can't touch." I give myself a couple of vigorous tugs, swelling even larger in my hand.

"The way you do that... it's so manly." She swallows hard.

"You've never seen a guy jerk off before?"

"Only online."

My eyebrows hit my forehead.

"Porn?"

Her cheeks flush.

"Phoebe's fault," she says in a whisper.

I laugh.

I stroke harder, stifling a groan.

"Soon, your lips will be wrapped around my huge cock, my generous girth stretching your limits."

Her eyes never leave my cock as I slowly pump my fist up and down. My cock strains under her inspection, veins bulging thick.

"You like what you see?"

She nods.

My length is slick. My fist works up and down, sliding from base to tip. I squeeze out a pearl of pre-cum, scoop it up with a fingertip and reach my hand out to her.

"Wanna taste me, baby?"

She nods.

"I want to hear it," I tell her.

"Yes, I want to taste you."

Such beautiful words.

"Open wide for me," I say.

So willing.

So, fucking eager.

"Lick!"

Her tongue slips out, and she cleans my finger with a few sensual licks.

*Fuck.*

I mentally snapshot the image and store it in my spank bank for later use.

"Nice!" I nod my approval. I return to fisting my cock, stroking it back and forth. "This feels so fucking good. Join me, baby."

"I thought you said I couldn't touch you."

"I did. I want you to touch your pussy for me." Her eyes widen in shock. "You did tell me you were responsible for your orgasms—"

"Yes, but never in front of my ex."

"You want a repeat of what you had with him, or do you want something mind-blowing?"

"You're right," she says. "I'm due for more."

"You mean, you deserve more," I tell her.

She beams.

"When you play with your pussy, do you use toys or your fingers?"

"My fingers."

"Show me how you do it," I say.

With a wicked grin, Arianne slips a hand down her stomach and under her panties.

I let out a groan, crazy with lust, as I watch her fingers wiggle underneath the sheer fabric of her underwear.

I pump my cock faster in a torturous rhythm that threatens to drive me out of my goddamn mind.

The hedonistic sound of her slickness gliding around her pussy makes me jealous. I want those fingers to be mine. If I touch her, I doubt I could walk out of here without fucking her.

"Oh God," she says.

"See. There are so many mutual benefits to being friends."

Her wicked grin is epic.

She keeps working her pussy, moans of pleasure escaping her lips. When she closes her eyes, I don't protest.

I know I've already said it, but goddammit she's beautiful.

"I'm so wet," she says in a pleading voice.

"Let me taste you, baby."

It's been a while since I've wanted my mouth on a woman's pussy. This isn't quite it, but it's close enough.

She pulls her hand out, fingers wet with her juices and brings them up to my mouth like a gift. Without slowing my hand stroking my cock in a slippery grip, I stick out my tongue and lap at her fingers.

She lets out a whimper.

"Your *vulva* tastes as good as I knew it would."

She explodes in laughter.

"Maybe I shared too much," she says when she regains her composure.

"Not at all. I'm dead set on giving you what he never could."

I can't understand my determination, but I don't attempt to make sense of it. Not when a gorgeous, nearly naked woman is willing to play my dirty games.

"Feed me more."

She scoops up more of her juices and allows me to clean her fingers.

Her eyes shine bright with desire.

This time I suck her digits, making raunchy noises, as I memorize her taste on my tongue.

"Dear God. That is so wrong, yet so right."

I could come in the palm of my hand just from her bewildered expression.

Tasting her is a tortuous tease.

I fooled myself into thinking it would be enough.

An internal battle between wanting the one-of-a-kind bike and the girl rages inside me.

*Fuck.*

My mind is spinning, searching for another loophole because not having my way with this woman isn't even an option.

"Face the mirror," I tell her.

She does as she's told.

I let go of my cock and stand behind her.

She's nearly naked. Her lipstick is long-gone and her hair is freely brushing against her shoulders.

She's a vision.

I can't help my grin when my eyes land on the bruise on her neck. That wasn't planned, but I fucking love my bite mark on her.

I pull her body closer to mine, with my cock pressed against her ass.

*Jesus.*

The closeness is a reminder of how long I've been deprived.

She meets my gaze in the mirror, a devilish smile parting her lips as she brings her hand up around the back of my neck. The position stretches her body beautifully. Her vulnerability is on full display. I close my hands around her tits, my fingers pulling at her nipples before caressing them in circles with my palms.

Her open-mouthed grin tells me she fucking loves it.

I pinch and pluck her rosy nipples until they're stiff, dark-plum peaks and my girl is breathing hard.

Such beautiful handiwork.

"Damn. Your tits are fucking amazing."

Her head turns, seeking my mouth for a kiss. I allow it. It's not as fiery as earlier, so much more sensual. I kiss her thorough and dirty, devouring her mouth until she protests, then I punish her by ravishing her with increased fervor. Her sexy ass grinds against my hungry cock as I squeeze her tits hard.

"I'm not going to be able to hold back much longer," I tell her. "I want you to take care of your clit while I use your ass to take care of my raging hard-on."

They say necessity is the mother of invention. So is desperation.

She gasps. "Wait. What? No." She's positively frightened. "Beckett, I've never done that before."

"Calm down, baby. I didn't say I was going to *fuck* your ass. I said I was going to *use* your ass. Big difference."

She frowns her confusion. "I don't understand."

"You trust me to make it good for you?"

She ponders on my question for a beat.

"I do," she says.

"In that case..."

I pull her G-string to the side, nestle my cock between her cheeks and press hard.

"Oh boy," she says, relaxing back into me.

My cock fits perfectly.

The sight is hedonistic as fuck.

The warmth of her body permeates mine.

The feeling is sublime.

"Work that pussy for me."

As she strokes her pussy, chasing her orgasm, I glide my cock between the crevice of her sweet cheeks. My mushroom-shaped tip is dark purple, angry, needy and desperate. I close my eyes and groan, silently thanking God for her perfect ass. I've never longed for skin-on-skin contact this much with a woman in my entire life.

"How many fingers do you have inside your sweet pussy?"

"One."

"I want two in there."

Her body shifts as she complies with my demand.

"That's it," I tell her. "With your other hand, I want you to tease your clit and pretend it's my fingers instead of yours."

She's a little startled, but she doesn't argue.

"Oh God," she says.

"Faster!"

Her breath hitches.

"I said faster!"

She gives me what I want.

"Pump those fingers inside your wetness. I want to hear it."

I tear my eyes away from hers and fix them between her legs.

The frantic motion starts. So does that sweet sound.

"Good girl."

The helpless little mewls spilling from her lips are intoxicating.

"How wet are you?" I ask.

"I'm positively dripping." The words come tumbling from her mouth on the heel of a long exhale.

"Who are you wet for?"

"You."

"What's my name?"

"Beckett."

"Now answer my question like a good girl."

"I'm wet for you, Beckett."

"Your pussy is desperate for my cock?" She nods. Fuck Rhys's stupid challenge. "Next time, baby."

"We're going to do this again?!" she asks, her eyes wide with bewilderment.

"I see a long-lasting friendship between us."

We grin at each other.

"You're okay with that?" I ask.

"More than okay."

"Good. Now, I want the focus back on your pussy."

I don't have to repeat myself.

Arianne is unleashed.

She's the most arousing sight I've seen in a long time.

The way her eyes roll to the back of her head, I can only assume it's as good for her as it is for me.

I pick up my pace, gliding with more pressing need between her ass cheeks.

Her hips are swiveling and rolling like they did on the dance floor.

As her fervor ratchets, the pressure her bouncing ass exerts against my cock is my undoing.

"Oh fuck," I say as my balls tighten.

I dig my hands into her hips, controlling her movement, as my cock glides up and down like a savage beast.

My eyes glaze as the onset of an eruption looms.

"Are you close?" I ask.

"God, yes!"

"I want you to come hard for me."

She nods.

The potent sensuality I knew was hiding inside her, surges. Lost to lust, Arianne swings her hips back and forth in a series of hard thrusts that nearly make me lose my fucking mind.

She's wild.

Unrestrained.

Unapologetic.

*I fucking love it.*

Then everything stops.

Her body goes rigid, her mouth drops open, her eyes close and a low cry escapes from her lips.

It's a thing of beauty.

Arianne comes so hard, she jerks her head back and stumbles.

She grips the counter.

I grip her waist.

She's trembling.

"I got you," I say. "Place your folded arms against the counter for me." My voice is strained. It's a struggle to speak.

She does.

God knows I've jerked an embarrassing number of times over the last week and a half, but you'd never know from the geyser building inside me.

The sight of my cock jutting against her milky white ass, desperate to explode, is more than I can bear. One final thrust and I come with a loud roar as ropes of cum spill all over, painting her ass.

"Feeling you on my body like this is so hot," Arianne whispers.

She stirs underneath me, squeezing her legs together, tilting her hips forward. In doing so, she traps the base of my still seeping cock between her ass cheeks.

*Damn.*

"God, I'm coming again," she says, panting and squeezing her legs even harder. "Oh—"

Her head jerks back with force before her body slumps forward against the counter.

*Jesus Christ.*

I didn't expect this from her and I'm caught off guard.

*Wow.*

It's a struggle to catch my breath.

She isn't faring much better.

She's a beautiful trembling, sweaty mess, spent and satiated.

I lower my chest to her back and wrap my arms around her body as I drop a trail of soft kisses across her shoulders. "Talk to me."

She turns her head to the side.

I lift my eyes to meet hers.

"I like being your friend," she says.

"It's mutual." I chuckle. "We're going to have a lot of dirty, naughty fun Love that book."

# Chapter 20

## *Arianne*

E urope is Europe, but it has nothing on the breathtaking sight stretching before me—LA at dawn. The canvas of warm colors painting the skyline in the early morning hour is sublime.

The City of Angels is barely waking up, but I've been standing on the balcony of my sublet for half an hour in nothing more than a loose-fitting t-shirt—no panties—a first—as I enjoy the view. Since I couldn't sleep, I figured what better way to ease into my day.

When sleep eludes me, it's because of my never-ending to-do list on a project, the stress of not letting people down, the worry of not measuring up to my last stellar performance or the anxiety of potentially failing.

Not today.

My body is still humming from my sizzling-hot encounter with a blue-eyed god. As much as I wanted things to go further, Beckett insists the wait will only make it better. He's already given me the most thrilling sexual experience of my life. I can't imagine what better even looks like.

After Beckett slipped out of my apartment, I went to sleep wet and aching, remembering the feel of his thick cock between my ass cheeks. God, that was so perverted. I've never done anything that kinky, and I'm not ashamed to say I want more. Pleasuring myself alone isn't nearly as earth-shattering as pleasuring myself under his watchful eye.

It's no surprise he's an insane lover, but I didn't expect the bad boy to make me feel like I was the most beautiful woman in the world. *Thank you, Beckett Christensen!* To add icing on the cake, I sure as hell never knew a few hours of filthy pleasures with the right guy could make me feel invincible.

*Take that, Chance. My vulva IS good enough!*

I know better than to send my ex a snarky text message to inform him that germ-filled bodily fluids are heavenly, but I'd love nothing more than to rub my newfound brazen-self in his jackass face.

My phone rings.

I rush inside to grab it.

Since Phoebe is already on a plane back to LA, I know it isn't her calling. And I doubt it's Beckett. He sent me a text message when he reached his car after leaving my place and another one when he reached his home to thank me for an incredible night.

My feet won't be touching the ground anytime soon.

"Mom," I say, picking up.

"Oh, honey, I didn't expect to catch you. Isn't it a little early for you?" she asks.

"Good morning, Mom."

"Where are my manners? Good morning, honey. It's only five-thirty your time. Why are you up so early?"

"I couldn't sleep."

"Too much partying with a hot guy will do that to a lassie," she says in an exaggerated Scottish accent.

*Huh?*

"What are you talking about?"

"Moira was all up and mighty on her high horse when she called this morning to tell me off."

"I thought you weren't on speaking terms with your estranged sister."

"We aren't."

"Then why is she mad at you?"

"You usurped her wee baby daughter's royal wedding announcement. The youngest Golightly is in town, making the rounds, flashing her big gaudy rock. So distasteful."

"Mariah is in Philadelphia?"

"Yes!" Mom makes this sound of disgust. I can see her crossing her arms over her ample chest, unimpressed.

"Unbelievable."

"You're telling me. It's like she's auditioning for a reality TV show. She arrived Tuesday morning just before her freakin' publicist pushed the news out about her pending nuptials. What a farce!"

"Mariah has a publicist?!"

My morning was going so well.

"Yes, she's going to be a freakin' princess, don't you know? So, of course it's newsworthy."

"She's just going to marry a multimillionaire, not a freakin' prince." I can't help but adopt Mom's Scottish accent.

"She's a bloody nitwit, that one," Mom says. I stifle a laugh. "In her delusional mind, it's the same freakin' thing. I'm surprised she hasn't taken to walking around with a freakin' tiara on her head—not that she'd find one big enough to fit that inflated ego of hers."

I roll my eyes. "I still don't understand why Aunt Moira thinks I care enough about stupid Mariah to give a damn about her wedding announcement."

"Good for you for not giving a flying fuck," Mom says.

"So, what's this about me stealing the limelight from her precious child?"

"You haven't been online?" Mom asks.

"No. It's still early here."

"Ooohhh, that's why you don't know."

"You're not making sense, Mom."

"From the photos and the in-your-face headlines, you're the new it girl, child."

"What?"

"Get on the internet and see for *yerself*."

"Okay, give me a second." I rush to my laptop, open it, and fire it up.

"My sister has some nerves," Mom says. "As Moira was losing her freakin' shit on the other end of the phone, I reminded her we were done as sisters before hanging up in her bloody face. I didn't mince words, I tell ya. Daddy was on his back laughing."

I still don't know what this is all about, but I can't help the laughter bubbling from me.

Daddy is always quick to defend me against the nasty Golightly clan.

Aunt Moira and her three daughters are witches, I swear.

I type the URL of a popular celebrity blog to make sense of what my mom is saying.

I gasp when I catch a glimpse of the headlines.

*'CEO OF SCORE HEADPHONES "SCORES" LAST NIGHT WITH SEXY MYSTERY WOMAN.'*

*'BECKETT CHRISTENSEN SMILING FOR THE CAMERA WITH GORGEOUS MYSTERY WOMAN.'*

*BECKETT CHRISTENSEN CAUGHT CANOODLING
WITH MYSTERY HOLY CHICNESS AT REGGAETON
KING CESAR NAVARRO'S ENGAGEMENT PARTY.'*

*'IS BAD-BOY, BACHELOR-FOREVER BECKETT
CHRISTENSEN WALKING DOWN THE AISLE?'*

*'BECKETT CHRISTENSEN, WHO'S THAT "HOLY
CHIC" GIRL?'*

*'FEVERISH NIGHT OF DIRTY SALSA DANCING FOR
BAD BOY BECKETT CHRISTENSEN!'*

The candid photos of Cesar, Diana, Beckett, and I smiling at the camera are a reminder of an enchanting evening. Never in a million years did I think they would go viral.

*Holy shit.*

I scroll through the photos, jaw-dropped.

The ones of Beckett and I dancing in an intimate embrace spark my lady parts.

"You've finally escaped from your self-imposed prison sentence." Her words bring me back to the moment.

"Huh?"

"The handsome lad," she says. "I guess you were waiting for *the one.*"

I'm stunned.

"Your father isn't perfect, but Gregor and I have weathered so many storms together. I want that for you. Every woman needs a good man. Not a spineless moron like Chance. You found yourself a live one, honey." She keeps talking. "This Beckett is quite the looker. A fine fellow, if you ask me." Muriel Buchanan is on a roll.

"Mom, you have it all wrong—"

"This lad seems to be doing quite well for himself—far better than Chance could ever dream of."

She's right about that.

"And he seems quite smitten by you."

"Smitten?"

"Yes! It's obvious. Even a blind man can see it."

"Mom—"

"Ari, don't argue with your mother! Look at the bloody photos. You two are a glamorous Hollywood couple. What a great match." Mom blurts that out in one breath. "When do I get to meet this gorgeous Beckett Christensen?"

And this is where I burst her bubble.

"He's my new boss-slash-client."

"The new company you just started working for?"

"Yes."

The silence stretches on the other end.

"Mom?"

"Oh, honey, do you really want to go down that road again?"

# Chapter 21

## *Arianne*

I woke up this morning basking in glorious bliss.

Now, my mood is dampened.

Mom's warning weighs heavy on my shoulders.

I should've known better.

I'm too levelheaded to allow another charming CEO to blindside me.

*Didn't I learn my lesson the hard way?*

One definition of insanity is repeating the same mistake over and over again, expecting different results.

*Get your shit together, Arianne.*

*Don't let those pretty blue eyes derail you.*

I sigh as I get out of the cab after paying the driver.

*I need to buy or lease a car.*

Since Rhys had already made arrangements on my first day at SCORE to tour Tekknika Audio, I spent the first ninety minutes of my day immersed in the ins and outs of the company's production. Now, I'm back at the office. As I make my way to the front door of the office building, I can't help but notice people staring.

I look down at my outfit, worried.

*Nothing is out of place.*

*No coffee or food stains.*

Maybe they're staring because I'm the new girl?

I shrug it off and keep walking.

When I enter the lobby, I receive the same treatment.

More stares.

"Good morning, Arianne!" Paula, the receptionist, says. "Love, love, love the new look! Very *Holy Chic!*"

"Good morning, Paula. Thank you. Have a good day." I head with a determined step to the elevator, not bothering to stop at her desk.

I'm in no mood to chitchat.

As I make my way to my office, I'm keenly aware of the stares.

*What are they looking at?*

Then Paula's comment hits me.

*Oh. My. God.*

If my mother and aunt—who live on the other side of the country—know about my evening with sexy Beckett, and Paula is aware of my wardrobe selection from last night, everyone else knows I was out with the boss and that it had little to do with business.

*Crap.*

I quicken my step.

*I'm sure it'll blow over by lunchtime. I hope. I pray.*

The walk through the executive floor proves to be an interesting experience. Women shoot me glances. At first, I'm certain they're shooting daggers at me, but they're not.

*Could it be... admiration?*

I'm not sure if it's because of my new outfit or last night, but I don't linger to find out.

When I walk inside my office, I freeze.

*What the hell?*

I'm so shocked, I step out to make sure I've not entered the wrong office by mistake.

*Nope. This is mine.*

I walk in again, close the door behind me, drop my handbag and laptop case on my desk.

My eyes bounce to every corner in shock.

I can't believe my eyes.

Everywhere I look, stunning bouquets of yellow roses greet me.

*Wow.*

I step up to a vase and inhale the delightful fragrance.

*Sublime.*

I spot a little white envelope with my name scripted on it with decisive cursive penmanship.

My curiosity gets the best of me.

With impatient hands, I rip the envelope open.

*No way.*

I'm speechless and in awe.

*Holy Chic,*
*You're fucking beautiful.*

*Your new friend.*

A blush creeps from the tip of my toes to the top of my head.

I was firm in my earlier decision to march into Beckett's office and tell him we needed to cool things off, citing the many disadvantages and pitfalls of an office romance, but now, I'm so enchanted I don't know what to do anymore.

My phone flashes a text message just before the phone on my desk rings, I jump.

*It's coming at me from all sides this morning.*

I drop the note and rush to grab my phone.

*Beckett.*

With a huge smile on my face, I round my desk to pick up the office phone.

"Hey, Valerie," I say.

"Hey, Arianne."

"Can I call you back in ten minutes?"

"Did you get the breathtaking flowers?" she asks, ignoring my request.

*Err... I hope she doesn't ask too many questions.*

"I did."

"It took the delivery guy three trips to bring them all up."

*Wow.*

"They're from Blooming Thrill—the best flower shop in the city. Everything is super expensive there. No wonder. All the rich people, celebrities and socialites get their flowers from there."

*This is unbelievable.*

"I see," I say, doing my best to sound as detached as possible.

"I texted my husband to let him know some girls have all the luck... present company excluded," she says.

I don't know how much she knows, so I tread carefully. "It's just a small thank you."

"I'll play along, but just so you know, those photos on the internet tell a different story. That said, I don't get paid to pry."

"Let me call you back."

"Sure thing," she says.

I put an end to the conversation before it gets out of hand.

Giddy, I turn my focus to my phone.

Beckett: Hey, Holy Chic!

I laugh.

> Arianne: Hey, you!

> Beckett: Did you get the flowers?

> Arianne: I did. You're insane.

> Beckett: You don't like them?

> Arianne: I love them! Thank you!

> Beckett: I was told yellow roses mean friendship.

> Arianne: That's so sweet.

*And unexpected. And mind-boggling. And amazing. And oh, my freakin' God!*

> Beckett: Turns out not even top-notch florists sell flowers that say, 'I woke up this morning with an overwhelming urge for a repeat of last night'.

I bite my lower lip as my nipples tighten with need. An electric current zips through my body, bulls-eyeing its way straight to my clit.

> Arianne: You're crazy.

> Beckett: I'm dead serious. You're my first.

> Arianne: Your first?!

> Beckett: I've never done anything that was both sweet and dirty before.

> Arianne: I don't know what to say.

Beckett: I do. I'm in meetings all day to cover for Rhys. I won't be back in the office until end of day. Swing by my office at six-thirty to retrieve your panties.

Arianne: What are you talking about?

Beckett: The panties you're wearing now.

Arianne: I don't follow.

Beckett: Did you go commando?

Arianne: It'll be a cold day in hell before I walk around without panties.

Beckett: Bundle up, buttercup. Winter is coming.

Arianne: Did you lace your coffee with a bottle of whiskey?

Beckett: I want you to remove your panties, fold them neatly, find a reason to walk into my office and leave them—preferably damp and permeated with your heady scent—in the last drawer of my desk.

Arianne: What?

Beckett: I want you to spend the entire day commando and thinking of me.

Just like that, I'm wet.

Arianne: You've lost your mind.

Beckett: Is that your way of saying you want to put an end to our friendship?

Arianne: This goes beyond being friends and you know it.

Beckett: I didn't hear you complaining last night.

He makes a good point.
The wheels in my head are churning fast.

Arianne: But here? At the office?

Beckett: Why be predictable?

I'm dumbfounded.

Arianne: We're playing with fire.

Beckett: Is there any other way to live?

Arianne: What if someone catches us?

Beckett: Newsflash. I'm the boss. If my door is closed, no one in their right mind would dare to walk in without knocking. Even Valerie knows better. One of the many perks of signing paychecks.

Arianne: You have an answer for everything.

Beckett: I'm a determined man, Holy Chic.

I grin like a fool.

Arianne: Yes, you are.

Beckett: You. Me. My office. Six-thirty p.m. I want you wet. And don't be late.

*Dear God.*

# Chapter 22

## *Beckett*

I admire people who go at it alone. I would've never been able to do this without my business partner. Today, I'm feeling Rhys's absence. My day was already packed, but I had to tack on important meetings he couldn't attend. That not only meant I was away from the office, but it also prevented me from catching a glimpse of my new friend.

As I get out of the chauffeured car and make my way to the garage's elevators, my phone rings.

"Rhys," I say, picking up. "Are you dying of heat yet?"

"Don't get me started. I'm fucking sweating my balls off," he says. "The humidity in Vietnam is oppressive."

"Better you than me—"

"Things aren't looking good for us, Beckett," he says.

"Talk to me."

"It's worse than I thought. This strike has no end in sight."

"Good thing you planned on heading to South Korea."

"Our production costs are going to skyrocket over the next few months."

"It may mean smaller profits for a short period of time, but we can handle it," I say. "Business has been on fire."

"That's the only glimmer of hope preventing me from losing my shit."

"That bad?"

"Leland waited way too long to warn us. We could've had this shit nipped in the bud a week ago."

"The strike has been going on for a week?"

"Two. Going on three."

"What?" I'm dumbfounded.

"If our production schedule wasn't so far ahead, we'd be screwed."

*Jesus.*

"You have it under control?"

"Not yet, but I'm working on it. It means I'm going to be stuck in Asia for longer than I thought. This also means you're going to have to shoulder a lot more work."

*Shit.*

"That's why we're partners," I tell him.

"On another note, I called Cesar to apologize for my absence," Rhys changes the subject. "Glad to hear you were representin' last night at his engagement party."

"I had to step up to the plate," I say.

"Rumor has it you have a *lady friend* now? I told Cesar he was drunk, but he assures me otherwise."

"Are you calling me to give me a hard time?"

"Are you skirting the question?"

"I went out for dinner with Arianne. She's new to LA and her best friend is overseas," I tell him. "Diana's birthday-slash-engagement party slipped my mind. It was only gentlemanly of me to take Arianne along. It would've been rude to just dump her."

"I understand, but you two looked like long-lost friends on the selfies Cesar texted me."

*You have no idea.*

"It was a big night. What did you expect me to do? Frown at the camera?"

"Don't twist my words, Christensen. You know exactly what I mean."

"No, I don't."

"What about those photos of you two dancing? That looked pretty intimate."

"It's salsa! Every couple at that club was dancing the same way."

"I'm sure I don't have to remind you of our agreement."

"You've already done a stellar job at reminding me." *Every. Single. Damn. Day.*

"So, you're still committed to your vow of chastity?"

*More or less.*

"My cock hasn't been inside a woman's pussy in the last fourteen days. And before you ask, no, I haven't fucked anyone's ass either." Using Arianne's crease wasn't on your list of no-nos.

"Any blowjobs or handjobs?" he asks.

"What do you take me for? Arianne just started working for us. Do you actually think I'd ask her for a blowjob or to jerk me off on day two of her contract?" He doesn't need to know of my recurring dream of Arianne on her knees in front of me with my cock between her plump lips, sucking me dry until I come like a fucking animal in the back of her throat.

"Has your cock been between a woman's tits?"

"No!"

"No need to shout or get your boxer briefs in a bunch. It's a legitimate question."

"I'm incensed you'd think so little of me, Hartford."

"You think with your cock, Christensen."

"Says the guy who can match me fuck for fuck."

"Don't even go there with me. Other than Collin Dennison, no one I know fucks like you, Beckett."

*He's right. My buddy Collin surpasses me.*

"Your sexual appetite is legendary."

*It is.*

"That's until you cock blocked me," I tell him.

"Someone had to rein in your dick before it accidentally created another PR scandal. Speaking of which, did you find a new publicist?"

"No! And to your earlier point, you're making way too much out of the photos floating on the internet."

"I'm just double checking."

"Thank you for your thoughtfulness, Dad," I say.

"Now you sound like a five-year-old who should be grounded."

"Fuck off!"

"I have good reason to worry," he tells me. "I saw the way you were looking at Arianne when she first started. I've never seen you look at a woman with such intent."

"You said it yourself, she's a gorgeous woman."

"Yeah, and I also said you have a weakness for gorgeous women. I must admit, I'm a bit surprised you haven't tried anything sneaky. I even checked with Arianne to make sure—"

"You talked to Arianne?"

"Yes."

"When?"

"Earlier today. I wanted to know how the tour at Tekknika went. She told me she got a lot out of it, and then I shifted the conversation to last night."

"What did she say?"

"She said she had a great time. It was a real treat you took her since she's a fan of both Cesar and Diana's music."

"I see."

"I also wanted to catch up with her. I miss not seeing her *gorgeous* face," I hear the amusement in his voice.

*Fucker.*

"Just so we're clear, I'm still playing by your rules." *While finding as many loopholes as possible.*

"I'm impressed, Christensen."

"You should be."

"I guess I'll have to get used to the idea of living without my cherished bike."

"Guess so."

*I hope I don't crack before the thirty days is up. Gliding between Arianne's sweet cheeks was hot as fuck.*

"My only consolation is knowing you still have sixteen very, very long days of suffering to go. I hope your wrist will be able to sustain the strain."

"I have to go. I have a business to run."

He explodes in laughter.

# Chapter 23

## *Beckett*

When I reach the executive floor, Valerie is closing shop. She informs me Arianne is on the second floor, still caught up in a meeting with the design team. She also mentioned something about Arianne's surprising new look. I'm not sure what she means, but there's no point in digging further since I'll be seeing her beautiful face soon.

*Thirty more minutes to go.*

I barely have time to drop my ass in my seat when my phone rings.

"Easton!" I say, picking up.

"Beckett! I'm sorry I wasn't able to get back to you earlier. It's been one of those days."

"I get it. I have a habit of collecting those as well," I say.

We laugh.

"Are you still at the office?" I ask.

"No. My fiancée would have my balls. I'm back at the penthouse. Since time is of the essence, I wanted to make sure to get back to you. Is this a good time?"

"It is."

"I hope you were able to sort out the situation you were dealing with yesterday?"

"Rhys is in Vietnam trying to sort things out as we speak."

"That doesn't sound too good," Easton says.

"We're dealing with a plant-wide strike."

"Ouch."

"Rhys has a game plan."

"Never a dull day when you're at the top of the mountain."

"You can say that again."

"Before I get to the reason for my call, I assume you're still happy with Arianne?" Easton asks.

*More than words can say.*

"She's amazing!" I tell him.

"I knew it would be a perfect fit."

*In more ways than one.*

"She's going to do wonders for you, Beckett."

*She already has.*

"Wait until she gets really down and dirty"—*been there, done that*—"and starts dissecting your numbers, highlighting staggering cost-saving improvements. That's when it really gets exciting."

*It was pretty exciting last night.*

"I have no doubt," I say, biting off a smile.

"She'll have you salivating and your juices flowing in no time over the possibilities."

*We've already crossed that bridge.*

"I'm looking forward to it," I say.

"Anyway, to the reason I'm calling."

*It's best to move on.*

"You've heard of the Sennheiser HE 1?"

"Of course, that's a top-of-the-line luxury gadget that's inaccessible to most people. Only the filthy rich can entertain the idea of dropping nearly ninety thousand dollars on headphones. Our cash cow headphones cost five hundred dollars. Our top-of-the-line product tips the scale at twenty-five hundred dollars, and only the elite can afford them."

"Even with my colossal wealth, ninety thousand dollars is outrageous, however, that doesn't stop Sennheiser from manufacturing them and selling three hundred of them a year."

"Surely you aren't suggesting we follow in their footsteps?"

"Not at all," Easton says.

"Why bring it up?"

"What if you could spend five minutes with one of the designers or sound engineers responsible for the design?"

"I'd give my right arm for the opportunity, but it's unlikely to ever happen. We're competitors to their mid-range lines. Why would they want to talk to me?"

"In the right setting, everything is possible."

"Easton, that sounded German to me."

"So apropos," he says. I'm confused. "One of my investors owns the company that creates the marble console for the Sennheiser HE 1, that's why he's in the know. What I'm about to tell you is hush-hush. Only a handful of people in the world are in the know."

"In the know about what?"

"Are you sitting down?" Easton asks.

"I am."

"Sennheiser will unveil the most expensive headphones on the market. They're more expensive than the Focal Utopia by Tournaire."

"You're kidding me?"

"I'm not."

"That's borderline insane, but I still don't see how that relates to our company."

"There's a two-day affair in Germany next week, including an opening gala. It's by invitation only. My client can't make it due to a conflict in schedule. He gave me the tickets as appreciation for the way his portfolio has ballooned. I'm holding them right now."

"Wow! You want us to go together?"

"It would be pointless for me to go when Arianne would make for a much better travel companion," Easton says. "I'm dead certain the two of you will get a lot out of it."

*I'm sure we will.*

"That's incredible. We're definitely going."

"I'll get my executive assistant to courier the tickets overnight," Easton says.

"Sounds great."

"I have to go, but I wanted to make sure to share the good news."

"Thanks again, Easton!"

"Anytime, Beckett."

I hang up.

My head is already swimming with ideas, and I'm basking in the glory of how much of a game changer this could be for our company. An unexpected overseas trip with Arianne is also a definite plus.

Speaking of Miss Holy Chic...

I pull open the last drawer of my desk, curiosity revving my engine.

Nothing.

*Huh?*

I rummage through my drawer, but I can't find what I'm looking for.

I search again.

I sit back against my seat as realization sets in.

*Someone disobeyed me.*

# Chapter 24

## *Arianne*

I'm immersed in my meeting with SCORE's design team when a text message flies across my screen. I do a double take when I notice Beckett's name.

*Shit.*

Dread twists my stomach. Worried I'll get busted, I snatch the phone from the table and place it on my lap.

It vibrates again.

Unable to contain my curiosity, I unlock it, and try to read the message as inconspicuous as possible.

"Do you need to get that?" Flora Crandell, the head of design, asks.

"I'm sorry," I say, embarrassed. "I'll be just a minute."

"Sure. We've had you trapped in here for the last two hours," she says.

"Thanks," I say with a small smile.

I drop my eyes to my phone.

> Beckett: I thought we had an understanding. After a long and demanding day, I expected a reward, but I won't get one because you ignored my command.

My cheeks burst into flames.

> Arianne: Your request is totally unreasonable and it would compromise me.

> Beckett: In what sense?

> Arianne: It's too long to explain via text.

Walking commando when you're wearing a white skirt is the kiss of death.

> Beckett: When I give you a command, I expect you to follow it.

> Arianne: What's up with this 'command' business? You're technically not my boss! I'm a consultant.

> Beckett: Semantics, dear friend. Semantics. You know as well as I do, I **AM** the boss of you. I proved it last night.

Not that I needed any more incentive than last night's saucy images incessantly flashing in front of my eyes, but the reminder just soaked my panties.

> Arianne: You're exerting excessive power, Mr. Christensen. What kind of friendship is this?

> Beckett: By the time I'm done with you, Miss Buchanan, you'll learn. You're mine. Mine to boss around. Mine to command. MINE! Enough with this back and forth. Get your fine ass up here.

The dominance in those words is my undoing.

> Beckett: Just so we're clear, I want you up here ASAP! Don't make me come down there and get you.

The warning is so forceful. So thrilling.

I don't have an ounce of rebellion in me, but for some strange inexplicable reason, I'd love nothing more than to test his limits.

"Is everything okay?" Flora asks.

My eyes fly up.

Everyone in the room is staring at me

*Get a grip.*

You don't want the five people around the table to read you like an open book.

"I'm sorry, Flora. It appears Beckett has an urgent matter he'd like to discuss."

"Of course. It's getting late anyway. Let's wrap it up and we can have another meeting tomorrow."

"That sounds great," I say.

The other team members nod their agreement.

*Meeting adjourned!*

I gather my things and dash out of the conference room.

Another message flashes across my screen as I head to the elevators.

> Beckett: Someone is in big trouble. I hope you're on your way.

I quicken my step.

When I reach the executive floor, it's almost deserted.

I shimmy as fast as I can to Beckett's office.

I catch my breath before knocking.

"Come in." His deep voice penetrates the door.

I open it and peek inside.

He's sitting on his throne—I mean, seat. His elbows rest on the desk, his fingers intertwined together, his chin resting on them, his gaze lasered on me.

He looks like a king.

A ruler who holds my fate in his hands.

I swallow hard.

"Who do we have here?" The sarcasm in his voice doesn't go unnoticed. "Oh yeah, the bad girl who disobeyed me."

I ignore the snide remark. "You wanted to see me," I say, stepping into his office.

He jerks his head back, arching his eyebrows in surprise.

"I see you've made 'holy chic' a permanent motto. I like it. A lot."

I grin like a fool.

"When I bought my outfit for last night, Andrea had a number of selections she thought would look good on me," I tell him. "I really liked this one, and it's so hot in LA, my three-piece suits were unbearable."

"Come here!" Beckett wiggles a finger, beckoning me.

I drop my iPad, notepad, and handbag on the console table near the door and approach him.

"I want you right here," he says, swiveling his chair to the side.

I round his desk and stand in front of him.

"You look fucking amazing!" Admiration shines bright in his eyes.

"Thank you." I blush.

"Turn around," he tells me.

I give him a twirl.

"Damn, woman."

He reaches up for my blouse, but in my nervousness I step back.

"I want you right here I said!" He points between his parted legs.

I reposition myself.

He reaches up and undoes two buttons.

It was a struggle to leave one open. Three? I feel naked.

I bring my hands up in an attempt to cover up.

"Don't hide from me," he tells me.

I hesitate, but lower my hands.

"Look at you, baby. I barely recognize you." He runs a hand through my hair, flirting with my shoulders. "A sexy silk blouse. A flirty white skirt. Your hair flowing freely. Impeccably applied makeup that showcases your gorgeous eyes. And those lips..."

His appraisal and compliments make me giddy. Sure, I hoped he'd notice, but I didn't expect this much.

Phoebe and I intend on spending most of Saturday at Neiman Marcus shopping our heads off. That said, I couldn't leave the store yesterday without this outfit. The champagne-colored silk blouse is so feminine and nothing like the stiff cotton shirts I usually gravitate towards. The white asymmetric skirt with ruffled hem that hits me below the knee is such a departure from my usual conservative pencil skirts. Since I already owned the nude Cedrics patent leather high heels, they were the logical choice. And not a vest in sight. In fact, I didn't even bother with a blazer this morning.

"What's the story behind the buttoned-up suits?" Beckett asks. "I sense it's more than a fashion statement."

I didn't expect his question.

"A suit sends a message."

"What kind of message?"

"It says I know what I'm talking about. People take me seriously when I dress the part, despite my age."

His eyebrows hit his forehead. "Arianne, your brain works

in a way that's unparalleled. People will take you seriously because what comes out of your mouth is pure genius. They'll be hooked when they find out you're the full package—brains, beauty, and charm. I know I was."

*Oh, wow.*

"The buttoned-up suit is a distraction."

"You're full of compliments," I say with feigned detachment.

"It's the truth," he says.

My brain tends to scare people away—including members of my own family. To hear a powerful man who can have any woman he wants talk about me like this is overwhelming.

"Is the new look here to stay?" he asks.

"I won't wear suits every day anymore... unless I want to suffocate."

"I approve," he says.

I bite my lower lip.

"Does this mean anything?" Beckett asks, caressing the star pendant dangling from my neck.

"Not really." I shrug. "I bought it at a high-end jeweler in Carmel when I got my first big bonus. It's an antique brooch that was transformed into a pendant. I liked the contrast between the white gold brooch encrusted with diamond and white pearls combined with a modern yellow gold chain. I figured it's the kind of piece a grandmother would pass down as an heirloom," I pause and swallow hard. "I don't have a grandmother per se, so I figured why not..." I let my words trail.

Beckett's blue eyes search mine. "Why do I feel there's a story behind that?"

"Because there is." I don't offer more.

"Maybe one day you'll tell me."

"Maybe," I say in a small voice.

"Why did you disobey me, Arianne?" He gets down to business.

I avert my gaze.

He places two fingers under my chin, forcing my attention back to him.

"I expect an answer from you."

"I'm wearing a white skirt, Beckett."

"So?"

I clear my throat. "A wet spot would be... noticeable."

"Just thinking of me makes you wet?"

"Yes," I say in a murmur.

He nods. "It's mutual."

"I make you wet?" I giggle.

"No, silly. You make me fucking hard."

Without warning, Beckett reaches for my skirt and pulls the fabric up until it bunches around my ass.

"Pull it up further. I want to see what you're hiding," he tells me.

His words cause my heart to beat at an infernal rate.

Still, I do as I'm told.

The cool air caresses my skin as I bare myself to him.

"Lace the same color as the blouse," he says. "Very. Nice. Take them off and hand them over." His hand is already extended. Waiting.

I spent the day in a constant state of arousal, but now, I'm about to combust.

I'm so nervous, I almost fall off my heels in my attempt to step out of my panties. Beckett reaches out and holds me steady. I ready myself to bend down, but he beats me to do it. He picks up my panties, brings the scrap of champagne-colored lace to his nose and inhales with his eyes closed.

The sight makes me dizzy.

"And they're soaking wet. You're right, a wet spot would've

been like a bulls-eye." *Thank God he understands.* "Still, you disobeyed me and I can't let it slide."

*Uh oh.*

My eyebrows draw together. "What does that mean?"

"Bad girls who can't follow orders get punished."

"Like you're going to send me to my room?"

"No. Like I'm going to put you over my knee and redden your ass."

"No, you're not," I say, horrified.

"You're putting an end to our friendship?" he asks with a cocked eyebrow. "Think of the benefits you'd be giving up..."

My clit weeps.

"Is it going to hurt?" I ask.

"So, this was your plan all along. You wanted my imprint on your ass. Admit it."

I roll my eyes at his mocking words. "You're out of your mind. Until a minute ago, it never crossed my mind."

"Yet, you're curious."

I offer a one-shoulder shrug.

"To answer your question, it's the best kind of pleasure and pain," he says. "It'll sting, but I promise I'll make it go away."

I ponder his words.

"It sounds kinky."

"That's because it is. Here's how we're going to play this game. You get ten slaps if you count. Twenty, if I count."

"I don't need two college degrees to figure out which one is the best option—"

"Keep up with the sass and it'll be thirty."

I gulp.

"What if I can't make it up to ten?" I ask, worried.

"I'll give you an incentive."

"I'm afraid to ask."

This guy is dangerous. I doubt I'll be able to handle whatever he has up his sleeve.

"Remember what I said about pleasure and pain?" I nod. "I'll angle your body so your pussy rests on this." He cups the bulge between his legs and squeezes. "That's your incentive to come hard for me."

The devilish glee glaring in his eyes should come as a warning, but obviously, my pussy does all the thinking when I say, "Only ten, right?"

"I won't ask for more."

"What if I really don't like it?" I ask.

"Everything stops."

"Okay."

"Strip. Keep only the bra and heels. Since we're going out for dinner after I'm done perverting you, we don't want your clothes to get wrinkled."

"We're going out for dinner after?!" I can't hide my surprise.

"Of course," he says. "Two people breaking bread is a healthy sign of a long-lasting friendship. Not to mention, you said you didn't know anybody in LA. I figured you might not want to eat alone."

"That's so thoughtful of you."

"That's the kind of guy I am," he says.

"I won't have to eat alone for much longer. My best friend will be back tomorrow."

"Does it mean you won't have dinner with me anymore?"

"I'll still have dinner with you," I say with a laugh.

"I like the sound of that." His boyish smile is disarming. "You're making me wait!" He waves an impatient finger up and down the length of my body. "Every minute that ticks by is an extra slap."

*Good grief.*

He's back to being Beckett, the uncompromising ruler.

I undress under his lustful gaze.

"Let's move over there." He points near the window. "It'll be more comfortable."

He gets up and extends a hand.

I take it and he walks us both to the couch.

He removes his jacket, places it on one of the modern leather side chairs and sits on the long couch.

"Bring your sexy ass over here," he orders. Beckett fixes me with a look that could compel the most devote and pious nun to moonlight as a stripper.

It's pure, adulterated carnal lust.

Pure filth.

Pure wantonness.

It's like the Big Bad Wolf eyeing Little Red Riding Hood.

Chance never made me feel wanted or desired like this.

Not even a two-thousand-dollar bespoke corset from an upscale San Francisco lingerie shop got a reaction from my ex. Mariah walking around braless in a cheap tank top with her ginormous melons spilling from every corner did.

"I feel like I lost you." Beckett forces me back to the moment. "Where did you go?"

"It's nothing," I say.

"Why do I have a tough time believing you?"

Old insecurities creep up. "I feel so sexually inadequate."

"What changed since a minute ago?" His boomerang question catches me off guard.

I can only answer with a one-shoulder shrug.

He stands up and approaches me, places a hand on my shoulder and uses the other hand to lift my chin.

"Does this have to do with your ex?"

I hitch a breath.

"Maybe."

I hate myself for allowing Chance to ruin this moment.

"It took forever to clean the river of cum dripping down your legs after I released myself all over your ass like a wild animal, Arianne. Would a sexually inadequate woman do that to me?"

"Men fake it," I say.

"Your ex must be quite the magician because even if you OD on Viagra, you can't fake cum. Plain and simple."

"You can fake attractiveness."

He grabs my hand and places it on his cock. "Does this feel fake to you?"

*Jesus, he's rock hard.*

"What about this?" he asks before crushing my lips in an all-encompassing kiss that steals my breath away.

"I guess not," I say when he breaks our embrace.

"I never see a woman twice. I never have dinner with women I've been with. And until this morning, I had never walked into a flower shop to buy flowers for a woman who wasn't related to me. I usually order flowers online for female staff members."

*Oh.*

*My.*

*God.*

"You're throwing a lot at me, Beckett," I say.

"Don't you ever question my attractiveness towards you. You hear me?"

My heart could burst right now.

"I do."

"Can we forget about your idiot ex and get back to the program?"

"Poof!" I do a hand gesture simulating an explosion. "He's gone."

Beckett chuckles. "Another thing. If I didn't think you were fucking hot, I wouldn't have craved you all night long." *Oh, wow.* "Halfway to my house, I wanted to turn my car around and go back to your place for round two."

*No way.*

I grin wide.

"We're good?" he asks.

I nod. "We're good."

He goes and sits on the couch.

"I want you right here." He taps his thighs, beckoning me over.

I take a deep breath, filling my lungs with as much air as possible. I'll need courage—and maybe a Higher Power—to go through with this.

I take a step, but he stops me with one word. "Crawl."

*Holy Jesus.*

When I don't move, he points to the floor.

I hesitate, but drop to my knees and do something I never thought I'd do in my life.

"Good girl."

How can an act feel demeaning and powerful at the same time?

"Get on my lap," he says when I reach him.

He helps me assume the position.

My fear turns quickly to arousal.

"You feel that?" he asks, tilting his hips up, pressing his bulge against my pussy.

"God, yes."

"Sliding my cock between your ass cheeks last night was a beautiful thing."

"We could have a repeat instead of you punishing me."

"Yesterday you were a good girl. That's not the case today."

Two strong hands grope my ass.

I moan.

I turn my head to watch.

He wets his middle finger and with his eyes locked on mine, he slides it into my desperate pussy.

A throaty groan escapes me.

He slides his finger in and out of me before retracting it all together.

"So fucking wet for me," he says, examining his slick finger. "I gather you've never tasted yourself?"

I shake my head.

"Open wide for me."

I do.

He sticks his finger into my mouth.

"Clean it up. And I want to hear it."

*Holy dirty.*

With one hand on my ass, pinning me in place, his bulge rolling against my pussy, I lick his finger clean with a series of loud slurps.

That's all it takes to push me off the cliff.

Taken by surprise, I squeeze my thighs together as the fizz of an orgasm makes me cry out.

*Oh, dear sweet Lord!*

"Did you just come?" Beckett asks. The warning in his voice makes me shiver all over again.

I don't answer.

"Arianne, I asked you a question."

"I... well... you..." Evidently, my MBA does nothing for my ability to string a cohesive sentence together.

"Try that again."

"It was totally unexpected," I tell him.

"Did I tell you to come?"

"I couldn't help it."

"Did I tell you to come?"

"No," I say in a meek voice.

"You disobeyed me. Again."

"You can't hold it against me," I say. "How do you expect me to keep it together when you keep doing these raunchy things to me?"

"I expect you to come when I tell you to come!"

"You're such a hardball!"

He squints and his lips form a slow grin. "Congratulations. You just got yourself an upgrade. It's twenty slaps now."

"Wait! What? You can't do that!"

"My building. My office. My rules."

Before I can plead my case, the first slap cracks against my ass.

"Shit!"

"No, baby, that's not how this game is played," he says. "Let's try that again."

*Slap!*

"Jesus!"

He sighs. "Arianne, I can keep doing this all night long," he says. "Is that what you want?"

"Beckett—"

*Slap!*

"Ouch! Ouch! Ouch!" I yelp, kicking out my legs, the move grinding my pussy against him.

"Stop moving," he says, pinning me in place.

*Slap!*

"One!" I blurt out. "That was one."

"You're a quick learner."

I turn around.

His evil laugh is demonic.

"Eyes up front."

I obey.

*Slap!*

"Two."

*Slap!*

"Three."

He slaps me from right below my cheeks. Quivering sensations travel all the way to my needy clit.

On and on he goes.

Each slap makes me more and more delirious.

I can't even explain it.

*Slap!*

"Twelve," I say in a shaky voice.

"You're doing so well, baby."

I meet his gaze. "Beckett, I don't know how much longer I can hold on."

"It hurts?"

"No. Yes."

"Which is it?"

"It hurts in a good way."

"What's the problem, then?"

"I need to come."

My pussy is pulsating, matching the thud of my heart. Not to mention my ass is on fire.

"I thought we already had that discussion."

"What am I supposed to do?"

"Wait for my command."

"But—"

"You come without my consent and we start back at one, Arianne. Your choice."

I consider him.

He arches an eyebrow, daring me to protest.

I look away.

*Slap!*

"Thirteen!"

As further punishment, Beckett tilts his hips, rubbing his impossibly hard cock against my pelvis.

My clit is practically weeping.

*Dear God, save me.*

Between each count, I coax myself to hold on. My body is trembling like a leaf from the herculean effort it takes not to dissolve all over this man's mighty cock.

*Slap!*

"Nineteen."

*One more.*

*Finally.*

I wait expectantly, but nothing happens.

I turn my head to see what's holding him back.

He's just grinning at me.

"You're playing me," I say.

"I'm playing *with* you. Big difference."

"What more do you want from me? I did everything you asked. I just want to come. I have to come. I need to come. Please let me come."

I don't even recognize the woman begging for sexual release.

"I wanted to make sure you were still with me."

I open my mouth to beg some more, when his hand comes down on my ass like thunder.

*Slap!*

*Thank you, God.*

"Twenty!" I exhale.

"Don't come yet."

"No, no, no."

"Yes, yes, yes." He has no problem torturing me.

"You're a tyrant! You said twenty! That was twenty!"

"I did."

I watch bewildered as he lowers his head and bites my ass.

I yelp, pleasure coursing through me like a raging river.

My other cheek receives the same treatment.

Then, he starts kissing my cheeks all over.

The sensation is sublime.

"Oh dear almighty God." The words fall out of my mouth, as my head tilts back, relishing his lewd actions.

Just when I think Beckett can't shock me more, he does.

He spreads my ass cheeks open, sticks two fingers deep inside my dripping pussy, scoops my juices, and brings his hand coated with my slickness to his mouth.

He slides his fingers into his mouth and sucks.

There are no words to describe the veil of lust coating his blue eyes. And that lewd sound...

*Don't come.*

*Don't come.*

*Don't come.*

He must read my mind because in a blink of an eye, his hand travels between my pussy lips until his fingers skate over my clit.

Round and round he goes.

"Yes! Thank you! Yes!"

"You're going to give me what I want?"

"I'll give you anything," I tell him. "Everything."

"Be careful. I might take you up on your offer," he says. "Are you going to come hard for me, baby?"

"I am."

"I'm not convinced."

"I'm going to come so hard. So, so hard."

"Show me you're a good girl."

He squeezes two fingers around my clit, trapping all the blood there and I go off like a rocket.

"Beckett! Oh, God! Beckett! Becket! Beckett! Beckett!"

# Chapter 25

## *Beckett*

The second I caught a glimpse of her sexy new look, I knew the likelihood of surviving the next sixteen days without fucking Arianne was pretty much nil. As much as I'd love to watch Rhys's defeated face as he hands over the keys to his vintage four-hundred-thousand-dollar bike, there are things I want with more fervor—like riding Arianne.

I need to dominate and own her.

I don't know how I managed to hold back after she came so beautifully. All I wanted to do was sink balls deep inside her pussy and lose myself in there for days.

Patience.

Two weeks without sex is an eternity for a guy like me. I don't think she would've survived what I was likely to unleash on her.

I never thought the day would come where I'd feel the need to mentally prepare myself to be inside a woman again.

*Thanks for nothing, Rhys Hartford.*

After some naughty fun, we're now at the Quintus Hotel for dinner.

"Mr. Christensen," Larkin says, approaching our table.

I get up to greet the elegant man who's as tall as I am. "Larkin." I shake the hand that's extended to me. "It's always good to see you."

"Likewise," he says. His gaze slides to the beautiful woman sitting at my table. "'*Holy Chic*' indeed," he says with an appreciative glance. "I hope you also bought the '*Holy Gorgeous*' t-shirt."

I still can't get over how the photos and headlines spread all over the internet like wildfire. My evening with Arianne went viral so fast, it dethroned the speed with which everyone was talking about my forbidden night with the pastor's daughter.

"She'd also need the '*Holy Freaking Smart*' t-shirt." I add to Larkin's cockiness.

"The whole package?" Larkin nods, already answering his own question.

"The whole package," I tell him.

"Okay, I officially don't know what to do with myself," Arianne says, her cheeks flushing in a lovely shade of pink.

"Larkin Gallagher, I'd like to introduce you to Arianne Buchanan. Arianne, Larkin owns the Quintus Hotel."

Since Arianne thoroughly enjoyed last night's dining experience, I decided to treat her to the same level of excellence. Except tonight, we're sitting at a corner table in Moonlight restaurant, one of the four five-star restaurants located inside the hotel.

"It's a pleasure," Larkin says with a slight head nod.

"The pleasure is mine," Arianne says.

Larkin's amber eyes bounce from mine to a blushing Arianne.

"It's no surprise the press can't seem to shut up about you two," he says.

"Everything got blown out of proportion," Arianne says.

"I disagree, Miss Buchanan. It's not every day a notorious bad boy like Mr. Christensen steps out to a private function with a mysterious beauty."

Arianne's eyes widen like saucers.

I chuckle.

She looks flawless. She meticulously reapplied her makeup and smoothed down her hair. It's still loose, flirting with her shoulders. You'd never know two hours ago I had her across my lap, submitting to my wicked ways, and begging me to let her come. I've never done anything like this before. My relationship with the women I work with is always strictly professional. Arianne is my rule breaker. In my defense, she's the perfect playmate.

"I can't stay," Larkin says. "Since I wasn't able to catch you yesterday, I wanted to make sure to come by."

"Always great to see you," I tell him.

His eyes ping-pong between Arianne and me.

"Well done, Mr. Christensen." Larkin taps me on the shoulder. "I hope I'll see you and Miss Buchanan at the club sometime soon. We have a theme party coming up. It could be a lot of fun."

"What club?" Arianne asks, curiosity coloring her eyes.

"We haven't talked about the club yet," I say.

"I hope you'll rectify that," Larkin says.

"The night is still young," I tell him.

"As it should be," Larkin says. "Please, enjoy your dinner. Good night."

And he's off.

Two beefy security guards who were standing at a distance follow close behind him.

When I sit back down, Arianne leans into me. "Wow. He's a bit intimidating."

"He exudes power. You don't want to mess with Larkin Gallagher."

"Noted." Arianne nods. "What club was he talking about?"

"Dark Compulsion."

"Is it a dance club?"

Such innocence.

"There's dancing, but there's a whole lot more that happens there. Dark Compulsion is a private members' only club located behind the hotel. It's a place where the biggest celebrities, Hollywood's Who's Who, the rich and famous come for a night of no strings attached hookups with the guarantee that whatever happens behind closed doors, stays behind closed doors. There's an understanding among members. No one is there looking for a soul mate."

"Like a swingers' club?"

"Some members are married and they're into that, but a lot of members are single and looking to hook up with other singles. At Dark Compulsion you can have an illicit encounter for a few hours, a few days, or a few weeks. There are different shades of kinky, but nothing hardcore and nothing demeaning."

"Oh," she says with a frown.

"Women there know better than to expect forever."

"You're a regular?" she asks.

"Yes."

She nods.

"I really don't know what you see in me, Beckett," she says so softly, if I weren't this close, I would've missed it.

"Whatever shit your ex did to you to erode your self-confidence pisses me off—"

"His fiancée didn't help."

"Fuck them both!" I say.

A few patrons look our way.

I lower my voice. "I'm not going to lie, Arianne, I'm used to fast women."

She winces.

"It's easy. I don't have to work hard for it."

"That's what I—"

"You didn't drop your panties in the elevator. The same applies for the first day we officially met. You told me off on your second day at SCORE. I didn't know what to make of you. You were a challenge."

She smiles.

"I couldn't resist you last night... even if I tried. Corrupting you has become my new favorite pastime."

"You're funny."

"Now that Larkin has extended an invitation, I'll have to take you as my date to the next theme party."

"Really?"

"Don't be so excited. You have no idea how kinky it gets."

She gulps.

"Who thinks of these things?" Arianne asks, her eyes glued to her empty dessert plate.

"I gather you liked it."

"I've died and gone to heaven." She lets out a dramatic sigh. "I'm tempted to chain myself to this table because I've never tasted anything like this."

For a minute there, I thought she was going to lick her plate clean. Then again, I don't blame her. Moonlight's signature dessert—chocolate chunk cookies stuffed with fudge brownies served with a heaped serving of homemade vanilla ice cream—is heavenly.

"Larkin's motto is 'above and beyond'. It applies to every single aspect of his many businesses."

"No kidding."

"More champagne?" I ask, grabbing the neck of the bottle.

"Just a little," she says, pinching her fingers together. "The champagne is also amazing." I top up her glass and then mine.

Larkin sent us a complimentary bottle. Although I've been a longtime member at his club, I doubt this is about me. My guess is, Arianne had quite the effect on him.

"I have a question," she says.

"Shoot."

"How did you get into the music business? You mentioned your father is a businessman. Is your mom a singer or musician?"

"No. Mom is Dr. Blythe Christensen. She's one of the best neurosurgeons in North America. She's also a caring and loving mother."

"I see."

"My older brother Holt, my cousin Jace, and I were obsessed with the idea of becoming the next big musicians. We didn't just want to be good. We wanted to dominate. We'd spend hours practicing. Our parents didn't object because our focus kept us out of trouble. After sending God knows how many demos to record companies and agents, and a crushing number of rejections, we got our lucky break when we least expected it. Not long after that, drummer extraordinaire Rod Wolfe joined our band when our former drummer's dad forced him to step down. The rest is history."

"Your band didn't win a TV talent show?"

"We went at it the old-fashioned way."

"I can't believe you've had two formidable careers and you're only thirty-one."

"I can't believe it myself." I chuckle. "I don't take it for granted, though."

"It shows. You take your company very seriously."

"I do." It fills me with pride she'd notice. "So does Rhys."

"You two have a great partnership."

"I'm very lucky. What about you? Can I ask how old you are?"

"Twenty-nine. I'll be thirty soon."

"The big 3-o."

"Yeah."

"Good? Bad? Not sure?"

"Not sure."

"What's missing to make it good?" I ask. "Better yet, what's missing to make it fucking good?"

"The last two years have been like starting from scratch. I saw myself at a different place in my life by now."

"Sometimes a detour can be so much better than a well laid out plan," I tell her. "Another stay at rehab wasn't part of the plan for me."

"I doubt anyone has that on their bucket list," she says.

"No one does." I shake my head. "I was just hoping to come out of there clean and more in control of my life. Meeting Rhys was totally unexpected. I wouldn't have a second career—that could trump the first one—without that detour. Rehab was a godsend in many ways for me. Maybe it's the same for you. Maybe LA has a lot to offer... you just don't know it yet!" I tap the tip of her nose.

"Maybe."

She doesn't sound too convinced.

I don't push.

"What else is there to know about the great Beckett Christensen?" she asks, changing the subject.

"I doubt there isn't anything you haven't read online. Other than my legendary partying,"—*and fucking*—"and my troubled days struggling with drug dependency, my life has been pretty easygoing. My parents have had their ups and downs, but they still love each other and they're still together after so many years. My brother and I are tight. Same goes for my cousins and my boys."

"What brought on the name of your company?" she asks.

"SCORE, as in music score."

"Oh, that's so smart. Was it your idea or Rhys's?"

"Mine, obviously."

"Obviously."

We laugh.

"I know you're from Philly and I know your parents are Scottish. Do you have any brothers or sisters?" I ask.

She hitches a breath.

For some reason, I feel like I committed a faux pas.

"I never knew my older brothers. They were twins and died in a swimming accident at Pymatuning Lake."

"I'm so sorry, Arianne," I say.

"My parents were devastated for a very long time."

"Understandably."

"They blamed themselves for the accident."

"Why?"

"Let me start from the beginning," she says.

"Okay."

"My mom's youngest sister, Aunt Moira, has a history of dating losers—she still does. She took Rylan and Dylan—the twins—with her daughters Marley and Mirai for a weekend camping. Weekends were so busy at the restaurant, my parents thought it would be good for the boys to be away. At the time my aunt was on a hiatus from her on-again, off-again main squeeze and father of her three girls, Fraser Golightly. He didn't want to put a ring on it, so she was on a rebound, using—I mean, dating—this guy Arvin Judas Dive—"

"His name is Arvin Judas Dive?"

"Yes," she says. "Arvin was supposed to be the adult, instead, he turned out to be a real douchebag and a bully." She pauses. "Dylan was the shy and introverted twin. Mom said he was scared of his own shadow. Arvin decided to poke him by provoking him. He dared Dylan to man up by taking a swim in the lake because only wimpy crybabies still wet their beds. Aunt Moira told Arvin Dylan was still wetting the bed at eight—"

"She betrayed her own nephew?" I ask.

"She wouldn't know a private matter even if it hit her across the face," Arianne says.

"Sorry to interrupt."

"Not at all," she says. "Aunt Moira was napping—her second favorite activity after stirring up shit. Marley and Mirai were with Arvin and the twins. Poor Dylan jumped in the lake. When he started to panic, Rylan jumped into the water, but he never surfaced. Marley and Mirai were so freaked out they didn't know what else to do other than to run and get their mother. Dylan drowned and got swept away by the current."

*Jesus Christ.*

Sad eyes meet mine. "Mom said Arvin told the police later he didn't know how to swim, so he couldn't even save them."

I'm dumbfounded.

"Dad wanted to kill him."

"Did Arvin go to jail?"

"No. It's not like he pushed Dylan in the water, and he wasn't responsible for Rylan hitting his head on a rock."

"He was the adult in charge," I say.

"There was no recourse." There's such finality in her words. Such injustice.

I shake my head.

"What about your aunt?" I ask. "Your mother left your brothers in her care. Her lazy ass shouldn't have been napping, leaving four kids under the supervision of her idiot boyfriend."

"Morally, she's a lowlife—just like Arvin—but in the eye of the criminal justice, she wasn't a killer. Aunt Moira was responsible for the well-being of my brothers. She dropped the ball big time, but she didn't commit a crime, per se."

"Unbelievable."

"Arvin denied having any involvement in the accident, but Mirai, who was seven at the time, was the whistleblower. Marley was five."

"Asshole."

"That, he is," she says. "For a long time, Mom couldn't stop mourning my brothers."

"Of course."

"Eventually, she got in a better place in life where she wanted another child. She just didn't want to get pregnant because she didn't want to risk having a boy—she couldn't handle the reminder. She was getting older as well, so that's another reason that pushed her to consider adoption. That's where I come into the picture. From what Mom told me, my birth parents dropped me off at a teen center in a laundry basket, wrapped up in blankets. They left a note. My biological father was fifteen. My biological mother was fourteen."

*Good God.*

"They didn't want to keep me." She takes in a lungful of air. "It was late November, and I was just a few weeks old."

*Jesus.*

"Mom and Dad had one restaurant at the time, and things were tight. Mom used to work as a cleaning lady at the teen center at night to make ends meet. She found me crying at the top of my lungs. A lengthy adoption process later, and I became Arianne Buchanan."

I'm rarely speechless.

She powers on. "There's a tradition in my family. All the girls' names start with an M. Even after Mom and her three sisters immigrated to America, they continued the tradition. My great-great grandmother was Morag. My great grandmother was Maude. My grandmother was Meredith. Mom is Muriel. There's Aunt Moira and her three daughters—Mirai, Marley, and Mariah. Aunt Maeve has six boys and Aunt Margot has four, so they're exempt." Her lips twist. "Aunt Moira never missed a day reminding me I was different and Mom stamped it on my forehead by breaking with tradition."

"She has some nerve putting you down," I say.

"I've always called them the Golightly witches behind their backs, including my aunt, even if her baby daddy refused to marry her." She smiles wide. I like that rebellious side of her. "Dad calls them go-fuck-yourself hags. Of course, Dad had to make the insult a wee bit Scottish."

I laugh.

"Did your parents meet in Philly?"

"No. Muriel MacDowall came to America at twenty-one. She left her longtime sweetheart behind. It took a little longer for Gregor Buchanan to follow, but he did. They got married soon after he arrived."

"I see. From the sound of it, there's no love lost between you and the Golightly witches."

"None whatsoever. Although, I've warmed up to Mirai given the horrible thing her baby sister Mariah did to her."

"Mariah sounds like a go-fuck-yourself hag," I say in the best Scottish accent I can muster, imitating my buddy Collin Dennison when he's drunk.

She laughs.

"Yeah, she's a queen bitch. Even though we were born the same year, we're worlds apart."

"You'd think you'd be closer," I say. "Jace and I are practically the same age and we're like brothers. Same goes for his cousin Loki. Growing up, the three of us were as thick as thieves."

"Mariah was born seven months before me. Even as a baby, I swear she hated me and always found ways to hurt me... as early as when we were in the playpen. For a long time, I was a people pleaser in my family. Mom told me at a young age I was adopted and of course, Aunt Moira drilled it into me. Growing up, even though Mariah was always quick to belittle me, I always helped her with her homework, hoping she'd come around. She always repaid me by being a total bitch. When I started at Maccabeus Learning, I decided I had enough—"

"What's Maccabeus Learning?"

"A school for gifted kids in Philadelphia," she says.

"I see."

"It was my ticket to a more challenging education and my excuse to stop helping my cousin with her homework. Dad was so proud of me for cutting her loose. Mom always treaded carefully with her youngest sister. Mariah's grades slid, and she hated me even more. I held my ground. Aunt Moira preferred to focus on fostering her daughters' outer-self. Finding a man to support you is a heck of a lot easier than studying or working a job, hence why a woman should really put emphasis on her *assets* and not her intellect. Because men can't see a brain at first glance... breasts on the other hand, jump out at you. And huge breasts are the way to a man's heart, aka wallet."

"I won't deny we're wired like that—we're visual—but I'd be willing to bet my entire fortune when I say the vast majority of men want the perfect combination of brains and beauty!" I wink at her.

She blushes. "Aunt Moira would vehemently argue your point. She's a piece of work and her daughters—"

"The apple doesn't fall far from the tree."

"No, it doesn't," she says. "As the years rolled by, it became clear my scholastic abilities were different from other kids at Maccabeus. One of my math teachers noticed. With his help and guidance, I was able to secure a scholarship."

"He believed in you," I say.

"He did. Without him, I doubt I would've ever made my way to New York. My grades at Maccabeus Learning and the school's stellar reputation allowed me to get a full scholarship for my bachelor degree and get the hell out of Philadelphia—"

"And away from the Golightly witches."

"Free at last... so I thought..." Her words trail. "When my proud mother started to tell anyone willing to listen how her daughter was a lot more intelligent than most, the Golightly witches turned up the bitch factor. They became mean bullies. The months preceding my departure to college were atrocious. Mom cut ties with her sister. She didn't ostracize Aunt Moira after the twins' death—I still don't know how she managed to do that—but Mom wasn't going to standby as the Golightlys destroyed me."

I would never have guessed all this about her.

"Your mom sounds like a strong woman," I say.

"She's been through a lot, but she's still standing. The same for Dad. Just like your parents, mine have also had their ups and downs."

"But they're still together."

"As Mom loves to say in her still pronounced Scottish accent, they still love each other hard."

I laugh.

"Going back to your cousins and your aunt, it sounds like they're jealous of you."

She shoots me a side gaze.

"What?" I ask.

"Dad has been saying that for years. I didn't believe him at first, but now I know he was right all along. Especially, Mariah. She's an envious cow, willing to steamroll you for the sake of one-upping you."

"Remember what I said yesterday about sluts?" I ask. "They don't have much going on for them. You've achieved impressive milestones. Clearly, they weren't rooting for you."

"They weren't. I'm the first person in our family to ever go to college and I'm the first to hold a master's degree. No one even knew what a CFA was until I acquired the professional credential. The Golightly witches made me feel like an outcast and an ugly duckling my whole life. Then, one day, I grew out of my awkward teenage years with two university degrees and a coveted accreditation in hand at the tender age of twenty-three. After that, I landed a ridiculously high-paying job in Silicon Valley. In other words, I left them in the dust. They hated me even more."

"All those milestones made you untouchable," I say.

Her face contorts in disgust.

"What's that expression about?" I ask.

She shakes her head. "Nothing."

I don't believe her, but I don't push.

"What kind of restaurants do your parents own?" I ask, changing the subject.

She looks around the room. "Nothing like this fancy eatery. Scots are renowned for their love of fried food. My parents own two chicken nugget restaurants."

"Just chicken nuggets?" I ask.

"Chicken nuggets are the main attraction at Wee Nugget," she says. "We also serve sweet potato fries, onion rings, fried pickles, French fries, and homemade coleslaw. It's not haute cuisine. The menu is simple. Dad concocts eight tasty seasonal dipping sauces that keep the crowds coming back. On weekends, the desserts outsell the chicken wings."

"What's on the dessert menu?"

"Two British donut favorites—the Isle of Wight doughnuts and Jersey wonders. Deep fried Oreo cookies are also super popular. A restaurant owned by Scotts, wouldn't be Scottish without the famous deep-fried Mars bar. Dad took it one step further by deep frying other chocolate bars—a different one every weekend."

"You'll have to take me sometime."

Her brown eyes grow so wide, I'm surprised they don't pop out of her head. The shock emanating from them, forces me to bite off a smile.

"Our friendship involves meeting the parents?!"

I reach out and brush a strand of her hair behind her ear.

She trembles under my touch.

"Why not?"

# Chapter 26

## *Arianne*

For the second morning in a row, I'm up early enough to watch the sunrise.

"Cali sure is pretty." I bask in the warmth of the wee hours.

I'm well rested thanks to Beckett Christensen's phenomenal fingers and his ability to make me come like never before. And to think, two weeks ago, I was trapped with him in an elevator. He was a stranger then. Now, he's anything but. After dinner, I was hoping we'd come back upstairs for a repeat of what transpired in his office or an encore of the naughty things we did in my bathroom a few nights ago. Both were so illicit. Dirty. Forbidden. And so totally sizzling hot. Beckett refused to indulge me, reminding me that predictability wasn't in his vocabulary. He assured me I wouldn't see the next round coming.

I'm giddy beyond belief.

Since the night was still young when I got home—and I was charged with so much energy—I did what I do best. I worked. Beckett's demanding ways cut short the design meeting, so I decided to go over my notes. An hour into it, my mind was percolating with ideas.

"Maybe there's more in Los Angeles than even I could wish for," I say out loud.

I shrug off the fairytale as quickly as it pops into my head.

"He's a notorious bad boy, Arianne. You two are just having a little fun." The voice of reason reminds at me.

*Sigh.*

One might argue I'm not the best judge of character because Chance blindsided me in such a humiliating way, but I doubt Beckett would do anything that hurtful or demeaning.

But... he's a handsome, powerful, sexy, confident, coveted, rich, and very eligible man who has a membership at an adult club.

"Keep it in check, girlfriend."

My phone rings.

I rush inside to grab it.

"Phoebe!"

"Hey, you're already up," she says.

"I am."

"Since it's only six, I expected you to still be in bed. I was going to leave a message."

"When I first arrived, it took me a week to get over the jetlag, so I didn't roll out of bed until I absolutely had to, aka when my alarm rang. Now that I'm on Los Angeles time, I get up without the alarm and welcome the new day."

"Very Zen. Very California," she says.

"I guess you're calling me this early because you want us to grab breakfast before we head off to work. I'm so up for it!"

She lets out a loud sigh. "I landed from Hong Kong, but I won't be in LA for long."

"I don't understand."

"I was counting the hours before I got home and slid next to my boyfriend's warm body, but instead, I'm at LAX waiting for a flight to Seattle."

"What's urgent in Seattle?"

"When I turned my phone on, I was bombarded with messages from my boss," Phoebe says. "We have a situation at the Seattle plant and I need to get my ass over there."

"Oh no, I was so looking forward to seeing you and spending the weekend with you."

"I can't tell you how disappointed I am, Ari," she says. "I have to bail on us hanging out together tonight at my place, our Saturday shopping spree, and our Sunday spa day."

"Crap."

"The worst part is that Oscar and you still don't know each other," she says.

"It's unfortunate, but it's not like it's your fault," I tell her. "When are you back?"

"Tuesday first thing, which means... drum roll, please."

I oblige by doing my best impression.

"I'm claiming you!" she says. "I've already talked to Oscar and since Tuesday nights are quiet at the bar, we're going to throw a little party in your honor."

"Come on, Phoebe, you don't have to go to all that trouble—"

"Hush. You're my best friend and I'll fuss if I want to," she says.

"Okay. Fuss all you want."

We laugh.

"I was really excited about the shopping and the spa weekend," I say. "I guess I'll play tourist instead, and we can postpone it until you're back."

"Oh no you don't. You're still going shopping *and* you're still going to the spa!" Her authoritative tone is a surprise.

"It won't be as fun without you."

"I'd say Andrea did a stellar job. Clearly, you don't need me."

"Andrea sent you photos?"

"No. After buying an inflated ticket for Seattle, I caught up with social media. It's amazing how much you miss when you're wrapping up a conference, and then you're on a stopover flight back home."

*Uh-oh.*

"The world knows of your best friend's transformation from three-piece-suit-armor-worshipper to a sexy goddess, but you're oblivious."

*Here we go.*

"The world caught a glimpse of the flurry of salacious photos of said best friend entangled in a hotter-than-hell dance with her new boss-slash-client—her blue-eyed hunk of a boss-slash-client, may I add—but you're in the dark. The world witnessed a torrid affair in the making. You, on the other hand, just found out."

*She's on a roll.*

"From my recollection, said best friend kept swearing up and down on a stack of bibles she was blind and unaffected by her hottie boss-slash-client. What gives, best friend?"

*Did she even take a breath?*

"Oh, you're done with the drama?" I say. "I thought you had more to get off your chest."

"Don't even go there with me, Ari. When I suggested a little night of fun with a guy who is as single as you are, you shot me down. Now, Miss Holy Chic and Mr. Sex-God-Former-Rock-Star-Turned-CEO are an item?"

"We're *not* an item." I roll my eyes at the phone. "Beckett was just being a gentleman. We were out for dinner and he invited me to the engagement party. He forgot it was happening that night."

"Dinner is a far cry from the photos floating all over the internet, Ari," she says.

"The press has a knack for blowing things out of proportion."

"You're telling me your pussy wasn't fluttering?" She doesn't give me a chance to answer. "Because the photos of you dancing sex-to-sex with Beckett Christensen suggest otherwise."

I'm a little caught off guard.

I didn't expect her call and I surely didn't expect to be besieged this early in the morning. I thought I'd have a couple of glasses of wine in my system before I had the courage to share my night of debauchery with Phoebe.

"Arianne?" she says when I don't answer.

"Yes."

"What aren't you telling me?"

"My pussy wasn't fluttering—"

"Don't you dare—"

"My pussy was beating harder than shutters flapping wild in the middle of a raging hurricane for sexy Beckett Christensen," I tell her. "When I'm around him, I don't know what to do with myself. It's like I'm always turned on like a freaking light switch." I pause to catch my breath because my heart is beating like a drum. "Frankly, I have no idea how I'm going to survive next week's business trip to Germany without melting in a pool of lust every time he looks at me."

"Wh—what?!"

# Chapter 27

## *Beckett*

Ignoring the pleading look on Arianne's face—and my protesting cock—last night when I dropped her off at her place, I retreated to my home and jerked off at the memory of our dirty encounter in my office.

I had a repeat this morning when I woke up with a mighty morning wood and again in the shower. I didn't know you could come so hard, you fear blacking out.

I've given up the pretense I could win this challenge.

I'm not even interested in trying anymore.

Celibacy is inhuman. Especially, when God sends a sweet temptation like Arianne Buchanan your way.

I held back for another reason—one I struggle to make sense of. For once in my life, my naughty thoughts are centered around the pleasure I give a woman and not my cock's enjoyment and what I get in return.

It's unheard of.

Yet, here I am, three days after Miss Buchanan started working for me, a changed man.

After a string of morning meetings offsite, I find myself

trapped in another one with the head of the legal team. We're going down a long list of important matters. Covering for Rhys while he's away is a juggling act. In the meantime, Arianne is keeping herself busy in a follow-up meeting with the design team.

I can't wait to catch a glimpse of Miss Holy Chic.

*Did she fall asleep remembering my thick hard cock pressing against her pelvis as I reddened her ass?*

I hope she played with herself, pretending the fingers plunging in and out of her dripping pussy were mine. Maybe she woke up this morning searching for release, flashing back to images of me licking my fingers clean of her slick, sweet juices.

*Fuck.*

Now, I'm all worked up again.

"Beckett?!" The sound of my name snaps me back to reality.

Rupert Cahill's expectant gaze is trained on me.

*What did he say?*

I rack my brain, but come up empty.

*Shit.*

Instead of focusing on the meeting, my mind is in the gutter.

"I'm sorry, Rupert. I missed that last part."

"Do I have the green light to ask our lawyers in Hong Kong to go after the copycats threatening to cheapen our brand?" our head of in-house counsel asks.

*Got it!*

"Absolutely! We need to send a message. A strong one! I want to deter other idiots from following the same sleazy path."

"We're on the same page," he says.

"It's one thing for them to steal our design—as cheap looking as it is—it's another for them to use a near-copy of our logo. It dupes customers."

"Agreed," Rupert says. "Thanks to astute private investigators, the lawyers in Hong Kong have already zeroed in on the culprit's plant. They're just waiting for an answer from you."

"Whatever it takes," I say.

"Excellent!"

Rupert takes trademark infringement seriously.

"For the next item on the list, I'd like to tackle—" I stop mid-sentence when I catch sight of the silhouette striding behind Rupert.

I lose my train of thought.

The advantage of having clear glass conference room walls is you don't feel like you're trapped in a dungeon. The disadvantage is you see everything that's happening outside and it can be quite distracting.

Like now.

Arianne trails past the conference room with Flora by her side, laughing her head off. Her exuberance isn't what catches my attention. What she's wearing has my cock on alert.

"Beckett?!"

In a matter of minutes Rupert catches me not paying attention twice. Not good for the CEO of the company.

I force myself to gather my thoughts. "I'm sorry, Rupert. As I was saying—"

*What. The. Fuck?*

My attempt at focusing goes to shit when Arianne comes to stand with Flora right across from the conference room, her back facing me.

My eyes are glued to her ass and I can only picture myself reddening said ass, leaving my mark with every slap. My cock swells at the idea of a mouth-watering encore.

I proclaimed predictability was such a bore, but damn if I don't want to drag her to my office for a repeat of yesterday's naughty play.

I shift in my chair to adjust myself.

"Beckett, if this is a bad time, perhaps we should reconvene later?" Rupert's eyes bounce from mine to the two women standing outside the conference room.

"It won't be necessary—"

Arianne turns around.

My gaze lands on her feet.

*Dammit.*

I'm not sure how to describe what she's wearing other than a cross between a pair of smoking hot black booties that hit her just above the ankle and open-toe high heels.

In other words, her shoe selection is sexy as all fuck.

Her toenails painted in hot pink only ratchet the hotness level.

My eyes glide up her black pencil skirt.

*My cock approves.*

As I continue my inspection my gaze lands on her black t-shirt.

I read the slogan printed across her chest.

*Well, well, well.*

*Someone is sending me a not-so-subtle message.*

Yesterday's outfit was outrageously feminine.

Today's is laced with effrontery.

Yesterday, she disobeyed me.

Today, she's provoking me.

*Let the games begin!*

I bring my attention back to Rupert. "On second thought, what I was going to tackle next can wait."

"Not a problem," he says.

"You know, you should get started with the weekend. You're a hard worker. You deserve it," I tell him.

"It's not even lunchtime yet," he says.

I look at my watch.

He's right.

"It's Friday," I say. "Have an extended weekend on me. Enjoy your time with your new wife."

"I'm not married. You must be thinking of Hubert."

Arianne—and not fucking—has me so discombobulated I can't even keep facts straight about my employees. Of course he's not married. I know that. Hubert Ferguson tied the knot not long ago.

"In that case, take advantage of the extended long weekend to find a partner."

Rupert looks at me like I have two heads. "Is everything okay, Beckett?"

"Never been better," I tell him.

"Okay." Rupert's eyes shift to where Arianne is standing. "I've been dying to get to know her better. Maybe I'll invite her out for lunch."

My head whips in his direction. "Come again?"

"Rumor has it Arianne is new in town. I'd love to show her around... maybe take her to my favorite spots." *I don't think so.*

"Do you really want to spend your extended weekend playing tour guide?" I ask. "Who the hell wants to be stuck in LA traffic when they can avoid it?" I'm fully aware of how ridiculous that sounds.

"You just pressed me to find a partner. Arianne is extraordinarily attractive."

*Congratulations. There's nothing wrong with your eyesight.*

"She's definitely partner material."

I used to like Rupert. Now, I'm not so sure.

"Since she's a consultant, I wouldn't be stepping all over the non-fraternization clause in my contract."

*Well, hell.*

"Who knows? Lunch could lead to dinner and then..."

*And then I chop off your fucking dick.*

"Rumor has it she might be involved with someone," I tell him. Okay, technically, it's a white lie, but it's not hurting anyone. I'm not affirming this as a fact, I'm simply planting the seed of doubt.

"Oh." Rupert looks genuinely disappointed. "It figures. A woman like that wouldn't be single."

"You know what they say."

"Yeah, all the good ones are taken or married."

*Too bad, buddy. I saw her first.*

"She wouldn't be available for lunch, anyway. Since I've been wearing two hats with Rhys in Vietnam, I intend on spending the rest of the afternoon with Miss Buchanan to make sure she's up to speed."

"Of course," Rupert says.

Just then, Arianne walks away with Flora.

*Shit.*

I stand up and gather my things.

*This meeting is adjourned.*

Rupert mirrors me.

"I guess I'll be on my way and get started on that extended weekend, even if it isn't with Arianne," he says.

*Exactly the way it should be.*

"Do you have any big plans for the weekend?" he asks as we walk to the door.

"I have a weekend-long date with an adorable blue-eyed blonde and her best friend."

"Wow. Women can't resist you," he says.

I scour every corner of the second floor as I inconspicuously search for Arianne. Many staff members are already spilling out of the office building for lunch. Good. The fewer people, the better. Still, I don't want to draw too much attention to myself. After searching the lunchroom-slash-break room, the kitchen, all the meeting rooms, and the sample room without any luck, I head to the intelligence room. We keep a prototype of every single one of our headphone models in the sample room. The intelligence room is like a lab. It's dedicated to tracking our competitors' bestselling headphones. When I get there, the door is ajar. Arianne's silhouette traverses the room.

*Gotcha!*

I look around to make sure the coast is clear before slipping inside. Arianne has her back to me as she searches the shelves.

I lock the door as quietly as possible.

For a few short seconds, I admire her, enjoying how she's oblivious to my presence.

*How will I survive the trip to Germany without fucking her every minute of the day?*

"I have a big problem with what you're wearing, Miss Buchanan," I say.

She jumps.

"Good God, you scared the living daylights out of me," she says, flipping around, a hand pressed against her chest.

"That wasn't my intention," I tell her. I approach a shelf and drop my belongings.

"I nearly jumped out of my skin."

I respond with a wide smile, as my eyes travel up and down the length of her body.

"You frighten me when you look at me like that," she says.

"Like what?"

*I take a step toward her.*

"Like, you know..." she waves a furious finger at me.

"No, I don't."

*Another step.*

"Like you're harvesting unholy thoughts."

There's no hiding what's brewing inside me. "It's your fault."

"My fault?"

"Yes, your fault."

*One more step and we're up close.*

We're breathing hard.

I lift a hand and run a light finger over her cheek. "For the second day in a row, you leave me speechless with your wardrobe selection."

She blushes.

"It's only a skirt and a t-shirt," she says.

"Bullshit!"

"I made a commitment to avoid wearing a suit every day. This is me trying my darndest." The slight pull at the corner of her mouth doesn't go unnoticed. Neither does the glee of malice shining bright from her eyes.

I take a small step back and my gaze falls to her chest. "Is the slogan meant as a warning?"

"Do you read it as one?"

"Don't you dare answer my question with a question."

"What was the question again?"

Now she's playing me.

I narrow my gaze at her.

"'*You Can't Touch This!*' is my way of letting you know yesterday was a lot to handle."

She didn't say she didn't love every salacious minute of yesterday's encounter. Nor did she say it can't ever happen again.

"And you think a freaking t-shirt is going to prevent me from taking what I want?"

"We're playing with fire."

"Didn't we address that yesterday?"

"I'm not as daring as you."

"Are you telling me you don't want to come as hard as you did yesterday ever again?"

Her eyes flinch. "I—I didn't say that."

"What are you saying, then?"

"We can wait until after work?" Her meek response holds no conviction.

I grab her by the waist and slam her body against mine, pressing my erection against her stomach, grinding hard, allowing her to feel every inch of me.

"You sure about that?"

She pants.

"That's what I thought." Satisfaction courses through me.

I cup her breast and grope it hard.

She gasps.

"Let me remind you how this game is played, Arianne. My building. My rules. My way. That means I can touch any part of you whenever I trap you in a corner or when we're behind closed doors, unless you tell me to my face you don't want my hands on your delectable body. If you don't want this as much as I do, I'll back off."

Her eyelashes bat a mile a minute.

She just stares at me.

"I'm sorry, you're going to have to speak louder."

"I want this," she says in a whisper.

"I didn't catch that." Yeah, I'm being a bastard.

"I want this."

"What exactly do you want?"

"Your hands on my body."

"With pleasure."

I capture her mouth in a burning kiss, sliding my tongue between her bright pink lips.

*So damn sweet.*

I fill my hands with her ass as I press our bodies together and grind so hard against her, I groan into her mouth.

Her desperate moans go straight to my balls as she bucks against me, seeking relief.

*My need to devour this woman is going to make me lose my fucking mind.*

I break the kiss.

Her glazed eyes tell me everything I need to know.

I step back.

I unfasten my cufflinks, place them inside the pocket of my pants, and roll the sleeves of my crisp white shirt halfway up my forearms, exposing my ink.

"Wh—what are you doing?"

She's worried.

She should be.

I flash her a predatory smile. "Getting comfortable."

"For what?"

"For what I have in store for you."

"And what might that be?"

"Let's just say, when I'm done with you, don't expect to be able to stand unassisted. Don't worry, though, I'll be here for you, baby."

"Beckett."

"Beckett, what?"

She looks over my shoulder.

"The door is locked." I answer her silent question.

"What if someone needs to grab something in here?"

"On my way to find you, I texted Valerie. I asked her to send a companywide email—and text—to let everyone know they're getting an extra half hour for lunch. Who doesn't want ninety-minutes of free time on the boss's dime? That should mitigate the risk of us getting busted."

"This was planned?"

"Yes and no. I was determined to find you because..."—my eyes trail up and down her body again—"you look so fucking hot. I'm glad I sent those instructions to Valerie. When I spotted you in here, I wanted a little one-on-one time with you. I didn't know what that meant. Now, I do."

"You're crazy, Beckett Christensen."

"You keep saying that, yet you keep coming back for more."

She rolls her eyes.

"I guess it won't be a repeat of yesterday since there isn't a chair or a couch in sight," she says. "No tables or counters either. There isn't much we can do in this room."

"Such innocence."

"Other than shelves stocked with headphones, there's nothing." Her eyes travel around the room before meeting mine. "Unless you locked me in here for..." Her eyes drop to my bulge.

"No. This is about you," I tell her.

"I don't get it. I really don't," she says.

"Enlighten me."

"You do all these really naughty things to me, but you don't expect anything in return. I know I haven't been out there that much, but shouldn't it be a two-way street? You know... you give... and I give." She's pointing at my cock.

"It *is* a two-way street. I get my pleasure from giving you pleasure."

She shoots me a skeptical side gaze. "That doesn't sound right."

"Did you hear me complain?"

She ponders for a minute.

"No."

"You have your answer."

"Wow. It's never been about me before."

I have some formidable skills, but from what she's told me

so far, I doubt I have the superpowers to undo all of the shit her ex did to her. I can only try.

"Aren't you glad you met me?" I wink.

She laughs.

"What are you going to do to me?" Her voice is coated with lust.

"Hmm. So many possibilities," I say, tapping my chin. "I want it raunchy today."

"Everything we've done so far is raunchy, as far as I'm concerned."

"I want to taste you, but not on your fingers or mine. I want to drink straight from the cup."

Her jaw drops.

"I want to gorge on your sweet pussy." I lean in, my breath hot on her cheek. "I want you to come in my mouth, your juices coating my tongue."

Just saying the words makes me fucking hard.

I pull away, allowing my filthy proposal to sink in.

Her eyes take over her face.

I continue with my wicked promise. "I want to lick your pretty little clit until you want to scream."

"Jesus," she says.

"But here's the catch, you won't be able to make a sound."

She shakes her head.

"You know why?" I ask.

"Why?" Her voice is trembling.

"Most people might be out for lunch, but we don't want to take a chance, right?"

She nods.

"You promise?"

"I won't make a sound," she says.

Her eyes bounce from one corner of the room to the other. "There's no furniture in the room."

"I don't need furniture."

Before she asks any more questions, I push her until her back rests against the shelves. Good thing they're bolted to the floor and ceiling. I sink to the floor, kneeling between her thighs.

"Dear God," she says.

"Look at that. With your sexy heels on, my face is level with your sweet pussy. Lucky me. Lucky you!" I grin up at her.

"I'm going to remain standing up?" she asks.

"Yes."

"How's that going to work?"

"Stop thinking so hard. Your job is to enjoy the ride."

She offers a jerky nod.

I reach out and slowly, deliberately push her skirt up her creamy thighs until it's bunched around her waist. I tuck the hem, so it doesn't obstruct my view—or pleasure.

"Oh, my God," she says.

"Hot pink panties to match the lettering on your t-shirt?"

"I've never been this turned on in my entire life." The confession spills from her lips, surprising us both.

I run a finger from the top of her lace panties, tracing between her pussy lips and back. Her panties are already damp. I blow warm air against her pussy.

She gasps, her legs trembling.

"I like you like this, baby... completely exposed to me," I say.

She looks down at me.

"What is it about you?" she asks.

"You mean, what is it about *us*? Remember what I told you about connection. You and I"—I wave a finger between us—"we have a great connection."

"We do."

We both grin at each other.

"I'm going to make it good for you."

"You always do," she says.

"I like hearing that." I tease a finger across the band of her panties. She shudders at my touch.

"I love the shoes, by the way."

"Thanks."

"You'll have to wear them when I fuck you."

"Dear God, Beckett. The stuff that comes out of your mouth—"

"My mouth is part of the reason you've never been so turned on in your entire life."

That gets me a wide smile.

*I'm done talking.*

I grasp the front of her panties in my teeth, yanking them down and letting them fall in a heap of sexiness around her feet.

"Holy Jesus!" Arianne says.

"Step out of them."

She obeys my order.

I toss them to the side, the bright shade against the gray cement floor, a testament to the naughtiness to come.

"Spread them wide for me!" I tap between her legs.

She does.

"Hold on tight," I say.

"Okay," she says.

She reaches up and clings onto the edge of a shelf.

*Good girl.*

She's naked from the waist-down and ready to play.

I ease her into it.

I grab her foot in my hand and trail slow kisses up one leg, caressing her soft skin along the way. I kiss every one of her dainty toes peeking from her heels.

She giggles.

"Ticklish?" I ask.

"A bit."

I smile.

Her other leg receives the same treatment.

She moans.

I drop her foot to the floor and slide my hands up the inside of her legs in an agonizing and slow stroke.

She closes her eyes and tilts her head back.

"No, baby, eyes on me."

She snaps them open and fixes her gaze on mine.

"I want you to watch me lick your pussy."

"Oh, God."

"Oh, *Beckett*." I correct her.

I slip my hand between her legs and lightly stroke the strip of hair. I glide a finger between her pussy lips, scooping up her slickness. She trembles under my touch.

"Oh, Beckett." She's a quick learner.

I do it again.

And again.

She moves her hips back and forth, matching the sensual strokes of my fingers. Suddenly, her body convulses.

"No, Arianne, you can't come before I tongue-fuck you," I tell her.

She ignores me.

I ease the pressure against her clit.

She shoots me a death glare.

"Patience, baby. I promise it'll be worth it," I say, my thumb skating around her clit again.

She nods her agreement.

"Good girl."

I dip my head between her thighs and inhale her heady scent.

*God, it's been so long.*

I slide my tongue between her pussy lips.

She cries out.

"Shhh."

"Okay. Okay," she says.

*Back to the program.*

I probe her pussy, my tongue hot and wet between her lips until I find her hard clit again.

She gasps as her body jerks.

She clamps one hand over her mouth. Her eyes are so fucking huge.

"I'm about to let loose," I tell her. "Can you handle it?"

"I'll be quiet," she says.

I'm not sure if I should believe her, but I'm not about to stop now.

I resume my mission.

My tongue is gentle at first, swirling around in slow circles, but I pick up speed. I lap and probe, over and over.

Her little, desperate moans ratchet my own desire.

She looks down at me like I'm a unicorn.

That does it.

I go fucking crazy.

I devour her, sucking at the tender flesh.

It's as agonizing for her as it is for me.

I pull her towards me, angle my head and plunge my tongue deep inside her.

I'm voracious.

"Holy shit, holy shit, holy shit," she chants in a low voice, sinking against me. It goes on for a while, alternating between prayers and curses.

"Fuck, fuck, fuck."

Her legs give way.

I wrap them around my neck, lifting her up and positioning her back against the shelves.

"You okay?" I ask.

"Hell, yes."

There's nothing stopping me now.

With her pussy spread wide, I plunge my tongue deep inside, fucking her, wishing it were my cock.

In and out.

In and out.

The sound of her slick juices coating my tongue reverberates around the room, trumped only by her sensual moans.

My desperate cock presses against my boxer briefs. With my hands full, there isn't much I can do. She's my only source of pleasure.

I double my efforts and slide two fingers deep inside her pussy, as my tongue rubs her clit with urgency.

My heart is racing.

"Oh!" The point of a heel digs into my back.

*Shit.*

That's going to leave an imprint for sure.

I curve my fingers, fucking her with the same insane rhythm as my tongue laps at her clit.

She struggles in my arms.

*Where the hell do you think you're going?*

I tighten my grip.

I lap harder, more determined. More unrepentant. I take it up a dozen notches by sliding a third finger into her soaking wet pussy. The more her slickness drips down my chin, the more I'm ravenous. I wrap my lips around her clit and suck hard.

*This is so fucking hot.*

She clamps her legs around my head, bucking in my hands. "Oh, Beckett!"

My eyes shoot up to her.

*That's it, baby.*

*Feed me.*

*Take your pleasure from me.*

*Come hard for me.*

Arianne shudders against my wicked tongue with a muffled groan.

Watching her climax so beautifully is a torturous punishment. My cock is so hard it could break concrete. The need to slide balls-deep inside her pussy in one hard shove is so strong, I can't think straight.

*Fuck.*

*What is this woman doing to me?*

This is Arianne's fourth day in my life and already she has me hooked.

# Chapter 28

## *Beckett*

It was quite the challenge to dive back into work after my salacious encounter with Arianne, but I had to. I spent the rest of the day briefing her on our marketing strategies and the massive upcoming promotional campaigns the advertising agency has been working on.

She gobbled it all up, not missing a beat.

There's something so darn sexy about watching her in business mode, legs crossed, and attention on me, while visions of her dissolving all over my tongue were still running rampant through my mind. Our salacious interactions at the office are so illicit, which makes them that much more forbidden... and scorching hot.

*It's our little secret.*

As much as I would've loved to continue playing with her all weekend long, I already have a date.

"Hey, Beckett!" Holt says when he opens the door.

"Hey!" I enter my older brother's home and drop my weekend bag on the floor next to his luggage.

"Uncle Beckett!" A tiny blonde princess comes racing

towards me. She zigzags in front of her dad, her arms wide open and ready to greet me. I bend down just in time to catch her. She jumps into my arms and giggles as I turn around in circles. I bring her close to me and shower her beautiful face with kisses.

She giggles harder.

"Too many kisses," she says.

"There's no such thing as too many kisses," I tell her before resuming my mission.

"You forgot to kiss Luna," my niece tells me.

I drop her to her feet.

She adjusts her tiny tiara and her yellow princess dress.

"*Woof! Woof!*" The eager Staffie lets me know she's waiting.

I bend down to pat her head. Well, I'd like to pat it, but I can't because she's wearing a tiara. She's also wearing a doggy-princess dress and her neck is garlanded with doggy jewelry. Not one to be left out, Luna jumps into my lap in search of a kiss. I oblige.

"Princess Luna, how are you?" I ask.

"Luna isn't a princess today. She's a lady-in-waiting," my niece says.

My gaze shifts to my big brother's. "I sense a theme for the weekend."

"Sorry. I had to pick my battles," he tells me. "I couldn't talk her out of the princess costume even though it's only Friday night and movie night isn't until tomorrow."

"It's going to be fun, Daddy! Uncle Beckett is going to be the bodyguard. I'm going to be the princess and Luna is my best friend."

"I've been downgraded to bodyguard? Why can't I be a princess?" I ask, pretending to be offended.

Naomi giggles. "Princesses need bodyguards. That's the rule."

I guess I don't have to wear Luna's jewelry or her tiara for our play date. *The things I'll do for this child.* Not that I'm complaining much. It's a small price to pay for my little niece, who believes I can hang the moon.

"A weekend of fun awaits," I say with a laugh.

"Uh-huh." She nods, sending her tiara flying. She bends down, picks it up and places it regally on her head. Holt and I watch in amusement. "Tonight, we're going to have donut high tea. Tomorrow, we're going to have cupcake high tea, and on Sunday, we're going to have pancake high tea. We should also have waffles on Sunday. And strawberry-flavored unicorn funfetti cake!"

Naomi is five.

For two years she lived in London while my brother was building his recording label across the pond. She still has traces of her British accent, and high tea remains a staple in her world.

"That's a lot of dessert," I say. "What about food?"

"Dessert *is* food," she tells me, her little eyebrows furrowing.

"No, it's not!" Holt says.

"But it is," Naomi says.

My brother levels me with his blue eyes. "Don't let her eat too much sugar or else you won't know what to do with her. Make sure she eats *real* food. And no sugar for Luna. She's only allowed doggie treats."

"No problem," I say.

"Naomi, while I'm away, you listen to Uncle Beckett," my brother says.

Huge sparkling blue eyes look up at us, her mass of blonde curls, a little wild, a mischievous grin stretching her lips.

*She's up to no good.*

"What did I just say, Noni?" Holt says.

"I'm always a good girl, Daddy. I always listen to Uncle Beckett." She clasps her little hands in prayer under her chin and bats her eyelashes at her father.

I swear she's a breath away from growing angel wings.

"I want to hear it, Noni," Holt says.

"Luna and I will eat *real* food, Daddy."

"Good." My brother turns his attention to me. "Thanks again for doing this." He pats me on the shoulder.

"I'm just doing my job as her uncle. You need to attend an important last-minute business trip. Your fiancée is in Jersey, Mom and Dad left this morning for Santorini, and coincidentally, Jace is out of town with his kid, and Jagger is on the East Coast with his daughter."

"What are the chances everyone would be gone at the same time? The beauty of living in a Manhattan Beach gated cul-de-sac, on the same street as your cousins is you always have back-up babysitters."

"Good thing I'm only a five-minute ride away, so I'm not too far when the Halsey brothers can't watch Noni. You know I'll never say no to babysitting my favorite niece." I wink at her. That earns me a huge grin. "That's what makes me the best uncle in the world," I say, puffing my chest out.

"Uncle Beckett, you're the *bestest* and my most favorite uncle ever!" my biggest fan says.

"Make sure she gets a bath," Holt says. "She's going to be covered in sugar by the time she's ready for bed. Luna will need one tomorrow."

"Got it!"

"Don't forget, she has ballet tomorrow morning and music lessons in the afternoon. You already know Saturday night is movie night."

"I do. Pizza?"

Holt runs a hand through his brown hair. "Noni is currently obsessed with charcuterie and cheese boards."

"Fancy palate for a tiny human."

"Tell me about it. I need to cut her off Food Network."

*Right. She has you wrapped around her little pinkie finger.*

"Since we're away, I won't fight her on it," Holt tells me. "All the ingredients are in the fridge. You have French baguettes in the freezer."

"Copy that."

"You decide what you want to do on Sunday morning, and in the afternoon, she'll go play with her friends on the street with Luna."

"I can handle that," I say.

"Don't forget, on Monday morning you have to drive her to school. Her nanny will pick her up in the afternoon."

"I won't," I tell him. "I left the Alfa Romeo at home for that reason."

I didn't buy my Mercedes-Benz G 550 Luxury SUV for my niece, but it comes in handy when I have to be her chauffeur.

"I'll be back from New York by Monday, early evening."

"I got it covered," I say.

I have no idea how Holt keeps it straight while running a successful recording label on his own. Rhys has been gone for a few days, and already, I feel the pressure. And I don't even have to worry about tiny princesses—human or canine ones.

There's a honk outside.

"That's my ride," Holt says. "I have to go."

"Love you, Daddy!"

My brother lowers himself to his daughter's height and wraps her in his arms.

"Love you, too, Noni."

"What about Luna?"

Holt rubs his dog's head. "Love you, too, Luna. Be good," he says to Noni.

"I promise, Daddy! Kiss! Kiss! Kiss!" She plants a big kiss on his cheek with dramatic sound effect and all.

Holt stands up. "Thanks again," he says. "I owe you."

"Don't worry, I'll come knocking at your door when I need you to babysit my kid."

Holt's eyes widen.

"What?" I ask.

He squints at me. "What did you just say?"

I replay my words in my head.

*Shit.*

"I don't remember." Blatant lie.

"Are you going to be a daddy?" Noni asks. She continues before I can answer, "Luna, Uncle Beckett has a girlfriend, and he's going to have a baby. We're going to be big cousins!" She's already jumping up and down. "When are you getting married, Uncle Beckett?"

*Wait. What?*

"Luna and I are going to be flower girls! Yay!"

*No, no, no!*

Holt's face contorts in myriad expressions. "Is there something I need to know?"

I shake my head. "Absolutely not!"

He leans into me and whispers in my ear. "Did you knock up a woman?"

"No! I didn't!" I take a step back. "I just said that in passing."

He studies me.

"Beckett, you've never alluded to having kids before... even in the very, very, very distant future."

"It was just a figure of speech," I say.

"Words like babies, toddlers, kids, and children frighten you."

"You're exaggerating."

"Are you feeling okay?"

"Why does everybody keep asking me that?"

"Maybe because what's coming out of your mouth is so out of character, it's worrisome," Holt says.

"Please..." I roll my eyes.

"Seriously, Beckett, if you fell and hurt your head, I need to know. I'm about to fly across the country and leave you in charge of my only child. If you're suffering from a concussion or temporary insanity, you're in no position to take care of my daughter."

"Get off it! She's in good hands and you know it."

"So, Uncle Beckett, you're not going to have a baby with your girlfriend and you're not getting married?" Noni asks.

"No, sweetie. There's no girlfriend, no baby on the way, and I'm most certainly *not* getting married."

"Oh."

I'm ecstatic my bachelor status remains intact. My niece, on the other hand, is quite disappointed. She'll get over it.

"Does this have to do with the *'Holy Chic'* woman?" Holt asks.

I conceal my surprise and tread carefully.

"What are you talking about?"

"Bree was going on, and on, and on about it. You know how much of a celebrity-watcher she is."

I shake my head. "Teenagers."

"Jagger's daughter was so obsessed, he became curious. Until he brought it up, I was unaware you were the talk of the gossip rags."

"Why did Jagger go through you when he could've asked me?"

"He wanted a straight answer," Holt says.

"I'm offended."

"I understand where he's coming from," he says.

"What is that supposed to mean?"

"Jagger sent me photos. Miss *'Holy Chic'* is stunning. She's also nothing like your usual type... If those photos are more than smoke and mirrors, I'd say, it's about time, little brother."

# Chapter 29

## *Arianne*

After a busy weekend filled with pampering and shopping, I make my way from the kitchen to the living room with a glass of red wine in hand after polishing off a delicious Italian meal.

My phone rings.

I rush to the coffee table, drop the glass, snatch it, and answer the video call as I plop myself on the couch.

"Phoebe!" Her smiling face appears on my screen.

"Ooohhhh! Your hair is amazing."

"It's not too blonde?" I ask, swirling a strand around my finger.

"No. It's not like it's platinum blonde or anything that dramatic. It's a stunning shade. It brings out your brown eyes."

"Thank you. I hesitated at first, but I'm thrilled with the result. Giuseppe said dark blonde highlights complement my complexion much more than the chunky blonde highlights I've been sporting since Silicon Valley."

"I'm so glad you didn't cancel. Giuseppe is one of the best stylists in LA. His waiting list is ridiculous. The man knows his stuff. Without him, I'd still be a mousy brunette instead of this," she says, shaking her dark chocolate brown hair with a flattering bang. "It seems you've also scored in the wardrobe department. Andrea worked her magic."

Phoebe has been extinguishing fires since she landed in Seattle on Friday morning. This is the first time we've had a chance to catch up. I've been updating her via a series of text messages, including photos.

"She's amazing. I love everything I bought. I even got all new makeup. The spa day yesterday was heaven. I feel like a new woman. I'm happy I listened to you and I didn't cancel."

"Look at you!"

"I know, right?"

"You'll look incredible at your party on Tuesday night."

"Oh, that again." I roll my eyes.

"Are you saying you don't want to see me?"

"I totally want to see you and you know it. I also can't wait to meet Oscar after hearing so much about him. It's just the whole idea of having a party in my honor..." I shrug.

"Look at it as a 'have a great trip' sendoff party since the next day you're flying out to Germany. That way you won't feel so self-conscious about it."

She knows me well.

"You're funny."

"Speaking of pending business trips with your super sexy and very naughty boss-slash-client, did you hook up over the weekend?"

"No. He spent the weekend with a blonde and her best friend—"

"Motherfucker!" Phoebe's eyes shine bright with fury.

"Calm down, guard dog. He was spending the weekend with his niece and her dog."

"Oh. Okay, that's officially the sweetest thing I've ever heard."

"Ditto that," I tell her.

"What a dichotomy—the caring uncle and the unwavering lover."

He's not my lover, but I don't correct her. I also don't admit my ovaries nearly burst when Beckett told me of his plans.

"I was worried Beckett might be cut from the same cloth as Chance," Phoebe says.

"Mom has the same concerns."

"What do you mean?"

I tell her about my conversation with Mom when she called to tell me Mariah was in Philly flaunting her big ass engagement ring.

"The two men couldn't be further apart," I say. "Beckett didn't have to tell me he was spending the weekend on uncle duty. We're not in a relationship. He doesn't owe me anything. Yet, he insisted on explaining the reason he wouldn't see me until tomorrow. I was touched beyond belief by his attentiveness."

"He showed you the respect you deserve. That says a lot about him."

"It does," I say with a small smile. I'm fully aware of the blush creeping up my cheeks, but there isn't much I can do about it.

"*Arianne likes Beckett. Arianne likes Beckett.*" Phoebe singsongs like a five-year-old.

"Oh, stop it!"

"Well?"

"Well, what?"

"Do you like Beckett?"

What's there not to like about the delicious hunk? But no way am I losing my head over another man.

"I'm just getting to know him," I tell her.

"That doesn't answer my question," Phoebe says.

I ponder for a beat. "I don't want to create a silly fairytale in my head just to end up being crushed and devastated when my make-believe castle comes crumbling down."

"You like him."

It's not a question.

"Me and pretty much every woman who's ever been in contact with the charismatic CEO," I say.

"Okay," she says. "I get it. You're not going to answer my question. I won't push. You've come a long way. I'm proud of you."

"I'm just glad Chance Taboras is no longer the only man on planet Earth to have seen me naked."

Phoebe laughs.

"And Chance Taboras's cock isn't the only one I've seen in real life," I say. "And contrary to his delusional mind, he isn't the size of an English cucumber—a baby cucumber, maybe, but not a full-grown one. I can attest to that first-hand."

Phoebe laughs harder.

I'm on a roll.

"And now I know Chance Taboras was dead wrong when he proclaimed genital fluids don't belong in one's mouth. They do. They really do."

Tears stream down Phoebe's face.

"And Chance Taboras—who doesn't have a vagina—is a moron for believing eating pussy is overrated and totally unnecessary."

"Yeah, idiot Chance needed to shut his mouth about that one," Phoebe says. "I doubt Slut Mariah is getting her pussy serviced the right way, even if he supposedly changed his views on the matter."

An evil grin stretches my lips. "I doubt Slut Mariah knows

the indescribable pleasures of having her pussy devoured by an impossibly gorgeous man, on his knees looking up at her with piercing blues eyes as he tongue-fucks her until she's hit with the most earth-shattering orgasms of her life in the middle of the afternoon while she's still at the office and she could easily get caught." I take a breath. There. I said it.

"No. You. Didn't." Phoebe's shocked expression is priceless.

"You told me to put myself out there. I did. In so many filthy ways."

# Chapter 30

## *Beckett*

After dropping Naomi at school, I drove back to my place. Instead of rushing, I decided to have a long leisurely breakfast and enjoy a cup of coffee before taking a shower and heading to the office. I miss being at my place, but I know better. It's much less of a headache for me to stay at Holt's place than to have Naomi pack her entire existence—and Luna's—to come over to my place. Not to mention, my house isn't very childproof.

I miss the quietude.

I love Naomi to pieces, but when you're on uncle duty, it's a twenty-four-hour job. There's no such thing as taking a break until the princesses you're guarding are so exhausted, they crash. Since I didn't have to monitor the whereabouts of said princesses, I was able to knock off quite a few things from my to-do list. After answering a batch of emails and catching up with Valerie on important matters, I had a long talk with Rhys. He was so preoccupied by the urgent need to find a backup manufacturer, he didn't even ask about my commitment to abstain from temptation. I'll tell him soon enough I'm no longer in the running for his bike.

By the time I get to the office, it's lunchtime, which means the executive floor is almost empty. Even Valerie is out. When I sit at my desk, a little white envelope with my name scribed in impeccable penmanship catches my eye.

It's sealed.

Eager, I open it.

> Dear new friend,
>
> I hope you had a great weekend. I couldn't give you what you wanted last week, but I can today. Check the last drawer of your desk. I hope you like my little gift.
>
> Holy Chic!

I grin.

The temptation to text her was ever present throughout the weekend, but I refrained. What stopped me?

Holt's reaction.

His words.

The way I pissed around Arianne like a fucking dog to ward off Rupert.

The fact I didn't hesitate a second to eat her out at the office and how close I came to fucking her.

The way those candid selfies on Cesar's engagement night elicited such interest, considering the parade of women I've been seen with.

And finally, because I couldn't get her out of my head no matter how much I tried.

It all freaked me out.

I've never craved a woman this much, and I'm not sure what to make of it.

"Maybe I did hit my head." I mutter to myself.

Curiosity takes over and I open my drawer.

I don't have to search.

My gift is staring at me—a scrap of cobalt blue lace. I hold the lingerie with both hands and admire it.

My cock twitches with need.

My mouth salivates, eager to taste her again.

*Little devil.*

She didn't go for regular panties. No. She went for the heavy artillery—a G-string with three straps on each side.

Images of them adorning her sexy ass assault me, followed by a vision of her shimmying out of them.

*Goddammit.*

I bunch the fabric in my fist.

*Shit.*

*They're damp.*

She must've just put her wicked plan into action.

*Bad girl.*

I guess I should say, good girl.

I bring the fabric to my nose and close my eyes.

Her headiness hits my senses full force.

I let out a low groan.

My cock swells.

Since the intelligence room encounter, I've been a choirboy. When I'm on uncle duty, I'm on my best behavior. So now, I'm about to snap like a twig.

I grab my phone to text her.

> Beckett: You're itching for my hand to slap your ass.

Her response is fast.

Arianne: Happy Monday! And good afternoon to you!

Beckett: Don't happy Monday me and don't try to change the subject!

Arianne: What did I do?

Beckett: Your playing coy isn't amusing.

Arianne: I'm just trying to understand why you're so upset with me.

I roll my eyes.

Beckett: I gather you aren't wearing a white skirt today?

Arianne: You gather correctly.

Beckett: What are you wearing?

Arianne: Clothes, obviously.

Beckett: Your cockiness is going to get you in trouble, Miss Buchanan.

Arianne: Maybe I'm looking for trouble, Mr. Christensen.

*Well, hell.*

My cock is in urgent need of relief. All thoughts of behaving fly right out the window.

Beckett: Get your ass to my office!

Arianne: Are you sure you don't mean the intelligence room?

Beckett: Oh, you're asking for it.

Arianne: We've already established that.

I stand up, stuff her panties into the pocket of my pants, and remove my jacket. I'm so jacked up—and my cock is so hard—I can't sit back down.

I pat the prize in my pocket, a sense of satisfaction washing over me.

I demanded her panties on Friday. She delivers them on Monday, and she has the gall to give me sass over it.

*Who the hell does she think she is?*

I pace the room as I await her arrival.

Minutes tick away.

Someone is defying me again by taking her sweet ass time to get over here.

There's a knock at my door.

*Finally.*

I eat the floor and open it.

When I do, I freeze.

*Who's that girl?*

*Holy transformation!*

"What happened to you?" I ask.

"Good afternoon, Mr. Christensen," she says.

She's playing me like a fiddle.

I grab hold of her wrists and pull her into my office.

I stick my head out and look left, then right to make sure there are no witnesses.

*The coast is clear.*

Satisfied, I close the door and lock it.

I turn around, lean against the door and drink in every sinful inch of her.

Her angelic smile betrays the spark of mirth flashing bright in her eyes.

"Good afternoon, Miss Buchanan," I say. "What prompted this?" I wave my finger up and down the length of her body.

"Something new," she says with a coquettish one-shoulder shrug.

"The dress is a knockout."

"Thank you. I love it, too. Once again, Andrea steered me in the right direction."

*Bless Andrea.*

Arianne is adorned in a long-sleeved wrap-around dress that reaches her ankles with a sexy criss-cross at the chest that show-cases the swell of her breasts. The long sash wrapped at her waist makes my fingers itch. The slit at the front doesn't go unnoticed. Neither does the pair of nude strappy heels she's wearing. The same pendant she wore the other day rests against her chest.

Then, there's the cascade of highlighted shoulder-length hair framing her face.

*She's blonder than she was on Friday.*

Her wide, eager brown eyes stand out behind the rim of a subtle plum and gold eyeshadow combo and the flared out black eyeliner around them.

And the muted pink kissable lips beg for mine.

Her mere presence throws me off-kilter.

*God, she's more beautiful than ever.*

"The vibrant color of your dress makes quite the state-ment," I say. "You wear it well."

"Thank you."

"New hair and a new wardrobe." *Like I wasn't already screwed.* "Way to start the week on the right foot."

"*And* new lingerie. *A lot* of new lingerie... many are quite skimpy and naughty. A big departure for me. The sales lady at French Appliqué insisted their selections are designed to bring men to their knees."

*She had to go there.*

"Not that I'd know what that means, but I decided to take her word for it and I bought all the flattering combos. Why the hell not, right? Now, it's a matter of finding a man who would be a willing victim. Hmmm... who could it be?" She grins at me.

I narrow my gaze at her.

What the fuck did she have for breakfast this morning? A seduction smoothie with an extra scoop of vixen protein?

"Bathroom! Now!" I tell her.

I don't give her a choice. I grab her hand and drag her behind me.

When we enter my private bathroom, I close the door and lock it for good measure.

"Oooohhhh! A repeat of what we did at my place?" she asks, her eagerness evident.

"No. No repeat."

"What are we going to do, then?"

Her excitement bubbles over.

"I need an audience."

Her eyebrows knit. "I don't follow."

"Your little shenanigans put me in a state of unbearable arousal." My confession elicits a triumphant grin. "Now, I have to do something about it." I allow for a pregnant pause. "You're going to watch what you do to me."

She squints. "I still don't get it."

"My cock is about to fucking explode and it needs my immediate attention. And it's going to get it under your watchful eye," I tell her.

Her jaw drops.

"You're going to jerk off in front of me?"

"I wouldn't be in this dire situation if it wasn't for you and your damp panties," I say. "So yeah, you're going to watch me come."

"That's it? I'm just going to stand here?"

"That's it."

"Do you expect me to clap when you're finished?"

"That's entirely up to you, but I promise to make it worth a standing ovation."

She doesn't look impressed. "How do I get pleasure out of it?"

"Trust me, you will."

"What we did at my place was way more enjoyable than me just standing here."

"Consider this your punishment."

"For what?"

"For your smart mouth. For the unexpected transformation. For looking so damn good. For turning me on. Pick one. Pick them all. You're the culprit."

A slow grin splits her lips. "Really?"

I grab her by the neck and pull her to me before crushing her lips. I kiss her until we both run out of air. The chemistry between us is potent. I break our embrace and take her hand in mine. "Check it out for yourself." I close her hand over my cock.

"God, you're so hard."

"I'm in pain," I say.

"Then you better do something about it." The sass is back in full force.

*Damn her.*

Two can play that game.

With my eyes locked onto hers, I slip a hand between the slit of her dress and find her pussy. It's already dripping for me.

"You think?" My voice is gruff.

"Oh, God, yes!" Her head lolls back.

I remove my hand as quickly as I put it there.

She shoots daggers at me.

"You're welcome to take care of yourself while I relieve my raging erection."

She makes a face. "It's not the same."

"Perhaps a little less sass next time if you want me to take care of you."

She's still glaring at me.

"You can stand there, or you can join me. The choice is yours."

She's thinking.

I unfasten my cufflinks, take the shirt off, and hang it on the door. I kick off my shoes. Then, I fumble with my belt buckle before unzipping my pants. I remove them along with my boxer briefs at the same time as I pull my socks off.

"Fuck," I say as my erection is finally, finally let free from its confinement.

I fist my cock and stroke it.

Arianne's breathing quickens.

*I need more.*

I bend down, fish inside my pocket, and pull out her panties. I bring them to my nose and inhale deeply.

"I love how you smell and how you taste, baby."

Wide brown eyes with a mixture of shock and lust blink at me.

With my free hand, I reach between her legs and glide my fingers, scooping her juices.

"Good God," she says.

I bring my hand covered in her slickness to my cock.

The next thing I know, Arianne is undoing the sash around her wrap-around dress. With quick hands, she removes it and tries to place it over my shirt. She can't reach.

"Allow me," I tell her.

"Thanks."

The cobalt blue bra is next to go.

She's in such a rush to get naked, I barely have time to appreciate the sexy as fuck cutout design on top of her breasts.

"So, you decided?" I ask.

She nods. "Yes, I'm going to join you."

She readies herself to kick off her heels, but I stop her.

"Those stay on."

"You have a thing for heels."

"I have a thing for *you* in heels."

That earns me a beaming smile.

My hand goes back to my cock.

She walks to the granite counter, leans against it, parts her legs, and slides a hand down her flat stomach until she reaches her pussy.

"Not yet!" I stop her right before she plunges her fingers between her lips.

She frowns. "Why not?"

I step right up to her.

"Because I said so."

"I thought you wanted me to join you."

"Sit. It'll be more comfortable for you."

"Okay."

I help her up on the counter.

I gesture at her legs. "Open wide."

She obeys.

I position myself between her parted legs.

The view is salacious enough to give me a fucking heart attack.

"I want my eyes on your beautiful pink pussy while I work my cock," I tell her. "Show me how you take care of yourself."

She bites down on her bottom lip.

I expect her to squirm and maybe refuse. Instead, she plunges her fingers between her pussy lips.

She moans with every stroke.

"That's it, baby," I say. "Make it dirty for me."

She does.

Her hand moves in a dizzying circle.

Round and round.

*Shit.*

Without warning, she reaches for my cock.

"What are you doing?" I ask.

"I want to touch you."

"You want to jack me off while playing with your pussy?"

"I just wanted to touch you," she says.

"You don't want more?"

"I'd like more, but..."

"What's stopping you?"

"I don't think I'm very good at giving a hand job."

Given what she's told me about her ex, I'm not surprised she hasn't had much practice.

"Give me your hand."

She does as she's told.

I place it around my cock and close mine on top of hers. "I'll show you."

"I'd like that," she says. "I just hope I do it well."

"We'll do it together."

"Okay."

Her eyes are trained on my cock, but her hand doesn't move.

"What are you waiting for?" I ask.

"You said you'd show me."

"I did, but you can start pumping my cock."

She does.

She's tentative. Careful.

"You want me to come or not?" I ask.

Wide eyes meet mine. "I'm not doing it, right?"

"You are, but you're being too gentle."

"Oh, okay."

"You're not going to hurt me. You have to grip my cock really hard and stroke it up-and-down with vigor."

She tries again.

I grope her breast, squeeze hard, lower my head, and pull her nipple between my teeth.

She gasps.

"Did you feel that?"

"Yes," she says.

"That's the reaction you want from me."

She nods.

Her hand closes tightly around my cock as she starts stroking.

She still has her training wheels on, but she's getting there.

I let out a low groan.

"Am I doing it right?" she asks before worrying her lower lip.

My eyes drop to my strained cock.

"You are, baby."

"I shouldn't be this proud, but I am," she says.

I laugh before dropping a soft kiss against her lips.

"I loved watching you come the other night." She picks up speed.

*Damn.*

*She's a quick learner.*

"Yeah?"

"It was so hot."

"What did you love about it?"

"Your face as you got all worked up."

"Like now?"

"Yes," she says.

I take over, guiding her hand.

She gets the message.

"What else?" I ask.

"I loved how your entire body started to shake just before you came."

"All guys shake right before climax."

She shakes her head. "Not all guys. My ex didn't even make a sound. He was always in control. The only reason I knew he had reached orgasm was because he'd remind me it was time for a shower and time to change the sheets."

Just when I think the jackass can't sink any lower, he surprises me.

Since I can't erase her unfortunate sexual past, I do the only thing I know—I kiss the hell out of her.

"What else did you like about our first time together?" I ask when I break our embrace.

"You're the first guy I've seen naked since my ex."

"Good? Bad?"

"Fucking amazing!"

I can't help my wide smile.

"Conversely, you're the second guy who's seen me naked."

She's distracted enough for me to pick up the pace, pumping my cock, forcing her to match my rhythm.

"That goes without saying."

"Good? Bad?" She worries her bottom lip again.

"Fucking amazing!" I borrow her words.

She laughs.

"Any other firsts?" I ask.

"It was the first time I felt a guy's cum dripping down my body."

"Did you like it?"

"I did." She pauses. "A lot."

My hips swing back and forth as I fuck her fist.

"What I loved the most was watching you in the mirror. It was naughty."

"What did you see?" Speaking the words is a struggle.

"The helplessness and lack of control, the pain and pleasure. I didn't know men went through all those emotions."

"You did that to me," I tell her. "Just like you're doing now."

Our gaze drops to where my large hand covers her small one, as I pick up speed around my cock to a frantic pace.

"You know what I'm looking forward to?" I ask.

"What?"

"You, kneeling in front of me, lapping at my cock."

"I'm not sure I'd be very good at it."

"Don't worry, we'll do it together."

"Are you sure?"

"We're doing it together now, and I'm not complaining."

She answers with a shy smile.

"Okay."

"Good. Because I can't wait to look down at you sucking my cock until I come undone and explode in the back of your throat while watching with satisfaction as you struggle to swallow my river of cum."

"Your mouth is lethal."

"My desire for you is lethal."

Her thumb glides over my engorged cock head.

My cock jerks.

"When—" she shakes her head.

"When what?" I press.

"When do you—" she hesitates again. "Never mind."

"When do I fuck your pussy?" I finish her sentence.

"Maybe you don't want to."

"Oh, I want to fuck your pussy and shoot my cum inside you. Badly. But I love our little games. Don't you?"

"I do."

"When I fuck you, I'll be so desperate, I'll destroy you."

Her mouth drops open.

"You asked." I wink.

"Noted."

Look at that. She's eagerly awaiting my assault.

I've lost the brainpower to continue this conversation because it feels like all the blood in my body is pumping into my straining cock.

"I need you to work it harder." I loosen my grip. "Jerk me like you fucking mean it."

"Like this?"

"Harder."

"Harder?"

"Yes. Can you manage that while still playing with your pussy?"

To my chagrin, she got a little distracted.

"Yes, I can," she says.

She doesn't disappoint, jacking me faster and harder while taking care of her pussy.

She's so fucking wet, dripping all over the counter.

How I wish I could lick up all her juices going to waste.

"I want two fingers pumping inside your pussy," I order. "And I want to hear it."

Arianne's fingers dive in and out of her at the same feverish velocity as the hand pumping my cock. Her body is already pulsing with pleasure. So is mine.

I catch a glimpse of my heavy-lidded eyes in the mirror.

*Pure sin.*

The slick sound of her fingers working her pussy travels to my balls and the fuse ignites.

*Goddammit.*

"Faster, baby!"

Her urgency is intoxicating.

She slaps her pussy as if trying to contain the inevitable.

She pulls out her dripping fingers and lifts them to my mouth.

I lift my gaze to her hooded eyes.

There's nothing left of the strait-laced, buttoned-up woman who walked into my office less than a week ago. 'Absolute control' is no longer the only thing she seeks.

"I didn't even have to ask," I say.

"I like when you do that."

I grab hold of her wrist, stick my tongue out, and wipe her fingers clean, my eyes locked with hers.

My balls tug, reminding me they're loaded full of cum and busting for release.

"Not that I needed any more incentive, but that just made me harder," I tell her. "The problem is, I can't come."

She frowns. "Why not?"

I kiss the tip of her nose. "Because you get to come first."

"Oh."

"Get to it."

Her fingers press her clit as her hand rotates in a sinful circular motion.

Her little mewls let me know she's close.

Unable to contain myself, I pinch both her nipples hard.

She gasps and squeezes my cock so tight, it's hard to hold back.

Her finger skates over her clit as her other hand strokes me from balls to tip.

*Fuck!*

"Make it dirty for me," I tell her.

And she does.

Alternating between plunging her fingers in and out of her pussy and massaging her clit, she brings herself closer and closer. I press my hand over hers around my cock, controlling the movements of my hips.

"Yeah, that's it, baby. Faster."

"Dear God. It feels so, so good." Her hand is glistening with her dripping juices.

I grunt every time her other hand slides back up over the head of my meaty cock, eliciting the sweet hedonistic sound of being jacked off. She pumps me like crazy, and I'm blinded by my need for release.

"Oh, fuck, fuck, fuck." My eyes roll to the back of my head as my hands clamp around her tits.

"Oh, God," she says. Her hips gyrate back and forth against the granite counter. "Beckett, I need to come." Desperation coats her voice.

"You're going to come hard for me?"

"I—I—Oh—"

"I asked you a question."

"Yes—"

Her body jerks.

The pressure around my cock ceases before she lets go altogether.

Her head falls back and a long, shuddering moan escapes her lips, her slicked-up fingers pressed to her pussy, her ass cheeks wet with her juices.

*Fuck!*

The vibrations of her climax shoot straight to my balls and the fuse is done.

"Christ!"

Arianne slumps her spent body back against the mirror. "Come all over me, please, Beckett," she says in a ragged breath.

*Fuck. Me.*

I point my cock at her pussy and shoot my load, legs trembling as spurt after spurt erupts, marking her perfect pale skin with ribbons of hot cum.

"Holy Christ!"

"Holy Christ yes," she says.

She spreads my release all over her stomach, around her tits and finishes her kinky little tease by sticking her fingers inside her mouth and licking them clean. Her eyes never leave mine.

*Jesus.*

Arianne Buchanan is going to be the end of me.

# Chapter 31

## *Arianne*

Bang. Bang. Bang.
*What's that loud noise?*
I'm semi-conscious, no longer sleeping, but not quite awake.
*Bang. Bang. Bang.*
*Please. Stop.*
"Arianne!"
*Huh?*
*Bang. Bang. Bang.*
"Arianne! It's Beckett."
"Beckett?!"
I peel open my dry, sticky eyes.
*My head. Ouch.*
After several long seconds of panting through the pain, the agony subsides long enough for me to move.
I try to sit up, but the room is spinning.
*God, please make it stop.*
I try again.
I finally sit up on the bed, completely disoriented.

My clothes are sitting in a condemning puddle of mess on the floor.

*What the hell?*

I always hang-up my clothes. Without fail.

*Bang. Bang. Bang.*

The noise rattles my brain, jarring a flood of memories.

My muddled brain sparks to life, as I struggle to piece together the previous night.

*Oh, yeah. Thanks for nothing, Phoebe.*

*Bang. Bang. Bang.*

"Arianne! Are you in there? Are you hurt? Open up or I'll call the police."

*Shit.*

I push the sheet off my body and pull on a t-shirt as I waddle to the door.

*Dear God.*

My stomach feels like a sinking ship.

I grip the doorframe to avoid face planting, my step unstable.

"Arianne!"

"Coming!" My voice is so hoarse.

*Serves me right for throwing caution to the wind.*

When I open the door, blue-eyes squint at me, then they widen.

The sexy man standing before me takes me in, and chuckles.

"What's so funny?" *Am I slurring my words?*

"You," Beckett says. "Your morning hair is wild." Freaked out, I try to tame it, but I already know it's a losing battle. "And your t-shirt!" He points at my chest.

My eyes follow his finger.

*Great.*

"'*Where the hell is Prince Charming? That douchebag is severely late!*'" Beckett reads out loud.

"No one was supposed to see that," I say.

"Walt Disney fucked you over from the grave, huh?" He's still laughing.

I give him a onceover.

Of course, he has to look fucking hot.

So far, I've only seen him wearing pristine bespoke suits or a dangerously sexy black-on-black look. This is a departure... one I approve of. Beckett is wearing a fitted white t-shirt that exposes his full-sleeve of colorful tattoos.

*His forearms are so. . . defined.*

My eyes travel to his legs.

*His muscles are so thick.*

I'm sure his casual outfit cost a fortune. He's sporting fitted dark wash jeans and navy suede leather-trimmed sneakers with a bronze tag on the tongue that reads the name of an Italian designer.

*He has such impeccable taste and style.*

I have no doubt this man's mouthwatering body is a combination of great genes, a kickass personal trainer, and hours of dedication at the gym, but damn.

Our eyes lock, our gazes lingering on one another for several beats.

"You're done with your inspection?" he asks, a sly grin lifting the side of his mouth.

"You drove all the way here before heading to the office to wake me from my sleep, make fun of me, *and* give me attitude?"

"No."

"Why are you here, then?"

"Germany. Remember?"

I blink.

And blink.

*Huh?*

"We have a flight to catch."

"That's tomorrow—"

My eyes widen in horror, as a panic attack threatens.

"Oh my God! Oh my God! Oh my God! Did I oversleep?! What time is it? I'm so sorry."

"Calm down. It's okay," Beckett says. "I got here early. I thought we could enjoy a nice breakfast at one of my favorite eateries before heading to the airport, but judging by the look of things, we'll be cutting it short."

"Shit, shit, shit." *How did I allow this to happen?*

"I tried to call you, but you didn't answer," Beckett says.

I'm dumbfounded.

"I tried numerous times."

*I must've been passed out cold not to hear my phone ring. And why didn't my alarm wake me?*

"This is so unlike me," I say. "I'm always early. Without fail. I can't believe we're going to miss our flight because I can't hold my liquor."

Beckett steps inside my apartment and closes the door. He places his hands on my shoulders.

"It's a private jet. The plane leaves when I say so. I can always get the pilot to schedule a later takeoff time, if needs be."

"Still." I shake my head. *This is so embarrassing.* "I blame Phoebe and Oscar for forcing me to party like there's no tomorrow. Here we are *tomorrow*, and I'm not so sure it was a great idea. I also blame the overflowing, expensive champagne and the hours of feverish salsa dancing—"

"Who was your dance partner?"

I cock an eyebrow at his slicing tone. "Jealous?"

"It depends who you were dancing with. I might have to rearrange someone's face."

"I was with my bestie."

He stares at me long and hard.

"I swear. I'm telling you the truth. I really was with her."

"No guys?"

"Just her boyfriend."

He cocks a brow. "No one else?"

I roll my eyes, but secretly I'm tickled pink. "Beckett, we don't have time for this. I'm a hot mess and it feels like there's a construction crew jackhammering in my head." I bring a hand to my temple.

"Glad to hear you had fun and you weren't—" he doesn't finish his sentence. Instead, he settles for, "It sounds like you had fun."

*Huh? That didn't make any sense.*

"That's not what you were going to say."

"Never mind," he says.

There's something about the way he's studying me. I just can't put my finger on it. Maybe it's nothing, but it sure feels like something.

*Your system is soaked in booze. So is your brain.*

My mind is still fuzzy and my stomach is seesawing as if I was on a yacht in the middle of a raging storm, so I'm not thinking clearly.

"My night of fun and partying is no excuse for my unprofessionalism," I say.

"Do you still have to pack?"

"God, no. I packed on Sunday. I just have a few items to stuff in my carry-on."

His eyes widened. "You packed three days in advance?!"

"Always."

"I always pack last-minute. Case in point, I packed a new set of clothes at one o'clock in the morning when I got back from Nashville. Same when I flew out first thing yesterday morning for the day-long business trip."

"Don't let the new look fool you. I'm still a control freak."

"Noted." He chuckles. "How long will it take you to get ready?"

"A quick shower, hair and makeup, and then it's a question of jumping into an outfit. Twenty minutes?"

"I'll be outside in the car."

"You don't want to stay?" I can't hide my disappointment.

"I'm going to do a quick pit stop. I'll be back before you know it."

"Okay."

He drops a soft kiss against my forehead.

*I love it when he does that.*

I close my eyes, relishing the contact and his closeness. The touch of his lips heats me from head to toe after going without since Monday. I can't believe how much I've missed him.

"If we had more time..."—his fingers pull at the hem of my t-shirt—"I'd want to know if you sleep with or without panties."

Beckett slips a finger between my pussy lips, and I fold over.

"You wild child. You sleep commando." Amusement coats Beckett's voice.

*I never did until you corrupted me that night in my bathroom.*

"Too bad I can't do anything about it."

*Can you come from just a touch?*

Because I swear, I just did.

"Thank you," I tell the chauffeur as he reaches for my luggage and drops it in the trunk.

"My pleasure," he says.

He opens the door behind the driver's seat.

"Thank you." I slide into the car.

My attention is quickly grabbed by Beckett.

He's sporting a wide grin and holding up two large jugs with handles. I remove my big designer diva sunglasses and furrow my eyebrows before meeting his gaze.

I freeze.

*Holy magnificence!*

I've never seen Beckett's eyes under the sunlight before. His eyes are arresting. As blue as the ocean. As mesmerizing, too.

*Wow. Of all the pantie-melting hunks walking the planet, Beckett Christensen is the sexiest man ever.*

I point at the jugs. "Breakfast?"

"So much more than breakfast," he says. "These are life-savers. A Love Your Liver smoothie to start." He lifts the glass jug holding a green liquid to eye level. "And a Post-Party Pick-Me-Up smoothie because its creamy, coconutty sweetness, goes down easy and coats your stomach." He lifts the pink one.

*Exactly what the doctor ordered!*

"That's so thoughtful of you," I say.

"Been there. Done that. I have the t-shirt, poster, Mp3 download, CD, *and* vinyl LP."

I laugh.

"In other words, I knew where to go to get you a fix," he says. "Tonics + Elixirs is the place to score much-needed liquid medicine food for late-night partiers."

"You're the sweetest."

"I aim to please." He hands me the green smoothie.

"Thank you," I say. When the car starts to move, my queasy stomach churns.

*Oh, God.*

I place a hand against it, willing it to settle. It's to no avail.

*No more champagne. Ever.*

"You okay?" The concern in his eyes his touching.

"Yes, thank you for asking."

"The champagne hit you harder than expected?"

"Yes. I'm sure I'll be fine with a few sips of this." I lift the smoothie. "What about you?" I ask before latching my lips around the straw.

*Wow! This tastes way better than it looks.*

"There'll be plenty to eat during the flight, but since I'm already starved even after a blueberry and peanut butter smoothie, we'll make a pit stop on the way as we head to Van Nuys Airport."

"Okay."

"You clean up nice, kiddo," he says, leaning forward and dropping a kiss against my exposed shoulders.

I giggle at the unexpected tickle of his lips against my skin.

"This might come as a shock, but usually, I travel in a suit."

He pulls back. "No shit." His huge grin lets me know he's making fun of me.

"I always like to arrive at my destination ready"

"What if you're going away for a fun time?"

"I tend to wear something..." I hesitate. "A lot more put together than this." I wave a finger at my body.

"What you're wearing *is* put together. Nicely, too."

"A dress and sandals aren't my calling card," I say. "Same with this." I point at my head.

As the minutes were ticking by and the embarrassment over my tardiness was weighing heavy on me, I panicked and grabbed an off-shoulder navy-blue maxi dress. It has a pretty ruffle running at the front and practical pockets. I paired it with low wedge silver sandals. I bunched up my wet hair in a bun at the top of my head, gave myself a two-minute face and I was out the door.

"Is this Andrea's doing?" he asks.

I shake my head. "Between being rushed and being a little shaky on my feet from last night's drinking, I didn't think I would be steady enough to slip into a pair of pants or jeans."

Beckett laughs.

"The dress looks amazing on you. And it's easy access for me." He drops another kiss on my shoulder.

"Are you going to kiss my shoulders the whole flight to Germany?"

*Not that I'd object.*

"It's also easy access for other things." His eyes drop to my lap.

A heated blush creeps up my cheeks.

# Chapter 32

## *Beckett*

When we boarded, Arianne was chatting up a storm while leafing through a few travel magazines. Soon after taking off, she crashed. I didn't expect to get a lot done during the flight, but since she was out, I put my time to good use.

I unfolded the seat tray from the armrest, pulled out my laptop and went to work. I was in the zone when a heavy weight landed on my arm. Arianne seems to prefer my shoulder to the pillow the flight attendant brought her. I tucked the pillow under her head, three times, but she's now curled on her side, hugging my bicep like a koala bear. This is the closest I've ever been to sleeping next to a woman.

Because of her closeness and the lovely floral scent of her perfume, I've been sporting a raging hard-on I can't do anything about other than curse under my breath. Now, I need to use the bathroom. Badly.

I brush her hair from her cheek. She untied it earlier, letting it cascade around her beautiful face.

I kiss the top of her head.

She moans and clings a little harder to my arm.

My eyes move to her phone still charging in the power outlet. I pull up the article that caught my attention on the flight back from Nashville last night on my laptop and re-read the over-the-top headline.

*I doubt this is a coincidence.*

Arianne startles awake. "Oh, God, my bladder is screaming at me."

I laugh. "You go first."

She frowns. "What do you mean?"

"I've been dying to go for a while, but Sleeping Beauty needed her sleep!" I tap the tip of her nose.

"Sorry."

"Don't be. Now, go!"

She rushes to the rear of the jet.

She's back as quickly as she disappeared.

I close my laptop, get up and run to the bathroom.

I take care of business and return by her side.

I slide into my seat. "Are you hungry?"

"Starving," she says.

"Me too."

I call the flight attendant.

In no time, she delivers our food and drinks.

Arianne and I dig in.

It doesn't take long for us to polish off our delicious meal.

"My phone must be charged by now," Arianne says, grabbing it. "God, we've only been in the air for three hours?"

"Nine more to go!"

"Maybe I should follow your example and get some work done instead of being lazy."

"You needed it."

"Henceforth, I'll avoid expensive champagne that goes down way too smoothly on a work night. Goodbye, Dom

Perignon," she says, resting the back of her hand against her forehead. It's a little dramatic.

"You were drinking Dom?" I ask. "You have great taste."

"Phoebe insisted we had a lot to celebrate. Since Oscar buys the stuff at cost, she splurged. I drank."

"Don't sweat it."

"It feels wrong, though," she says.

"Well, I thoroughly enjoyed the experience."

She furrows her eyebrows. "What do you mean? You weren't even there."

"Thanks to Dom Perignon, I was able to see a very different side of you this morning."

"I'll never be able to live that one down, will I?"

"It's unlikely. You looked so vulnerable. So unhinged. The only other time I've seen you let go of control is right before you scream out my name."

She clears her throat, her eyes shifting from left to right to see if the flight attendant is in earshot.

"Okay," she says, fanning herself. "Well..." she clears her throat again. "I'm going to pretend you never said that by losing myself in work."

"It's our little secret!" I wink.

Her cheeks redden.

"You've been spending a lot of time with Flora lately," I say, changing the subject.

"We've had three meetings so far and I've been brainstorming. I want to go over the proposal I'm putting together for an idea that's been bouncing around in my head."

"I can't wait to see what you come up with," I say.

"The trip to Germany will only solidify the idea or kill it altogether."

"I have no doubt we're going to get a lot out of this business trip."

"Leave it to Easton for scoring something this monumental."

I nod. "I agree."

"Before I jump into the proposal, I want to check my messages. I'm sure Phoebe must be worried sick," she says, connecting to WiFi.

"Sounds good." I open my laptop and close the article I was reading before Arianne sees it.

"Whoa!"

My head whips in her direction. "What is it?"

"My mom sent me like ten text messages." Her eyes are glued to her screen. "So did Phoebe. What's going on?"

Her jaw drops.

*I guess she just found out.*

"What a publicity whore." Arianne mutters that under her breath.

"Chance and Mariah?" I ask.

Her head jerks back. "What?"

"I read about it last night." I reopen the tab I just closed and angle my laptop so she can see my screen.

She closes her eyes, shakes her head, and lets out a heavy sigh.

"*FAIRYTALE CASTLE WEDDING FOR CHANCE TABORAS AND MARIAH GOLIGHTLY!*'" She reads the headline out loud before letting out a sarcastic laugh.

She doesn't read the rest of the article that goes into details on how Chance Taboras' fiancée, Mariah Mandoline Golightly, hints at an extravagant royal-like wedding at the Biltmore House—a French Renaissance-inspired castle in Asheville, North Carolina. They're expecting a whopping five hundred guests.

"How did you know?" Arianne asks in a low voice.

"I remembered your reaction on your second day when I

asked you out for dinner. You said something along the lines of, *office romances turn into disasters*. Since Easton had mentioned you were instrumental in shaping Glach Tech into the industry giant it is today, and you made it clear your cousin was a back-stabber, I put two and two together. I confirmed by Googling your name and Chance's. I saw a lot of photos of you together, but none hinted at a relationship. Still, I felt strongly about my hunch."

"Chance frowns upon PDA. No public display of affection for the CEO."

"I see."

"I should say that was his motto *before* Mariah came along. How quickly people change." The sarcasm doesn't go unnoticed.

"Earlier, you mentioned you drank too much last night. At first, I thought it might've been because you were upset—"

"I'm glad I didn't find out last night. It would've ruined my night with my best friend." She lets out a frustrated grunt. "No matter how far I run, it seems I just can't get those two idiots out of my life."

"You didn't want to have dinner with me because of your past relationship with Chance?"

"Yes," she says.

"I'm not him."

"I know. I'm sorry if I put you in the same category."

"Was it serious between you two?"

"We were dating and living together. Everyone in the company knew it, but we were discreet."

I nod my understanding.

"Chance and I were good together, especially when it came to business," she says. "What we shared was nothing like a Fourth of July firework show, but at the time, I thought those types of relationship were like a match—they ignite fast and die as fast. Honestly, I always thought passion was overrated—"

"You still feel that way?"

She shakes her head. "My parents love each other, but it's because they stuck it out. I wouldn't call what they have, passion. It's more like deep loyalty. From what I witnessed last night, Phoebe, on the other hand, has passion. My relationship with Chance was comfortable. Steady. Predictable. Reliable—"

"That sounds like the top-rated SUV of the year."

She attempts a small smile.

"Maybe that's why he chose Mariah." Sadness pulls down the sides of her mouth. "This isn't the first time she stole one of my boyfriends. She made it her mission. I was the brunt of the Golightly witches' jokes—I was *just* a nerd. What could I offer a guy? Mariah was a stunning head-turner so, of course, men would choose her over me. That snarky attitude changed really quickly when Mariah sank her claws into her oldest sister's husband."

"What a cunt."

"Yeah. Mariah seduced her older sister's husband as she was struggling to get pregnant. Mirai was frustrated and depressed she couldn't have a baby. Her husband was getting irritated and annoyed with the regimented sex and lack of spontaneity. Mariah offered an outlet."

"Mariah has no shame."

"None whatsoever," Arianne says. "Mirai promptly divorced Steve and ostracized her baby sister."

"What happened to her is horrible."

"Yes and no," Arianne says. "Mirai hooked up with a high school crush not long after her divorce was final. He was also divorced. Fast forward a year and they're expecting twins any day now. They're planning on getting married next year when the twins turn one."

"Great news, but that doesn't justify Mariah's callous actions or her selfishness."

"Absolutely not," Arianne says. "Mind you, all three Golightly sisters have always used their very generous *assets* to get what they want, but Mariah takes it to another level. When she turned sixteen, it's like her breast size quintupled—no joke —and the size of her tops shrunk proportionately. A lot of guys only cared about getting their hands on her breasts. She was happy to oblige. She even dated a wealthy guy in his late sixties —she was twenty-one at the time—and he was too eager to pay for a long list of cosmetic enhancements, including her ass."

"Butt implants?"

"Yup. She went for the reality TV star size—this monstrous bubble butt. Between her enormous breasts and giant ass, you can't miss her when she walks into a room... especially because she wears skin-tight clothing."

"How did Chance and Mariah meet? I thought you left Philly for New York and then Silicon Valley to escape the Golightly sisters?"

"After a few acting lessons and small parts in local productions in Philly, Mariah moved to New York. I was already in California by then. Thank God. She got a few parts, but nothing noteworthy or capable of sustaining her. Discouraged, she set her sights on Hollywood. While she was working on the set as an extra on an episode of a popular TV series, another wannabe actress told her porn paid her bills and afforded her the luxuries she couldn't get with her lackluster acting parts. Mariah jumped on the bandwagon."

"How did that work out for her?"

"She never made a movie."

"That's a shame." My words drip with sarcasm.

Arianne laughs.

"What happened?" I ask.

"She chickened out because her first casting was a girl-on-girl scene, followed by one with four guys."

"That's hardcore."

"It sent her running," Arianne says. "At the time, Mom was proud of my accomplishments, and she might've rubbed Aunt Moira's face in it. My aunt must've been the one who tipped off her daughter that Chance and I were dating and living together. That's how she knew where I worked. Imagine my surprise when I returned from a business trip to Japan to find Mariah in Chance's house, lounging in a skimpy negligee on the couch, channel surfing, while eating popcorn at five in the afternoon."

"Didn't he know how you felt about your cousin?"

"He did."

"In that case, why didn't he discuss things with you before inviting her to stay with you guys?"

"Mariah is manipulative. She came knocking at his door with a sob story and crocodile tears. She had no money and nowhere else to go. Chance caved in—"

"Whose side was he on?"

"Mine until he met Mariah," she says.

"I get the part about Chance feeling sorry for her, but why didn't you kick her out on her surgically enhanced ass soon after she arrived?"

"I tried, but Chance fell for her act," she says. "I didn't want to come across like a heartless bitch, so I gave Mariah three months. That decision started the demise of my relationship. After a month of Mariah living with us, I lost it. I got into a fight with her because she would constantly walk around the house in skimpy form-fitted dresses, without any underwear on. Her protruding nipples were impossible to miss. Same for her butt crack. She was quick to tell me my insecurities clouded my judgment."

"Did you bring it up with Chance?"

"Phoebe suggested a different approach. She pushed me to ask Mariah to go away for a weekend so I could spend a few romantic days rekindling things with Chance to solidify our relationship. To my surprise, my cousin agreed."

"She gave you space?"

"She did... just because she was planning to drop a bomb on me."

"What kind of bomb?"

"A nuclear one." She hitches a breath. "The romantic evening was perfect. Chance and I were reconnecting. I was filled with hope. So much so, I planned on telling Mariah she had to move out by the end of the upcoming week. Her presence was undesired from day one and I was unwilling to accept any of her lame excuses. As Chance and I were finishing dessert, she waltzed in—of course, my boyfriend gave her an extra key—"

"Your ex is an absolute moron."

"He was under her spell."

"No! He was an absolute moron."

She nods, but I wonder if she's convinced.

"Mariah came strutting to the table where we were sitting, plopped her ass on a chair and a plastic bag on the table. She then waited, her eyes bouncing from mine to Chance's. He turned as white as a ghost. All the blood drained from his face. She grinned like a hyena before an attack. When I mustered the courage to ask what was in the bag, Mariah suggested I see for myself. Chance reached for the bag first, but I reacted quickly. The bag ripped and boxes of pregnancy tests came flying out."

"Shit."

"Exactly! Mariah looked at my boyfriend and asked him if he wanted to tell me or if she should. I told them to spare me the bullshit explanation. Chance had the gall to suggest a *Sister Wives* living arrangement—we'd each get him for one week and we'd all be living under the same roof. It was with herculean effort I didn't spit in his face or pour scalding boiling water over his cock."

I shake my head.

"Mariah was open to the idea." Her words are dripping with disgust.

"Un-fucking-believable."

"I almost slapped her."

"I don't know how you held back."

"I decided to walk away before things turned ugly," she says. "As Chance and Mariah were arguing in the dining room over her little ruse, I packed as much as I could in suitcases and called a cab. Since I had shattered his *Sister Wives* dreams, Chance told me not to let the door hit my ass on the way out."

"He's as disturbed as she is," I say. "How long ago did that happen?"

"Two years ago." There's fire in her eyes. "Going to Europe was a way of distancing myself from their venom."

"Is that why they're getting married? Because of the baby?"

Her features go from dark to thunderous. "Mariah was never pregnant. It was part of her master plan to break up our relationship. She made sure to text me to let me know."

"And Chance is still with her?"

"She has a way of weaving herself into your life."

"Chance didn't deserve you, Arianne."

"Thanks for saying that, Beckett. The betrayal stung like vinegar on an open wound, but it was nothing compared to what I was about to find out."

"There's more?"

She nods. "Chance cheated on me and then he fucked me over."

"How?"

"I worked tirelessly to put his company on the map. Those crowdfunding campaigns were my doing. He couldn't even spell the word until I put together a proposal. I came up with the ideas. I managed the campaigns. I rallied the troops within his organization. I trained them. I amassed the money. On top of that, I took care of all his marketing and oversaw the product development team. He had someone in place, but the guy was useless. Just like the Apollo Project, I had my eye on the prize—make his company attractive to a potential buyer. He was generating six million dollars in sales when I started. By the time Mariah fucked everything up, his company was churning out eighty million dollars a year in sales."

I whistle, nodding my head. "That's impressive."

"I thought so," she says. "So did he for a long time. But then, just like that!" She snaps her fingers. "He did a turnabout. Chance always promised he'd take care of me once he went public or when he got bought out—"

"Please don't tell me he didn't keep his word."

"I believed him." His betrayal still leaves a bitter taste in my mouth. "Phoebe wasn't as trustworthy. She demanded I get his promises on paper. I asked him numerous times, but I was afraid to push too hard."

"Why?"

"If you don't have faith in the person you're with, you have nothing," she says.

"I see your point, but when it comes to dollars and cents, sometimes, loyalty goes out the door when there are multiple zeros behind numbers."

"Are you speaking from experience?" She arches her eyebrows.

"I am. It's a lesson my father instilled in my brother and me, but that still didn't prevent us from getting blindsided by an unscrupulous manager. He stole millions from our band. My cousin Jagger had to step in after we fired his ass. Jagger also hired a team of ruthless lawyers who went after the asshole."

"Did they recoup the money?"

"He'd burned through a lot of it, but lucky for us he had assets—expensive cars, houses, boats, and collectors items. We didn't get back all the money he stole, but we got a lot back and, more importantly, his ass is rotting in jail."

"At least you got vindicated."

"I couldn't believe someone we trusted would pull the wool over our eyes," I say. "After that incident, I was a lot more careful of the fine print on a contract. When Rhys and I decided to go into business together and created SCORE, I made sure we had a solid contract. Even though he was walking into the partnership with little financial backing, his father created our golden ticket. A contract ensured our partnership would always be on equal footing."

"Rhys is lucky you're so upstanding," she says. "I wasn't as lucky. I learned the hard way."

"You got nothing?"

"Not a cent."

"Chance is a lowlife."

"I'll never be able to know for sure, but I'm certain Mariah influenced him—"

"I disagree, Arianne."

She frowns.

"The guy never had the balls to put your agreement in writing. Someone pulling those annual sales has an army of lawyers working for him. How complicated can it be to draft a contract since he knew full well without you, he would never have half the success he had?"

Sadness morphs her beautiful features.

"How long were you together?" I ask.

"I was working at Glach Tech for five years and we were together for four of those years."

"You have your answer," I say. "He was stringing you along. Maybe Mariah was the catalyst, but he had devious intentions well before your cousin showed up at his door. He planned on screwing you over from the get-go."

"I should've listened to my parents and Phoebe. He made millions because of me and I have nothing to show for it. I didn't expect he'd give me half of his profits, but you don't go from six million to eighty million by chance. Phoebe suggested I contact a lawyer. I did. And I told Chance I would come after him. He promised he'd bury me in legal papers and it would cost me far more than I had. I backed off."

"Don't let these photos upset you." I point to my screen. "Those two are a match made in hell. No matter how lavish the wedding, it will never make up for their downright appalling personalities."

She looks at me funny.

"What?" I ask.

She tells me about Mariah's recent trip to Philadelphia, about her new publicist and how her cousin freaked the hell out over the selfies we took with Cesar and Diana. The photos of us dancing salsa didn't go down very well either.

"Mom is certain the royal wedding news is to trump the fact I was trending so much on social media, it drowned the news of her engagement," Arianne says. "You and I both know we were having fun that night, but to the outside world, those photos ignited *a lot* of interest and rumors—"

"Miss Holy Chic and the Bad Boy CEO!"

She shakes her head. "You're more than that, Beckett, and you know it. Mariah is marrying a multimillionaire. Whoopty ding-dong!" She rolls her eyes. "I'm hanging out with a badass rock star and the CEO of a company pulling several billion dollars in sales and poised to double, if not triple that. Furthermore, said CEO is pretty easy on the eye. Chance isn't ugly, but it's unlikely women will ever drop their panties when he walks into a room. And he'll never grace multiple covers of men's fashion, business, or music magazines. And let's talk about those smoking hot calendars the Dennison brothers produce you've been featured in several times. Oof!" She fans herself. "Pigs will fly before that ever happens to my ex."

I almost blush. Almost.

"Chance lacks your swagger, charisma, cocksureness and perfect white teeth." I can't help my smile. "Chance is a joker..." Her eyes bore into mine. "While you, Beckett, you're a king."

*Your king.*

# Chapter 33

## *Arianne*

After getting the Chance-slash-Mariah mess off my chest, I had great expectations for the rest of the flight but I kept dozing off. I fought it as much as I could, but eventually, I gave in. My body was in desperate need of rest. Too much boozing and too much wild partying will do that to a girl who tends to color within the lines.

Speaking of fucking mess, I didn't expect to open up like that. Other than my mom and Phoebe, no one knows of my humiliating story. I never told Easton why I hightailed it out of Silicon Valley in such a rush, but the day Chance's company got bought out for a ridiculous amount, Easton sent me a short text message that spoke volumes.

> Easton: The asshole fucked you over, didn't he?

I responded with a simple yes.

Easton promised he'd back me up financially to go after what was rightfully mine. I passed, to his chagrin. Fighting Chance was only going to end up killing me inside. The idea of seeing him and Mariah together as a couple was too nauseating. I pray karma will be a bitch when it comes to them.

Arriving in Europe on a private jet is different from arriving on a commercial flight, even when flying business class. The luxury treatment of traveling with a billionaire extends to the mode of transportation when we land—the chauffeured Bentley is a classy touch.

The short ride from the Hannover-Langenhagen Airport into Wedemark is dedicated to soaking up the German countryside. Even though I lived on this continent for two years, I never made it to Germany. Now, I wonder why.

On the flight over, Beckett mentioned Valerie tried to get us a room in one of the handful of hotels, but since we're last minute, we lucked out. At least, she was able to book us rooms in a quaint inn.

"*Guten tag und herzlich willkommen.* Good afternoon and welcome to the Lindelglück Gasthaus," a smiling blue-eyed blonde with noticeable silver streaks says.

"*Guten tag und herzlich willkommen,*" Beckett says and I follow suit.

"You speak German?!" the woman says.

"Oh, God, no," Beckett tells her. "So far, those are the only words I've mastered."

"Same here," I say.

"We had a crash course on the flight over here," Beckett says. "Thanks for not making fun of us, even if we butchered your language."

The woman laughs.

"I speak English. So, we are okay," she says with a pronounced accent. "My name is Astrid, and you are?"

"Beckett Christensen and this is—"

"*Herzliche Glückwünsche!* Congratulations on your

wedding! We have the nuptial suite ready for you. You're going to love it."

*All cohesive thought comes to a screeching halt.*

"The nuptial suite?" Beckett asks.

"Yes," Astrid says. "Love... so exciting and new!" She clasps her hands in prayer under her chin and sighs dramatically. "I still remember when I married my Günter—my prince—at twenty-three. Thirty wonderful years later... we're still in love." Another long sigh.

She's so busy reliving her life story, she's oblivious to the way Beckett is staring at her in disbelief. I'm sure I'm sporting the same shocked expression on my face.

She leans forward, a proud smile stretching her lips. "Do you want to know the secret to a long marriage?" Beckett and I are still speechless when she continues. "Tattoos," Astrid says as her eyes lower to Beckett's colorful forearms. "Husband and wife tattoos, to be precise. He has my name etched on his chest. I have his on my..."

When Astrid slaps her very plump ass, both Beckett and I flinch in surprise.

"I have Astrid + Günter on the right cheek." *Slap!* "And *Für Immer* on the left." *Slap!* "That translates to Forever in English. My husband loves it... especially when the love making happens." She giggles.

*TMI.*

"He has Forever tattooed here!" She points to her hipbone. "When I'm giving him... you know..." She purses her lips. "I can see it."

We're just passing through town. That is way more than we need to know about Astrid and Günter. Seriously, on a scale from one to ten of overshare, that was a solid three thousand.

Beckett and I are still rooted in silence.

"If you want, I can direct you to the shop. *Gestempelt* is close by. It means stamped."

*Whoa, lady!*

*You might want to start with must-see local landmarks first.*

"I'm sorry, Astrid, but we have a problem." Beckett finds his voice.

I'm still searching for mine.

"A problem?" she asks.

"Yes," Beckett says. "As in, you might've made a mistake."

"At the Lindelglück Gasthaus, we do not make mistakes!" She shakes her head with a small smile. "We only give top service!"

I think Beckett offended her.

"Sorry to burst your bubble, but in this case, there's a mistake," Beckett says.

"Burst my butt hole?" Astrid's eyes widen with indignation. "No, no, no. I am married. And happy. I told you about the tattoos." She adjusts her glasses.

Something got lost in translation.

"It is not good for you to say that in front of your new wife. Your marriage will not last, sir," she says, her drawn-on eyebrows furrowing, and her finger wagging in disapproval. "Yes, I am very sexy for my age." She caresses the sides of her body from her ample bosom to her wide hips. "But your offer is not right." She shakes her head vigorously. "You, sir, will not burst my butt hole. Günter will not like that."

I can't keep it together.

Laughter erupts from me.

I turn around so Astrid doesn't see me.

My whole body shakes and tears stream down my face.

Once I find my composure, I turn around.

"I said burst your *bubble*—Forget it!" Beckett waves it off.

"What you need to focus on, Astrid, is the fact there's been a mistake."

To contain another outburst, I bite against my lower lip because who knows what else will get lost in translation.

"No, no, no!" Astrid shakes her head. "No mistake."

Beckett lets out a frustrated sigh.

He pinches the bridge of his nose before speaking again. "Astrid, perhaps you might want to double check the reservation. I'm *Beckett Christensen* and this is *Arianne Buchanan*. We're here on a two-day business trip and we should have *two* separate rooms reserved."

"You're not here on your honeymoon?" she asks.

"No," Beckett says.

"Ah. You are not married to her?"

"No!" Beckett's voice rises.

"Ah!" Astrid nods. "You are sure?"

"If I were married to Arianne, I'd remember," Beckett tells her.

And why am I seeing images of me walking down the aisle in a beautiful flowy princess-like white dress to the soft sound of Pachelbel's Canon in D to a waiting dashing Beckett Christensen clad in a bespoke tuxedo? I can even hear the church bells. *'Dearly beloved, we are gathered here today, in the presence of God and these witnesses, to join in matrimony—'*

*Stop it, girl!*

*You're losing it!*

"Ah." Astrid's go-to word pulls me out of my reverie. She types like a mad woman on her keyboard. "Hmmm..." She's not as certain as she was a few minutes ago. "You are not Berg Christiansen and Arielle Bohannon-Christiansen?"

"I'm afraid you have us confused," Beckett says.

"Ah." I'm starting to understand when she says that, it's a

precursor to bad news. Astrid frowns before typing on her computer some more. She's sweating bullets.

"The Lindelglück Gasthaus *does* make mistakes after all," Beckett says.

Astrid glances up, smoothes her hair, gathers the front of her blouse, and fans herself as if the temperature in the room is unbearable.

She goes back to her research, her fingers flying on the keyboard.

It's pretty comical to watch.

"We're not in your system?" Beckett asks.

She types more feverishly.

"Ah." *Bad news is coming.* "It is a very busy time of year here with the very popular annual *Bier und Käse Fest*."

"What's that?" I ask.

"The beer and cheese pairing festival. People come from all over the country," she tells me.

"What does that mean for us?" Beckett asks.

"This is not the big city, sir," she says. "I see here you have a last-minute reservation."

"So?" Beckett says.

"We have you as coming tomorrow," Astrid says.

"That's not possible," Beckett says. "My executive assistant is on top of things. Are you saying we have a gala in a few hours and nowhere to shower or change?"

"We will accommodate you, sir," Astrid says. "It is just that... we only have three rooms left. The nuptial suite—"

"We're not married!"

"Yes, yes, sir!" Astrid nods. "The only accommodation we have left is the *Familienhöhle*."

I knit my eyebrows. "The what?"

"The *Familienhöhle* offers a stunning view of the area—"

"What's the catch?" Beckett cuts to the chase.

Astrid frowns her confusion.

"You're hiding something. What exactly is the *Familienhöhle?*"

"We are talking about two rooms—"

"We'll take them!" Beckett says.

"I must warn you, sir, the *Familienhöhle* only offers partial privacy and not everyone adjusts to the ceiling slant."

*That was German to me.*

"Is that all you have left other than the nuptial suite?" Beckett asks.

"Yes."

"Then we don't have any other choice, Astrid," Beckett puts an end to the most awkward check-in of my life.

"Hey, roomie," Beckett says.

"Hey, you."

Neither of us moves, our eyes fixed on one another from across the Jack and Jill bathroom.

Beckett and I are sharing a large space split into two by a very large enclosed connecting bathroom. The *Familienhöhle*, located in the attic of the inn, is top choice amongst parents traveling with teenagers, hence the partial privacy Astrid alluded to. The slanted roof may be whimsical and picturesque from the outside, but walking around hunched over isn't all that charming.

*I don't know how the tall, gorgeous man standing across from me will manage.*

Unable to contain myself, my gaze wanders down Beckett's sculpted torso without an ounce of shame until it rests on the white towel wrapped around his waist. It's set low enough to offer a peek of his lip-smacking V.

Even his feet are sexy.

Beckett's half naked body is on full, carnal display. My pussy muscles clench in appreciation.

Every part of me yearns.

When I lift my gaze to his again, his lips pull up into a knowing smile, before he returns the favor. He traces his eyes up and down the length of my body, his gaze so searing, it's as real as a caress against my skin—softly trailing down my neck, over my chest, down my stomach, my legs and up again until he stops right between my thighs.

I bite off a moan.

Just like him, a white towel wrapped around my chest acts as a shield.

"Figures we'd meet here," he says.

"Seems like we have a thing for bathrooms."

We laugh.

"How's your side of the *Familienhöhle*?" I ask.

"A bit small, but it'll do. What about you?"

"Same," I tell him.

Beckett pushes off the doorframe he's leaning against and crosses the bathroom in a few short steps.

The sexual tension between us is palpable.

"Now, Mr. Christensen behave, or else we'll be late."

"I keep telling myself that, Miss Buchanan, but looking at you..." His burning gaze travels across my body once more. "I wouldn't mind being late."

My heart pounds hard against my ribcage.

"Beckett."

"I'll be good. For now."

"Do you want to use the shower first?" I ask.

Our living arrangement makes it that much harder to behave.

"Who says we can't take one together?" he says, his gaze dark and feral.

He cups my face in his hands, pinning me in place.

"I haven't kissed you in two days." He doesn't give me a chance to respond. He leans down and takes ownership of my mouth.

I lose track of everything.

I can't even remember which continent I'm on.

The kiss is hard, insistent, forceful.

I kiss him back with as much fervor, my arms wrapping around his neck. He sucks my lower lip into his mouth, bites down just hard enough to force a surprised gasp out of me. I part my lips so our tongues tangle together in a wild fiery dance.

I could kiss this man all day, every day.

If I were willing to be honest with myself, I'd admit I want our illicit encounters to become more. But there's no point in hoping for a notorious bad boy bachelor to change his ways for a girl like me.

"Just a quick shower," Beckett says, releasing my mouth.

I should protest, but my mind is too busy relishing his closeness.

He trails his tongue along my neck, his hands sliding down my back, groping my ass, causing my pussy to clench. I arch my hips, eagerly rubbing my tummy against the hard length of his massive cock.

*God, I'm soaking wet.*

A delicious pulsating twinge shoots from my bellybutton straight down to my clit. I go at it like a bitch in heat. The sensation is pure bliss.

*I need this.*

"Weren't you the one telling me to behave a minute ago?" His voice is as low as gravel, as smoky as the finest whiskey.

Without warning, he yanks the towel from around his waist and tosses it to the floor.

Mine is next.

Instinctively, I bring my hands to my breasts to cover them.

"I've enjoyed it all before," he tells me. "Come on." He's already pulling me by the hand.

An assertive man is a huge turn on.

"By taking a shower together, we're being earth-conscious and eco-friendly. Imagine all the water we'll conserve," he says.

I giggle like a silly girl.

"Not to mention, I can do a better job than you can washing your back."

"Do I get to wash your back?" I ask.

"Baby, you can wash any part of me you want... with a sponge or your tongue. I'm easy."

*Sold!*

# Chapter 34

## *Beckett*

"Knock, knock!" I rap my knuckles against the bathroom door on Arianne's side.

"Come in!"

There's no way in hell I would've been able to ask Valerie to book connecting rooms without waving a red flag. Astrid's mistake is a godsend.

I enter the room and freeze.

*Holy shit, she's gorgeous!*

I take her in.

She does the same.

"My God, you're hot enough to get any woman pregnant on sight," she says, almost in a daze.

"I didn't know I had such superpowers," I tell her.

Her eyes widen in horror. Her cheeks flame up, matching the same vibrant color as her pretty dress.

"That came flying out of my mouth without my permission." She closes her eyes and shakes her head. "This is so embarrassing," she says. "I blame my overshare on how well you wear a tuxedo."

I approach her.

"If we're exchanging compliments..." I give her a salacious onceover. "Without seeing any of the women attending the gala, I already know I'll be the envy of every man there."

She brushes a fictitious hair behind her ear.

"Thank you," she says. "I wasn't sure if I should've selected something a lot more formal given the expected guests."

"Is Andrea responsible for the look?"

"Yes. I had picked a handful of more conservative dresses, but she pushed me to live on the edge. I hope it's not too much. Or not enough." The tremor of nervousness in her voice is audible.

I place my hands on her shoulders. "Stop stressing. You look perfect. You could be wearing a purple velour tracksuit or overalls and you'd still be hot."

"That's a little extreme," she says. "I'd never make such a fashion faux pas. I just don't want to look homely."

"You're pure elegance in this, baby."

"You're not just saying that?"

"I'd never bullshit you."

"Thank you."

Arianne's sleeveless red dress with a high neck is red carpet perfection. The lower part is slightly flared and pleated, hitting her well below the knee. The intricate red heels suit the dress to a T. Her hair, which she's been wearing out a lot more lately, is pulled back in a low bun. She's only wearing a veil of makeup.

Rhys has hinted at it. So has Holt. She's a departure from every woman I've ever been with. The more I'm with her, the more I want to be with her. I can't explain it. That said, there's no way I'll attempt to make sense of it while we're in Germany. I have a lot more interesting things on my mind.

I allow my hands to glide down her back. "You know what I like the most about this dress?"

"What?"

"Easy access," I say as I slide the zipper down a little.

"Don't you dare."

"I'm practicing for later."

"Aren't you a little cocky?"

"Are you telling me you had enough earlier?"

She doesn't answer.

*Yeah, I thought so.*

The shower was a tease—lots of kissing, touching and stroking. I didn't want to take things too far because after so many weeks of celibacy, a quickie was out of the question.

"We start the day at eight a.m. sharp tomorrow morning," she says as an excuse.

"So?"

"With the jetlag, I'll need my beauty sleep."

"That's lame."

"What do you want from me?" she asks.

I grab her hand and place it over my throbbing cock.

She hitches a breath.

"I'll tell you exactly what I want from you after the gala."

# Chapter 35

## *Arianne*

The opening gala for the upcoming release of the six-figure headphones is taking place at the Schützenweide reception hall—a building on the premises of Sennheiser's headquarters. I almost passed out when Beckett told me people were willing to fork out ninety thousand dollars for headphones. It's preposterous the new model is even more expensive. I suppose when money isn't an object, you wouldn't balk at the exorbitant price tag. I'm not their target audience. That said, most of the people I'm rubbing elbows with tonight, are. Including the good-looking guy standing next to me.

After shaking too many hands, Beckett and I are standing near the piano, enjoying a glass of champagne, accompanied by some delicious finger food. It's the only exciting part of the evening. For all the money in the room, tonight is a bit of a snooze fest.

"Let's give it another half hour and we'll call it a night," Beckett says.

"I second that."

"If it isn't Mr. CEO in the flesh," a voice says.

I turn around to see two tall men approaching us.

I do a double take and my jaw drops.

*No way.*

*I mean, no way.*

*I must be imagining things.*

"Beckett!" The tall man with coffee-colored hair and coffee-colored eyes I know as Tomas Lazović extends a hand.

"I didn't know you two were attending," Beckett says, shaking it.

"We couldn't get here earlier because we were performing a sold-out concert last night in Vienna," Tomas says. "On top of that, our publicist had a full day of publicity appearances across the Austrian capital booked for today. Hence, why we landed an hour ago. We barely had time to drop our luggage at the hotel before rushing here."

"That explains it." Beckett turns his attention to the equally handsome man standing next to Tomas. "Good to see you."

"It's good to see you, too," the man I know as Anders says, patting Beckett on the shoulder.

They exchange a bro hug.

I'm too shocked to even breathe.

Tomas playfully punches Anders' arm. "It appears tonight, we'll have to be satisfied with the other attractive single women in the room." His eyes brush up and down the length of my body. "Since Mr. CEO already snatched the most gorgeous one."

I blush furiously. My only saving grace is the color of my dress, competing for attention.

"Knock yourself out," Beckett says.

"Joker," Tomas says. "Are you going to introduce us, Christensen?"

"I wasn't planning on it, but if you insist," Beckett says.

*Okay, I officially don't know what to do with myself.*

"Fucker," Tomas says.

"Arianne Buchanan, I'd like to introduce you to Tomas Lazović and Anders Benković the duo behind Cello2Cello. Gentlemen, please meet Arianne."

We exchange greetings.

I try to keep my cool and not come across like an awestruck fan.

"Remember, I told you about Jam Session, the talent show I'm a co-judge on along with Stasia van Gameren?"

"Yes," I say.

"Two judges had to pull out because of international concerts and tour schedules. These two will be the new judges in the upcoming season."

"Your music is incredible," I tell them.

"You know our music?" Anders asks.

"Who doesn't?" I manage without jumping up and down with giddiness.

"You didn't know anything about my former band or my music. I'm a little insulted," Beckett says with a grin.

"Tomas and Anders' music touches your soul."

"So does rock music when it's played right," Beckett says.

We all laugh.

"I'm sorry I didn't know who you were before I started working for you," I tell him. "Please don't take it personally." I pat his forearm.

"I like her," Anders tells Beckett.

"So do I," Tomas says. "A lot."

They exchange a knowing look.

"Perhaps you might want to join us for a nightcap, Arianne."

"I like the way you think," Tomas tells Anders.

"I thought so," Anders says before returning his attention to me. "It would be our pleasure to play something just for you. Let's call it a private concert..."

"Gentlemen, we've already gone through this." Beckett's tone is borderline icy. "There are tons of other women in the room to choose from. Just not Arianne." His response startles me. That tinge of possessiveness does something to me.

Anders holds Beckett's stare.

Beckett arches an eyebrow defiantly.

"My apologies," Anders says with a slight bow of the head.

"Noted." Tomas does the same.

"It's a shame, though," Anders says.

"Indeed," Tomas says.

"That's just the way the cookie crumbles," Beckett says with a tight smile.

All three men stare at each other, and it's as if I'm excluded from a silent conversation.

*What am I missing?*

The testosterone floating around us is overwhelming.

Tomas turns to me. "We're honored you like our music."

"When you play, it's like you lose yourself to the music," I say. "There's so much passion in each note. It's amazing how you've turned an instrument that was almost relinquished to becoming a relic, forgotten by so many, into something hot and sensual. And let's not forget how well you navigate from classical to hard rock. It's uncanny how you do that. Without you, I wouldn't appreciate rock music."

"What a compliment," Anders says.

"You have a way with words," Tomas says. "Is she your new publicist?" he asks Beckett.

"No. Rhys and I brought her in to expand SCORE," Beckett says.

"Speaking of the devil, where is he?" Tomas asks.

"Urgent business in Vietnam," Beckett says.

"Got it," Tomas says.

"So, who did you pay—or sleep with—to get on the invitation list for tonight?" Beckett changes the subject.

"Guess who's going to be the face—and the face—of Sennheiser's new international advertisement campaigns?" Anders answers Beckett's question with a question.

"Congratulations!" Beckett says.

"Thanks!" Anders says. "I'm surprised they didn't want to use your pretty boy face, Christensen."

"I don't even plaster my pretty boy face on SCORE products," Beckett says. "Not to mention, I'm Sennheiser's competitor—"

Anders and Tomas jerk before pulling their phones out of their pocket.

"Gage just arrived," Anders says, lifting his gaze from his screen.

Beckett turns to me. "Gage Hollingsworth is Jam Session's executive producer. He's also the owner and CEO founder of the music streaming service StreamTunes."

"Didn't Gage Hollingsworth buy out his early investors eight months ago?" I ask.

"Yes," Beckett says.

Wow. Beckett rubs elbows with big players. Not that he's a small fish. Still, I'm impressed.

"I was also on that list, but I requested an early buyout because I was worried about conflict of interest." Holy shit, Beckett is incredibly wealthy. "It's the same for my older brother Holt. Once I no longer had financial ties with Gage, it was easier to work together. In Holt's case, it was to ensure his artists wouldn't be accused of favoritism."

"I see."

"Gage's company is behind the StreamTunes Music Awards—"

"What a trio!" A short man wearing a forest-green tuxedo jacket with a large camera in hand interrupts Beckett as he approaches us. "I'm Douglas Tovey with The New York Times Style Magazine. Could I get a few photos?"

"Absolutely," Beckett says.

"I'm always up for a little publicity." Anders chuckles.

"Christensen, your popularity rating is about to skyrocket because you'll be seen with us," Tomas says.

"You need to lay off the cheap booze, Lazović." Beckett shakes his head. "You're talking shit."

All four men laugh.

I step aside to get out of the way.

"You too!" Douglas points at me.

I hesitate.

"You're Miss Holy Chic, right?" Douglas asks.

My jaw drops.

"I recognize you from those viral photos," Douglas says.

Earlier, Beckett and I were accosted by photographers from several media outlets, but none of them seemed to have recognized me.

"You're right, Douglas." Beckett answers on my behalf. "That's the one and only, Miss Holy Chic, aka, Arianne Buchanan."

I'm stunned.

"That's what I thought." Douglas nods, satisfied. "Pleased to meet you, Arianne."

"Likewise." I manage that one word with a timid voice.

"I absolutely want you in the photos," Douglas tells me.

*Unbelievable.*

When I'm still rooted in stupor, Beckett extends an arm. "Come on, Your Holy Chicness, the photographer is waiting."

I oblige.

He wraps his arm around me and brings me close to his body.

I look up at him, smiling warmly.

He returns my smile.

One photographer turns into several.

They seem to come out of nowhere, all clamoring for the money shot. We're talking about some of the biggest media outlets in the world.

Every time I tried to step aside, Beckett, Anders, or Tomas would pull me back into their circle. Some of the shots were hilarious. Those three guys do a good job at riling each other up.

When it's all said and done, I'm dizzy from the overload of attention.

*This is a lot to handle.*

"If you'll excuse me, I'm just going to run to the bathroom," I tell the guys.

"Sure," Beckett says, squeezing my hand.

I squeeze his back.

"It was a huge pleasure and an immense honor," I tell Anders and Tomas. "I'll remember this day forever."

*God, I sound so lame.*

"You say that like we won't see each other ever again," Anders says. "If you're hanging out with this guy"—he points to Beckett—"chances are this is the first of many encounters."

"Anders is right." Tomas cuts in. "Not to mention, we'll be at the two-day event and the closing gala."

"I'll see you around, then."

With a bright smile, I wave at the musical genius duo before I make my escape.

*I need some air to compose myself.*

I fan myself as I weave my way through the crowd on my

way out of the elegant room. I follow the signs until I reach the bathroom. There's a line when I walk in. A quick glance tells me it might be a while because there are only two stalls.

*Why are women always short-changed?*

I exit, determined to find another bathroom. After asking around, I head to two other bathrooms without much luck. The third one is the charm.

"All yours," a diminutive redhead says, as she exits the bathroom, kindly holding the door for me.

I take in the white evening power suit she's wearing without anything underneath—aka, no top and no bra—and her super high heels in the same color.

*Wow.*

"Thank you," I say.

When I enter the bathroom, I nearly shout in excitement because I'm alone.

I inspect my surroundings, nodding my approval.

From the granite counter, to the crystal chandelier, to the intricate gold frames around the mirror, this bathroom screams opulence.

I enter the stall, place my evening bag on the hook behind the door, lift the bottom part of my dress and hover over the seat, praying to God in gratitude as I take care of business.

As I pull up my panties, the bathroom door slams open and then shuts.

*Someone is in a rush.*

"Lock the bloody door," a woman says.

"Did you check to see if we're alone?" a man asks.

*Wait. What?*

"I'm tired of jumping from one loo to the other," the woman says. "This is it."

"You've been itching for an audience for a while." The man chuckles.

*Huh?*

"With good reason," the woman says. "This is our care-free weekend without the twins. Let's make it wild, big daddy."

I peek through the crack of the door to get a glimpse of the couple. When the woman walks in front of the stall, I scoot out of the way.

"How dare you tease me like this?" the man says. His foot-steps are loud against the stone floor.

"As posh as this evening is, it's dreadful and boring as fuck. I had to come up with a way of livening things up. I figured my pussy would do."

*Whoa!*

"You can't wait until we get back to the hotel?" the man asks, humor lacing each word.

*I commiserate with how boring the evening is, but he's right. Get a room!*

"We don't do lame, big daddy," the woman says. "A public fuck is exactly what we need."

*She did not just say that.*

"I tucked my creamed knickers inside your pocket because my cunt is desperate for your big fat cock."

I swallow my gasp.

I didn't know British people were this daring. Phoebe is right. Two years in London and I spent all my time working, leaving little room for socializing and closing the door to dating and sex. Now, I'm starting to think I missed out.

"Be careful what you wish for, gummy bear." There's a warning in the man's voice.

"I don't want to be careful!" the woman says. "I want to be savagely fucked. I don't want it later. I want it bloody right now!"

The man lets out a feral growl. "Show me that beautiful

cunt, you slut. Hands on the counter and pussy ready to be stuffed."

*What the—*

"I thought you'd never ask." The woman sounds giddy.

I'm so stunned, I'm uncertain if I should storm out of the stall or keep hiding.

I peek through the crack just in time to see the woman assume the position. She bends over the granite counter with her bare ass and pussy staring at me. The expression on her face reflecting in the mirror is so carnal, it's unsettling.

*Oh. My. God.*

The man fumbles with his belt and zipper before lowering his pants and his boxer briefs to his knees.

I jerk back and clasp my hand over her mouth to stifle a gasp.

Beckett is huge, but this guy is of eye-popping proportion.

*The man is a horse!*

"I'm going to ram this beautiful cunt until you give me what I want," he says, vigorously stroking his cock with both hands.

It's like he's polishing a very long rod.

"You're ready for my huge cock?"

"Yes, please, big daddy." The woman gyrates her hips in circular motions.

*This is obscene.*

A part of me wants to flee, but another is fascinated beyond words.

The man positions himself behind his wife and rams into her in one thrust.

It's so forceful, *I* feel it.

She moans at the intrusion.

I bite down against my lip.

*Holy shit... just... HOLY! SHIT!*

"Oh, yeah, pound my cunt, big daddy," she says.

The husband growls as he gives her what she wants.

"Fuck me with your very big dick," she says.

"You love being on display," the husband says. "You love swallowing my pole."

She lets out a wicked laugh.

"You filthy whore," the husband says.

*Slap!*

*Slap!*

*Slap!*

"Do you have any idea how much I love this fucking cunt? How much I love this beautiful body that gave me two beautiful babies? How much I fucking love you?"

"God, I love you, big daddy."

*Wow. They have a hell of a relationship.*

"I'm close." The man grunts. "You're going to come for me?"

"Oh, yeah! Oh, yeah! Oh, yeah!"

"Say it!" The man barks his command.

"I'm going to come hard for you, big daddy."

I'm surprised security hasn't busted through the door to find out what's happening in here.

On second thought, thank God they haven't.

Talk about embarrassing.

"That's right, filthy whore." The satisfaction in the man's voice is unmistakable. "You give me what I want every. Single. Bloody. Time."

*Slap!*

*Slap!*

*Slap!*

"That's it, clench that juicy cunt all over my big fat dick, you filthy slut. Make me bloody come."

The woman is panting so loud, her pleads reverberate throughout my body.

My clit is on fire.

Every part of me tingles.

A war between morality and immorality rages inside me.

Judging by the woman's whimpers and the skin-on-skin slapping, they're going at it like jackrabbits. The grunting sounds crescendo and then it slows to muffled groans and a series of *fucks*.

I can only assume they've climaxed.

I've watched porn a few times, but this live performance takes the cake.

Their heavy breathing takes over the room.

I pray they can't hear mine.

It takes everything in me not to make a sound.

My heart is hammering through my chest, my body trembling from the forbidden experience.

"Fuck, that was hot," the husband says.

"Oh, big daddy, you made me come so hard."

"Good girl, gummy bear."

Their kiss is as passionate as their lovemaking.

*I hope they don't go for round two.*

The sound of ruffled clothing and the clinking of a belt suggests the show is over.

Thank God. I couldn't handle an encore.

"Gorgeous shoes, darling," the woman says.

My heart lurches.

*Oh, no.*

"I hope you enjoyed it as much as we did."

"I'm sure she did," the man says. "I heard her heavy breathing over ours."

*Busted!*

"Come on, gummy bear, big daddy needs a stiff drink."

"Good night, darling. Sweet dreams. I hope you'll think of us when you play with yourself later," the woman says.

*She's talking to me again?!*

Their footsteps carry them across the stone floor, as they both laugh at my expense.

I hang my head in shame.

I shouldn't have witnessed that. I should've let them know they weren't alone in the bathroom, but nooooooo, I watched, listened and dare I say, enjoyed that naughty episode.

*Arianne Buchanan, you're a vile, filthy, lewd woman.*

I'm also turned on like a light switch.

I'm so fucking wet, I'm surprised my juices aren't dripping down my legs.

I'm taken aback by how my body reacted to something so forbidden.

When I'm certain I'm alone, I flush, grab my evening bag, and step out of the stall.

I look left, then right.

*The coast is clear.*

I approach the counter and study my face in the mirror. Pure carnal lust stares back at me.

It only takes a split second for me to make the decision.

I place my bag on the counter, search underneath my dress and pull down my panties before stepping out of them.

I'm sure if I were to wring them, I could soak the floor.

With my heart still beating hard and my panties bunched up in my hand, I rush out of the bathroom, and race back to the ballroom. I spot Beckett the second I walk in. I find my composure and approach him.

"Where the hell were you?" he asks. "I've been looking everywhere for you. I was just about to send a search party. It's like you disappeared into thin air. I even tried calling your phone without a response—"

"The organizers asked us to put our phones on vibrate before walking into the room. I turned mine off." I'm fully aware I avoided answering his question.

"You had me worried," he says.

My heart stutters.

He's someone I could really like.

*You already do, you fool.*

"I didn't mean to," I say.

He caresses my cheek. "You're forgiven."

A swarm of butterflies dance in my belly as I debate if I have the courage to do what's been playing in my head since the salacious peep show.

"Arianne, what's going on?" he asks.

"I think maybe we should cut the evening short."

I don't recognize the brazen woman speaking.

He cocks an eyebrow.

"You in a rush?" The unholy sexy hunk flashes me a wide grin.

My pussy is way too needy for a long explanation.

With one hand, I pull the lapel of his tuxedo jacket and with the other, I slip my wet panties inside his pocket.

I give it a few taps for good measure.

His eyes widen.

Beckett pulls the lapel of his jacket and inspects his gift.

The splash of red lace stands out against the black.

His face screams disbelief. Then, his features morph into something dangerous. His ocean-blue eyes, now the color of dark rough seas, meet mine.

"You dirty girl. I didn't even have to ask," he says. "Looks like I'm rubbing off on you after all... and soon... I'll be rubbing you off."

I have to contain the glee of excitement bubbling through me.

He leans closer until his lips touch my earlobe. "And that's just the warm-up. I want my mouth on your pussy until my face smells like you."

The words send a thrill up my spine. He grabs my hand and pulls me after him.

*Yes!*

# Chapter 36

## *Beckett*

What I read in Arianne's eyes unhinged me. The expression on her face—a tempting combination of boldness and vulnerability—when she placed her wet panties inside my pocket was so fucking potent, my cock jerked to attention. No way was I going to waste another second at that stupid gala when I could be balls deep inside her. I didn't even attempt to find Gage, Tomas, and Anders in the crowd. I hightailed it out of there with the lady in red who had the audacity of throwing my salacious promise right back in my face.

The short ride back to the inn is torture.

Arianne doesn't speak.

Neither do I.

All I can do is hold her hand in mine, willing myself to control the volcano building up at the pit of my stomach.

Upon arriving at the inn, I jump out, round the front of the car, watching her all the while through the windshield—to the chauffeur's bewilderment—and open the passenger door to let her out, leaving her no choice but to trip after me in her high heels as I race inside.

My overwhelming desire is so all-encompassing, good manners fly out the window. I barely acknowledge Astrid and Günter as I rush us back to our rooms. I pull out my key card, scan it, and push her inside. I close the door behind me and whirl her around, placing her back against the door. I move closer, right into her space. I tip her chin up, my eyes narrow thoughtfully on her face.

"Where did you disappear to?" I ask. "And don't even think of lying to me."

She tells me all about the risqué British couple and how she became a participant to their kink.

I'm incredulous.

I never would've pegged her as a voyeur.

Just when I think I've figured her out, she pulls a fast one on me.

"You've done the impossible—you struck me speechless," I tell her.

"I know. I should be ashamed." Her eyes are downcast.

"Remember when we met Larkin you asked me questions about the private club?"

"I do."

"Congratulations, you just got a crash course. Now, you know exactly what happens at Dark Compulsion."

"Oh."

"There's a lot more than that, but watching others get down and dirty is part of a long list of kinks you can satisfy."

"Oh."

"Now, I understand the urgency. The Brits performed. You enjoyed. And then you didn't know what the hell to do with yourself."

"Yes," she says.

I reach for her panties, still safely tucked inside the pocket of my jacket, bring them to my nose and inhale deeply.

*Damn.*

"You decided my cock was your only salvation and came looking for me because you want me to wreck your pussy like that man drilled his wife's cunt?"

"Yes," she says in a whisper.

Raw desire flares, scorching hot, and rips right through me.

"You're lucky. I'm in a giving mood," I tell her. "Where do you want it?"

Her eyes avert mine, shifting from left to right.

I tighten my grip on her chin.

I lean in, my breath feathering against her cheek, then against the corner of her lips where I speak in a coaxing voice. "I asked you a question."

She lets out a pleading sound, but still doesn't give me an answer.

I pull back from her and examine her face.

Her long black eyelashes bat furiously.

"Arianne?"

"The bathroom?!"

"Is that a question or an answer?"

She shakes her head and then nods. "I want it in the bathroom."

Her response holds more conviction.

"I can work with that."

My hand slides underneath the hem of her dress, traveling up her inner thighs before cupping her pussy. Her head falls back against the door and she moans. My middle finger slips between her pussy lips, grazing her hard clit. Arianne cries out as her hips jerk forward. I bring my lips to hers and swallow the sound in my mouth as I continue teasing her.

*Fuck, she's so wet.*

"You need me inside you," I tell her.

"God, yes."

"I have one question before I give you what you need."

"What?" she asks.

"When was the last time you were with a guy?"

"Is it a turn off?"

"Did I say that?"

"Why else would you ask?"

I change tactics. "I haven't been with anyone in a while."

Shock registers on her face. "You haven't?"

Three weeks is an eternity in my world. "I haven't. I keep saying I'm going to destroy your pussy, and yes, the thought is sexy as fuck, but I don't want to hurt you. I need to know how far I can take things."

She swallows hard. "It's been close to three years."

"I thought you broke things off with your ex two years ago."

"I did," she says. "The last few years of our relationship, the focus was on building Chance's company. We lived at the office, returning to his house to sleep, shower, and change. There wasn't much energy left for romance or sex. I comforted myself with the hope that once he made it big, all the stress and anxiety would dissipate and we'd be a couple again instead of the boss-employee friendship we'd drifted into. Well... you know how that story ends."

That moron short-changed her in so many ways.

He used her and then dumped her.

*Asswipe.*

"And no one else since your ex?" I ask.

"No."

"Okay."

"Beckett, we don't have to—"

"The fuck we don't." I frown. "You provoke me and you think I'm not going to fuck you senseless? Your prolonged celibacy has no bearing on how damn much I want you, Arianne."

"Really?"

"Really, baby." She offers a dazzling smile. Her short bout of insecurity dissipates. "You've proven time and time again you can keep up with me. Tonight, we aren't putting the brakes on until my raging hard-on fills this pretty little pussy." I slip two fingers inside her, pumping them in and out.

She lets out a groan and her thighs tremble around my hand, as if coaxing me to continue torturing her.

"Oh, Beckett." Her words end in a shaky breath.

Her hooded eyes drop to my lips.

She bites down hard against them and lets out a low whimper.

"Goddammit," I say when her hand gropes my massive erection. I wasn't expecting her bold move.

She squeezes again, but I grip her wrist and push her hand away.

"Don't. Unless you want me to come in my pants. And that would be a damn shame and a waste of a good load."

Her lips pull down in disappointment.

"Let's go to the bathroom so we can put my cum to good use." I

scoop her up in my arms.

"Beckett!" she shrieks. "I've never been swept off my feet before!"

"Fair warning, there will be *a lot* of firsts tonight."

"I'm so ready," she says with a mischievous smile.

I march us through the dark room to our shared bathroom, turn on the light with my elbow, and drop her to her feet. I remove my tuxedo jacket and place it on the chaise longue in the corner. I fumble with my bow tie until it loosens, slide it off and fling it so it lands somewhere on the bathroom floor. I couldn't care less.

As I untuck my shirt from my pants, I catch a glimpse of

her watching me with rapt attention. Her breath roughens when I pull the shirt off my shoulders, exposing my abs, arms, chest, and ink.

"Your body is a work of art... until you, tattoos scared me."

"And now?"

"They arouse me."

*Good answer.*

"Strip! Keep the heels on."

She reaches around and unzips the dress, letting it slide down over her slender hips to pool at her feet, exposing her bare ass to me. She unhooks her red lace bra and tosses it to the side. Then she picks up the dress, walks across the bathroom, and places it neatly near my tuxedo jacket. Her eyes never leave mine.

She comes and stands in front of me.

I pause in the midst of unbuckling my belt to admire her.

Her glorious nakedness is too much to bear.

It isn't the first time I've seen her without clothes on, but it's the first time I know with certainty I'm finally, finally going to know what it's like to come with her pussy gripping my cock.

"Hurry," she says, waving a finger at me.

I chuckle, shaking my head.

With a pressing sense of urgency, I toe off my shoes and remove my socks before pushing my pants and boxer briefs down my legs. I step out of them. When I stand up straight, my cock snaps against my stomach, pointing north.

*Fuck. I'm hard.*

"Give me a sec."

I rush to my luggage, rummage through it until I find a box of condoms. I grab a packet and run back to the bathroom.

She's leaning against the counter, waiting.

I stalk towards her and drop the condom to her side.

She smiles and pushes off the counter, but I place a hand against her chest.

"Stay."

She does as she's told.

"Spread your legs for me," I say, kicking them further apart.

I grasp my heavy cock, stroking it from root to head.

Her eyes drop to my grip.

The tip of my cock is swollen and flushed in a deep red purple shade of anger. All the veins running along its length pop, filled with blood as if reminding me how cruel abstinence has been.

"Are you still dripping wet?" I ask.

Before she can answer, I guide my cock between her pussy lips, dragging the head through her slickness, circling her clit with the engorged tip. The movement is slow and agonizing.

"Oh, God." She grips my forearm and dropping her head to my chest.

"You're my first."

She looks up at me, confused.

"I've never dipped my cock between a woman's lips without a shield."

"I like knowing I'm your first," she says.

"Don't worry, I'm clean. I get tested regularly and I always wrap up."

"I'm clean, too," she says. "After finding out Chance was cheating on me, I got tested."

"You're on the pill?"

"I am."

"You're okay with me playing with you like this?"

"More than okay."

I resume my mission.

The head of my cock skates over her hard clit in torturous

circles. I apply more pressure, eliciting carnal groans from both of us.

As if to punish myself, I press my cock inside her entrance, sliding in.

The sensation is mind-blowing.

I pull out before the urge to sink balls deep becomes too overwhelming to back away. I grab the condom from the counter and bring the packet to her mouth.

"Help me open it up," I say.

Her teeth clasp against the foil and I pull against it to rip the packet open.

"Good girl."

Pushing away the pleasure of feeling her bareback, I resign myself to sheathing my imposing length.

I lift her up. "I want you up here." I place her against the flat surface. "Use the top of the counter as leverage if you need to."

"Okay."

"Wrap your legs around my waist."

She does.

"I've wanted you since I saw you in the elevator." My voice is strangled. "I know this is our first time together, but it might be hard and fast. You okay with that?"

"More than okay."

When my heated gaze lands on her tempting lips, I take her mouth with a growl, biting and licking. I force her mouth open, demanding to be let inside. Our tongues tangle like crazy as I devour the hell out of her.

She whimpers.

I kiss her with ardor until we have no other choice but to come up for air. Not that I'd mind dying with my lips locked with hers.

"You ready for me, baby?" I ask.

"I've been ready since I slipped out of my wet panties."

The little shred of restraint I had around her fizzles faster than the explosive fuse of a bomb.

*Kaboom!*

I push inside her with such force, I swear the counter shakes beneath us.

Arianne cries out, the sound mingling with my own strangled grunt.

"God, you're huge," she says as I thrust in and out of her.

All movements stop.

"Am I too much to handle?"

She shakes her head, and then nods.

I'm not sure if that's a yes or no.

"You want me to stop?" I ask.

I really don't want to pull out of her, but no way am I going to hurt her.

"Don't stop," she tells me, her eyes boring into mine. "I'm just not used to this sensation of fullness."

I know what I'm packing, but her words flare the alpha in me.

"Let's just say my ex never *literally* took my breath away when he entered me." She lets out a little laugh.

I can't help mine.

I drop a soft kiss on her lips.

Her body relaxes enough to accommodate my size. Soon, the tension rolls off her.

"It's okay if I keep wrecking your pussy?"

She clenches around me in response.

"Oh, shit!" I say.

She does it again, this time with more intent.

"You feel me real deep inside you?" I ask.

"Uh-huh."

Arianne circles her hips, moaning as she presses her clit

against the base of my cock buried deep inside her. She tightens her thighs around my waist, gyrating her lower body in a frantic rhythm.

"Good girl. That's it. Take your pleasure from me."

I reach up and fumble with her hair until her locks cascade around her beautiful face.

She lets out a sharp gasp as her head falls back.

I grip her ass, digging my fingers into her flesh as I move her up and down my rigid cock, torturing her—and me.

My eyes drop to where her pussy is swallowing my cock.

*Damn.*

"God, your cock. Your fucking amazing cock."

I pick up the pace.

I fuck her like an animal, a part of me considering taking it down a notch or two, another part knowing full well that's just not possible.

She places a hand behind her on the counter and thrusts against me with fervor. She slams into me, bouncing up and down my erection. The points of her heels dig into my ass cheeks.

"Goddammit," I say.

*Pain and pleasure.*

She does it again.

*Fuck.*

By the third time, my balls are ready to fucking explode.

I look down between us, amazed at their size. I've never seen them this swollen.

With herculean effort, I keep it together.

My hips move like a piston, sending my aching balls crashing against her ass with each swing. The sensation nearly short circuits my entire body, the thudding sound shooting straight to my brain.

*Christ.*

I pull her body closer to me, and grind, and grind, and grind.

"Oh, yeah! Oh, yeah! Oh, yeah!"

I absorb her cries with my lips.

With our tongues intertwined, I slide my hand between us and close two fingers around her clit and press hard.

Her body goes rigid.

She breaks the kiss and gasps inside my mouth.

"Come for me, baby."

Her eyes glaze over right before her head lolls back. Arianne lets out a desperate cry as she comes apart in my arms, her orgasm washing over her.

I'm a breath away from following her off the cliff.

I thrust harder and harder.

My balls pulse, eager for relief.

Arianne slumps her body against my chest and circles her arms around my neck.

She whispers, "Beckett, I need you to fuck me like this every day with your huge cock."

She's probably still riding the climactic wave, but every cell in my body responds to her invitation.

One, two, three thrusts.

"Arianne, baby! Oh, fuck."

No amount of mental coaxing can muffle my shouts as I repeat her name over and over again. I shoot my load deep inside her, wishing there was no barrier between us.

*Jesus Christ.*

Satiated beyond belief, I bury my face in her neck with a low groan.

We both struggle to get our breathing under control.

It takes a long while.

I straighten up, remove the condom, and toss it to the floor. I lift her in my arms. On shaky legs, I carry her to my room. I drop her to her feet and pull back the cover and sheets.

"Get on the bed."

She does.

I climb next to her and start trailing kisses down her stomach.

"Beckett?"

"Shhh, I'm not done yet," I say. "Remember, I told you earlier I want my face to smell like your pussy."

She lets out a satisfied moan.

"You're making it hard for me to ever forget this trip—or you—Beckett Christensen." Her voice is low and groggy.

I'm sure her mind is still hazy and I doubt she's conscious of what she just said. Well, that's what I tell myself. Admitting her words do something to me would make this hookup a lot more complicated than it is. Why rock the boat?

# Chapter 37

## *Arianne*

Phoebe lifts her glass. "Here's to the girl of the hour!"

"You're way too excited," I tell her.

"Stop being so rational," she says. "Lift your glass, woman, and clink it with mine!"

I oblige.

"Cheers!"

"Cheers!"

We both take a long sip of our martini.

Beckett and I arrived late last night. I'm totally jetlagged, but no way was I going to miss an evening out with my best friend.

What a trip.

On Friday and Saturday, Sennheiser shared a few well-guarded secrets behind the jaw-dropping success of their six-figure headphones. I took copious notes, as my mind was spinning with ideas on how I could borrow some of their innovative strategies and apply them to SCORE.

On Saturday night there was another gala with the same

army of reporters and photographers. Contrary to the opening gala, the last night in Germany was a lot less buttoned up.

On Sunday, we were back on Beckett's private plane, heading home. Since our time in Germany was jam-packed with presentations and social gatherings—and a hell of a lot of naughtiness—Beckett declared Monday was a day off for both of us. I didn't argue. I spent most of the day unpacking and running errands.

Phoebe insisted on drinks to celebrate my return, so here we are at Nic's Martini Lounge in Beverly Hills.

"My bestie is the envy of every woman on the planet," Phoebe says, dropping her glass on the table.

"I was at the right place at the right time."

"You've been in LA for five weeks and you're more popular than the most coveted actress in La La Land." Phoebe's big brown eyes shine bright. "You weren't hanging out with one smoking hot musician. Noooooo. You had your pick of three." She lifts her fingers to drive her point. "Beckett Christensen, Tomas Lazović, *and* Anders Benković?" Phoebe shakes her head. "No wonder the media won't shut up. You're lucky you're my best friend and I'm madly in love with my Peruvian god. You don't have to worry about me being jealous. However, if I were you, I'd start walking around with bodyguards because I'm pretty sure there will be many women eager to claw your eyes out."

Her hilarious comment catches me by surprise and I have to drop my martini glass on the table before spilling its contents.

The press found a million ways to twist a candid moment in time into screaming headlines.

*'MISS HOLY CHIC HAS A NAME! ARIANNE*

*BUCHANAN CAUGHT PARTYING WITH THREE OF
THE MOST ELIGIBLE BACHELORS IN THE WORLD.'*

*'MISS HOLY CHIC AND CEO ROCK STAR STEP OUT
AT SENNHEISER GALA.'*

*'IS MISS HOLY CHIC CHANGING BECKETT
CHRISTENSEN'S BAD BOY WAYS? STAY TUNED!'*

*'MISS HOLY CHIC, THE ROCK STAR AND THE
CELLISTS. WHAT A LUCKY GIRL.'*

*'HAS HELL FROZEN OVER? IS BECKETT
CHRISTENSEN OFF THE MARKET?'*

I still can't get over the tsunami of attention.

"I called it!" Phoebe says, pride washing off her. "I said the city of Angels was your new beginning. I was right."

"You're taking a little too much credit for this."

"I disagree. I'm the one who pushed you to live a little, and after two years of living like a nun, you took my advice. Eat your heart out, Slut Mariah!"

I explode in laughter.

"I couldn't have predicted I'd end up on the front page of so many publications, but I thank God everything so far has been positive," I say. "I would've been mortified if any of them had criticized my sense of fashion."

"I take full credit for that as well! Andrea turned you into Cinderella. That dress was so regal looking."

The press agrees.

*'MISS HOLY CHIC TRADES BEJEWELLED T-SHIRT FOR
STUNNING RED DRESS.'*

*'MISS HOLY CHIC TRANSFORMS INTO THE LADY IN
RED AT SENNHEISER GALA.'*

*'MISS HOLY CHIC SETS THE BAR WAY HIGH IN
ELEGANT TRAFFIC-STOPPING RED DRESS.'*

"I'm still a bit baffled by how a new wardrobe and an updated hairstyle make such a dramatic difference," I tell her. "I barely recognized myself when I looked in the mirror before Beckett walked into my room."

"You certainly looked the part of the successful CEO's date," Phoebe says.

"Thanks."

She takes another sip of her espresso martini.

I do the same.

Something wicked flashes in her eyes as she examines me from over the rim of her glass.

"What?" I ask.

"You're poised."

I expect her to elaborate, but she doesn't. She just stares at me with a goofy smile on her face.

"I'm poised for what?" I ask.

She has this smug look on her face now.

God help me because something tells me what's about to fly out of her mouth is going to floor me.

"Reverse harem is the new ménage. Why have two guys when you can have four—two execs and two musicians. Bravo, girlfriend. Bravo!"

I nearly choke.

"Rhys is still in the running, right?"

I glare at her like she just grew two extra heads.

She shrugs. "Just sayin'."

"What is wrong with you, Phoebe? The idea of me with

two guys is preposterous. Four? I'll swim across the Atlantic before that ever happens."

"So, all that pent-up sexual energy that was practically jumping from the opening and closing galas photos is *just* between you and Beckett?"

"How do you come up with this crazy stuff?"

"It's quite obvious from that photo of you looking up at him with goo goo eyes and him looking down at you with as much lust."

I shake my head, amazed.

Phoebe leans forward and places her hand on top of mine. "Arianne, I've known you forever. You texted up a storm about mundane things related to your trip. You even made light of the comical situation surrounding the mistake in the reservation. You've already had some dirty fun with Beckett. I can just imagine two people in connecting rooms, a continent away... no one has to know..." She pauses. "And of course, there's the tell-tale sign."

"What telltale sign?"

"Your eyes are sparkling, Ari. Either you scored some amazing shopping deals in Germany, or you got laid. My money's on the latter."

My back hits the seat.

"Am I wrong?" she asks.

There's no point in lying.

"You're not."

"Why did you keep it from me?" she asks. "Is he an asshole? So help me God if he is—"

"He's not." I shake my head. "On the contrary. Beckett is a gentleman, through and through." I hesitate. "The trip was a lot to handle and..." I let out a long sigh. "I'll start from the beginning."

I spill my guts to my best friend.

"Holy hotness!" Phoebe fans herself. "Oof..." More fanning. "I thought Oscar sexed me up pretty good, but you two leave us in the dust."

"Like I said, it was intense."

"In capital letters!" Phoebe laughs at her own joke. "Since you two didn't work today, I assume he spent the day rocking your world?"

*I wish.*

I shake my head. "It was a day filled with chores. Sex with the CEO wasn't on the list." I offer a small smile to hide my disappointment.

"How come?"

"The man plays with my body with as much finesse as he masterfully strums a guitar, leaving me bone-tired and satiated after countless toe-curling orgasms. When he dropped me off, I was hoping"—*and praying*—"Beckett would want to come up to my place and even stay the night, but he didn't."

"Did you invite him up?"

"I didn't."

"Arianne, you were bold enough to ask for what you wanted on the first night of the gala," Phoebe says.

"That was different."

"In what sense?"

"We're back in LA now—"

"This smoking hot hookup started well before Germany."

"True, but it was never at this scale. In Germany, things became intimate. I'd spend my days with him, and at night after dinner and socializing, it was just the two of us. We were insatiable. We'd go at it until the point of exhaustion... and then we'd pass out—"

"Why didn't you ask him up?"

"He seemed a distant by the time he dropped me off last night. I wasn't going to humiliate myself by begging for sex because of a few heated trysts that might not mean much to him," I tell her. "True, he has a nice cock and everything—"

"You want more." It's not a question.

*I'm afraid to hope for more.* "I don't want to get hurt again."

Phoebe squeezes my hand. "From everything you've told me, he's a far cry from your ex—"

"I'm not the best at reading or understanding men. Chance made me believe, but it turned out I was just a commodity with a brain that helped him achieve the success, clout, and financial wealth he yearned for. Once he was done with me, he discarded me, and replaced me in a New York minute. How do I know Beckett won't do the same thing? Maybe when he dropped me off last night, he remembered he was the CEO and I was *just* a consultant."

Old insecurities creep up.

"You make him sound like Jekyll and Hyde," she says. "You're reading too much into it, Ari. Maybe he was just exhausted."

I drop my eyes to my glass and circle the rim with my finger, as if to soothe myself. "There's not a woman in the world who wouldn't want to jump Beckett Christensen—"

"Perhaps, but not all of them end up in his bed. You did... three nights in a row. From what I gather—thank you, Google —Beckett is a once and done kinda guy. It's well documented."

"I'm sure the repeat performance was because it was convenient." I shrug. "My room was next door—"

"You're so full of shit, Arianne."

My eyes fly up to hers.

"Even if Chance and Beckett aren't cut from the same cloth, you said it yourself, he's a once and done kinda guy. After our uncomfortable goodbyes last night, I'm starting to second guess my decision to throw caution to the wind because right now…"—a lump forms in my throat—"I feel like his office booty call."

~

As I make my way from the cab to my place, I try not to remember Phoebe is going to fall asleep in Oscar's arms tonight. I'll be cradling a pillow. It never bothered me before, but after three nights sleeping nestled against Beckett's strong chest and wrapped in his arms, my bed will feel cold and lonely.

The downside of opening your fortress is you put your vulnerability under a spotlight.

*Sigh.*

When I get to my apartment, I peel out of my clothing, slip into a silk robe, and stroll to the balcony. This is my new nighttime routine.

What's the point of living in LA if you're not going to take full advantage of the warm weather?

You'd never know we're in October.

I'm not even out here a minute when my phone rings.

I rush back inside and scramble for it at the bottom of my bag. Without any hesitation, I accept the video call.

"Mom. Is everything okay?" I ask when her smiling face pops on the screen.

"Of course, honey. Why would you ask that?"

"Because you rarely do video calls."

"I had to see it with my own two eyes," she says.

"See what?"

She squints her green eyes at me. "If this Miss Holy Chic the press keeps talking about is the same person as my daughter, Arianne Buchanan."

I laugh.

"Even your father insisted on me calling you. He's certain someone kidnapped you and is duping the world by passing as you. When did our daughter become such a freakin' gorgeous model?"

I laugh even harder.

She joins me.

"You're so dramatic," I tell her, regaining my composure and wiping tears from my eyes.

"Honey, your it-takes-a-hell-of-a-lot-to-impress-me dad is beside himself. So am I," she says. "You wear glamour well."

I beam.

"You like the new look?"

"I love it! Now, you look like mini me," she says, smoothing her natural blonde hair. "All kidding aside, I was starting to wonder if I didn't have to call your publicist to get through to you," Mom says. "Didn't you get my text messages?"

"I'm sorry. I was going to call you back. I was out with Phoebe."

"Oh, how is she doing?"

"She's acing all areas of her life. As usual."

"Nothing new there. You two are such go-getters," Mom says. "Hence, why you've been best friends since the first day you met."

I walk to the couch, sit down and stretch my bare legs on the coffee table.

"Are you calling to catch up or is this about Germany?" I get right to the point.

"Everywhere I turn, there you are with that gorgeous man with the beautiful blue eyes. But then, you have to go all Hollywood on me. I can't believe you spent three days in Germany with Cello2Cello! They're huge stars!" Mom shouts that last part.

"So is Beckett."

"That may be the case, but I've never heard his music. You know how much I love, love, love Cello2Cello." The second I introduced her to their music, she was hooked. "Did you get me an autograph?"

"No, Mom. I didn't want to come across like a crazy fan girl."

"Oh." She does little to hide her disappointment.

"I might meet them again—"

"You can't be serious." Her eyes grow as wide as saucers.

"Yes, they're part of Beckett's circle of friends, and soon, they'll cohost a talent show with him. So, it isn't entirely impossible."

Mom's head jerks back. "Are you and the CEO dating?" she asks, a huge grin slicing her lips.

"No, we're not."

"Oh." She does this thing with her head, tilting it left to right with her lips pursed together. Something is brewing in there.

The last time she called, she offered a cautionary warning. Now, she genuinely looks bummed out.

I don't get it.

"What is it?" I ask.

"It'll be our little secret." She places a finger in front of her lips. "Shhh."

"I don't follow."

"I'll tell Daddy, but I won't tell Moira. I'll let her believe you and the CEO are the new it celebrity couple."

I knit my eyebrows together. "Why would you do that?"

She shrugs in a noncommittal way.

"Mom, what's going on?"

"Everyone in the neighborhood is talking about those photos of you and the hot CEO. For the past few days, people have been cramming into the restaurants, waving their phones at me in excitement. As you can imagine, it's impossible to contain such big news. Since I wasn't answering her incessant calls, Moira marched into the restaurant, livid—"

"Why?"

"She demands I force you to back down."

"Back down from what?"

"She wants you to put an end to your well-orchestrated media campaign designed to steal the spotlight away from Mariah."

"What?" I shout in disbelief.

"Apparently, Mariah's press release about the big hoity-toity fashion designer who will design her wedding dress fell on deaf ears because everyone has been talking about Miss Holy Chic."

"She had a press release for that?" I can't believe it. "She really thinks she's royalty."

"I told you last time, Mariah is delusional. Her mother is no better. My stupid sister believes you're doing this to be spiteful because Mariah is the 'love'"—she uses one hand to do the quotation marks—"of Chance's life, and vice versa, and they were meant to be together." If this weren't the most preposterous thing I've ever heard, I'd laugh. "Of course, Mariah backstabbing you to get with said love of her life is irrelevant." Mom's tone is dripping with sarcasm.

"Aunt Moira needs new meds because the ones she's taking now clearly don't work for her!"

"You should've seen her. She was jabbing an angry finger in my face, telling me you were ruining everything."

"Forget about prescriptive meds, she must be high."

"She became so belligerent, your father and another employee had to wrestle her out of the restaurant. She was creating such a scene."

I'm dumbfounded.

For a beat I'm stunned into silence, then I burst out laughing.

"What?" Mom asks.

"Even if those photos of Beckett and me don't tell the full story, Mariah is foaming at the mouth and bursting at the seams with jealousy." *Take that, bitch!*

"It's payback for all the shitty things she did to you," Mom says. "She's stuck with Chance... and you have a *chance* with sexy Beckett. Pun intended."

I stare at her confused.

"Mom, weren't you the one telling me to keep my wits about me?"

"I know, but..."

"But, what?"

"Perhaps I spoke too quickly, Ari."

"What brought on the change of heart?"

"The way that man looks at you in those photos suggests there's more there. A mother knows, honey." She says that last sentence with a strong Scottish accent, reminiscent of my youth.

"Those photos are smoke and mirrors, Mom."

I expect her to drop the subject, but instead, she drops a bomb on me.

"What if they're not?" Her green eyes stare intently at me.

I'm speechless.

# Chapter 38

## *Beckett*

I picked up my phone a hundred times to text Arianne. I changed my mind as many times. In an attempt to calm my tormented mind, I went into the office to lose myself in work and stop replaying R-rated scenes from our steamy evenings in Germany.

The day whizzed by, and it's only when Valerie knocked on my door to tell me she was closing shop, it occurred to me it was getting late. I gave it another hour, and then I called it a day.

Focusing on something other than Miss Holy Chic put an end to my irritable and surly mood. However, by the end of the day, I was back in the same predicament—Arianne was front and center in my mind.

I headed to the Quintus Hotel for dinner and to clear my head. My plan bombed. Just being at the hotel reminded me of the last time Arianne and I were there together. I knew I was in trouble and needed a solution. Fast. Certain that going back to my old bad boy ways would be a foolproof cure, I headed to Dark Compulsion, determined to find a distraction for an hour or two. A half hour after entering the private adult club—and being accosted by half a dozen willing souls—I'm behind the wheel of my Alfa Romeo, driving back to Manhattan Beach.

*Fuck. This needs to stop.*

*Arianne is cock blocking me.*

After stripping down to my jeans, I make my way barefoot and shirtless to the bar cart. With a stiff drink in hand, I collapse on the couch, and dial for help.

"Hey, Holt," I say when my brother accepts the video call.

"Hey," he says.

"I thought of dropping by, but decided against it."

He frowns. "Why? You're always welcome at my house."

"I know..." I hesitate. I'm not sure how to explain what's going on to myself, let alone explain it to someone else.

"What's up?" he asks.

"I hope I'm not calling at a bad time?"

"I'm free."

I check my watch. "Is Naomi already sleeping?"

"No. I was banished from bath duty *and* nighttime reading tonight." He hangs his head low and shakes it. "The estrogen level in my house is too high. They're ganging up on me, little brother. I'm losing the battle."

I laugh.

He joins me.

"Had I known, I would've dropped by. It's not too late. I can be there in five with some beer or something stronger." I lift my tumbler.

He laughs. "Don't feel too sorry for me. I wouldn't change anything in the world. I love my girls and I love my life."

My brother has officially hung up his bad boy boxing gloves. He's so domesticated now.

"Are you going to tell me why you wanted to come by, or are you going to keep beating around the bush?" he asks.

"I have a problem."

His eyes widen in surprise. "Rhys isn't making any headway in Vietnam?"

*I've been putting off talking to Rhys about Arianne, but I'm going to have to fess up.*

"That's not it. The workers went back to work. The strike is over—management saw to it. I'll get the full briefing when Rhys comes back next week. He's in South Korea right now, looking for backup manufacturers, just in case this happens again."

"It makes sense," Holt says. "What's troubling you?"

I rub my hand over my face.

"Beckett, what's going on?"

"I just got back from Germany—"

"Oh yeah, how did that go?"

"It was worth my time."

"I still can't believe people are willing to fork out that kind of money for headphones," Holt says.

"Trust me, you have to see it to believe it. Those beauties are a work of art. Even though Rhys and I don't have any plans to produce a six-figure headphone, there's a lot I can borrow from Sennheiser and apply to SCORE—things that aren't obvious from the outside."

"Excellent! How was it for Arianne?"

"She got a lot out of it as well. She swears she already has a plan she's perfecting that will explode our sales and set us apart from our competitors—including Sennheiser."

"That's incredible! She hasn't been at SCORE long and already she's hitting it out of the park."

"She's a go-getter."

"She sounds like it. Did you know any of the attendees?"

"The guys from Cello2Cello were there. So was Gage. I didn't know anybody else, but I made some great contacts."

"I'm surprised Jagger didn't mention anything. Bree is so

die hard about keeping up with celebrity news affecting her uncles."

I laugh. "Most of the coverage was in the business and life sections because of the prohibitive price tag of those head-phones and because Sennheiser was making history."

"I see."

"Arianne's dress made the fashion and style sections, though. Fashion bloggers adore her. The press dubbed her, *Holy Chic in red*. Her dress was exquisite. She was equally breathtaking on the closing night in a stunning emerald show-stopper—"

Holt squints at me.

"Why are you looking at me like that?" I ask.

"There's something about the way you talk about her."

"What do you mean?"

My brother stares at me. "Is *she* the problem?"

"Fuck, yes."

"I'm going out on a limb here. Your relationship with her isn't strictly business."

I shake my head. "Not anymore."

"Beckett, what the hell were you thinking?" he says. "I thought you never crossed that line."

"Technically, she isn't an employee."

"Perhaps, but you have to work with her."

"I know that."

"Is your problem related to you fucking her one night and then moving on to another woman the next?"

I shoot him a stern glare.

His daring gaze zeros in on me.

"Don't look at me like that, Beckett. That's how you operate."

"I've never spent the night with a woman—"

"Is that supposed to be news?"

I shake my head in frustration. "We ended up having to share accommodation of a sort—"

"There was a shortage of rooms?" Holt asks.

I tell him about the inn's mix-up.

"Got it!"

"We ended up in rooms flanking a Jack and Jill bathroom... except she never slept in her bed."

Holt's head jerks back. "You're kidding?"

I've been with plenty of drop-dead gorgeous women like Arianne before. I've also been with unattainable women, kinky women, downright nasty women, two women at a time, and somehow my nights of pleasure with Miss Holy Chic were more stirring and unforgettable than anything I've experienced in the past. The first time I allow a woman this close and she blows my fucking mind.

"I'm dead serious, Holt."

"Did it start in Germany?"

"No. We started hooking up right here in LA."

I give him the lowdown.

"It was fun and games at first, but what happened in Germany was unexpected," I say.

"That doesn't even make sense," Holt says. "If it was hot and heavy before you left, surely, you knew it would escalate since there would be no witnesses."

I shake my head. "Not like that. It was so intense." I close my eyes for a beat as my balls tingle at the raunchy memories.

When I open my eyes again, I read Holt's shock loud and clear.

"It's never been like that with a woman," I say. "The first night... it wasn't even a consideration for her to leave my bed. After that, it was a given."

"Is it still as intense since you got back?"

"I threw a bucket of ice-cold water over the flames."

"Why?"

I let out a long sigh. "I should've been looking forward to the next conquest, but when we got back last night, all I wanted was to spend the night wrapped around her."

"Why put the brakes on?"

"Holt, I've never been with a woman multiple nights in a row. And I sure as hell have never missed a woman when I wake up in the morning, nor have I spent all day thinking about her." More like obsessing, but that's beside the point.

Arianne Buchanan has done a number on me.

For a few long seconds, neither of us says a word.

"Why are you wasting my fucking time, Beckett?"

My eyebrows hit my forehead.

"Are you shitting me right now?"

"I'm not," he says. "You told me you wanted to come by my house because you had a problem. What you just described isn't a problem."

"The hell it's not."

"Beckett, you're making this unnecessarily complicated."

"It *is* complicated."

Holt rolls his eyes. "You see something. You want it. You go after it. That's how you've operated since birth. You're the one who pushed us to take our garage band to superstardom. In doing so, you became a rock star sensation in your late teens. By the time you were a young adult, you were already a rock star god. Then it all slipped between your fingers. You hit rock bottom and ended up—like so many in our industry—in rehab. When Jace and Rod came out of rehab, they were without a compass for many months, lost and uncertain of what the next phase of their lives would look like. A lot of people leave rehab in the same predicament. Not you, little brother. You walked out of there like the undefeated champion of the world—with a solid business plan *and* a trustworthy partner. Who does that? Only you. Today, you're sitting on a multibillion-dollar company—that's on top of the billions you made from selling your StreamCloud and StreamTunes shares. You're by far the most successful member of our family. And that says a lot considering how many successful family members we have."

"Are you lecturing me?"

"You asked for it."

"No, I didn't. I asked for help."

"You sound like a child."

"You're irritating the hell out of me."

"You've known me your entire life. I don't bother sugar-coating things," he tells me. "Arianne isn't your usual buffet of socialites, starlets, wannabes and brainless fast women. Wanting to spend time with an attractive woman of substance isn't a problem, Beckett. It's just an opportunity for you to man up, little brother."

He's throwing a lot at me.

"If you're unwilling to go there with Arianne"—his eyes move away from the screen and scan the distance—"why aren't you balls-deep inside another woman?" His gaze meets mine again. "Is Dark Compulsion closed?"

"I was just there."

"How come you're sitting talking to me, then?"

I shake my head.

"Let me guess," he says. "You went. You saw. You considered your options. Since I'm also a member and until recently, I know what it's like to be on the prowl at the club, I'm willing to bet there was a bevy of tempting women, all vying for your attention... but none of them were Arianne."

"Fucker," I say under my breath. "Aren't you supposed to be in my corner?"

"Please," he says. "You're way too intelligent to need my help finding a solution to your fictitious problem. I suspect you already know what you want to do. The question is, do you have the balls to do it or not?"

# Chapter 39

## *Arianne*

I tossed and turned all last night.

Between yearning for Beckett and what Mom revealed about Aunt Moira's tirade, my mind wouldn't shut down. Even my morning ritual, communing with the City of Angels as she wakes up, brought me little joy. I was too troubled. Since I was up really early, I decided to get dressed and head to the office.

If I lose myself in work, there's no room in my head to reminisce about the irresistible CEO who did sensual, naughty, and lewd things to my body for three consecutive nights. Our morning quickies were a bonus.

I didn't hear from Beckett all day yesterday.

I was hoping for a text message last night, but he remained radio silent. I didn't initiate any contact. The last thing I want is for him to gently—or not so gently—dismiss me with a one-liner response. Dread eats at me at the thought I've made a monumental mistake. Again.

*Sigh.*

"I need a break." I stretch my arms over my head. "Nah, I

need strong coffee!" I stand up, smooth down my dress and head to the kitchen.

I step outside my office and bump into Valerie.

"I was just coming to get you," she says with a bright smile.

"You found me!" I say with exaggerated lightness.

"I surely did," she says, gracing me with an approving head to toe glance. "I absolutely love your dress."

"Thank you. I did a little shopping before going to Germany."

I opted for a pale pink dress and matching heels. It's feminine, yet business appropriate.

"You have great taste in fashion."

"The credit goes to my personal shopper," I tell her.

"Fancy. When you're a mama to three chipmunks, you can't afford such luxuries," she says. "Speaking of the business trip, I need all your expenses so accounting can pay you back. The boss just brought his in."

*Oh, he's here?*

"Beckett took care of everything. I didn't have to pull out my credit card once."

"One less thing to worry about," she says. "The other reason I was coming to see you is because the boss came in with a sugar high, aka three flavors of blondies, an equal number of chocolate brownies, and chewy peanut butter brownies for the entire executive floor. They're to die for. Perfect with coffee. They're in the 1938 Crocker conference room."

"I still can't get over the names of the conference rooms."

"I know, right," she says. "In any case, Paula mentioned the security log shows you arrived at seven." Paula checks them every morning to track employees who work outside regular hours.

"I did."

"Honey, you're setting a bad example for the rest of us,"

Valerie says. "Soon, the bosses will get it in their minds we should all arrive at Arianne-time."

"After so many days away, I had a lot to catch up on."

"Well, you can't do it without caffeine or sugar. Come on, you need a break." She's already pulling me by the arm.

As we pass in front of the 1916 Traub conference room, my heart starts tripping as if I were a contestant in a Double Dutch championship when a pair of blue eyes lifts up to mine. I nearly stumble as Valerie keeps dragging me behind her, unaware of my growing trepidation. Of course, he looks five-alarm hot in another impeccable suit. Only Beckett Christensen can make pinstripe look edgy. He holds my gaze as we traverse the hallway. His face is unreadable. There isn't even a hint of a smile.

*Bad news is coming.*

I avert my gaze so he can't read my disappointment.

When Valerie and I enter the conference room, a crowd of employees are chatting as they chomp down on blondies and brownies, cups of coffee in hand.

To avoid being impolite, I plaster a smile on my face and join in.

After a few minutes of water cooler conversation, I can't keep up the charade. My heart isn't in it. I excuse myself and scurry back to my office. I close the door and rest my head against it.

I can't believe I put myself in this predicament again.

The phone on my desk rings, putting an end to my self-wallowing. I march to my desk and pick up without checking the display.

"Yes?"

"It's Beckett."

My heart stops.

"Good morning!"

"Good morning," he says. "Do you have a minute?"

If he's calling the landline instead of calling my phone or texting me, things aren't looking good.

"Hmmm... I'm in the middle of—"

"Let me rephrase that. I need to see you in my office right now."

"I'll be right there."

I take my courage in my own two hands and head to his office in a series of trembling steps. When I get there, I take in a deep breath and exhale before knocking.

"Come in!"

I enter.

He's leaning against his desk, looking every bit the ruler he really is.

He looks good enough to eat. *Who needs blondies?*

The man turns a well-cut white shirt into a drool-worthy experience. Too bad for me, I know what's hidden underneath is even more delicious.

We stare at each other without saying a word.

He gets up.

*The hot ruler is about to seal my fate.*

He walks right past me.

I turn around to see where he's heading.

He locks the door, turns around, leans back, and crosses his arms over his wide chest.

It doesn't go unnoticed how his eyes are undressing me.

I grow uncomfortable under his inspection.

I clear my throat and brush a strand of hair behind my ear. "You wanted to see me?"

"I did, but I needed a minute to admire you." Another onceover. "You look amazing."

"Thank you."

He pushes off the door.

"Let's sit down." He points to the seating area.

I head towards one of the large chairs, but he stops me.

"I want you to sit next to me on the couch."

"Okay."

These theatrics are only delaying the inevitable.

The second I sit down, memories of the day he reddened my ass come flooding back.

My cheeks burn up in flames.

"Valerie, hold all my calls. I'll be in a meeting for a while."

*Not good. Not good at all.*

He sits down next to me. "I don't want any interruptions."

My nerves get the best of me.

"You don't have to worry about me turning into a psycho crazy bitch." I can't bring myself to look at him, so I stare at my lap, playing with my fingers like a child.

"Look at me."

I'm steadfast in my decision to avoid reading anything that might destroy me in his ocean-blue eyes.

"I said, look at me."

Ignoring his command, I keep staring at my lap. "Beckett, I get it. What happened in Germany, stays in Germany. You're the CEO and you have a company to run. I made a commitment to you. I will be the picture of professionalism in executing my role—"

"For the love of God, woman. Look at me!"

I slide a weary gaze his way.

"Your plan was to seduce me and then forget about me?"

I'm startled by his question.

"Wh—what?"

"I'll have to get HR involved."

Panic seizes me. "Wh—why?"

"You took advantage of me in Germany. You used my body for your own pleasure and now you just want us to be all business and shit?"

My jaw drops.

*Is he high?*

"What are you talking about? I never used you."

"You did," he says, "and I enjoyed how you *used me*."

*Thank God he's kidding.*

"We need to talk," he says.

The four most dreaded words in the English language.

"Okay," I say, already accepting the inevitable.

He places a hand on top of mine on my lap.

His warmth seeps right through me.

I have to hold back a moan.

"You must be wondering why I've been MIA?" he asks.

"I understand. You've been busy—"

"Stop bullshitting, Arianne. You and I both know it has nothing to do with work."

I swallow hard.

I twist my fingers together. "Beckett, I don't understand what's going on here."

"Thank you for finally being honest."

"If you have something to say, just spit it out."

*Make it quick. Put me out of my misery.*

I don't know if I can handle the truth, but it beats staying in limbo.

"When I dropped you off at your place on Sunday, I wanted to come up and spend the night in your bed, but I chickened out."

My eyes nearly bulge out of my skull.

"You did?"

"I did... and that's the problem."

"You lost me."

"I don't do sleepovers and I don't do repeat performances with the same woman."

"That last part makes it sound like we were part of a Vegas circus act."

He laughs.

"Given the way we were going at it in all sorts of crazy positions, I'd say it qualifies."

"Ha. Ha."

His expression changes. All lightheartedness dissipates. "I tend not to sleep with the same woman more than once."

I wince.

"You took me by surprise. I didn't expect to crave you so much."

I don't know what to say.

"I needed time to think because all this is new to me," he says.

I'm still unable to speak.

He brings a hand to my face.

"Arianne, I want to go out on a date with you."

"A date?!" I find my voice.

"Yes, a *real* date. We've been fooling around, but that's not enough anymore."

"It's not?"

"No. I don't want to sneak around to be with you."

"You don't?"

Well, there goes good money thrown out the door. With two college degrees under my belt, I can't even form a cohesive sentence.

"I don't know what it is about you, but I can't get enough of you."

"Dear God. I must be dreaming. This can't be happening."

"You're not dreaming, baby."

*Damn inner voice.*

"I can't believe I said that out loud." I'm so embarrassed.

"Can I assume we're on the same page?"

I nod. "Yes."

"Yes, what?"

"Yes, to everything you said and hell yes to going out with you on a real date!"

"Good!" He smiles wide.

I grin like a fool.

*Beckett Christensen wants to go out on a real date with me? Holy amazing!*

"I'll have a meeting with Valerie to let her know about us and I'll do the same with Rhys's executive assistant. I'll speak to him when he gets back."

I blink. "Oh, you want to make it official?"

"What part of *I don't want to sneak around to be with you* didn't you understand?"

*I'm taken aback.* "This is a big step, Beckett."

"That's why I was MIA," he says. "I needed time to understand what I wanted with you. I'm not a half-measure kind of guy. It's all or nothing with me."

Oh my God, I'm going to pass out.

"What about everybody else in the office?" I ask.

He runs the pad of his thumb across my lower lip. "The rest of the staff doesn't need to know about my private life. We'll be discreet in the office. I'm not going to send a mass email letting everyone know my relationship status has changed."

I bat my eyelashes at him. "Relationship status?"

"Yes. If we're dating, that implies you're my girlfriend."

*I'm dead.*

# Chapter 40

## *Beckett*

The doorbell rings.

*She's here!*

Since Arianne doesn't have wheels, I hired a car for her.

I drop the bottle of Italian red on the dining room table and eat up the floor underneath me on my way to the door. Eager to see her again, I fling it open.

All the blood in my brain travels south so fast, I falter back.

A ray of sunshine greets me.

Arianne's brown eyes sparkle and her sunny smile dazzles against the darkening sky as the sun sets behind her.

I give her an appreciative onceover. Her hair is now up in a messy updo with loose strands flirting against her cheeks. Her makeup is as subtle as it was earlier. She's wearing a vampy, off-shoulder dress with a frill ruffle running at the front that hits her right above the knee in a light shade of yellow that displays her tempting slender curves to perfection. She completes the look with a pair of open-toe high heels in gold.

My cock twitches in approval.

"The plan was for us to have dinner before I have my way

with you, but you're making it hard in that dress," I say in lieu of a greeting. "You look like my naughty dreams come true."

This newfound monogamy thing is unheard of for a guy like me. Lo and behold Rhys's scheme changed me. Arianne is the only woman I've been with in a while and she's the only woman I want to be with. I'm used to scratching an itch and responding to my basic carnal needs without a second thought. My cock usually does all the thinking. Not since this woman walked into my life.

No-strings-attached-Beckett is now attached.

Un-freaking-believable.

I fucked her on Sunday morning before leaving Germany, since then I've been horny as hell. Her looking as good as she does now doesn't help my case.

She works her lower lip.

Those mischievous eyes tell the whole story.

"This was planned," I say. "You didn't show up here looking like a goddess by mistake."

"I wanted to look pretty for our first date."

I give her another onceover.

"Sorry, cupcake, you failed miserably. Forget about pretty. You look fucking hot!"

She beams.

No more sedate business suits for my girl. I'll never admit it, but I sometimes miss obsessing about what she's hiding underneath her armor.

"Let's talk about the elephant in the doorway," I say.

She looks behind her.

"I'm talking about those, silly." I point to the bags she's holding in each hand.

"Just a few gifts," she says with a coquettish one-shoulder shrug.

"Arianne." I shake my head. "What did I tell you?"

"I know you said just to bring myself—"

"I said just to bring your fine ass."

She blushes.

"Well, my fine ass grew up with Scottish parents. Showing up empty-handed isn't in their DNA—hence, it isn't in mine. Since you took care of the food and dessert, I figured I'd supply the drink."

"You didn't have to."

"I know, but I wanted to."

"I already have wine covered—"

"I figured you'd say that."

"What did you get us?"

"I took care of champagne," she says, lifting one hand.

"I already bought champagne to celebrate tonight."

"Oh." She frowns, but bounces back. "You can never have too much champagne!"

"I agree. What else did you bring?"

"Since you thoroughly enjoyed cognac while we were in Germany"—she lifts the other bag— "I thought I'd get you a bottle. I'm sure you must have some in stock, but just in case you run out."

"You kill me."

"I wanted to be more original, but..."

"But?"

"There's so much I don't know about you."

"Hence, why we're dating, baby. Get your fine ass in here."

She steps inside, and I grab the bags from her.

"Thanks," she says. "I got a crash course in cognac today. Who knew there was so much to learn?"

I drop the bags on the console table, close the door and lock it before returning my undivided attention to her.

"What did you learn?"

"Well, you just don't walk into a liquor store and ask for a bottle of cognac. You have to know what you're looking for. You have different levels of sophistication for different price points and different palates," she says. "The salesperson told me if I wanted to impress my host, a bottle of Louis XIII would make for an unforgettable gift. When I saw the staggering price tag, I nearly choked. I swear, my eyes popped out of their sockets. Three thousand seven hundred dollars for booze? I *settled* for a refined bottle of Rémy Martin XO—"

"You did the right thing by *settling*."

"Glad to hear I dodged that bullet. It would've been embarrassing had I showed up on our first date with something subpar," she says.

"You know, I would've been more than happy with just your fine ass."

"Scottish parents, remember? To finish my story, I told the salesperson, the Louis XIII was too rich for my blood. I explained how my current client didn't pay me nearly enough to be able to afford such luxury. That said, I made a mental note to speak to said client first thing tomorrow morning about beefing up my fees so I can have discretionary income for pricier booze."

*Tease.*

I pull her to me.

"Why wait until tomorrow? You can talk to your current client about your fees as early as tonight... preferably in his bed, naked and willing. I'm sure he'd be far more receptive than he'd be at the office."

She looks up at me, batting her eyelashes like an innocent debutante.

"My word, sir. I'd never dream of crossing the line. That would be wrong. Not to mention, I doubt my new boyfriend would approve."

My hands rove down to the small of her back. "You sure about that?"

Lust ripples through my body, feeling her this close.

*Damn. I've missed her sexy little body.*

"On second thought, I'm sure my new boyfriend would understand that my client drives a *hard* bargain." Her coated voice and lidded eyes are my demise. An endless list of priorities made it easy for me to be a good boy today, the gloves are off.

I crush her lips, plunging my tongue deep inside her mouth, searching for hers. I ravish her mouth, making up for the last three hours since my lips were on hers. I cup her ass and squeeze hard, forcing her to feel the length of my desire as I grind my hard cock against her stomach. I let out a low growl as the passion between us ratchets.

*Fuck.*

I break our embrace. "Let's have dinner before I devour you."

"I think you already started."

"Let's put a pause on things while we're still ahead, then."

"If we must," she says with feigned affliction.

"Eager much?"

"Very." She pauses. "Not that I'm counting, but it's been three days."

I shake my head. "I've created a maneater."

We both laugh.

I grab the bags and with our fingers interlaced, I drag her to the kitchen.

"Wow! Wow! Wow! Oh, WOW!" she says, her head turning left to right as we stroll through the house.

I chuckle. "You'll get the grand tour after dinner."

"I'm surprised you didn't feel claustrophobic in the diminutive bathroom at my place. Your house is palatial."

"I was focused on only one thing, baby," I tell her. "Not to mention, the small size of the space made my cock look even bigger so I can't complain."

She laughs.

"That didn't sound vain at all."

"Not at all!" I smile. "Welcome to Casa di Beckett," I say with a ceremonious bow when we enter the kitchen.

"Did you buy a restaurant out of business?" Her eyes take in the multiple bags sitting on the kitchen island.

"I'm not as good as my brother or my cousins in the kitchen. They're all single dads, so they have an incentive. I thought I'd leave it to professionals."

"I'm not a great cook myself."

"Look at that, we already have so much in common," I say.

"So, so much," she says. "If you didn't whip all this up, who's responsible for the spread?"

"Belloni is one of the best Italian restaurants in the city."

"Ooohhh!"

"They're pretty strict when it comes to their food."

"What do you mean?"

"You won't find them listed on any food delivery services' website," I tell her. "You want their food? You show up. And it's not like they're next-door. It's a trek to get there. That said, every delicious bite makes up for it."

"I'm starved just inhaling the amazing aroma, and your glorious review makes it worse."

"Wait 'till you sink your teeth into the food. It's an experience. I got small portions of their most popular dishes and all of my favorites. I also bought a platter of Italian charcuterie and cheese. Dessert at Belloni is equally unforgettable. I stuck with the classics—tiramisu and cannoli. Belloni add their twist to cannoli by flavoring the mascarpone cream. It's a thing of beauty."

"Good thing I brought an appetite."

"Good thing, indeed."

"What can I do to help?" she asks, assessing the mountain of food.

"Nothing. You're my guest. Sit and enjoy." I point to a stool in front of the granite kitchen island.

"I can give you a hand."

"Tonight, my job is to take care of all of your needs. I don't want you lifting a finger, unless you're about to wrap your hand around my cock."

She swats my chest. "You're impossible."

"I know." I grin. "Not to mention, your dress is way too pretty to play the role of sous-chef."

"I feel like a princess."

"You *are* a princess. *My* princess."

"Lucky me."

I open my mouth to say something, but I hesitate.

"What is it?" she asks.

It suddenly hits me. I have zero experience in dating.

"I'm flying blind here, Arianne," I tell her. "Maybe this first date is a little too low key. Ideally, we'd be sitting at a Michelin-starred restaurant and I'd be serenading you with expensive wine and a meal to remember, but we're so high-profile these days... I wanted tonight to be about us. No audience. No photographers. No celebrity bloggers. No paparazzi. No auto-graphs to sign. Just Arianne and Beckett."

Her mouth twists into a small smile. "Being *with* you is more important than being *seen* with you. And for the record just Arianne and Beckett is perfect."

She gets on her toes and offers her lips.

No way am I going to say no to that.

# Chapter 41

## *Arianne*

**B**elloni's food can be summarized in two words—holy delicious!

It was out-of-this-world amazing. When I was in Europe, Italy was my guilty indulgence and our dinner transported me right back to a place I love. Every bite was succulent. In fact, the whole Belloni experience is irreproachable—including the charming, dashing, sexy host. Once my belly was so full I could barely breathe, Beckett thought of an ingenious way to burn calories.

I couldn't stop oohing and aahing as Beckett and I trailed the hallways of his majestic mansion. His abode is so big, the tour was like a workout. If he wasn't holding my hand, I swear I would've gotten lost.

It's good to be Beckett Christensen.

We kicked off the evening in his restaurant-like kitchen and then discovered the rest of his big ass pad. His Manhattan Beach mansion is like a little oasis, complete with home office and gym in a separate wing. The mini home recording-studio is badass. Ditto for the home theater. The wine cellar would be the envy of many restaurants around the world.

And then there are the upper floors.

Beckett's modern bedroom is huge, easily the size of my sublet. The spectacular ocean view from the upper deck that opens from his bedroom is breathtaking. The bathrooms are like a succession of high-end spas. And a few of them have steam rooms. I could totally lose myself in one of those bathrooms for days without any hope of ever emerging. A stellar home wouldn't be complete without *recherché* artwork on the walls. Beckett has that covered.

The man knows how to live large.

Now, we're back in the main living room, lounging like pashas on his extra-large L-shaped dark-gray couch. He greeted me at the door earlier looking like he jumped out of the pages of *Strut* magazine. He's long lost the expensive black Italian shoes and he's now barefoot. The stylish black shirt and dark wash jeans remain.

This guy is my boyfriend.

I was steadfast in my resolve to keep men at bay.

I stopped believing because I couldn't open myself up enough to trust.

My fortress was shut tight.

Then, a serendipitous encounter in an elevator turns out to be one of the most fortuitous events of my life.

Not even in my wildest dreams could I have imagined anything this amazing.

Arianne and Beckett.

Un-freaking-believable.

Since this relationship status is brand new, I'm still trying to wrap my head around it.

I gaze into his eyes and bring a hand up to his face and stroke his jaw, dusted with a smoking-hot 5 o'clock shadow.

"Thanks for an unforgettable first date," I say.

"Thanks for making it unforgettable." He taps the tip of my nose with his finger. "Do you want dessert?"

"Is it okay if we wait a bit?"

"Sure," he says. "Just say the word when you're ready."

"I will."

"You look good in my t-shirt, by the way." There's humor dancing in his eyes, but he doesn't let the smile form on his lips.

"I kinda like wearing your t-shirt." I pull on it.

"I already know you'll look even better without it on," he says.

A wave of heat washes over me, coating my skin and engulfing me whole.

"Who says you'll get to see me without it on?" I dare to ask.

"Weren't you going to negotiate with your client for more discretionary income to buy expensive booze?" he asks. "How exactly do you think those negotiations are going to happen without a little skin-on-skin action?"

I furrow my brows. "Are you using my words against me?"

"I am."

I try not to give him satisfaction by staring, but my eyes waver to his firm chest and the hint of ink flashing back at me.

"You like what you see?"

"You already know I do."

"Sit on my lap and tell me more."

He robs me of the decision when he reaches out and lifts me off the couch onto his lap.

For a second, I can't think because good God, sitting like this on his cock ignites every cell in my body. It's a good thing I kept my panties on or else his jeans would be soaked right now.

"Looks like you're using me for sex. Again."

His words snap me back to the present.

I'm gyrating back-and-forth against him like a bitch in heat, unaware my hips are moving of their own volition.

*It's like I can't control myself around him.*

His eyes flash a dangerous glare, veiled with lust and a hell of a lot of unholy thoughts.

I clear my throat. "Can I ask you a question?"

He brushes the strand of hair behind my ear. "Of course."

"Since the beginning of our illicit hookup, you've always insisted it was about me first—"

"And that's a problem how?"

"Hear me out."

"Fair enough."

"After our hot episode in the intelligence room and God knows how many scorching trysts in Germany..." My earlier burst of courage deflates like a balloon without any air.

"Finish what you were saying," Beckett says.

"I love how you take care of me with your hands, mouth, and cock, but if..." Another pang of nervousness takes over.

"Talk to me, Arianne," Beckett says.

"If I'm your girlfriend, I should be able to return the favor... minus the cock part... because I don't have one."

He laughs.

"Thank God for that because I much prefer pussy—yours to be precise," he says when he finds his composure.

I blush.

"So, you want to suck my big cock, baby?" he asks at the same time as he tilts his hips up against my hungry pussy.

"Yes."

It's ironic someone with such little experience and confidence when it comes to blowjobs would be begging for it. The truth is, I've been obsessed with the idea of making him come with my mouth since I saw the intoxicating expression on his face the first time he came inside me on the night of the gala.

He leans forward and runs his nose along the side of my neck.

"You sure you can handle it?"

*Absolutely not.*

"Yes."

"I don't know if I can be gentle with your beautiful mouth."

"I—I'm okay with that."

"You have no idea what you're getting yourself into."

I know I'm biting off more than I can chew. The old me wouldn't even have the courage to ask. Since meeting Beckett, it's like I've been walking on the wild side.

I lift my chin in defiance. "I'm okay with that."

He considers me for a beat, almost as though he's giving me a chance to backtrack.

I hold his gaze.

He takes my hand, placing it against his hard bulge between us, and presses his hips up.

"I want to hear you beg for it."

"I want to suck your cock," I say in a low voice.

"You're going to have to be a lot more convincing than that, baby, because right now I'm not certain you deserve my cock."

His stubbornness makes me want it even more.

*Bastard.*

"Beckett, please, let me suck your cock."

"Much better," he says, a wolfish grin stretching his lips. "I'm willing to honor your mouth with a river of cum."

The uncompromising ruler emerges.

And if my pussy doesn't tingle with excitement.

He rewards me with a slow, provocative kiss, nudging his mighty erection between my legs. I respond with as much fervor, grinding my pussy against his cock.

He breaks our embrace. "On your knees." His firm tone, a departure from what just transpired between us.

He unbuttons his shirt before removing it altogether

I lower myself to the floor, the plush rug acting as a buffer against my knees.

"Take my cock out."

I reach for his belt and work the buckle before unzipping his jeans.

"Remove them fully." He lifts his hips.

I pull his jeans—and boxer briefs—down his legs before tossing them to the floor.

His cock springs to life, more mouth-watering than the last time I cast my eyes on his magnificent length.

I move my gaze up to his and wait for his next command.

"You've done this before?"

My stomach twists. "Not very well."

"It's not going to take much for you to get the hang of it."

"Okay."

"First thing first, use your tongue to explore my length. When you're ready, wrap your beautiful lips around my cock and let nature take over. I'm in no rush."

I nod. "Okay."

"When I think you're ready, I'll fuck your mouth, but until then, you control the pace."

"I hope I don't suck at this."

"Sucking is a good thing... as long as you're sucking my cock, that is."

I'm sure he's lightening the mood by making a joke, but I don't crack a smile. I was full of sass a minute ago, but in reality, I'm clueless. I'd never given Chance a real blowjob. I grab Beckett's hands in mine and place them on either side of my head.

"Show me how you like it," I tell him.

Beckett blinks in surprise.

"That way I won't screw up," I say.

He's stunned.

"We just talked about this, baby. You suck. I come. I can assure you, just having your mouth on me is enough."

"I want to be amazing at it... for you."

"Let go of my hands, Arianne."

Dread washes over me and I firm my grip over his hands.

"I said, let go."

I shake my head.

"You asked me to show you how I like it," he says.

I lower my hands.

Beckett grips the thick base of his cock with one hand and grabs my hand with the other.

"Let's do this together," he says

"Okay."

I'm a ball of nerves.

"Stick your tongue out and explore me, baby," he says.

I squash my insecurities and go for it.

I run my tongue up and down the length of his cock. I taste every inch of him with my tongue, lips, and teeth.

He growls.

*Good job, Ari!*

The saltiness assaults my taste buds, but it doesn't take long for me to get used to his taste. From his low groans, I know I'm not the only one enjoying this.

"Look at that greedy little tongue."

Pride washes over me.

*I can do this.*

I double my effort.

I lick along his length in a slow languorous tempo before focusing my attention to his head. I swirl my tongue around it.

Feeling greedy, I close my lips in a tight vice, sucking the engorged head.

A series of curses falls from his lips.

*Yes!*

I move lower, licking his balls.

More curses.

Brimming with courage, I take one of his balls between my lips and suck the whole thing into my mouth.

*Oh wow.*

I close my eyes as I relish the sensation.

"Jesus Christ!" Beckett says. "Do that again!"

I obey.

"Goddammit," Beckett says. "Fuck, that is amazing."

I do a triumph lap in my head.

I lick my way back to his tip, my tongue dancing over his cock with gleeful pleasure.

Strangely enough, even though I'm on my knees, I feel empowered every time he growls.

"You're ready for the next level," he says.

My eyes fly open, lifting up to his.

The validation means so much.

"I need your mouth around my cock." His voice is like gravel.

"Okay."

He positions his cock like an offering and I take him in my mouth, placing my hands on his thighs. I already know Beckett is huge, but that doesn't prepare me for what comes next.

He thrusts his cock deep into my mouth, hitting the back of my throat.

I gag, my eyes tearing a little.

"You're okay?" he asks.

I've come too far to back down now.

I nod with his cock still trapped between my lips.

"We're going to take it nice and slow at first," he says.

I nod again.

"Work your warm mouth up and down my cock. It's that simple."

And I do.

The more I suck him, the more my arousal ratchets.

Beckett grabs my hair and wraps it around his fist, clearing my view, and making it much easier for me to give him pleasure.

"Take me all the way, you dirty, filthy girl."

*My God, this is hot.*

I do as I'm told.

Up and down.

Up and down.

I can't get enough of his taste. Ditto for the sounds of pleasure spilling from his lips.

He pulls my hair hard, as if he wants me to stop.

I latch onto his cock, unwilling to let go.

"Stop!"

Determination fuels me as I take in a few more inches of his impressive cock. In my overzealousness, his cock hits the back of my throat with force.

This time, I gag so much, I'm certain I'm going to throw up, but it's not enough to deter me from my mission.

"Baby, I said stop!"

*Goddamnit, he's going to come inside my mouth if it's the last thing he does.*

Like a stubborn mule, I go at it with more fervor.

"Oh, fuck!"

He's no longer asking me to stop.

"You want my cum?" I nod again before swirling my tongue around his shaft. "You're going to get it." No sooner the warning leaves his mouth than he presses my head, leaving me no choice but to take him fully.

*My God.*

Beckett rocks his hips back and forth, fucking my mouth deeper. I don't gag when he hits the back of my throat for the third time.

This is so raw, so lewd, and so incredibly hot.

Sharp inhalations accelerate as my eyes water and my chest heaves with the filthy thrill of it all.

Up and down.

Up and down.

I close my hands around his balls and squeeze them with care.

"Jesus!" he says.

He clamps a hand firmly at the back of my head and tilts his hips up.

"Fuck, baby. Yeah. Suck me."

I answer with a whimper.

I'm no longer in control.

I'm forced to submit to him completely as he fucks my mouth over and over again like an animal. I should hate the forcefulness of his thrusts, but I don't.

He dictates the cadence.

And by God, do I ever love it.

"Oh, shit," he says. "That's it. Fucking take my cock, baby."

I'm so turned on, I don't know what to do with myself. It's a bit tricky, but I manage to keep my teary eyes fixed on his gorgeous face as I watch him take pleasure from my mouth. I slide a hand between my legs in search of relief.

His eyes fly open. "I make you come, or you don't come at all," he says.

I hesitate for a second because I really, really need to come.

"I mean it, Arianne. The decision is in your hand, pun very much intended." His words leave no room for negotiation.

I move my hand away.

"Good girl," he says. "I was trying to ease you into it, but since you're determined to go all the way, finish sucking me off with your filthy mouth."

His words travel all the way to my desperate clit.

*Damn.*

I roll my hips side to side, seeking some salvation.

"Which part didn't you understand?" he asks. "I. Make. You. Come."

Like a docile pupil, I behave.

*I can't believe the hold this man has on me.*

I guess he's pleased because he resumes fucking my mouth.

The cadence of his thrusts is almost frantic now.

I moan into his cock, my whole body rising and falling with every stroke and my saliva dripping off my chin.

His breathing grows ragged each time he slams to the back of my throat, but I'm a pro now. I don't gag.

Beckett is relentless.

Saliva runs down his cock, down my hand and my arm.

"I'm close," he says.

He pumps harder into my mouth.

This is so unbelievably hot.

The man rocked my world in Germany, but what he's doing now takes the cake.

His hips jerk, and all movement stops.

I lift my eyes up just in time to watch his head loll back.

"Oh, Christ! Your fucking beautiful mouth, Arianne."

Beckett comes, and comes, and comes.

A jet of warm cum floods my mouth.

He wasn't kidding about dumping a river of cum in my mouth. I swallow every last drop, even though it's a struggle.

"Good girl," he says in a low voice.

Beckett grips my shoulders, forcing me to tear my mouth away from his cock. He pulls me to my feet and looks intently into my eyes when he says, "I need to feel you come around my cock."

I lick my lips still coated with his cum. "Oh, okay."

"Let me run upstairs to grab a condom." He stands up.

"If you need to feel me come around your cock, wouldn't it be more powerful without a condom?" I ask in a confident voice that makes his eyebrows hit his forehead.

"What are you saying?" he asks.

I offer a one-shoulder shrug. "I already know what it's like when you come all over my pussy... I'd love to know what it's like when you come inside me."

A low, guttural caveman-like noise rumbles from his throat, his eyes flashing with heat.

# Chapter 42

## *Beckett*

I swear to God, my cock spews cum at her unexpected suggestion. Asking me to fuck her bareback is like handing me the keys to Paradise.

"You're sure about this?"

I can't believe I'm asking her this question, but I don't want her to walk into this blindly.

"I'm sure," she says.

"This is a big step for us."

"I know."

"If I fuck you bareback, there's no going back."

"I wouldn't dream of it."

"It also means you belong to me because there's no way I'll ever allow another man to enjoy what's rightfully mine."

"I wouldn't want to belong to anyone else, Beckett."

Fuck, if those words don't do something to me.

"Judging from how much cum I released into your pretty mouth, this couch won't survive what I'm about to unleash on you," I tell her.

Her eyes are so fucking wide, I bite off a smile.

"Bend over the couch."

She's just about to climb on the couch, but I stop her.

"Not over the armrest," I say. "It's too low. I want your body bent over the back cushion."

She obeys.

I come and stand behind her.

"Legs spread apart," I say at the same time as I kick them open. "Use your elbows as leverage."

"Okay." There's an unmistakable tinge of nervousness in her voice.

I like it.

A hiss of pleasure escapes her lips when my chest presses against her back and my cock slides under her wet pussy.

"How do you want it?" I murmur my question close to her ear.

"You decide."

I press my hardness against her. "I need it rough."

"I—I'm okay with that"

"You sure?"

"I am." Not an ounce of hesitation.

"Hold on tight, baby."

I slip one arm around her waist to hold her steady, grip my cock with the other hand and position it at her entrance, teasing her tender lips.

"Oh God!" She yelps when I thrust into her balls deep.

"Jesus Christ!" I'm so deep, she's forced onto her tiptoes.

She's so fucking wet.

And so fucking tight.

The skin-on-skin contact is mind-blowing—far more potent than I ever could've imagined.

I pull out, leaving her warmth, before thrusting deep once more.

She groans.

Because I'm a greedy bastard, I do it over, and over, and over again.

*Goddammit.*

I can't get enough of her.

"Fuck, your pussy," I say. "I'll never get used to how tight or slick you are. I can't get enough of this sensation."

She whimpers.

"Do you feel me inside you, baby?"

"Hell, yes."

"You like how your man is fucking you?"

"Ohhhh yes." Her voice is breathy.

Bracing herself on her elbows, she lifts up on her toes and grinds back against me, her hips gyrating in wild circles. I can't resist.

*Slap!*

"Greedy girl, *I* set the pace."

"Please, Beckett," she says. "I really need to come."

"You will... when I say so."

She lets out a little sob.

"Poor little lamb." I chuckle. "I promise, it'll be worth your while."

The way her body slumps in resignation, lets me know, she won't argue with me.

*Good.*

I resume my mission.

I fuck her long and hard.

The cadence is so frantic, I barely have time to catch a breath. Given how wet she is, I'm surprised I'm able to hold on this long.

This is pure wantonness.

"Please, please, please, please, let me come." She begs so beautifully, I can't refuse her.

"How bad do you want it?"

"I can't hold back anymore. I need to come. I'll do anything you ask."

Her pleading makes my balls tighten.

With my cock buried deep, I slide the hand I'm holding her with down to the damp strip of hair and I find her clit—hard and engorged with blood.

She gasps and grinds against my hand with determination, seeking the friction she needs as she chases after her climax.

She's wild.

I fuck her in sharp little thrusts, my hand pressed against her clit. "Come hard for me."

"I—I—" She's so close. I fuck her faster. "God—" Her body shudders and she lets out a long wail as she gives in to her climax. "Oh, Beckett, oh, Beckett." She chants my name over and over again, clenching hard against my cock.

"Baby, you're my drug!" I grip her hips tight and fuck that beautiful pussy like there's no tomorrow—like she's the last woman on earth and that's it, no more. "Fuckkkk!" I roar, slamming home one last time as my balls erupt. My turn to shudder and tremble, only just holding us upright as my cum fills her.

My body gives into exhaustion.

I can't do much more than catch my breath.

From the sound of it, she's in the same predicament.

When my breathing returns to normal, I pull out of her.

She doesn't move. She doesn't even make a sound.

"You're still with me?" I ask.

She holds herself up with her elbows. "I'm not sure."

I chuckle.

"Let's go upstairs for round two."

"Wait. What?"

She turns her head to look at me.

Her eyes are so huge, they nearly take over her beautiful face.

"Round two," I say.

"But you just came."

"I know," I tell her. "But now that I know how sweet it is to fuck you without anything between us, just give me a few minutes to fill up and I'll be ready for another round."

"Who's using who for sex, mister?"

She laughs.

I don't.

A strange new thud beats against my chest with enough force to make my breath catch.

"It was a joke." Concern causes her eyelashes to flutter.

"This is more than sex for me, Arianne. You know that, don't you?"

Silence.

I wrap my arms around her and hug her into me. "Answer me, baby."

More silence.

"Baby?"

"Now I do."

# Chapter 43

## *Beckett*

**K**nock, knock, knock.
"Come in!" I say.

"I'm back!" Rhys walks into my office. "Did you miss me, honey?"

"Keep that up and I'll ship your ass right back to Asia permanently."

"Is that any way to greet your partner after twenty-one days away?" he says. "I'm a little offended. And hurt. And sad. And a million other emotions."

He's so not funny.

"We were texting constantly and we had plenty of video chats. It's not like we haven't been in contact for three weeks."

"It's not the same. Nothing can replace the face-to-face."

I roll my eyes.

"Are you in my office to display your newly acquired passion for bad acting or are you here for a reason?" I ask.

He takes a seat in one of the chairs across from my desk and leans forward, placing his elbows on his knees. Amusement dances in his eyes.

"What is it now?" I ask.

"I didn't think the day would come, but you proved me wrong."

"What are you talking about?"

He reaches for his suit pocket, pulls something out and tosses it on my desk.

My eyes drop to it before settling on his gaze.

It's a keychain I'm very familiar with.

"While I was away, Cecelia was my eyes and ears. Other than your business trip to Germany—which made a nice splash in the business section and boosted SCORE—it seems you and your cock managed to stay out of the papers. Since you held your end of the bargain and you were a choirboy for the last thirty days, I have to honor my word. And for the record, I'm shocked. My vintage motorcycle is now yours."

My eyes drop to the keychain again.

I gave up one temptation for another. No regrets.

"We just need to make arrangements to figure out when I deliver my pride and joy to your door," he says. "I'm sure your fist must be killing you by now. I guess tonight, you'll be heading to Dark Compulsion to make up for the last four weeks." He lets out a boisterous laugh.

I don't crack a smile.

Rhys texted me an hour ago to let me know he was on his way, but I've been ready for this conversation for a week now. It's time to get it out of the way. I was waiting for his return to talk to my executive assistant and his. I know Cecelia well. She pledges allegiance to her boss. I wanted Rhys to hear it from me and no one else.

"I can't accept your bike," I tell him.

He's incredulous. "What do you mean?"

"Exactly what I said. I can't accept your bike."

"Has hell frozen over without my knowledge?" He actually

looks outside the window. "Are you telling me Beckett Christensen is passing up on a chance to gloat about a win?"

*Idiot.*

"Let's have this conversation over there." I point to the couch area.

"Okay," he says and looks at me suspiciously.

We both get up and cross my office. I sit on the couch. He sits across from me on a large chair.

"What's up?" he asks.

I inhale a deep breath.

"I'm guessing you didn't uphold your end of the bargain," he says.

"You left a lot of room to manoeuvre," I tell him. "I became really creative at finding loopholes."

"As in?"

"As in kissing. You left that one off the list."

"You don't kiss women, so I didn't bother adding it—" His eyes widen as realization sinks in. "Arianne." It's not a question. He soldiers on without giving me a chance to answer. "Another notch in your belt, Christensen? Is that it?"

"It's not like that at all—"

He jumps to his feet. "This is just another case of you pulling down your boxer briefs, grabbing a ruler and measuring your cock to prove you have a bigger dick—which you don't."

"That's not it—"

"You couldn't keep your hands off her? Everyone has to be your plaything?" he says. "I'm sure you've already moved on to another woman." His eyes radiate with rage.

"You're dead wrong," I tell him.

"Sure." He shakes his head.

In many ways, his reaction doesn't surprise me given my history, but I didn't expect him to be this slicing.

"You mean, your generosity extends to two nights now, instead of just one?" Sarcasm laces his words.

"No," I say. "I mean, Arianne and I are dating."

His jaw drops.

"I'm a 'one woman' kind of man now, Rhys."

"You? Dating?"

"Yes."

"You're not fucking other women? No more Dark Compulsion for you?"

"No to the first question, and yes to the second, but with Arianne."

"Are you shitting me right now?"

"I wouldn't joke about something like this. I really like her, and we have a great thing going on."

He comes to stand in front of me and studies me long and hard.

I lift my gaze to his and hold it.

I'm not going to bother getting up.

I can do this alpha shit from where I'm sitting.

Seconds tick by as we each stand our ground.

Rhys steps backward until he's sitting in the chair across from me.

"You're serious?"

"I am. I've never been compelled to date a woman before, but Arianne cast a spell on me, and frankly, I'm not itching to break it."

"Holy shit," Rhys says. "I guess I should say, *Holy Chic*."

We both laugh.

"That stupid t-shirt started it all," I say.

"Yeah, that and the steamy salsa dance."

"Arianne had me from the moment the lights were turned back on in the elevator, but Cesar's engagement party sealed my fate."

"I called you on it when we spoke the day those telling photos went viral, but you denied it."

"I answered your questions truthfully. It's not my fault you weren't asking the right ones."

"Omission is the same as denial," he says.

"Yada yada yada."

"I guess, that's beside the point now," he says. "Let's move on to the more important matter at hand... Beckett Christensen is off the market. What the fuck?"

"All this bullshit I've always heard about *the one*... it turns out it's just a question of bumping into her."

Rhys shakes his head in amazement. "I leave for three weeks and you're now pussy whipped."

"Guilty as charged!"

# Chapter 44

## *Arianne*

Rhys, Beckett, and I have been sitting in the 1938 Crocker conference room for the past thirty minutes. I've been dying to share my idea with them, but I wanted to wait for Rhys to return from Asia.

This is a month in the making. Thirty days of due diligence. Four weeks of thinking, planning and strategizing. Even though the ground-breaking idea was planted in my head well before our business trip, I can't deny the impact of the three-day conference in Germany. Looking at Sennheiser's success from the inside gave me the confidence to push forward.

"What do you think?" I ask when I finish my presentation.

"SCORE Yours," Rhys says.

"SCORE Yours," Beckett says.

I nod. "SCORE Yours."

They exchange a knowing look like they're having a silent conversation.

I've already walked Rhys and Beckett through the production aspect of the project, now it's a question of selling them on how this edgy concept is what their company needs to reach the next level.

"It has strong brand recognition and 'yours' brings forth the unique aspect of this new line of product," I tell them.

"I can see it," Rhys says.

"Everything on the market is a different shade of sameness," I say. "SCORE Yours stands out. There are two ways of getting customizable headphones—you either do it yourself or you scour the pages of Etsy to find a refurbished pair with a design you like. With SCORE Yours, we're talking about brand new out-of-the-box top quality sleek painted headphones customized to your customers' taste. True, there's a waiting time—so, no instant gratification—but the end result will be well worth it."

"Pricey headphones with a high gloss paint job!" Beckett says.

"This is how your company goes from a few billion dollars to eight billion dollars or more."

They nod their approval.

"We'd paint the outer brackets, the outer headbands and domes," I tell them. "The slogan I had in mind goes as follows, *SCORE Yours—top quality headphones combined with our signature customization... just for you. As unique as you.*" I'm on a roll. "If we can source out some cool artists, we could also offer cool artwork or graffiti designs via decals as another exclusive customizable line." My eyes bounce from Rhys to Beckett.

"Arianne, this is pure gold!" Rhys says. "I love it!"

"I agree," Beckett says. "I love every aspect of this concept."

Pride courses through me.

Even though Beckett and I have been dating for nearly two months, I've guarded this idea close to my heart, careful not to reveal anything before the presentation.

"I'm pleased," I tell them.

"We already have an unfair advantage, but this will leave our competitors in the dust," Rhys says.

"That's the whole point," I say. "There will be copycats. But SCORE will be the first on the market, therefore the leader."

"As long as everybody remembers who's number one, I can live with that," Beckett says.

We all laugh.

"Now that you're on board, let's talk about launching SCORE Yours with a bang!" I say.

I can hardly contain my excitement!

# Chapter 45

## *Beckett*

"This is so nerve-racking," Arianne says. She squeezes my hand hard. I squeeze back.

"Just a few jitters," I tell her.

We're in the back of the chauffeured car on our way to the gala to announce SCORE Yours to the press. The affair is taking place at Building 22—a luxury tower not too far from Waldorf Astoria Beverly Hills.

"It's more than that..." She places a hand against her stomach. "I think I'm going to throw up."

*Shit.*

"Do you need me to ask the chauffeur to stop?"

She lifts a hand up.

I don't rush her.

With her eyes closed, she inhales a deep breath. Then, exhales.

She does that a few times before speaking.

"It was just a figure of speech, but God my stomach is tied up in a knot."

"Arianne, this isn't the first time you've spearhead a massive project. You've done it several times in the past. You have more than enough experience under your belt."

"I've always been in the background. Chance insisted on presenting my ideas to the rest of the company and the press. According to him, having more than one spokesperson is confusing."

"You know that's utter bullshit."

"I know now it was just part of his ploy to hog all the credits for Glach Tech's growth. Still, I've never been in this position before."

"You just smile for the camera and share your kickass idea. That's it."

"You make it sound so easy," she says with a nervous laugh.

"Because it is, baby. Don't forget, Rhys and I will be right by your side."

She nods and then averts her gaze. "What if the press hates the idea?"

The question has come up a few times leading to tonight.

"Look at me."

She offers a tentative side gaze.

"Arianne!"

She focuses her big brown eyes on me.

"They won't hate the idea because it's innovative, edgy and unique. Who doesn't want that? The press will gobble it up and disseminate the good gospel to the masses who will quickly convert to hardcore worshipers," I say.

She frowns.

"Religion at a time like this? Really?"

Okay, she didn't like the joke.

"What I'm trying to say is, there's nothing like SCORE Yours on the market," I tell her. "It's a sure antidote to plain headphones. Not even Sennheiser came up with the idea first. You did. What's there not to like?"

She lets out a long exhale. "Okay, you're right."

Her words don't match the petrified look on her face.

"You got this, Arianne," I say. Trust finally shimmers in her eyes. "If the press is too jaded to get on the program, they'll change their tune once they see us laughing all the way to the bank."

That gets me an earnest laugh.

She's a beautiful mix of fearlessness and uncertainty—the dichotomy still catches me off guard. I don't know why she's this worried. Rhys and I aren't the only ones who think this is a shoe in. She ran the idea by Easton. He was so impressed, he flew to Los Angeles to tell us in person. My former bandmates can't wait to get their hands on a pair of SCORE Yours. Holt has already placed an order for custom ones for his top artists. Rod and Loki—who run a video production company—did the same for their roster of clients. Just within our circle, the frenzy is at a fever pitch. If this is a precursor of things to come, this new venture will be a game changer for our company.

And let's not forget about Arianne's mind-boggling esti-mates. Even Easton agrees. Rhys and I went the distance. We made sure Arianne knew we were behind her one hundred percent. We had the legal team draft a contract. Easton hooked her up with a LA lawyer to review our offer. She accepted the generous terms. My girl is set to get a big payday out of this.

I reach out and wrap a strand of her loose hair around my finger. "The idea is solid, but if all else fails, the press will be so blinded by your beauty and how hot you look in this dress, they'll forget why they're there in the first place."

She laughs.

"I really like this dress," she says, smoothing down the fabric.

"It's arresting on you." Although I'd love nothing more than to ravish her lips, I kiss her on the cheek instead. This night is too important. I don't want to fuck up her perfectly applied makeup.

"Thank you," she says. "Andrea came through, once again."

She certainly did.

Arianne is wearing a striking hot pink dress that fits her slender body like a charm. In her trademark style, the dress hits her below the knee. Even though the sleeves are long, the edgy design amps up the sex kitten factor by exposing her shoulders. Sexy strappy heels in the same bright shade and a pair of crystal-encrusted earrings complete the look.

She looks good enough to eat.

My cock nudges against my suit pants, aching for attention. From its eagerness, you'd never know I was balls deep inside her an hour ago.

*Down, boy.*

I brush my fingertips over her exposed shoulder. "It's the right dress for someone about to make history." This is exactly what we're doing tonight.

For the rest of the ride, I hold her hand. It seems to be enough to help calm her nerves.

"We're here." I point to the tall building in front of us.

This venue is as Hollywood as it gets.

The deluxe venue is located near Rodeo Drive and the Hollywood Walk of Fame—where my band have our own star. Six weeks ago, after her stellar presentation, Arianne said we needed a venue that was guaranteed to get attention for our big night. It had to be Building 22. This is lavish, with a capital L.

"We're here already?" There's a distinct tremolo in her voice. "That was much faster than I expected."

I arch my eyebrows. "You're the first person in the history of mankind to complain about *not* being stuck in LA traffic."

She giggles.

I pull out my phone and text the publicity team. I have yet

to hire a personal publicist, but since I'm a one-woman-man these days, I don't have to worry. When it comes to all things SCORE, Josephine (Joey) Boswell is the agency's point person. She responds to let me know she's already there with three of her employees. Then, I text Rhys. He's on his way with his date. Satisfied, I tuck my phone inside my suit pocket.

"Everything is in place?" Arianne asks.

"This night will go without a hitch."

"From your lips to God's ears."

As the car comes to a stop in front of Building 22, I bring her hands to my lips and drop a soft kiss. "It's showtime, baby!"

"This is it?!"

I lean into her. "I know of an effective way of mellowing you out."

"I'm all ears."

I lean in closer so she's the only one to hear what I'm about to say. "We find a quiet place inside Building 22, I drop to my knees, lift the hem of your pretty dress, and ravish your pussy until you come all over my face. That should do the trick."

I pull away from her and wait.

I already took care of my girl's pussy, but if she needs another round, I'm willing to sacrifice myself for the greater good. I'm that kind of boyfriend.

I expect her to scold me for my bad behavior, but the veil of lust glistening from her eyes lets me know she might take me up on my offer.

*Bring it on!*

"I'm tempted," she says. "But if we get caught, we'd end up making history for a whole other reason. A sex video on the internet isn't on my bucket list."

I don't miss the little squirm she makes in her seat as if trying to relieve an ache between her thighs.

*Damn.*

I want to relieve that tension gripping her.

"Can I take a rain check on the offer for later when we're back at your place?"

I laugh.

"You can count on it." I kiss her forehead. "Let's get out of this car."

On cue, a doorman helps Arianne out.

I receive the same treatment.

I round the vehicle and meet her on the sidewalk.

I circle a possessive arm around her waist.

"Come to think about it, we're making history in three ways tonight," I say.

She frowns up at me.

"I can only think of one. What are the other two?"

"One, the unveiling of SCORE Yours' lineup of proto-types." I lift one finger as I enumerate my points. "Two, this is our first big affair since dating. Three, this is our first time together walking the red carpet."

"You're right." She smiles wide. "I can see the headlines now—"

"'BREAKING NEWS: MISS HOLY CHIC STEPS OUT IN STYLE WITH SEXY-AS-FUCK CEO BOYFRIEND'," I say with a grand hand gesture.

She laughs, and laughs, and laughs.

"All right, Miss Holy Chic, get it together."

"I'm ready!"

I search the crowd until I see Joey.

She waves.

"The team is in position," I tell Arianne.

"At least we have backup just in case the piranhas decide to eat us alive."

The press can be heartless. Lucky for us, Joey is in our corner.

We barely take a step when the press assaults us.

"Beckett! Arianne! Over here!" A tall blonde photographer waving a hand is the first to catch our attention.

I angle my body so we're both facing her.

She points a lens at us, and a group of photographers huddle around her and follow her cue. For a few seconds, they're frantically taking photos while shouting our names.

"Who's on the invite list?" A well-known celebrity blogger shouts that question.

"Family. Friends. Influencers. Celebrities." I rattle off the list. "In other words, the usual suspects."

I'm downplaying it.

He'll find out soon enough since all of our guests will walk the red carpet. Given my contacts—and Rhys's—it's an impressive list.

Amongst the heavy hitters expected tonight, Cello2Cello will show up to support us. So will Gage, the executive producer of the show the three of us co-judge. My buddies Collin and his big brother Shane Dennison are among the lineup of illustrious guests. Cesar and Diana are among the stars coming out tonight along with a lot of people on Rhys's side.

"Are you two dating?" An older man wearing a pair of enormous glasses with a blue frame and yellow-tinted lenses shouts the question. The crazy colors of his glasses match his outfit—yellow pants and a blue shirt.

*Talk about making a statement.*

"It's official, we are," I say.

"Do you go by #BeckAri or #AriBeck?" he asks. "I tried other options—like #ArBe—but the first two are solid."

This guy has too much time on his hands.

"Neither," I tell him. "It's Arianne *and* Beckett. Please don't mash-up our names."

"Why not?" he asks. "I think #AriBeck has a nice ring to it. Very catchy."

*I don't give a fuck what you think.*

I just glare at him before moving my attention to my girlfriend.

"Come on, let's keep walking," I tell her, pulling her forward.

"Arianne, over here!" A striking black woman shouts. We stop right in front of her. With her statuesque height, it's impossible to miss her. That said, her copper-red afro, fitted white mini dress, and thigh-high leather hot pink-heeled boots make her stand out even more.

"Those are Cedrics!" She points to my girl's feet.

"Guilty as charged," Arianne says. "Cedric de Seignard shoes are my weakness."

"They're from the new collection," the black woman says. "I love them on you."

"Thanks. I love them as well," Arianne says.

"The question burning everyone's tongue is... who are you wearing?" the reporter asks, giving my girl an appreciative onceover.

Arianne blurts out the name of the design-duo.

"You have great taste," the woman says.

Arianne beams.

"I'm also a big fan," the woman says. "I hunt down their designs at secondhand shops. I get my dresses chopped off really short to showcase my best assets." She extends a leg to drive her point.

"You look amazing and confidence drips all over you," Arianne tells her. "There's no way I'd be able to get away with that. I'm not used to calling that much attention to myself."

"Oh, honey, you think hanging from Beckett Christensen's arm isn't calling attention to you? If so, think again," the woman says. Her eyes move to mine and she cocks an eyebrow.

I'm caught off guard by her boldness.

Reporters and bloggers laugh.

My girl's face turns a bright shade of red.

"I don't know how to respond to that," Arianne says.

"I'm sure you already know, but it bears stating the obvious, you're the envy of a lot of women in this country..." the striking beauty says, before shifting her eyes to me again, "present company very much included."

*She just goes for it.*

"How did you lasso him in, Arianne? After all, many have tried, but so far, Mr. Christensen has always remained a free agent." She's right on the money. "What's your secret, Arianne?"

My girlfriend doesn't know what to do with herself.

She looks up at me for reinforcement.

"The t-shirt!" I say, coming to her rescue. "Definitely the t-shirt." I nod. "Followed closely by her sultry salsa dance moves. I'm only a man. I couldn't resist."

Laughter explodes around us.

"Arianne and Beckett you look like a real power couple," a redhead says from behind a camera before popping her head up.

"Thank you," my girl says.

"Great suit, Beckett." Her amber eyes eat me up. "Impeccable as always. Bespoke, I'm sure."

"Thanks," I say. "And yes, tailored is the only way to go in my world."

The redhead shifts her attention to my girl. "Arianne, how is bad boy Beckett Christensen as a boyfriend?"

Arianne bites her lower lip before answering. "I know this sounds cliché, but I'm the luckiest woman in the world." Pride puffs up my chest, but she takes it one step further. "He's absolutely wonderful. I couldn't ask for more."

*Well, hell.*

"By the way, you two would make super cute babies," the redhead says. "I'm talking baby-model cute."

"Err..." Arianne hesitates and looks up at me, her eyes shimmering with something I can't read. Her cheeks are as rosy as her dress. She tears her gaze away from mine and sets it on the reporter. "Thank you?!"

I'm not sure if that's a question or an exclamation. I suspect, she's as thrown off as I am. Holt is right, words like baby usually scare the shit out of me. Why I'm now picturing my girl's belly swollen and tight with our child is beyond me.

A booming voice puts an end to my musing.

"I knew I saw a baby bump!" Enormous Glasses shouts.

My head whips in his direction.

*Where? Behind her ears?*

"Are you looking forward to fatherhood, Beckett?" he asks.

What an asshole for fanning a lie that has the potential of going viral even before we enter Building 22.

"Do you want a boy or girl?" a reporter asks.

"Any names for the baby yet?" That question comes from the celebrity blogger.

"What if you're having twins?" Another female reporter wants to know.

"Or triplets?" the male reporter standing next to her asks.

I'm floored.

The redhead's comment starts a wildfire and Enormous Glasses poured gasoline all over it.

The press starts shooting a barrage of questions at us, fishing for a scoop. Since they're speaking over each other, it's impossible to make sense of anything. Not that it matters.

*We're done here.*

"Ladies! Gentlemen!" I shout over the chaos, lifting a hand to silence them. "This is as much as we're willing to discuss about our personal life. If you have questions about why we're gathered here tonight, Arianne Buchanan—the mastermind behind SCORE Yours—has all the answers. If she's busy, our PR agency will be more than happy to schedule interviews." I point to the four women standing near the door, flanked by bodyguards.

Another frantic round of flashes ensues, blinding us in the process, as the press throws more questions at us.

"What about a kiss?" The provocative question comes from the reporter wearing the giant glasses. "After all, Arianne Buchanan makes history tonight by being the first woman to capture the elusive bad boy rock star turned CEO."

He was irritating the hell out of me a few minutes ago, but now, I'm warming to him.

I turn to face a blushing Arianne.

"The guy's right," I say. "If we're going to make history, we might as well seal it with a kiss."

She smiles, her eyes gleaming with mirth.

I reach out and dip her, Hollywood style.

It's dramatic and picture-worthy.

Arianne looks petrified. Her eyes take over her face.

"Oh my God. Oh my God. Oh my God." She struggles with the lower part of her dress. "Beckett, stop! Please, stop!"

It takes me a second to catch on.

*Fuck!*

I demanded she goes commando and now I'm about to expose her pussy to the world.

*Way to go, Christensen.*

I straighten her so she's standing.

Her eyes are still wide. Her flesh is so flush, I can't discern between her skin and her dress.

I bite off a smile.

"Sorry," I say. "We were going to reveal a little too much about our relationship."

"Way too much."

"That's for my eyes only. No one else sees it."

A little complicit smile plays across her mouth. "I should hope not."

"Kiss! Kiss! Kiss!" The group of reporters chant.

Arianne and I exchange a wicked glance.

"The first rule of show business is to give people what they want," I say.

"It's only good business practice," she says.

My girlfriend and I lock lips to a roaring and clamoring crowd.

*Fuck, yeah! History in the making!*

# Chapter 46

## *Beckett*

I hang up with Joey, pride washing over me.

*Wow.*

The PR firm can hardly handle interview requests. One week after the unveiling, and it's like the whole country is waiting with bated breath for the official release date of SCORE Yours headphones. We knew we had a hit on our hands, but the media's reaction is far more enthusiastic than we could've ever hoped for.

As I scroll down the latest search results, I can't help but shake my head, amazed and pleased.

*'SCORE YOURS HEADPHONES: THE NEWEST MUST-HAVE IN TERMS OF GADGETS!'*

*'SCORE YOURS HEADPHONES: UNIQUE WITHOUT EVER COMPROMISING ON QUALITY!'*

*'ARIANNE BUCHANAN, THE MASTERMIND BEHIND SCORE YOURS, HITS IT OUT OF THE PARK.'*

*'SCORE STEPS AHEAD OF SENNHEISER WITH THIS
LATEST COUP!'*

I particularly like the last headline.

It's not easy to step ahead of a giant.

Since time was of the essence, Arianne sourced a handful of local artists, graffiti artists, and even a badass mechanic—who does insane custom paint and design jobs on vintage bikes. The six artists put their talent to work by coating basic white headphones with top quality paint jobs or standout-art on the prototypes for the unveiling. As a result, pre-orders are coming in massive numbers. That's why my girl and Rhys have been at Tekknika Audio all week in endless production meetings while I hold the fort down here.

Our public kiss also caused quite the frenzy.

*'ANOTHER BAD BOY OFF THE MARKET. BECKETT
CHRISTENSEN IS TAKEN!'*

*'ARIANNE BUCHANAN AND BECKETT
CHRISTENSEN, LA'S NEWEST POWER COUPLE!'*

*'ARIANNE BUCHANAN AND BECKETT
CHRISTENSEN LOCK LIPS IN SWOON-WORTHY
HOLLYWOOD-STYLE KISS.'*

*'BREAKING NEWS: BECKETT CHRISTENSEN NO
LONGER FLYING SOLO, LADIES!'*

Just like Cesar, a lot of guys in my circle have been giving me a hard time about my new relationship status. My parents and Holt adore Arianne.

*Knock, knock, knock.*

There's a rap at the door.

"Come in," I say, lifting my gaze.

The door opens, and a blonde pokes her head in.

"Beckett Christensen, right?" she asks.

The day after the unveiling, the building was under siege by a swarm of reporters. It's not like we weren't expecting a certain level of excitement. We beefed up security accordingly. Things have somewhat died down, but I'm not surprised a sneaky reporter would do just about anything to get a scoop on a story.

"How the hell did you get in here?" I ask.

"Finally," the blonde says, letting herself in. "I've been bouncing all over this floor to find you. Where is everybody?"

It's lunchtime, which explains why the executive floor is nearly empty, but that's none of her business.

"You want an interview or information about SCORE Yours, contact our PR agency! As far as I'm concerned, you're trespassing—"

"I'm not a reporter," she says.

I arch an eyebrow. "Who are you?"

The blonde approaches, strutting with an exaggerated swing of the hips. She comes to stand right in front of my desk.

I knit my eyebrows together.

*Where have I seen her before?*

*And why is she even wearing a trench coat when it's hot outside?*

"I asked you a question," I tell her.

Her painted red lips break into a wide smile as her brown eyes—which seem too far apart—hold mine.

"Surely *she's* talked about me," the woman says.

"Who are you talking about?"

"The bane of my existence, that's who," she says, as if I'm supposed to clue in.

This woman looks a little too put together—and too coherent—to be high on drugs. Then again, I'm sure I looked like I had my shit together when I was in fact high as a kite back in the day.

I reach for my phone. "Listen, lady, I'm about to call security—"

"I wouldn't do that if I were you."

"You think you can boss me around? Whatever medication you're on, ask your doctor for a new prescription—"

"You'll want to hear what I have to say, Beckett."

I narrow my gaze and study her. Something about her demeanor suggests I tread carefully.

"I'm going to ask three simple questions. You answer them or I call the police," I tell her.

"Hit me with your best shot," she says in a flirtatious tone.

"Who are you? Why are you here? And how the hell did you get into my building?"

She slides a finger between her teeth and bites against it like you'd expect a shy little girl would do. She also does this thing with her shoulders. It looks like a rehash seduction tool from her lame bag of tricks.

"I'm Nerdy Ari's cousin," she says.

"Who?"

"Arianne Buchanan," she says.

*Then it hits me.*

"You're Mariah Golightly?"

"She *has* talked about me?" She beams gleefully. "Of course she would. She's a little obsessed with me because she wants to be me, but she can't."

It takes everything in me not to roll my eyes.

"Let me guess. You're here to order SCORE Yours headphones as wedding favors?" I ask.

"You're funny, but no," she says. "I'm here because you and

I can work out a deal that would be mutually beneficial for everyone concerned—"

"I doubt we have anything to talk about," I say. "You still haven't answered my last question. How the hell did you get into my building?"

She lets out a dramatic sigh. "I flew in from Silicon Valley late last week after your big announcement—and those stupid photos of you kissing Nerdy Ari—drowned *my* announcement."

*Nerdy Ari? How fucking condescending.*

"I secured the top celebrity baker to create a show-stopping piece for my wedding, and thanks to you two, the press practically ignored me."

*This woman thinks too highly of herself.*

"I've been hanging around your building for a couple days now, trying to figure out how to get your attention. It's amazing what you can get when you give great head. I just love giving blowjobs. Bonus, your new recruit has a pretty big dick. So, it was a win-win. I sucked him off twenty minutes ago, and in return, he snuck me in."

*Someone's about to get their ass fired—*

*Wait a minute?*

*Great head?*

*Blowjobs?*

*Isn't Mariah engaged?*

I don't know what this woman has up her sleeve, so I cut to the chase.

"If you're here to see my girlfriend, I suggest you leave your contact information with our receptionist on your way out—"

"Girlfriend?" The look of disgust on Mariah's face is quite telling. "Beckett Christensen can do so much better than Nerdy Ari—"

"Don't you dare call her that again." I wave a warning finger at her.

Mariah holds my icy gaze.

"Touchy," she says.

"*Very* when it comes to Arianne," I say, exerting as much self-control as I can muster. "Just so you know, I don't give a fuck what you think about my relationship. If you flew in to give me a piece of your mind, you might as well turn around—"

"Let's play it your way, Beckett." She flashes me an artificially wide grin. "I have something that could destroy your so-called girlfriend's pristine image and shatter her reputation to pieces if it were to go... viral."

"Are you threatening my girlfriend?"

She smirks. "I have your undivided attention now."

She takes a seat in one of the guest chairs without being invited, flashing me in the process. Her micro-length trench barely covers anything.

*Classy.*

She crosses a leg and dangles a foot clad in a thigh-high white leather boot, a demonic grin stretching her lips.

"You're not welcome here, neither are your empty threats—"

"I have video clips of your so-called girlfriend fucking on camera," she says.

*What the actual fuck?*

She opens her handbag, pulls out a phone and waves it.

I'm too shocked to speak.

"Nerdy Ari's—Oopsie." She flashes her too-white teeth. She's grating on my last nerve. "I mean, Arianne's face is clear, so there's no mistaking it's her." Mariah fixes her eyes on me, and all I see is hatred.

She arches an expectant eyebrow.

Everything in my body is buzzing with acute awareness.

If she's holding onto a bomb, I need to figure out how to disarm it before it explodes. Sex videos are no laughing matter when they're scattered across the internet.

I lean against my chair and bring my hands to my lap. In a slow, deliberate move, I slide my hand underneath my desk until I find three buttons. I press the middle one. With one simple touch, this entire conversation will be recorded. There are cameras and microphones in every corner of my office. When we started SCORE, Larkin suggested this set-up as an insurance policy. We didn't argue. Rhys's office and all the conference rooms are rigged in the same way.

I do a mental countdown before speaking.

"Mariah, those are some big claims." I play it cool even though my blood is boiling.

"I'm holding Arianne's life in the palm of my hand, Beckett." She waves her phone again.

*Smile for the camera, bitch!*

"If I understand correctly, you're saying you have a video of Arianne having sex on camera and the video is on your phone?"

"Are you deaf? I just said that!" she says.

"That's a lot to process. I just want to make sure I got it right."

"Just so we're clear, it's not just one video. There are several, and I also have a bunch of explicit photos."

*I have you where I want you, you scheming piece of scum.*

"How do I know you're not bluffing, Mariah? After all, how would you get your hands on videos of your cousin having sex with men?"

"Men? Please." Mariah rolls her eyes. "Nerdy Ari—"

"Watch your mouth!"

She stares at me.

I stare back.

We glare at each other for a few short beats.

"I'm still waiting for an answer," I say.

"Chance keeps them on a cloud. He also has hard copies on a memory stick in a safe."

My blood freezes.

"Are you saying Chance recorded videos of them having sex and he took pictures?"

"Something like that."

"Yes or no?"

"Yes."

"We're talking about Chance Taboras, CEO of Glach Tech, and Arianne's ex-boyfriend?"

"No, we're talking about Chance Taboras, CEO of Glach Tech, and *my* fiancé," Mariah says.

*This isn't about you, idiot.*

*Thanks for incriminating the asshole, though.*

Mariah keeps talking. "He placed several cameras in his bedroom to capture my stupid cousin in the most compromising situations."

"Was Arianne aware she was being filmed?" I ask.

"Of course not." Mariah rolls her eyes. "That would defeat the purpose."

"I don't follow."

She uncrosses her leg and sits up a little straighter.

"I'm sure Arianne told you tons of false lies about me. It's not my fault if I'm a lot sexier and I know what I'm doing in bed. Chance took a liking to me immediately. I mean, obviously."

*False lies?*

That negates her accusation.

She's so dense, she doesn't even get it.

"Arianne never told me any lies about you, Mariah," I say. *I'll believe her before I ever believe you.*

"In any case." She shrugs. "Arianne was jealous Chance

fell head over heels for me at first sight. Chance wanted to be with me, but he wasn't sure how to get rid of Arianne without any backlash—"

"In case she got pissed off, he broke things off?" I play along.

"That and also because Chance made a lot of promises..."

"What kind of promises?"

*Spell it out, cunt.*

"Arianne hasn't told you anything about her relationship with Chance or about me?"

*My God, this woman is so self-centered it's nauseating.*

"I know she played an instrumental part in turning Glach Tech into what it is today—"

"You're exaggerating," Mariah says. "Arianne helped bring in a few more sales" —*as in millions upon millions of dollars of increased revenue*—"Chance feels strongly he could've eventually figured it out without her." *When? Next century?*

"Okay, so Chance had it covered." *Moving right along.*

"Yes, but my stupid cousin became too greedy for her own good," Mariah tells me.

"Arianne was pressing Chance's hand to get a big payout?"

"Exactly! The company is Chance's. She worked for him, therefore, all the ideas she came up with under his employment are technically his."

*Talk about warped logic.*

"There was no reason for him to fork out millions of dollars to her."

"Is that what Chance promised?"

Mariah flashes her fangs. "It was all part of the game. Chance was willing to tell Arianne anything she needed to hear as long as she made him a very rich man."

"Basically, Chance dangled a golden carrot in front of Arianne's nose so he could exploit her?"

"She was so gullible. She actually believed they had a future together. He was playing her since day one. Once Chance got what he wanted, he didn't need her anymore... especially not after I came into the picture. A wildly successful CEO needs a woman who reflects his success... which begs the question, why would you get trapped with Arianne? Is she pregnant?"

*No, that kind of shit is right up your alley, though.*

I ignore her.

"So, Chance never planned on making good on his promises to Arianne?" I'm repeating myself, but I want this to be airtight.

Mariah lets out an evil laugh. "He put the money to better use. He bought a much bigger house here in LA, a vacation home in the Greek Islands and one in the Caribbean, along with several pricey cars. He also got me a nine-carat diamond ring."

My eyes drop to her hand.

*Interesting, she isn't wearing her big rock.*

"If Chance had forked out the money he had promised Arianne, I would've ended up with a much smaller stone, and that would've been a crying shame."

*Once again, this is all about her.*

"A man is only as good as his word, Mariah," I tell her.

"Please," she says. "Chance became very good at stalling, which is why he never signed any agreements or contracts. He's so smart."

*You mean, he's a despicable and dishonest scumbag.*

"It's her word against that of a prominent CEO. She's just a peon. Not to mention, it's not like she can hire lawyers to fight *my* man."

"I'm still confused as to how all this relates to me?" I move things along because with everything that's coming out of her degenerate mouth, my rage compounds. I can't trust myself to keep my cool much longer.

"You're dating her, which means she's hogging all the media attention from *my* pending wedding."

*My jaw drops because who the hell says that kind of shit?*

"You're here because you don't want us to be as public about our relationship?"

She shakes her head. "I'm here because I'm fucking tired of seeing Arianne's stupid, grinning face all over the place. I refuse to be overshadowed by Miss Holy Fucking Chic. I hired one of the top PR companies in New York to document the journey to my big day. This is supposed to be *my* time to shine. *My* year. *My* big moment. *My* opulent royal wedding." She slams a closed fist against her chest with each statement. Given the massive size of her breasts, I really should say, her shoulder. "All eyes are supposed to be on *me*, but nooooo. My loser of a cousin had to snag a multi-billionaire CEO who just happens to be a former rock star. Chance isn't repulsive per se, but let's face it, he's a far cry from a super hot and much younger hunk like you."

*Talk about stand by your man.*

"This aggravating media circus needs to stop and you're going to make it happen!"

There's a truckload of bitterness and dare I say, a scary layer of batshit craziness in that tirade.

"I don't see how I can help," I say.

"I'm going to give you an ultimatum."

My eyebrows pull together. "Are you high?"

She lifts her phone at eye level. "Remember, I can destroy Arianne Buchanan in a heartbeat." I'm this close from leaping across my desk to wrestle that fucking phone out of her goddamn hand. "Imagine the negative implications for your upcoming SCORE Yours and your company at large if I were to leak the sex videos Chance recorded of my dumb cousin."

*The bitch is threatening me on top of threatening my girl?*

Once again, I coax myself to simmer down the volcano raging inside me.

"What do you want me to do?" I ask.

"Finally, you're asking the right question." Mariah smirks.

I expect her to elaborate, but she stands up instead.

She drops her phone and handbag on my desk, undoes the sash at her waist, unbuttons her coat and exposes her body clad in a white mini see-through dress.

My head jerks back in surprise.

Her gigantic tits with huge areolas are just staring at me. Same for her full bush.

"These juicy melons are a hell of a lot better than Arianne's small oranges." Mariah cups her breasts, squeezing them with a moan.

*How can she walk without tipping over?*

"And what about this?" She turns around to expose her ass.

When Arianne said her cousin went for the reality TV starlet butt implant, she wasn't joking. That ass is a monstrosity, and it looks like it's made of rubber.

"I bet you want to fuck me," she says, looking over her shoulder.

*So my dick can fall off from the STDs? Yeah, I'll pass.*

I'm so repulsed, I want to barf.

Still, I maintain my composure.

"Thanks for the offer, Mariah, however, I'm in a relationship with Arianne. I don't stray."

Mariah flips around to face me. "Fucking Arianne again!" Her hands fly in the air before landing on her thighs in a loud thump. "Here's what you don't understand, I call the shots! You have two choices—you fuck me, or I leak the videos of your so-called girlfriend on the internet."

For the first time in my life, I consider strangling a person.

"Mariah—"

"Your cock!" She points at me. "My pussy!" She points to her cunt.

"What about Chance? I thought you were engaged?"

"I'm doing this *for* Chance! For us!"

"He won't mind?"

"He'll understand and support my decision. His face—and mine—should grace the front covers of magazines and websites. NOT YOURS AND NOT ARIANNE'S!" She shouts that last sentence so loud, I flinch. Her eyes are demented and it's like she's foaming at the mouth.

With extreme caution—and without breaking eye contact—I slide my hand under my desk, but this time, I press the first button, which alerts security of a code red situation. They'll get 911 on the line in a blink of an eye.

"After Arianne was out of our lives, I tried to convince Chance to get rid of the videos and images." She's not done spewing shit. "He refused, stating they might come in handy someday. We can finally put them to good use."

*This woman is out of her fucking mind.*

"Basically, either option would destroy Arianne," I say. "If I fuck you, you'll make sure Arianne knows about it and that would be the end of our relationship. On top of that, she'll be devastated—"

"Exactly."

*What a piece of shit.*

"You should've seen the despair on Arianne's face when my little ruse worked and she thought Chance had knocked me up. Priceless." The bitch actually laughs.

"If I don't fuck you—"

"I'd much prefer if you did."

My anger is about to erupt.

I bite down against my teeth so hard, I'm surprised they don't shatter inside my mouth.

"If I don't fuck you," I say, "Arianne's image will be destroyed forever because of the sex videos."

"I knew you'd understand!"

I nod. "Oh, I understand very well."

It's mind-boggling how Mariah is determined to hurt Arianne for no apparent reason other than jealousy and envy.

"Arianne will only be left with her three fancy-schmancy degrees to wipe her ass with. No one will want to touch her. No one will want to hire her. No company in their right mind will want to be associated with her. She'll have to crawl back to Philadelphia and work at Mommy and Daddy's tacky and God-awful chicken nugget restaurants."

"Let's make a deal," I say.

"I don't want to—"

"I'll buy the sex videos off you and we can call it a day."

"Err..." Mariah is caught off guard. "That's not an option."

"Why not?"

She hesitates again.

"Because..." Her words trail. "Because..." she repeats.

I lift the corners of my mouth into a fake smile. "Because... you don't like money?"

"Chance has money!"

"That's *his* money. Not yours," I say. "Do you really want to depend on a man for the rest of your life when you could be financially independent?"

She stares at me.

I sweeten the pot. "Technically, I should be paying off Chance, but he's not in my office, you are."

The wheels are churning in her head.

"How much would you be willing to pay?" she asks.

*Gotcha.*

"Life-changing money..." I set the stage. "Two million dollars under your name. I can wire the money anywhere in the world."

"That's not enough," she says.

*Now we're talking.*

"Name your price."

Her eyes shift from left to right.

She's thinking.

"For ten million dollars, you can have the stupid videos and the photos—"

The door busts open, interrupting her mid-sentence.

Mariah screams in fright.

Police officers pour into my office, followed by my security guards.

"LAPD! Hands up!" A female officer leading the pack, shouts, her gun pointing in front of her.

*This nightmare is over.*

"I didn't do anything wrong," Mariah says. "That man was trying to force me to have sex with him. You should be arresting him!" She waves an accusatory finger at me. "Look, he ripped my coat off."

I roll my eyes.

"Ma'am, I'm going to repeat this one more time," the female officer says. "Hands up!"

# Chapter 47

## *Arianne*

When an idea catches fire, it's a beautiful thing. It also means you have to strike while the iron is hot. Hence, why Rhys and I have sort of taken up permanent residence at Tekknika Audio. For the sixth day in a row, we're trapped in a conference room with Leland and his team. We've been at it all morning. I hope we'll stop for a lunch break soon. I need to run to the bathroom, replenish on food, and more importantly, text my boyfriend. Speaking of the very sexy CEO, I miss not seeing Beckett and I miss not being able to sneak around for some naughty fun without getting caught.

I was praying for last week's announcement to be a massive success.

God answered my prayers.

SCORE Yours scored big time!

The tidal wave of interest is overwhelming and humbling. As a result, the entire company is pedaling hard to start delivering SCORE Yours to an expectant crowd. Getting the prototypes done took a lot of strategizing, but going full-scale is a mammoth of a project. There are so many moving parts. Thank

God Leland and Rhys are confident we can deliver without fail.

*Phew!*

As Leland confers with his team about a question Rhys just asked, my phone chimes on the conference table. Beckett's name flashes across the screen. I can't help my smile of delight.

*Someone misses me.*

Out of respect to the people in the room, I ignore the text.

Another ensues.

Then, another.

And another.

And another.

*What's going on?*

My eyes shift to Rhys's phone, which is also flashing with Beckett's name.

Something is up.

"I'm sorry," I say, reaching for my phone. "I have to take this."

"Same here," Rhys says.

The opening line of his message has me on edge.

> Beckett: Drop everything and get here NOW!

> Arianne: Why?

> Beckett: It's too long to explain. This is urgent. Just get here! NOW! Same for Rhys.

I look up at Rhys, and he's sporting the same puzzled look on his face as I'm sure is reflected on mine.

"I don't know what's going on, but let's get out of here," he says.

"Yeah," I say.

"Leland, something urgent came up at the office and Beckett needs us back immediately," Rhys says.

"There's more than enough to keep us busy," Leland says. "Once you've extinguished the fires, shoot me a text or call."

"Will do," Rhys says. "Let me warn the chauffeur," he tells me.

"Sounds good," I say.

While Rhys shoots off a text, I gather my things and slip them in my handbag.

Once he's done, we make our exit.

Since it's a short ride from Tekknika to SCORE, there isn't much time to speculate. As the car approaches the building, my eyes grow wide.

"What the hell?" Rhys speaks first.

I blink in shock. "What happened?"

There are four police cars parked in front of the security gate—with officers standing guard near their vehicles.

"Do you think it has to do with the press?" I ask. "They've been overzealous. Maybe a reporter got a little too cocky."

"I doubt an eager reporter would require this many officers," Rhys says.

"I guess not."

Since the guards recognize Rhys and the chauffeur, they wave us by. We barely come to a stop, when Rhys and I jump out. We rush to the front door, passing groups of employees huddled together outside of the building. As much as I'd like to think I have psychic powers, it's impossible to read the expression on their faces.

"Is anyone hurt?" I ask Paula when we stop in front of her desk.

"I don't think so," she says. "The paramedics and the firefighters were on site, but they just left."

"Thank God," I say, relieved.

"Do you know what's going on?" Rhys asks Paula.

"I swear, I thought I was on the set of an action movie. About twenty minutes ago, the head of security came barging in here with a bunch of his guys and an army of police in tow," she says. "No one knows what's going on. We were just told to stay put."

"I can't rely on Cecilia to find out what's going on, but what about Valerie?" Rhys asks. "She must know."

Rhys's executive assistant is home, playing nurse to a sick child today.

"Have you talked to her, Paula?" I ask.

"Valerie is out of the office," Paula says. "She went out for lunch with a girlfriend. I texted her and she should be back any minute now."

"This is unsettling," I say.

"Well, you're about to get briefed because Beckett wants you on the executive floor asap," Paula tells me.

"Good stuff," Rhys says. "Let's go!" He grabs my hand and we head to the elevators.

When the doors close, my heart is palpitating so hard, I place my hand against my chest to calm my erratic heartbeat.

"Something tells me we're in for a shock," Rhys says.

I look up at him. "I think you're right."

When we step out of the elevator, a tall, bald man with piercing dark brown eyes greets us.

"Miss Buchanan. Mr. Hartford. You're finally here," Clyde Kendall, the head of security, says.

"Clyde, talk to me," Rhys says.

"Mr. Christensen asked me to usher you and Miss Buchanan to his office," Clyde says. "We have a situation on our hands, but I'm not at liberty to say much more. Mr. Christensen wants to be the one to fill you in."

Paula is right. There's the same frantic energy you'd expect from watching a nail-biting scene of a gripping action movie.

"Alright, lead the way," Rhys says.

"After you, Miss Buchanan." Clyde extends an arm.

I give him a tight nod.

As we rush down the hallway, I spot more officers posted on every corner of the floor. I can't imagine what kind of scenario would warrant this level of police presence.

*Did a competitor infiltrate the building in an attempt to steal market intelligence?*

*What else could it be?*

When we reach Beckett's door, a female officer lets us in.

I step inside the office and freeze.

Certain I just walked into the jaws of hell, I stumble backward, ready to run for my life, but I only end up bumping into Clyde.

"Careful, there, Miss Buchanan," he says, closing strong hands over my shoulders to prevent my fall.

I blink.

*What the hell?*

I blink again.

*This can't be happening.*

I blink once more.

*I'm losing my mind.*

*This is a mirage.*

I blink a fourth time for good measure.

*No, it's not.*

*Why are you doing this to me, God?*

The last person I ever expected to see is standing in my boyfriend's office, surrounded by officers, with her hands behind her back.

"Mariah?!"

"Hey, Nerdy Ari."

*God, I hate her.*

"It's me," she says before flipping her hair back. The ends

of her long extensions whip against an officer's arm. She doesn't look impressed.

It doesn't jump out at me at first, but now it does.

*Why is Mariah wearing a trench coat and thigh-high boots in this heat?*

*The damn coat is so short, why even bother?*

"Your cousin came all the way from Silicon Valley for a visit," Beckett says.

I tear my gaze away from my smirking cousin's face and shift my attention to my boyfriend.

"Wh—wh—what's going on here?"

"We"—Beckett waves a finger at my cousin—"spent the last half hour getting to know each other better. Isn't that right, Mariah?"

My existence wilts a little. Okay, a lot.

She lifts her chin up with a stubborn head jerk in response. When she does, the upper part of her trench coat opens, revealing what she's wearing underneath.

*A see-through top. Of course.*

Dread courses through my veins.

If Beckett spent the last half hour locked in his office with Mariah wearing one of her legendary slut outfits, it can only mean one thing.

"Your cousin is a hell of a woman—"

I lift a hand, interrupting him. "I don't need to know more, Beckett."

"This isn't what you think," he says.

*Here we go again.*

I let out a sarcastic laugh. "Isn't that what they always say?"

His head jerks back at the accusation.

"Are you putting me in the same category as your lowlife ex?" he asks.

"He's lying to your face!" Mariah says. "You're blind, Arianne. He was trying to have sex with me."

I shoot Beckett an icy glare and open my mouth to spit a tirade of anger in his face, but he precedes me.

He points a finger at Mariah. "Shut up, you lying bitch!"

I didn't expect that.

He fixes his gaze on me.

His eyes are as thunderous as a cyclone.

I stare at him, disappointment and hurt beating hard against my chest.

"Do you think I'm as reprehensible as Chance?" he asks.

I sigh.

"Answer me, dammit!"

"Beckett, this isn't the first time I've gone through this shit with Mariah. She's come after every boyfriend I've ever had. She pulverized my relationship with Chance within a matter of days... and now she wants you." I heave a heavy breath. "You want her?" I point at the slut. "You can have her." I swallow a lump in my throat.

Beckett's blue eyes turn dark gray as he studies me.

I grow uncomfortable under his piercing gaze.

"If you think I'd choose your cousin over you, Arianne, you know nothing about me and that's disappointing."

I'm taken aback by the weight of his words.

"What am I supposed to think?" I throw at him as my mind struggles to make sense of things.

Betrayal.

Humiliation.

Pain.

It all comes flooding like a raging river. It's all *déjà vu* in my world.

"You really think I'd want to fuck *that*, Arianne?" He points an agitated finger at Mariah.

"I... I..." *I'm confused.* "This is how Mariah operates..."

Beckett grabs me by the neck and pulls me close to him. "I'd never hurt you. I'd never betray you. And I sure as hell would never play you for a fool, Arianne."

His solemn words tighten my chest and tug at my heart.

I bite hard against my lower lip, but it does little to contain the tears rolling down my cheeks.

Beckett wipes them away with his thumbs.

I place my forehead and the palms of my hands against his strong chest, needing a few seconds to compose myself.

He kisses the top of my head and rubs my back with soothing hands.

"You okay?" Beckett asks in a low voice after a few long seconds.

"Not really." I murmur my response against his chest.

"Look at me, baby." He strokes my arms in long sweeping, comforting strokes.

My eyes meet his.

"I wouldn't fuck Mariah for a hundred billion dollars. I have zero interest in Chance's sloppy seconds—"

"Fuck you!"

"Shut the fuck up, Mariah!" Beckett shouts back.

He returns his dreamy eyes to me. "You and I have a good thing going on, and I'd hate for your repulsive cousin to ruin our relationship because of her deceptiveness and lies."

"So... there's nothing going on between the two of you?" My insecurity towards Mariah runs deep. I need the confirmation.

"No, baby," he tells me. "I didn't even know this woman until forty-five minutes ago. You either trust me or you don't." His tone is unwavering.

I hold his gaze for a beat.

Honesty shines bright in his blue eyes.

"I trust you."

"Good." He smiles. "Arianne, I care deeply about you. You're a gem and you're mine."

*Wow. Just wow.*

His declaration mends something in me that's been broken for so long, I thought it was irreversible. This wonderful man proves me wrong.

In an unprecedented move of public display of affection, Beckett drops a soft kiss on my lips.

I'm suddenly very much aware of all the people standing in the room.

I let out a girlish giggle when he pulls away.

"There's a reason for the police presence and it's not by chance Mariah is in handcuffs," Beckett says.

"What did she do?" I ask.

"Although jumping off the roof of the tallest New York City skyscraper would've been much less painful than having to endure your despicable cousin for half an hour while she spewed her venom, I did it to protect you," Beckett says.

I furrow my brows. "Protect me from what?"

"Your cousin came here to blackmail me," he says, "and destroy you."

"Wh—what?" This is the last thing I expected to hear.

"He begged me to come to his office for sex!"

Beckett turns his attention to my cousin who's fighting against her restraints. A female officer forces her to calm down.

"You're a walking red flag, Mariah," Beckett says. "Everything you said since you sat in the chair across from my desk was recorded. Every incriminating word. Every malicious threat. Every devious blackmail plot."

"You—you—" Mariah's jaw drops. "You recorded everything?"

"Audio and video," Beckett says.

Mariah looks positively petrified.

"That's right, bitch," Beckett says. "This is my house! You don't lay down the law here. I do! I let you believe you had the upper hand, which gave you enough rope to tie the noose around your neck... and you did."

"Threat? Blackmail?" I ask.

"Showtime!" Beckett says. "Clyde, can you please turn off the lights and pull the curtains closed."

"Certainly, sir."

Beckett walks up to his desk and grabs a remote control. He points it at the ceiling and the retractable screen lowers. The room isn't pitch black, but it's dark enough.

"There's thirty minutes of this shit, but before you got here, I pre-set the video to play the most incriminating part," Beckett says. "I want you to hear it from the horse's mouth. It's only three minutes, but it speaks volumes."

"Okay," I say.

Mariah's annoying voice fills the room.

I watch and listen in absolute horror.

"Clyde, lights back on, please," Beckett says when the snippet ends.

Clyde obliges, and then, he opens the curtains.

The office is immersed in silence.

All eyes are on Mariah.

I stare at my cousin in disgust.

I never knew the true depth of her malevolence.

It's worse than I could've possibly imagined.

And after all these years, I still don't know why she keeps beating me down with her animosity like she would a sworn enemy.

She holds my stare and smirks, proud of herself.

Up to this point, I didn't think I had a violent streak in my body. Then again, until now, I never knew how far she'd be willing to go to hurt me. Before I know it, I leap in Mariah's direction, ready to wipe that condescending smirk off her face.

Beckett's quick arms wrap around my waist, holding me back.

"Don't ruin it," he tells me. "This is as perfect as it gets."

I'm dumbfounded.

I wiggle out of his hold.

He doesn't resist.

"What's perfect about my cousin and my ex-boyfriend wanting to make my life a living hell... one so miserable, I may not want to live?" I'm so worked up. "Chance violated my rights to privacy and Mariah was itching to make it go viral because the press is paying more attention to me than to her." I throw daggers at my cousin.

An officer raises her hand as a barrier. She also gives me a warning look.

"Your spitefulness knows no bounds!" I wave a menacing finger at Mariah. "What have I ever done for you to hate me so much you'd be willing to do such an abominable thing?"

She doesn't answer.

"What the fuck is wrong with you?"

She's obstinate in her silence.

"Answer me!" I yell.

"You're a goodie-two-shoes-people-pleaser, which makes you an easy target, Arianne." Mariah finally speaks. "As we grew older, it became clear I'd never be able to beat you at life— fucking Miss Genius and all—so I made it my mission to screw up your relationships. You couldn't compete in that department and I knew it. I figured you'd hide in a hole for the rest of your natural life after Chance, but noooooo, you had to score him!" She jerks her chin in Beckett's direction.

I can't believe my ears.

This woman has no soul.

"Because you're jealous of me, you're entitled to destroy me?" I ask.

"I'm the pretty one in the family! Stop overshadowing me!"

"You sound pathetic. Grow up, Mariah—"

"I wish Aunt Muriel had never found you and let you freeze to death—"

My palm doesn't crack against her cheek like I intended.

Beckett pulls me away before I'm able to rearrange her smirking face.

"I get where you're coming from, Arianne, trust me I do, but don't give her any ammunition," he tells me.

*One blow. I just want one blow.*

*Okay, more like two dozen, but I'll be happy with one.*

"I'm going to sue you for assault and battery!" Mariah threatens.

"You wish, evil bitch!" I say.

She doesn't have a comeback.

"Mariah's jealousy is a gift."

My head whips in Beckett's direction.

My face contorts in myriad expressions, unable to understand the logic behind his statement.

"Without her confession, you wouldn't know Chance was holding a loaded gun to your head, ready to fire at the drop of a hat." Beckett's words put everything into perspective.

My shoulders slump in defeat.

I'm no match for evil.

"You're right," I tell him.

"You're protected under the state of California's nonconsensual pornography law, aka revenge porn law," Beckett says. "In other words, you can sue Chance for every penny under his name. The same applies to your cousin. By coming to my office, Mariah handed you everything you need on a silver platter. It doesn't get any better than this."

Rhys claps and whistles.

With everything that's unfolded, I forgot he was in the office.

"Take them to the cleaners, Arianne," he says. "Fuck them up like they intended on fucking you up."

I respond with a small smile.

I stare at my cousin's ugly face.

With anger burning my throat, I deliver my verdict through gritted teeth. "I'm going to make you pay, cuz."

# Chapter 48

## *Beckett*

---

*'GLACH TECH'S CEO CHANCE TABORAS GIVES NEW MEANING TO 'SEX, LIES, AND VIDEOTAPE!''*

*'CHANCE TABORAS AND FIANCÉE MARIAH GOLIGHTLY CONSPIRE IN EVIL BLACKMAIL PLOT.'*

*'ARIANNE BUCHANAN VIOLATED IN THE WORST WAY. SHAME ON YOU, CHANCE TABORAS.'*

*'GLACH TECH AT RISK OVER SEX VIDEO SCANDAL.'*

U*nbelievable.*

I move my gaze away from my iPad and look up.

Arianne is shaking her head, her eyes still riveted on her iPad.

"I can't believe the length Chance was willing to go to renege on his promise," she says. Her anger is still palpable. "I made him an incredibly rich man, and he was willing to steamroll me to avoid paying out what was rightfully mine." She pauses. "I wasted three years of my life with that asshole."

It's been two taxing days since Mariah barged into my office with her lame ass threats and ludicrous demands. Stupid cunt.

The media has been relentless since the scandal broke, the screaming headlines a testament to the frenzy. Yesterday, was a zoo at the office. Even though we beefed-up security, there was no holding back the army of reporters and bloggers or their litany of questions. Since Arianne is at the heart of the scandal, I recommended she hire a top-notch publicist to help her navigate through this nightmare. In the meantime, Joey handled the press with finesse.

Today, we have the luxury of extracting ourselves from all this shit. It's just Arianne and Beckett. Thank God.

We've just finished breakfast and we're lingering at the kitchen table on a lazy Saturday morning. I'm still in my pyjama bottoms and she's wearing nothing more than shorts and a soft pink t-shirt, her hair bunched up in a messy bun on the top of her head. She's as beautiful as ever, but I can tell this ordeal has taken a toll on her.

"I made some calls, and I found you a lawyer with a stellar track record," I tell her. "He feels this is an open and shut case."

"Really?"

"The video doesn't lie. It's not like I tricked Mariah into confessing. She was too happy to spew her venom. Good thing I held you back and prevented you from striking her."

She sighs. "I still wish I'd been able to get one blow."

"Arianne, it would've added a layer of complexity you don't need."

She nods.

While the police were babysitting Mariah, I slipped out of my office to phone my lawyers to secure a search warrant and an arrest for Chance. Given what Mariah had shared, I was afraid the asswipe would seek revenge by sharing the videos.

"I'm still not sure how I'm going to pay for a top lawyer—"

"I'll cover your legal fees."

"Beckett, you can't do that. It's too much—"

I place two fingers against her lips, silencing her protest.

"Chance has deep pockets. I'm sure he'll lawyer up with an army of sharks. But my pockets are much deeper than his. He duped you. He cheated on you. He cheated you. And to make matters worse, he was willing and ready to taint your reputation forever. What he did is reprehensible. Once a sex video is out there on the web, it's a nightmare and costly to get it removed from every website."

She nods.

"The law is on your side. Use it to your full advantage."

"Thank you." Arianne offers a shy smile. "Money—or lack thereof—is what prevented me from going after Chance the first time around. I'm glad it won't happen twice."

"No way." I shake my head. "The asshole and his bitch need to be held accountable. The lawyer I got you is ruthless when it comes to protecting his clients. I also reached out to Larkin. He knows some of the best investigators in the business. We'll put a team on the job to scour the internet as precautionary measures. We don't want to leave any stone unturned."

"Thank you," she repeats.

"Don't mention it." I squeeze her hand. "Let's talk about something else. We've already devoted enough brain cell matter to those lowlifes."

"I'm with you," she says before popping the last bite of muffin into her mouth.

"Do you want more coffee?" I ask.

"I'm good. Thanks."

"Another muffin?"

She shakes her head. "I know I've said it before, but these are to die for," she says in between chewing, pointing at her mouth.

She's had high praises for Mom's homemade dark chocolate and banana muffins. Not that I blame her.

"I'll make sure to tell Mom you like them."

"You mean, I *love* them," she says.

I laugh.

"What do you want to do today?" I ask, changing the subject.

"I wouldn't mind spending the whole weekend locked up in your mansion," she says. "Did you have something in mind?"

"I did, but if you're too tired..."

Her eyes light up. "I'm never too tired for sex!"

"I appreciate the enthusiasm, but this has nothing to do with my very big cock."

"Oh."

"Don't look so disappointed."

"What is this about?" Worry colors her words.

I push my chair back and angle it so I'm facing her.

I reach out for her hands and grab them in mine. "When was the last time you stayed at your sublet for longer than a few hours to clean-up the place and grab fresh clothes to come back to my house?"

She draws her brows together. "I can't remember. It's been a while—Am I crowding your space? Is this what this is about?"

I shake my head. "No."

She pulls her hands from mine and rubs them over her face. "If it's an issue, I don't have to stay here as much. I'll go back to the sublet so I'm not in the way."

"Give me your hands."

She looks at me funny, but she obeys my command.

"I love having you here, Arianne," I tell her.

"What's bothering you, then?" There's a tinge of nervousness in her voice.

"Nothing is bothering me, baby," I tell her.

"Then why do I feel like I'm waiting for the other shoe to drop?"

"Someone woke up on the pessimistic side of the bed this morning," I say.

"Whatever it is, just tell me."

She still looks petrified.

"We've been dating for nearly three months and we've been doing this back and forth dance—"

"You want to break up with me?"

My jaw drops. "You're putting words into my mouth—"

"It's your fault, Beckett. You're being all mysterious and shit."

It takes me a while to catch on, but I finally do.

I grab her chin.

"Arianne, I'm not about to dump bad news into your lap. We're talking. People who date, talk."

Stress lifts off her shoulders and she allows them to fall.

"Maybe I'm being paranoid—"

"Ya think?"

"Okay, I am."

"Let's drive to your sublet, grab all your belongings, stuff your entire universe in the back of my SUV and drive back here," I say.

She looks at me puzzled.

I cup her face, drop a soft kiss on her lips and spell it out for her in no uncertain terms. "Your stuff belongs in my house. You belong in my house."

She still doesn't clue in.

"Arianne, I want you to move in with me."

"Wh—what?"

"For all intents and purposes, we're already living together."

"Are you sure about this?"

I get up, walk to the counter, grab the little black box I hid first thing this morning and return to sit next to her.

Her eyes bounce from the box I'm holding to mine.

"I was going to give you this two nights ago, but you were dealing with a lot. That said, I don't want to delay things any longer." I hand her the box.

"What is it?" Her uncertainty is evident.

"Open it!"

This was planned. Same for the new set of wheels waiting for her in my garage. Phoebe was instrumental in the decision-making. It turns out, my girl is quite partial to German luxury vehicles. So, I got her an Audi R8.

She opens the box and gasps.

Her big brown eyes bounce to mine, searching my own, shimmering with bewilderment. "Beckett?!"

Her gaze drops to the box.

"Oh, my God," she says, teary eyes meeting mine. She pulls out the keychain and holds it at eye level. "Is this what I think it is?"

I smile at her.

I grab the box and toss it on the table.

I nod. "Those are all the keys to my house." I drop my eyes to her clinging hands. "Consider the keychain your entrance to my world, Miss Buchanan." She brings the set of keys close to her heart.

"I'm bursting at the seams!" she says.

"*Mi casa es tu casa, bebé!*"

She laughs.

I stare at my girl as if she's the only thing in the world... because she is. "You're now part of the small group of people I care deeply about. People I keep close. People I protect. People I'd go to war for. People I'd die for."

"Dear God," she says.

More tears roll down her beautiful face.

I wipe them away.

"I've never had a woman I called my own before—never wanted to and never felt the need... I'm damn happy you're it, baby. I love having you in my life and I love knowing you're mine."

"I can't believe you just said that."

"Silly girlfriend, I'm sure you already knew. It's obvious to everyone around us how I feel about you."

She rewards me with a lopsided smile.

"I love—" She stops mid-sentence. "I mean, I love being yours," she says in a trembling voice.

"Is that all you were going to say?"

"I love having you in my life?!" The uncertainty is back in full force.

I chuckle.

"That's it?"

She averts her gaze.

"I love you, Arianne," I say.

She blinks at me.

"I love you, baby."

"You love me?!" her voice breaks.

"Every sexy inch of you," I tell her.

"Oh, my God."

"I love you, Arianne Buchanan!" I shout my declaration at the top of my lungs.

She dissolves into a fit of laughter and tears.

I chuckle and I kiss her lips.

"You really love me?" she asks.

"I already told you I love your fine ass, woman. What more do you want?"

She jumps into my arms.

I catch her and cover her beautiful face with kisses.

"Guess what?" I ask, pulling away from her.

"What?"

"We're officially roommates!"

"We are!" She laughs.

"It's about time."

We stare at each other for a beat, smiling like fools.

Something passes between us.

This gorgeous and vivacious woman is all mine.

With my eyes boring into hers, I reach out and trail a finger down from her lips, over her collarbone, over her breasts. She sucks in a breath, my thumb teasing over her nipple. That's all it takes for me to have a raging hard-on.

"I like those, roomie," I say low and rough. "I like touching them." I reward her throaty moan by teasing her a little more. "I like how hard they are under my touch." I squeeze the tight pebbled bud.

She lets out a curse.

Or is it a prayer?

I lean into her and brush my lips along the underside of her jaw. "You respond beautifully to my tease. I know your body so well..."

A whimper escapes her lips.

I capture her mouth with mine and kiss her hard and hungry as if I haven't already kissed her half a dozen times this morning alone. Just like every time I take ownership of her mouth, the contact is potent, traveling straight to my balls.

We both let out a shuddering moan as our tongues dance wildly.

After a few heated seconds, I break the kiss, stand up, and extend my hand to her.

"Come on, roomie. We're going upstairs."

She eagerly takes my hand.

I help her to her feet.

"One of the many benefits of living with the woman I love is having access to her sweet pussy anytime I want."

"Oh, I'm more than okay with that, roomie," she says.

I lift her in my arms.

She wraps her legs around my waist, her thighs bracketing my torso. I'm trapped in my favorite place in the world. Her hands lace around my neck, and I'm second-guessing the idea of leaving my house today.

"I love our new living arrangement, Beckett." She tightens her thighs around me.

Her shorts are dripping wet, the heady smell of her arousal tickles my nostrils and hardens my cock.

With rushed steps, I eat the floor underneath me as I head to the staircase.

"Mine." I murmur the word low in her ear as I climb the stairs.

"Yours."

# Epilogue

## Arianne

*Eighteen months later*

**M**y parents, Phoebe, Oscar, and I are weaving our way through the crowd at the spectacular Walt Disney Concert Hall, aka home to the Los Angeles Philharmonic. It's the perfect venue for a big night like tonight.

"Oh my God, Gregor, can you believe it?" Mom can hardly contain her excitement. "This is living it large."

"Muriel, keep walking," Dad says.

"Stop rushing me," Mom says. "Oh, look at the ornate balconies!" She points. "And the curtains look so regal!"

"I see, dearie," Dad says.

"Let's take a selfie!" Mom says.

"Not now, woman." Dad pulls Mom's hand, forcing her ahead. "We're in the way."

"Mom, Dad is right." I cut in. "We need to get to our seats."

"All right, all right, I'm walking," Mom says.

Phoebe and I look at each other and laugh.

As my parents stroll in front of us, Mom's head whips to the left then the right, oohing and aahing along the way.

She's in awe.

And I'm as giddy as she is.

The buzz of excitement is palpable.

Given the smash hit of their latest album, Anders and Tomas are holding an exclusive concert. Beckett, his band—Random Misconception—and badass female guitarist Stasia van Gameren will join Cello2Cello on stage in an unprecedented musical collaboration. Since Cello2Cello, Beckett and Stasia are co-judges on Jam Session, they've performed on the show, but this kind of star power gathered on one stage is a first. Two thousand plus tickets sold out in the blink of an eye.

This will be a night to remember.

"Arianne! Over here!" Rhys waves at me.

Thank God the man is so tall. He's impossible to miss.

I wave back.

"Let's go, gang," I tell my parents, Phoebe and Oscar.

We make our way to our seats. Rhys's girl, and Blythe and Erik—Beckett's parents—are already there. Beckett's cousin Jagger and his daughter Bree are with them. So are Levi Aldridge, his very pregnant wife Jules—she's expecting their second child—his older brother Linc and his wife. Linc is a renowned stage designer. Levi was Linc's business partner until he had to focus all his attention on another successful company he helped Jules launch. They're also part of Beckett's entourage and responsible for the set design for tonight's concert.

We greet each other, exchange warm hugs and find our respected seats.

"Talk about being close to the stage," I tell Beckett's mom.

"It doesn't get better than front row seats," Blythe says.

She's sitting to my right. Beckett's dad is seated a little further down the row flanked by Jagger and Rhys.

I open my mouth to respond, but my mother precedes me.

"Not unless you're sitting on stage," she says. She's sitting to Blythe's right. "Blimey." Mom clamps her hands over her mouth and her eyes widen as her face turns a bright shade of red.

"Mom, are you okay?" I ask.

"She is." Dad, who's sitting next to her, responds on her behalf.

Mom averts her gaze.

Her coloring is still a concern.

"Dad, she doesn't look okay," I tell him.

"She just needs to keep quiet. That's all," he says.

"What do you mean?"

"Honey, it's impolite to have a conversation over people like that," Dad says. "Your mother and I raised you better than that."

*What's gotten into him?*

"The concert is upfront... not down here." He points to the stage.

"Okay," I say, nodding, but still not getting it.

He tears his gaze away from mine and fixes it on the empty stage to drive his point.

Mom gives me a tentative side gaze.

*My parents have officially lost their marbles.*

"Don't be so hard on them. We're all excited," Blythe says when I'm still staring at my father's determined profile, perplexed.

I accept her explanation with skepticism.

My parents have worked very hard their whole lives and I understand concerts are a novelty, but something about them is off. They've been having these hush-hush conversations since they arrived in LA two days ago. Actually, their strange behavior started when I called them to let them know about tonight. Mom worships Cello2Cello. I flew them in so we could spend time together and attend the concert. Imagine my surprise, when they insisted on staying at a hotel instead of staying with us. Mom blurted something about not wanting to cram our space. No matter how many times I insisted, she turned me down flat. Dad wouldn't budge either.

I turn to my best friend who's sitting to my left. "The Buchanans are acting strangely," I tell Phoebe in a pronounced Scottish accent.

"Och, leave 'em be," she says in a farcical Scottish brogue.

"If ya say so, lassie."

We laugh.

"I can feel it in the air," Phoebe says. "Tonight is magical. Your boyfriend is making history in so many ways."

She's absolutely right.

"That's the only reason I'm willing to give my parents some leeway about their bizarre behavior—"

"Miss Buchanan." A man approaching, calls my name.

"Yes," I say.

The camera hanging from his neck is of concern.

"My name is Mark Sutton from the LA Buzz—"

"My publicist already made a statement. I have no comments," I tell him.

"Come on, Miss Buchanan." Mark ignores my protest. "Two trials resolve in one week weighing heavily in your favor and you haven't made an official statement—"

"I have no comments."

Mark opens his mouth to ask another question, but Oscar stands up.

"Leave her alone," he says. "She's asked you twice. If I have to ask you a second time to get out of her face, I won't be as polite."

Mark ignores Oscar.

"Are you keeping quiet because you're planning on making a big announcement, Miss Buchanan?" Just to be a jackass, he lifts his camera and points it at me.

I hide my face with my clutch.

*Crap.*

Tonight, I'm hanging out with my favorite people while my man and his friends rock the stage. Even though this overzealous reporter is being annoying, I'm not going to let him ruin my mood or dampen my excitement, although it's getting pretty damn close.

Beckett suggested hiring security guards to shadow me. I laughed it off and refused. Maybe I should've listened.

"You don't understand English, is that it?" Oscar asks.

"Get away from my daughter." I hear Dad shout.

*Great. My presence is making a scene.*

"I'm here to cover the concert, but if Miss Buchanan wants to give LA Buzz a scoop—"

"You have two seconds to get out of her face before I call the police," Rhys's voice slices through the brouhaha.

I lower my clutch.

Rhys is holding up his iPhone, recording the mess. His blue eyes are dark and menacing.

"All right," Mark says with a slow nod. "I apologize, Miss Buchanan," he tells me. "Can I give you my card just—"

"Fuck off!" Rhys and Oscar shout at the same time.

Mark scurries off.

*Finally.*

"You okay, honey?" Dad asks.

"Thanks to you three, I am. Thank you," I say to my unofficial bodyguards.

Dad smiles warmly.

"Anytime," Oscar says.

"Phoebe, why don't you swap seats with your boyfriend," Rhys tells my best friend. "I'll swap seats with Beckett's mom. That way we can keep a close eye on Arianne—"

"What about—"

"She'll understand," Rhys tells me.

A pair of worried hazel-green eyes meets mine.

I smile to let her know I'm okay.

She smiles back.

"I feel so badly," I tell Rhys, returning my attention to him.

"Who knows how many Marks are here tonight?" He makes a good point. "I don't want your boyfriend to break my balls because I'm not watching over his girl while he pretends to be a rock star for the night."

Everyone laughs.

A few shuffles later and I'm flanked between two white knights.

Mark was itching to get my side of the story because I've been tight-lipped.

Yesterday, the California court awarded me nine point seven million dollars, in the biggest judgment ever in a revenge porn case. Earlier this week, another jury awarded me sixty-three point eight million dollars in expectation damages as retribution for the promises Chance broke. Usually, cases like those take longer to settle, but thanks to Mariah's little visit and her deep-seated vendetta against me, my lawyers had gold in the palms of their hands.

It took a while to get a trial date, but the verdict was swift.

Chance had promised me a quarter of a million dollars for my contribution to the massive growth of his company—I have copious notes of our discussions. I was more than happy with that number. Since he wasn't man enough to keep his word, he ended up paying through the nose for his sneakiness and dishonesty. He was dumbfounded by both verdicts. So was I. Since the scandal broke, he was removed from his position of CEO.

The press smeared Mariah's name and shamed her out of the country. I consider it vindication. The last I heard, the cantankerous bitch latched onto another rich, older man.

The lights turn low in the theater.

Rhys nudges my arm. "The concert is starting."

I lean forward to look at my mom.

She's like a kid on Christmas Day.

When I look to my left, Phoebe isn't faring much better.

"Good evening, LA!" Tomas and Anders shout as they walk on stage, electric cellos in hand. Stasia, Beckett, Jace, Rod, and Holt, follow close behind, holding their instruments. Cello2Cello's drummer is the last one on stage.

The crowd goes mental.

I jump to my feet and clap like a crazed fan girl. "Beckett, we love you!" I shout at the top of my lungs, waving my hands in the air.

I've watched Random Misconception's music videos a thousand times. I know the lyrics by heart and I always drool all over my boyfriend. He's a hotter-than-hell rock star with an insane swoon-worthy stage presence. Nothing compares to hearing the rawness of his deep voice or watching him in all of his elements than when he sings live.

Beckett looks freaking delicious!

He traded his bespoke suits in favor of an edgy look that honors his beginnings to a T—leather pants, motorcycle boots, and the form fitting t-shirt that showcases his muscles and ink. I also dressed for the part of the rock star's girlfriend. I matched his all black look, except I'm wearing killer bright pink strappy high-heels.

I've been his girlfriend for a year and a half now, but there are times like these it hits me how Beckett Christensen is so ridiculously out of my playing field. Still, he chose me. A nerd like me with a bad boy stud like him. Two opposites in so many ways yet, we fit so perfectly together.

*It's good to be me!*

# Epilogue

## Beckett

Anders and Tomas are done warming up the crowd.

Anders nods at me.

I nod back.

"We're going to deviate from the program tonight." He announces the change of plan to the crowd.

A low rumbling runs through the theater.

Anders turns to his creative partner. "If you're going to make history, you do it in a big way or not at all, right?"

"I couldn't agree more," Tomas says.

That gets the crowd fired up even more.

I look to my brother for support.

He smiles warmly at me.

Stasia, Jace, and Rod also offer sympathetic smiles.

That does little to untie the knot lodged in my stomach.

*I'm nervous as hell.*

I've played to sold out arenas around the world. Up to now, I've never been gripped with stage fright. Singing to twenty thousand adoring fans is vastly different from this moment, though. Thank God Anders and Tomas are behind me one hundred percent—in fact, they insisted I usurp their stage. All of our friends and family gathered here tonight have been helping me for months to make this special night happen.

"In true Cello2Cello fashion," Anders says, "we would normally kick things off with an edgy rock song, especially when we're performing with some of the best rock artists and one of the most powerful rock voices on the planet."

The crowd approves.

"Speaking of powerful voices"—Tomas takes the lead—"in my humble opinion, no one comes close to Beckett Christensen. His distinct voice is like no other."

Another round of enthusiastic applause ensues.

"Who wants to hear Beckett sing?" Tomas asks the crowd.

People cheer, stomp, holler, and clap.

The cacophony is fucking deafening.

It's deeply humbling.

"Should we start with the badass singer?" Anders fans the crowd by waving his hands in the air.

The cheers in the theater reach earsplitting decibels.

Anders turns to face me. "Beckett, my man, the public has spoken. The stage is yours."

I nod in gratitude and step forward, guitar in hand.

I swallow to find my voice.

"Hello, LA!"

The crowd offers a booming response.

It takes me a heart-pounding second to search the front row. To my satisfaction, I spot two empty seats. Rhys has already set the wheels in motion.

*This is it.*

Muriel has been a ball of nerves, tripping all over herself and her words, since I flew to Philadelphia to let Arianne's parents in on my little secret. We agreed Mom would be the one helping my girl up on stage. After the unwelcome interruption from that idiot reporter, Rhys texted me to warn me there's been a change of plan.

"We're making history in so many ways tonight," I say into the microphone. "It's more than just a performance tonight. On that note, I want to thank Tomas and Anders for allowing us to share the stage with them. It's pretty wicked. It's also always an honor to rock with the beautiful and talented Stasia van Gameren."

The crowd shows her some love.

My gaze shifts to the edge of the stage, behind the curtains, where the audience can't see.

Arianne's hands cover her beautiful face. Rhys is comforting her.

I wink at my girl.

"On a personal level, tonight is more than just rocking a crowd," I say. "It's about telling a woman I'm madly in love with how much she means to me."

The crowd doesn't hold back.

When our eyes meet again, I smile wide at the beautiful woman who's my world.

She just shakes her head, her hands still hiding her face.

"Come on stage, baby!" I wave her over.

She approaches on trembling legs, Rhys trailing right by her side. Thank God because she looks like she's about to faint.

"My big brother already serenaded his girl with our smash hit love song, *Until I found you.*" I go back to the script. "As perfect as it is, no way was I going to recycle that song. My girl deserves *her own* song. I had to convince songwriter extraordinaire, and my cousin, Jagger Halsey to write me a new song."

The crowd laughs.

I shift my gaze away from the crowd and focus my attention on the woman I love.

Finally, she uncovers her face.

"This song is for you, Arianne," I say. "*All Of You* tells our story beautifully."

Her expression is full of disbelief.

I strum the first cord to the song.

Stasia, Jace, Rod, Tomas, and Anders follow suit.

I belt out the first verse, the intense melody from the guitars and my brother's bass mixing with my emotions. Cello2Cello's instruments emanate warm, low, almost crying, pitches that ratchet the heartfelt lyrics.

Arianne loses it.

With each verse, she cries a little harder.

She's shaking so hard, Rhys embraces her by the shoulders, holding her tight.

I had a lot of input in the song. Jagger delivered more than I could've hoped for. The poignant lyrics express everything I needed to say to this gorgeous woman from the depth of my soul, on this memorable night.

When we hit the last verse, Arianne is nothing more than a pool of tears, but she finds it in her to clap, a huge smile stretching her lips.

I wink.

The crowd goes ballistic.

I thank them with a bow.

My friends do the same.

Then, a solemn silence settles around the theater, as if people are waiting with bated breath for what comes next.

I walk up to Rhys, remove my guitar and hand it to him. Holt hands me a small red box. I take it from him and place my arm behind my back. It's still too early. I approach Arianne and interlace our fingers together.

"This is more than just a concert, baby."

"You tricked me," she says.

"I didn't tell you everything. That's different. There's still going to be a concert, but there's no way I was going to be able to go through two hours holding back what I have to say to you." I squeeze her hand. "Arianne, we're total opposites in so many ways, but we fit as perfectly as a puzzle. Amazing, right?"

She nods.

"I fell for the melodic timbre of your voice since our first encounter took place in the darkness of an elevator in the middle of a power outage. The second the lights turned back on, I fell for *all of you*. I know you swore up and down we'd never see each other again once we were rescued. For the record, it was apparent you couldn't get away from me fast enough."

She laughs.

"Nearly two years later... here we are."

More tears roll down her face.

"I kinda don't want to live without you, baby."

"Neither do I," she says in a shaky voice.

"I love you so much, baby."

"I love you with all my heart, Beckett."

I flash her a coy smile.

"You and I are going to make beautiful babies one day soon I hope."

She laughs in between tears.

I drop to one knee.

She gasps, but the sound is muffled by the crowd's murmur of excitement.

"Arianne Buchanan, you're it for me. Will you marry me?"

She waves her free hand in front of her face, hyperventilating.

I try again. "Will you be my wife?"

She shakes her head.

The crowd gasps in horror.

"No, no, no," she says, waving a hand at the crowd.

"No?" I'm dumbfounded.

More petrified gasps from the crowd.

"I'm so tongue-tied, I'm screwing things up," she says.

"Oof!" I exhale. "That was going to be the most awkward moment ever known to mankind," I say. "'*BREAKING NEWS! MISS HOLY CHIC TURNS DOWN BECKETT CHRIS- TENSEN'S MARRIAGE PROPOSAL IN FRONT OF 2,000 PEOPLE!*'"

She giggles.

There's a collective round of laughter.

My girl takes a deep breath and straightens her shoulders.

With eyes boring into mine, she whispers. "Try again."

"Marry me, Arianne," I say. "By the way, this time you're supposed to say yes. You know... third time's the charm and all."

She laughs wholeheartedly.

"Beckett Christensen, I can't imagine a greater gift than being your wife. Yes! Yes! Yes! A thousand yeses! I'll marry you, my love!"

The crowd cheers so loud, I'm sure you can hear them all the way in Philadelphia.

I drop her hand so I can open the box.

I lift it up for her approval.

"Holy massive rock!" she says, eyes shining like stars.

Her reaction gets the crowd going again.

I pull out the ring and slip it on my girl's finger.

"Oh my God! It's so beautiful!" she says.

"You like it?"

"Are you kidding me? I absolutely love it! It's my dream ring," she says. "How did you know?"

"I got a little help."

"Phoebe?"

"Yes, Phoebe."

Thanks to her best friend and one of Larkin's contacts, I got my girl a dazzling five point two carat cushion cut round solitaire set in platinum with accent brilliant diamonds running along the sides. The ring is elegant and feminine... just like Arianne.

I stand up and wrap my arms around her.

"Guess what?" I ask.

She looks up at me. "What?"

"We're roommates forever now!"

"I wouldn't have it any other way," she says.

I turn with her in my arms so we're facing the crowd.

"She said yes!"

The crowd approves.

"Ladies and gentlemen, I'd like to present to you, soon-to-be Mrs. Christensen!" I shout even louder.

Friends, family, and two thousand strangers are witness to one of the most amazing days of my life. From here on in, I suspect I'll be accumulating a collection of unforgettable memories with the woman I love.

"Kiss! Kiss! Kiss!" The audience chants.

The first rule of show business is to give people what they want... so I kiss the hell out of my girl.

# Bonus Scene

## Rhys

*This scene takes place a few days after Mariah comes barging into Beckett's office.*

I stroll through an empty executive floor on my way to Beckett's office. The hours between six and eight o'clock in the morning—before most employees start spilling in—can be more productive than an entire day. There's nothing quite like showing up bright and early before the hustle and bustle to get a shit ton of work done. It's amazing what you can accomplish when you aren't constantly tripping over distractions.

I knock on Beckett's door.

"Come in, Rhys!"

"Morning!" I enter his office.

"Morning," His eyes drop to the bag I'm holding. "What's that?"

"You suggested a breakfast meeting." I say. "I figured you're still too high-profile for us to go out and grab a bite."

He texted me when he got into the office at six o'clock this morning. I was already on my way, but decided to make a pit stop.

He nods. "Good thinking," he says. "It seems the school of piranhas has dissipated—I mean, reporters are no longer harassing us as we try to enter our own fucking building."

"As usual, Joey worked her magic," I say. "She handled a sticky situation with finesse."

"Which is why she's worth every penny," Beckett says.

After last week's circus, aka Arianne's cousin Mariah trespassing and making a fool of herself, it seemed like every reporter in the country was camping outside our gates. Thank God it's over.

"My first coffee of the day is long gone, I could use a second," Beckett says.

"That's what I thought." I head towards the small conference table in the corner of his office. In no time, I display the assortment of French pastries I bought from our favorite shop and two large cups of steaming hot lattes from Thoroughly Hot.

I remove my suit jacket, place it on the back of a chair and take a seat. "Come on." I call him over. "I'm starving."

With a chuckle, Beckett gets up from behind his desk and joins me.

We drink our coffees and savor the pastries in record time.

Beckett leans back against his chair, a look I don't recognize veiling his eyes.

"What's up?" I ask.

He offers a lop-sided smile in response.

"What's going on, Beckett?"

"I did something I never thought I'd ever do in my life."

"You mean other than declaring and I quote, *'Arianne, I care deeply about you. You're a gem and you're mine'* in front of a room full of witnesses?"

"It's an even bigger statement than that," he says.

My eyes drop to his left hand. "You eloped to Vegas and got married without telling anyone?"

"Nah. My girl deserves better than a shotgun wedding in Sin City," he tells me. "When the time comes, she'll get a big ass wedding."

My jaw drops.

"The most notorious certified playboy I know—other than Collin Dennison—is talking about marriage?" Bewildered, I look around the office. "Have I entered an alternative universe without knowing it?"

"Fucker!" Beckett says. He scrunches up his paper napkin and throws it at me.

I swat it out of the way.

We both laugh.

"Okay, I'll bite. What did you do?"

"I made Arianne a bona fide roomie."

My eyes shift left to right before my confused gaze lands on him. "That can only mean one thing, and I reckon hell will freeze over before that ever happens."

"In that case, I hope you know how to skate, buddy."

My eyes widen.

"You asked Arianne to move in with you?"

A smug smile stretches his lips, and he nods. "I did. On Saturday morning over breakfast." No hesitation. No waffling. His certainty bounces off walls.

"Wow." I'm speechless for a few beats. "Does your family know?"

He shakes his head. "Not yet. You're the first one to know. I guess I should say, you're the third one to know. Arianne couldn't wait to tell her best friend and of course, Phoebe had to tell Oscar. I plan on inviting my parents and my brother over next weekend. We'll call her parents to make the big announcement to both families at the same time."

"Holy shit, Christensen. You're officially off the market?!"

"I've been off the market since Cesar's engagement party," he tells me. "It took me a little time to clue in."

"Cesar will never let you play that one down."

"No, he won't... and I'm okay with that," he says. "Cesar called it first, but I have to thank Mariah for pushing me off the cliff."

I frown my confusion. "Why the hell would you thank that woman for anything? The worthless conniving bitch is an instigator that thrives on destroying Arianne's relationships."

"Her unwanted presence served a purpose."

I cross my arms over my chest and lean against my chair. "This, I have to hear."

"Mariah's cunningness flared a protective nature in me I didn't even know I had," he says. "Furthermore, as she was shamelessly throwing herself at me, it hit me. Not only had I raised my standards when it comes to women, but I didn't want anyone other than Arianne."

I'm at a loss for words.

Beckett and I talk about personal stuff, but this is uncharted territory.

"Manwhores can be reformed," I say.

His eyebrows arch. "Takes one to know one."

"Touché." Given the changes in my life recently, I can't even argue with him.

"I'll accept your first born for my role in bringing you two together," I say.

"Fuck off, Hartford!"

I chuckle.

"I've said it before, but without my dare, forcing you to embrace celibacy, you two would never have been together."

"You're probably right." He shakes his head, almost as if having a conversation with himself. "I didn't see her coming. That woman just came crashing into my life."

"I know exactly what that feels like."

He laughs, shooting a knowing glare my way. "Of course you do."

"Except in my case, it's more like *she* came crashing *back* into my life..."

"You mean, *she* came crashing back into your life *and* turned it upside down," Beckett says.

"That, too..."

~

### Bonus Secret Chapter

For two bonus secret chapters about Beckett and Arianne (including Arianne's POV during the salsa dance with Beckett), subscribe to my newsletter!

**www.MyRomanceAddiction.com**

### *Who's The Next Filthy Rich Book Boyfriend in This Scorching Hot Series?*

Beckett's business partner Rhys comes across as the level-headed one. Of course, that all goes to shit when he finds himself in a compromising situation. Agreeing to allow his best friend's little sister to move in with him is a double-edged sword. It's easy to resist temptation... until *she* becomes your roommate...

### Binge-read now: Billionaire Mogul—Rhys

### *Psst... you can read a sneak peek of Billionaire Mogul—Rhys at the end of this book.*

### *Reviews are sweet as pie!*

It only takes a few minutes to leave a review, which makes a huge difference for an indie author like myself.

### Here's the link to leave a review for: Billionaire Mogul—Beckett

# Scarlett's Book Banter!

Dear Sexy Reader,

There's so much out there in terms of romance.

As a person who has a AAA personality, I'm driven by the need to hit it out of the park with each book. It's a hell of a lot easier to do if I zoom in on a sub-genre I master. Translation, a hell of a lot more dirty-talking, filthy rich book boyfriends with an alpha streak to come!

This opens the door to so much drama, twists, turns, and a hell of a lot of dominant-slash-submissive power play.

*Let's circle back to Beckett and Arianne.*

Holy hotness!

I must say, I really, really love this whole forbidden office romance theme. Trust me, there will be other books.

*Let's talk about Easton...*

His story was part of a royal romance box set that became my first *USA Today* Bestselling title. Hence, the trope, but I decided to make her the princess and him a billionaire. I folded the story under the Billionaire Factor series when I started putting my standalone books in series, but it took me a long time to understand I needed to write a chapter that connects Max's book to Easton's. In the meantime, I was feeling a little sorry for Easton because no one knew how addictive his love story was. His story is amazing. And so, so fucking sexy.

To remedy the situation, I decided I would make him an important character in Beckett's story to allow readers to get to know him.

Mission accomplished.

Easton has a brilliant business mind, a dirty mouth, and a jealous and possessive penchant. In other words, he's irresistible. He's also willing to move heaven and earth for the woman who captured his heart—his baby sister's best friend.

Easton's story is an engulfing billionaire romance laced with shades of royal romance.

Fair warning: This *isn't* a Hallmark princess story. It's way too naughty to be PG. Rather, you'll devour this romantic tale one steamy page at a time.

----------

★★★★★ "I can't even describe how much I love that book!"

★★★★★ "Scarlett Avery has fogged up the windows with this one!"

★★★★★ "Fantastic plot! Very exciting story! I loved it!"

★★★★★ "Holy Hotness! I couldn't put this down!"

★★★★★ "I loved the characters and the way the story just sucked me in!"

★★★★★ "I literally could not put it down. It had drama and passion, and chemistry!"

**Binge-read now: Billionaire Factor—Easton**

*Now, let's talk about Rhys...*

Beckett's business partner Rhys comes across as the level-headed one.

Of course, that all goes to shit when he finds himself in a compromising situation.

Agreeing to allow his best friend's little sister to move in with him is a double-edged sword.

It's easy to resist temptation... until she becomes your roommate.

Rhys's story is a smoldering hot older brother's best friend romance that will keep you reading well past your bedtime.

**Binge-read now: Billionaire Mogul—Rhys**

**(Psst... make sure to read the sneak peek of Billionaire Mogul—Rhys at the end of this book.)**

*So many more filthy rich book boyfriends to fall in love with...*

**The Billionaire Moguls are part of a binge-worthy series (and world) of sexy as sin LA movers and shakers...**

I invite you to fall head over heels for the forever bachelors who are responsible for this spin-off. Holt's story, aka, Beckett's older brother, is Book 4 of the series.

Fair warning: You're guaranteed it's going to be SCORCHING HOT!

*The Billionaire Hotshots Series*

Six sexy as fuck filthy rich book boyfriends. Six possessive alphas. Six unapologetic seducers. Six scorching hot lovers you'll fall hard for.

These hotshots will undoubtedly become your next string of

obsessions.

Proceed with caution... you won't get enough of these delicious, domineering alphas.

Fall in love with a whole new group of book boyfriends.

Start the adventure with Book 1.

**Billionaire Hotshot—Levi** kicks off the series with a naughty ball that's so hot it comes _**with**_ a warning.

★★★★★ "I am not sure how Scarlett does it, but these books just keep getting better and hotter! I need more of these playboys in my life!" —P. Turner's Book Blog

**Binge-read now: Billionaire Hotshot—Levi**

That's it for me.

Back to writing!

Much love,

_Scarlett Avery_

P.S. Reviews are always appreciated and let me know I wrote a swoon-worthy story! Thanks a billion in advance.

P.P.S. I keep writing because of your hunger for my stories. Thank you for your fervor, love, and loyalty. I'm humbled and incredibly grateful. Without you, there's very little reason to keep coming up with new stories.

P.P.P.S. For access to an EXCLUSIVE Secret Chapter, go to the next page!

# Get the Secret Chapter for Billionaire Mogul—Beckett!

Thank you for purchasing this romance!

I have a couple EXCLUSIVE Secret Chapters to share with you!

For Secret Chapter 1, get a peek into Arianne's POV during the salsa dance with Beckett.

For Secret Chapter 2, get a peek into the Conclusion To Beckett's Adventure At The Club From Jagger's Book.

Trust me, you're going to love the extra tidbits.

When you sign up on my list, you'll receive an email with further instructions!

Sign up TODAY!

**www.MyRomanceAddiction.com**

***If you've already signed up to my list from previous books, you can visit the same page to download the Secret Chapters and/or Storyboard for this romance. ***

# Sneak Peek of Billionaire Mogul —Rhys

## Chapter 1 | Rhys

Even though it feels like my balls are melting, I'm too starved to bother with a shower before filling my stomach.

*What a day.*

The maître d'hôtel recognizes me when I enter the hotel's restaurant and offers a slight head bow.

"Mr. Hartford," he says.

"Good evening."

"Let me show you to your table."

Dinner service ends at ten p.m. Unfortunately for me, by the time I got back to the hotel it was eleven p.m. This is my third hellish day in a row in Ho Chi Minh City. Thank God for the top-notch service at my usual stomping ground. One phone call, and I was set. No wonder the thirty-nine-story Reverie Saigon Hotel in Vietnam is synonymous with excellence.

I follow the maître d' through a bustling and animated crowd. Even at this late time, the luxurious restaurant is packed. As we pass a table, two gorgeous blondes rake their eyes up and down the length of my body, eyeing me like I'm a juicy steak.

"Nice," the one with the blue eyes mouths, touching her bare neck.

"Oh yeah," the other mouths, squinting her brown eyes at me, almost as if she's committing every part of me to memory.

I respond with a polite smile and keep walking.

*You're losing your touch, Hartford.*

The blatant desire shining bright in their eyes, is a reminder that I've been a little too serious about adulting lately. If my day hadn't whipped my ass—scratch that—if this week hadn't been a complete mind fuck, I'd invite them to my table. A red-hot night of raunchiness isn't on the cards for me. Not when I have more shit to shovel bright and early tomorrow morning.

"Since you pre-ordered your meal, a waiter should be out shortly," the maître d' says when we arrive at my table. "Can I get you a drink in the meantime?"

I need at least five drinks just to mellow out after the day I've had, but let's start with one. "I'll have a local beer, please—"

My phone rings.

I look at my screen and smile wide.

The maître d'hôtel excuses himself with a head nod. I respond in kind before answering.

"Noah!"

"Hey Rhys!" my best friend says. "Trolling bars for a victim?"

"Don't ever quit your day job," I say. "And for your information, I don't have to go very far. I already have *takers*."

"Plural?"

"Plural."

"Mr. Player," he says. "It's good to be you."

"Well, we can't all be Rhys Hartford."

I slide my weary body onto one of the seats and lean back, biting down a groan.

The blondes are still staring, throwing flirtatious glances my way.

*Sorry, ladies. I'm jetlagged, bone-tired, and my head is so crammed with stuff, it's about to explode.*

It's pretty pathetic when your bed is calling you more than two willing pussies.

I catch sight of a waiter approaching, balancing a tall glass of beer on a tray, and I let out a silent prayer.

*Hey, sexy thing. Come to Daddy.*

I thank the waiter before bringing the glass to my lips, guzzling down a quarter of my drink.

"Seriously, am I calling at a bad time?" Noah asks. "I know your trip has nothing to do with pleasure."

"Nope. I'm in Ho Chi Minh City to put out fires." I drop my glass on the table. "My day started at six a.m. and I'm just having dinner now."

"Ouch," Noah says.

"I'm brain-dead."

"Being the COO of one of the leading audio bass head-phone companies in the world isn't all it's cracked up to be," he says with a laugh.

"Tell me about it," I say. "I swear to God, I got gypped."

"In what sense?"

"I should've set my sights on the CEO title of SCORE MAX Audio Bass instead of being the chief operating officer. That's the cushy job—"

"One your business partner holds. You want to dethrone Beckett Christensen?"

"I'm thinking of it."

"Vietnam isn't treating your kindly."

"So far, the days have been interminable and punishing. And it's hotter than Hades down here—ball-melting scalding-hot is a more accurate description of the heat level. While I struggle to breathe in this oppressive humidity, pretty boy Beckett is in LA party-hopping and hogging the attention of the press."

"What's new about pretty boy Beckett getting the attention of the media? Isn't that an everyday occurrence?"

"Yeah, but he's making headlines for another reason these days."

"Trouble in paradise? I thought Beckett and you have the perfect partnership?"

"We do," I say. "That said, I sure as hell can't wait to get back to LA. The only plus side to this trip—other than dealing with this production crisis that blindsided us—is that we get to hang out for a few days. When are you flying in?"

"About that..."

"You can't make it?"

"I can't."

"What happened?"

"I thought I'd be able to steal four days while production is shooting another scene without special effects, but I have to stay put in Doubtful Sound. The freak storm in New Zealand delayed production, and now we're playing catch-up."

"Another time, then." I try to hide my disappointment.

"I'm really sorry. We haven't seen each other since I left LA, and I was looking forward to it, but this is my big break. I can't screw it up——"

"I know how much this opportunity means to you. This TV series will change your life. You do what you have to do. We'll connect eventually."

"Thanks for understanding," Noah says.

"If things weren't as hectic on my end, I'd try to make it to New Zealand, but after Vietnam, I'm heading to South Korea."

"The timing is off for both of us," he says.

"That's what happens when your best friend is the special effects supervisor on the most watched fantasy drama series set in a medieval fictional world. I hope UTV.com knows you're their secret weapon."

"Says the guy sitting on a multibillion-dollar company."

We both laugh.

"Listen, Rhys, I have a favor to ask."

"Shoot."

"Keira called me—"

"How's your baby sister's trip to Thailand?"

"So far, bumpy."

"What happened?"

"On the second day after she arrived in Bangkok, a little girl pretending to need help approached her and her friend. Turns out, the girl was a decoy for a group of thieves. Keira's bag, containing her iPhone, was stolen."

"Shit."

"Yeah."

"Did they steal her wallet?"

"They did," Noah says.

"Fuck."

"The thieves didn't get much. They made out with coins."

"What happened to her money?"

"Keira carries her ID and money under her clothing—a habit she acquired from living with the nuns."

"Sneaky."

"Yeah, my kid sister can be pretty smart," he says. "About that favor..."

"Does it have to do with Keira?"

"As a matter of fact, it does!"

"Do you need me to send her money for a new iPhone?"

"Nah. She bought a replacement flip phone that's functional. She can send and receive text messages. She says it'll do for now."

"Okay. How can I help?"

"It's a big favor."

*Why is he beating around the bush?*

"Noah, you're my best friend and you've been there for me more times than I can count. Unless this has to do with ordering a hit on someone, you can ask me anything."

"Keira decided to travel for another two weeks since she has a travel companion. She's going to Laos next."

"Good for her."

"She's ready to come out of hiding, Rhys." The weight of his words hangs heavy in his extended silence.

"This day was bound to come." I play it down, but this is huge.

"She doesn't want to go back to London—"

"With good reason," I say.

"No one can blame her for not wanting to set foot in that city ever again after everything she's had to endure," Noah says. The anger in his voice has somewhat faded. Still, a tinge of it remains. Not that I can blame him. His little sister has been to hell and back. "Keira visited me here right after leaving London, but New Zealand isn't her home." He pauses. "She's ready to go back Stateside..."

I remain silent.

"She insists she's doing better—and I'm sure she is... that was the whole point of her isolation—but I don't want her living alone in a house or an apartment. She's not ready yet." He lets out a loud sigh. "I know I'm asking a lot and I also know this favor might put a serious wrinkle in your pussy time." He laughs at his own joke. I don't.

"What's the favor?" I think I know what's coming.

"Can she stay with you?"

*There it is.*

"In between running your empire, attending fancy galas and holding onto your rank as one of the most eligible bachelor playboys in LA, I'm also asking for you to big-brother her... like you did when she was growing up." I rake a hand through my hair. "She looks up to you."

*I haven't been on her list of favorite people in a while.*

"I wouldn't ask if it wasn't important," Noah says. "It's not like she has anyone else. LA can be a big bad city. She just needs a little time to get back on her feet."

Myriad emotions conflict inside me.

"I don't want to have to worry about her when I'm on the other side of the planet." Noah soldiers on. "With you, I'll have the peace of mind she's safe because you'll watch over her."

I pinch the bridge of my nose before scrubbing a hand over my face in frustration.

I know I told him he could ask me anything. This wasn't on the list.

"I'll send you money to cover her expenses—"

"Shut up about that, Weatherly!"

# Sneak Peek of Billionaire Mogul
—Rhys

## Chapter 2 | Keira

I smile wide at my travel partner.

"I'm so happy you talked me into doing this, Mikki," I say. "I get to cross Thailand and Laos off my list! Yay!"

"This little jaunt was the best way to ease back into our urban jungles," Michaela says. "Imagine the shock of going from near isolation to living in a hyped-up mega metropolitan city like LA again, or in my case, going back to the City That Never Sleeps."

That's the understatement of the century.

"I can't believe we're a few hours away from leaving the sanctuary and the safety of being anonymous," I say. "These past two and a half weeks were a great transition, but I predict returning to LA will be a jolt to all of my senses." I take a long sip of my refreshing mango juice.

I'm dreading and looking forward to going back. Dreading, mostly.

"When you say jolt, are you talking about the frantic pace of the city or the frantic pace of your heart when you're near your new roommate?" She narrows her green eyes at me.

"Rhys is just doing Noah a favor," I say.

"I get that your big brother's best friend would open his door to you, but can you handle it?" she asks, genuine concern in her voice.

"It's no different from crashing with a family member," I say, trying hard to convince myself it's nothing more.

Michaela twirls a forkful of noodles, poking through an equal portion of chicken and shrimp, before bringing the perfect bite to her mouth. "But he's *not* family." She shoves the food in her mouth and chews, her eyes still glued to me.

"In many ways, he's the only family I have in the US right now."

"But he's *not* family."

"Fine. He's not family." She wins. "I lost everything when I left London. What other choice do I have? It's not like I have any money left to live on my own in a city like LA. Heck, I don't even have enough to rent a pantry in someone's kitchen for three months." I push around my food on my plate. "Nearly every wealthy neighborhood in LA has a guesthouse. I'm sure Rhys has one. He'll shack me up there and forget all about me. That way, I won't invade his space."

"What if he doesn't have a guesthouse?"

"He *has* a guesthouse," I say. *Please God, he surely has one.*

"Guesthouse or not, you'll be living really close to him," Mikki says.

"No big deal." *I hope.*

She stares at me like I'm blowing smoke through my ears.

Okay, maybe I am.

"Keira, you showed me photos. Rhys Hartford's gorgeousness is on a planetary scale. How are you going to live with—or near—that man without either tripping all over yourself or fanning yourself all day long? And, I'm not talking about fanning your face."

She's wrong.

Rhys isn't gorgeous.

He's DEFCON 2 degree of hotness.

When he walks into a room, I'm certain panties drop.

Mine have a few thousand times.

I cross my legs to stifle the pressure building. My body is keenly aware I no longer have to adhere to my vows of chastity.

*No, no, no, Keira. Just no!*

Hot embarrassment floods through me because once again Rhys is taking up every bit of space in my brain.

Despite the A/C in the restaurant, my whole body is flushing.

*Will I survive living that close to a DEFCON 2 state of emergency? How am I going to manage to avoid melting into a pool of heat when I'm around him?*

I've asked myself those questions a million times since Noah announced Rhys was more than happy to welcome me into his home. Since I can remember, those two have been as tight as brothers. I've often felt left out—and a little bit jealous—of their bromance. The age difference between my brother and me has never played in my favor.

*You can do this, girl.*

*You're not that silly teen and teenager who drooled all over your older brother's best friend like a loser.*

*So what if Rhys Hartford is insanely successful, wildly talented, and a self-made, badass mogul?*

*He's just a man.*

I flash back to that kiss I stole from my long-time crush—the kiss I'd longed for.

One kiss.

One dear-God-make-me-yours-because-no-way-can-it-get-better-than-this-with-any-other-man-on-Earth-or-any-other-galaxy kiss.

One passionate, sensual kiss that's been haunting my lips for years.

One kiss that didn't go further... no matter how much I begged.

One kiss that left me so undesired.

One kiss that crushed me.

"Keira?" Mikki's voice snaps me out of my trance.

"Sorry. What were you saying?" I ask, meeting her gaze.

"Are you still with me or are you already in LA?" she says.

"Smartass!"

"You know you're kidding yourself about Rhys?"

"I'll manage."

"Right," she says.

"I will."

I grab my drink and hide behind it, that way she can't see I'm lying.

"Okay, let's play your game," she says.

I don't like the sound of that.

"If you're that detached, you should use this perfect living arrangement with the sexy blue-eyed COO to your advantage."

"In what way?" I ask.

"Rhys can devirginize you!" I nearly choke on my drink. "You'd get your wish. You've been pining over him for years. Men love knowing they're the first to mark you. It's primal—centuries of alpha coding and all."

"But I'm not a virgin."

She ignores my protest. "Gifting a man with your *born-again virginity* is better than the first time you punched your V card. No pain. No fuss. No mess."

*She's put a lot of thought into this.*

My gaze lowers to her glass. "Did the waiter lace your mango juice with vodka or rum, or both?"

"Like you haven't thought about it!" Her response comes out faster than a whip crack.

"Rhys is my older brother's best friend, and he's made it abundantly clear he sees me like a kid sister—"

"That was then. This is now," she says. "You're twenty-three and you're all woman—"

"Mikki—"

"Guys get freaked out when their best friends are in the picture. Noah lives far, far away. What a perfect time to push the envelope!"

Perhaps I confessed too much to her.

She grabs her glass, wraps her lips around her straw, and sucks on her mango juice, her smiling green eyes locked onto mine.

She's so smug.

"Thank you, Dr. Knight, for your insightful assessment," I say.

"I might not hold a PhD, but I'm a great listener... and you've had a lot to say about sexy Rhys in the two months we've known each other." She grins around her straw.

I definitely told her too much.

"Rhys must have a girlfriend or a fiancée." It's really not something I want to think of, but I have to face reality.

"Your brother would've told you," she says. "Not to mention, when the press labels you Luva Boy Rhys, chances are, variety is your middle name."

*I'm sure he has them lined up.*

The parade of women hanging from Rhys's arm in photos on the internet is dizzying.

"Even if your idea wasn't preposterous—which it is, just so we're clear—Rhys would still reject me. I'm not subjecting myself to that again. His loyalty to Noah is unwavering, almost etched in his skin, tattooed in blood. The way I trip his best friend's kid sister meter has been the bane of my existence." I huff in frustration.

Mirth dances in Mikki's eyes. "Perhaps you need ammunition."

"I'm afraid to ask."

"You might want to buy a bottle of *'Eau de Vage'* at the airport and spray it on from head to toe to drive the message home that you're ready and willing. Think about it, perfume that smells like a narcissistic celebrity's private parts will help you seal the deal. What red-blooded man doesn't want that?"

She dissolves into giggles.

I can't help but do the same.

Our joyous outburst elicits suspicious glares from patrons trying to enjoy their meals.

I pray most of them don't speak English because our conversation is over the top and inappropriate.

It takes both of us a while to find our composure.

"Heck, I might have to take a page from that celebrity's book," I say. "After all, she sold out in a matter of hours. Since I have nothing to fall on when I land in LA, bottling my feminine scent and selling it to the masses might be my second wind."

"I can see it now," Mikki says with an exaggerated hand gesture. "Think bigger! Think a whole line of products— shower and bath gels, soaps, body creams... and even candles."

I play along. "Now you're talking."

Mikki taps her chin with her finger, her eyes lifted to the ceiling. "I wonder if you'll have to stamp a 'use by' date on your products? I'm sure over time, that shit smells nasty."

Her comment makes us lose it again.

More and more patrons glare at us.

It's a struggle to stop laughing.

"Seriously, Keira," Mikki says when she's able to talk again. "I'm jealous. I have to endure my stepmother while you get to play house with a dangerously hot artist-turned-billionaire."

She makes it sound like a fairytale.

It's anything but.

I haven't told her the whole story.

No amount of *'Eau de Vage'* will help Rhys warm up to me. Not after what I did.

It's complicated between us.

Alas, beggars can't be choosers, so now I'm stuck living with a guy I'm sure hates my guts.

**Binge-read now: Billionaire Mogul—Rhys**

~

## Billionaire Moguls Series

**Billionaire Mogul—Beckett**

**Billionaire Mogul—Rhys**

**Billionaire Mogul—Phoenix**

**Billionaire Mogul—Gage**

The Billionaire Moguls is part of the **Billionaire Hotshots'** world.

## Billionaire Hotshots Series

**Billionaire Hotshot—Levi**

**Billionaire Hotshot—Roderick**

**Billionaire Hotshot—Lochlan**

**Billionaire Hotshot—Holt**

**Billionaire Hotshot—Jace**

**Billionaire Hotshot—Jagger**

These sexy as sin Billionaire Hotshots are notorious bachelors forever... that's until they cross paths with the women who bring them down to their knees.

You'll find **all my books** and **reading order** on my site:
**www.ScarlettAvery.com**

I hope you enjoyed **Billionaire Mogul—Beckett**! Can't get enough of Beckett and Arianne? Subscribe to my mailing list and you'll get instant access to an exclusive **Billionaire Mogul—Beckett** secret chapter and/or storyboard. Just use the QR code below.

Already subscribed? You would've received the link in the first email I sent you. If you can't find it, you can email us. If you've changed your email address, simply resubscribe.

# About the Author

USA *TODAY* Bestselling Author Scarlett Avery unapologetically pens all-consuming love stories featuring sexy as sin billionaires who have the determination of a thousand warriors. These filthy rich heroes bow to no one. Only the women who steal their hearts can bring them down to their knees.

Scarlett's stories are intense and passionate, emotional and steamy, and leave you begging for more. In other words, they're the perfect blend of swoony and sinful. Once you start reading Scarlett's novels, there's no going back!

Fair warning...

You should always expect edge-of-your-seat twists.

Made in United States
North Haven, CT
22 March 2024

50338008R00311